THE STONEY MOUNTAINS

Sam J. Pisciotta

THE STONEY MOUNTAINS
Copyright © 2016 by Sam J. Pisciotta

ISBN 978-0-9915496-2-7

Printed in the United States

Lupo Publishing, Sam J. Pisciotta, Pueblo, Colorado

SAM J. PISCIOTTA

CHAPTER 1
BENJAMIN VOSS

Benjamin could feel the sun's heat reflecting from the golden stalks of wheat around him. The dust in the hot summer air mixed with the perspiration that rolled in rivulets down his face and back. It was not so much that he was tired as he swung the scythe back and forth, cutting the dry stalks, it was that he kept thinking how much he would rather be swimming in the river, or hunting in the woods near the farm. Even the thought of running through the cool green woods sounded like heaven. But, he was older now, and for the past five years his duties on the farm had become closer to those of a full grown man.

Since the planting of the crops in the spring a full day's labor of an adult had been expected of Ben. His father had taken him aside and again told him how the land would barely feed the extended clan of the Voss family. At sixteen years old, he could no longer be the baby of the family, the youngest son, free to do as he wished. It was expected that he carry the same weight as his brothers, all seven of them.

The Voss family had moved to western Pennsylvania from Frederick County, Maryland after Jacob's first wife, Elizabeth died in 1775 at childbirth, taking with her newborn twin sons. Jacob, with two young boys, then married to Willamette Sturm and she had given the tough Prussian seven more children before she succumbed to a fever and died. From this second union, Jacob lost two more sons, one at birth and one was caught under the wheels of a wagon before he had reached the age of five.

Like the biblical son of Isaac, Jacob Voss had

named his children after those God had given his namesake and intended to produce no less than a twelve sons. With this in mind, within a year of Willamette's death, Jacob had wed a third time. Rebecca Blake, a comely young woman with a kind heart, became the third and last wife of Jacob Voss. Though younger than half of the Voss children, she proved to be a good mother not only to the two children she bore, but also to those of her predecessors as well. The members of the extended Voss family respected her, and save for Joseph, a son of Willamette, each grew to love her in their own way. Joseph had known no mother other than Rebecca, but had never felt close to her. In some way he blamed her for taking his real mother's place and he transferred this enmity toward the two children she bore his father.

Of the two children born of Rebecca, the first had disappointed her husband by being a girl, Rosalinda. Like her mother, Rosalinda was kind and quiet. Compared to many of the young women her age she could not be considered an outstanding beauty, but neither was she plain. At eighteen years old, she should have been married, or at least courting with a line of young men at the front door of the Voss house waiting for her father's permission to see her. But, on the contrary, there was not a young man for miles around that dared to confront Jacob and the few who had shown interests were persuaded to look elsewhere by her brother Joseph. In his own selfish way, he thought that if she were kept at home to care of him, his father, and his brothers, there would be little chance of a new "mother" being brought into the Voss household.

One of the would-be suitors, William Hartmann though the most timid, and run off at first by Joseph, had still made some attempts to gain Rosalinda' favor. William knew there was little chance of gaining

2

permission from Jacob to court his daughter, but in his heart he loved the girl and vowed someday to find the courage to face the Voss men. His heart would pound when she smiled at him and she, in turn, was smitten with him, returning blush for blush. In the meantime, William would settle for wishing Rosalinda a good day when they met at church or at community gatherings.

Two years after Rosalinda, Benjamin was born, the thirteenth child to be placed down in the Voss family bible. After Benjamin there were no more children and Rebecca had lived as the matron of the Voss household for another fourteen years before she succumbed to the effects of what the doctor called liver colic.

The fact that not all of Jacob's children had lived to see their fifth birthday; such was accepted as a fact of life in the wilds of the west. The Voss patriarch accepted what he considered God's will. He was thankful in his own way for what he had received from the Creator and felt he had paid more than a fair price of four sons and three wives given back to God.

Ben looked at the row of his brothers, spread out as they crossed the field to his left, from Reuben down the line to him, each kept pace just a step behind their elder brother, swinging their blades in an arch, each swath leaving short stubble behind. They were each expected to cut an acre of wheat in one day's work, and Ben struggled to match his brothers in this accomplishment.

Wheat was not the only crop grown on the Voss farm. There was corn, beans, and squash, as well as oats and clover in the fields. These crops were rotated every four years to give the ground a chance to recover from the needs of any particular crop. With the crops, there was also the tending of a few pigs, and cattle for beef and milk. At the end of the summer's harvest, work began on the butchering and processing of the livestock in preparation for winter.

Ben stopped to wipe the sweat from his eyes with the back of his hand, and not a second had passed before his brother, Reuben remarked that he was slacking in his duties.

"The wheat will not cut itself, Benjamin," he chided. "If you intend to be treated as an equal in this family you must do your share." Twice Ben's age, Reuben had a wife and children of his own. His marriage had increased the size of the Voss family farm, as had the unions of brothers Simeon and Dan. The massive farm produced more than enough for the extended family of almost two dozen.

Other than hunting, Ben had one other thing that brought pleasure to his thoughts, Giselle Wise. The mere thought of the girl made Ben's blood warm, and even in the hot sun he flushed with visions of her in his imagination. Giselle was one year older than Ben, but she had never treated Ben as being younger. She had always had a smile for him, and when no one was looking she had even reached out and touched his hand. At the wedding of William Betcher the previous month, she had even kissed him on the cheek. He could still feel her hot breath on his skin. He could smell the scent of lavender soap and something else, a musky fragrance that drove him to imagine what it would be like to feel her bare flesh against his. She had said that she would be willing to offer more than just a kiss if the chance would arise. She said that she would let the man who married her touch her in a special way. She spoke often of how grand it would be to become part of the Voss family and Ben was sure that when he was a year, or maybe two older, she would be his bride. He would show his brothers and his father, he and Giselle would be married, and raise fine strong children. With her at his side, he would be the man that no one else thought he could.

Giselle had promised him that they would steal

away to be alone the first chance they had, and that chance would come in a few days. The whole community would gather to raise a house for his brother Issachar and his bride to be, Leyna Huffstutler.

Giselle said that there would be so many people there, that no one would miss them if they stole away for an hour or so. She assured him she would then allow Ben to touch her.

He was lost in thoughts of her, thinking what it would be like to have her in his bed when Joseph yelled, and swinging a fist knocked Ben to the ground. In an instant Joseph was on top of Ben, striking him again and again screaming, "You fool, you damn near cut my leg off!"

The others brothers had dropped their tools and were pulling Joseph off almost before Ben knew what had happened. He had swung the scythe too close to Joseph and caught his pant leg, tearing it and cutting Joseph's calf. Isaac and Zeb held Joseph back as Dan inspected the leg.

Reuben approached, while Ben was still on the ground, now sitting and holding his hand to his face, an eye already turning red and a split lip oozing blood.

"What happened?" he asked.

"That dunderhead liked to cut off my leg!" shouted Joseph.

Reuben looked down at Joseph's leg and then over at Ben, anger in his eyes. Shaking his head he held back the urge to strike Ben. He bent over, his face mere inches from the boy's and spoke, "You have come close to crippling your brother. You have also caused us to lose time and now Joseph will have to go to the house and have Rosalinda care for his wound.

"This takes him from his work and our sister from hers. How do you intend to make up for this? Get up and get back to work. If you were my son you would be punished here and now, but that is for father to decide. Joseph, go to the house and have Rosalinda tend you. The rest of you, get back to work, the day's not over yet."

Joseph bent down and picked up his scythe, and as he did so he looked at Ben. "I'll get even with you." Joseph spoke low and deliberate causing a chill to run through Ben.

Ben got to his feet, his hands shaking and his stomach churning from both the humiliation and the fear, not fear of Joseph, but of what his father would do. The biggest anxiety was not so much the beating that he would surely receive, for he had felt the razor strop across his back more than once. He was afraid that he would not be allowed to accompany the family to the house raising for Issachar and he would be deprived of seeing Giselle. Ben knew he could suffer anything but that.

Some of his brothers scowled at him as each one took up their scythes and went back to work. Ben moved over to where Joseph had been cutting and his bother Zebulun looked over at him. He shook his head and with a slight smile he leaned closer and placed a hand on Ben's shoulder.

"Why, Benjamin, do you always have your head in the clouds? You could have badly injured Joseph."

"I know," said Ben, "I didn't mean to hurt anyone."

"You never mean to do anything. How will you be respected if you do not grow up?" Zeb patted his little brother on the shoulder. "Now go back to work and try not to kill me." He smiled. Zebulun was the only one of his brothers who had ever taken the time to be close to Ben and treated him like a brother.

The sun was setting low in the sky when the sons of Jacob Voss left the hay fields to come up to the house. The wives of the oldest sons had come to Jacob's house and a large dinner would be waiting, not as sumptuous as the huge lunch they had provided for the midday's repast, but what appeared to be enough to feed an army.

They washed their faces and hands and all waited for Jacob to appear before they sat at the table. Their chairs sat empty until he came in to the room. The women and children had already eaten and those at this table would be only Jacob and his eight boys, from Reuben at thirty-two years-old down to Ben.

As would a king entering his throne room, so too did Jacob enter the large front room of his house. He was clean shaven save for a fringe of gray whiskers at his jaw line. His head was covered by a thick matt of hair matching the color of his beard and his cold blue eyes stared out from beneath bushy eyebrows that appeared like gray clouds over the his unblinking countenance.

He wore a boiled shirt with a stiff collar, a black cravat tight around his neck, and a dark tweed waistcoat. Covering all was a black wool frock coat and matching pants. His build was that of a wrestler, grown stout from years of heavy farm work. At sixty-five years old, he was still as strong as an ox, and it was said that he had single-handedly lifted a hogshead of tobacco from the ground and loaded it into a wagon bed down in Pittsburgh.

There was not a man in the county that would wrestle Jacob, even at his advanced years, and he would pass up no opportunity to challenge any comer to try and throw him to the ground. With no takers, he would be satisfied to force one of his sons into a match against one of the other young men and woe to the son that lost.

Jacob moved to the head of the table and sat down placing his hands flat on the smooth wood. This was the signal for his sons to take their seats starting with Reuben at his right hand followed by the next brother in line until Ben, the youngest sat at his father's left had. When all were seated, Jacob bowed his head and in his deep harsh voice prayed.

"God, all mighty, Source and Giver of all things, who manifests thine infinite majesty, and power in the earth about us, we give thee honor and glory. For the sun and rain, for the bounty we have wrenched from the fields with our labor, for the increase of our herds, we thank thee. For the enrichment of our souls with divine grace, we are grateful. Supreme Lord of the harvest, graciously accept the fruits of our toil as atonement for our sins, for the growth of our faith, for salvation to all.

"Though thou hast seen fit to take four sons from me before they were men, I give thanks for the strong hands of those sons seated here at this table. Give them strong sons of their own and bless the union of Asher and his wife Ruth, who after two years of marriage, have yet to provide children to this family. Bless and make fruitful the union of Issachar and Leyna Huffstutler who will join in marriage within a month.

"We also give thanks Lord, that our son Joseph was spared serious injury today in the fields. Help his younger brother to see thy path of righteousness and deliver him as a man to this family, not a wonton child, spoiled since birth by a frivolous mother."

The remark brought Ben's eyes up from the table where so far he had endured his father's words with down cast, and closed eyes. He glanced in the old man's direction, and as if possessing the ability to see through closed eyelids, Jacob swung his left hand, catching Ben across the face, sending him and his chair backwards to the floor. With not a moment's hesitation, Jacob resumed his prayer.

"Teach him also Lord, humility, so that he may know his place on this farm and at my table. He is a wicked son and a burden to his father and his brothers. Amen."

As his father spoke, Ben picked himself off the

floor and retrieving his chair set it back at the table, settling into it sheepishly. Jacob was the first to take food onto his plate and pass it to his right. As this first platter reached Ben, Jacob reached over and drew the plate away.

"Do you believe that you deserve to eat at my table?" he asked his son. There was no reply from Ben, save a look from watery eyes, one starting to swell from the blow he had just received. He hung his head and looked at his hands, now empty.

"It would be best that you went to your room and prayed for guidance, and prayer is best done on an empty stomach."

Without a word, Ben stood and headed up the stairs to the second floor. He went to the room that he shared with two of his brothers and sat on his bed. He knew he should be praying but all that could come to mind were questions. He had always been a great disappointment to his father. Ben hadn't a single memory of Jacob giving him a kind word, let alone a compliment. It had only gotten worse when Ben's mother died.

She had given Jacob a daughter, and going against his wishes, had named her Rosalinda after her grandmother. His disappointment was somewhat cooled when a year later Ben was born, giving Jacob his much sought-after twelfth son. Rebecca doted after the child who was born small and somewhat sickly. Because he began life so small, he was not expected to be as physically strong as his brothers, and he was constantly measured by his failures.

Ben didn't have the great girth of his older brothers, who were heavy of chest and short legged, but he did grow strong and straight limbed. While his siblings took more after their father he resembled his mother's people in stature, and by the age of twelve was as tall as his brother Joseph, who was more two years his elder. Ben could not match Joseph's strength but was faster afoot and quicker to dodge a fist if he anticipated its coming. This made the hostility felt by Joseph stronger and he took advantage of every opportunity to punish his younger brother. If Ben was unfortunate enough to fall into Joseph's grasp, his brother would pull him down, and with his superior strength, pin the boy to the ground, pummeling him unmercifully. Early on, Ben found that it did no good to complain to his father or other brothers as they advised him that he needed to toughen up, become a man, and take his lickings as a lesson.

When Ben had any free time it was spent in the woods hunting. As he brought game to the table, he was allowed this one pleasure for though his brothers were accomplished hunters on their own, Ben was far superior. He grew proficient with both the smoothbore fowler and a rifle. He was not the owner of these firearms, but was allowed to use those that belonged to his father, or a brother, receiving complaints that he wasted powder and lead when he was unsuccessful in a hunt, or when he provided too little game for what was expected for the table.

Ben was made for the woods. There, he was in his element, either hunting or just ranging through the forests. These were also the times he could meet Giselle. She would wander the woods much the same as him. They even had a secret place, known only to the two of them. They would meet and talk, in a small grassy glade shaded by the tall trees that filtered the sun's light, making the sheltered place seem magical. It lay on the brook that delineated the boundary between the Huffstutler farm and the Voss property. A small depression in the creek's course created a pool that on a hot summer days offered a cool place to swim. It was also close to where the house was to be built for Issachar and his bride-to-be. A perfect place for the two young people to meet, and Ben hoped, make love.

The next morning Ben was up before day break and started his chores before his brother's had risen from their beds. They would rise soon and begin their morning duties around the farm that were a daily routine before breakfast. Roslinda, of course, was the first to awaken each morning, for she was charged with the task of starting the breakfast that would feed the hungry men after morning chores. At eighteen years old, it was wondered by some why she had not married and obvious to others that her father wanted her to remain tied to his house to care for him and those under his roof. She was just placing a large coffee pot to heat, when Ben came into the kitchen.

"Ben! What are you doing up so early?" she asked.

"I have to make up for yesterday," he answered.

"Father should have let you eat." She shook her head. "I would have brought you something to eat, but Joseph or one of the others would have told him," she apologized.

"That's alright."

"Here," she stopped him, taking him by the arm. She opened a cupboard and withdrew a loaf of yesterday's bread. She cut a large thick piece of the heavy bread and then from a small crock spooned out butter, spreading it on the coarse slice.

"Thank you, Sister," Ben said as he leaned over and kissed her on the cheek.

"Well, no one can expect you to work without food in your belly." She smiled and patted him on the chest. "Now go about your business."

For the next three days, Ben worked harder than ever. He rose early, completed his morning chores, helped finish the cutting of the wheat fields, and spoke not a word, nor showed any outward sign of fatigue. He kept up with, and at times surpassed, Joseph's efforts. And though he received no praise for his efforts from his brothers or father, he felt that they could not complain either.

When the day of the house raising arrived, his father had not mentioned the accident of the previous week and Ben was allowed to attend. The neighbors for miles around had gathered to build a sturdy, little home. The men cutting and joining the lumber made fast work of erecting walls before the morning meal was set out by their wives and daughters.

Ben had worked, just as hard as any of the grown men there, again receiving no recognition from his own family for his labors. Mr. Huffstutler noticed Ben's efforts and remarked that he wished he had a second daughter as it appeared Ben would make a good husband. Ben blushed at the comment. Though Huffstutler's daughter was handsome, she could not compare to Giselle. Giselle was tall and willowy, with hair the color of corn silk and skin like alabaster. Her green eyes sparkled from beneath coquettish lids, and her smile had a way of melting Ben's heart while quickening his pulse. At times, just the thought of her made him shake.

As Ben worked, he would glance over to where the women were to catch a glimpse of Giselle. On her part, she too would be looking in the direction of where the men worked. He was sure she rewarded his glances with her smiles. At one time Ben struck his thumb with his hammer and she laughed. Ben swore at his own clumsiness, but the pain was worth seeing her smile, hearing her laughter.

As the men finished their morning meal and started back to work, Giselle found the opportunity to speak a few words to Ben.

"I'll be waiting for you in our place," she promised. "Watch for me to leave and then you come along, not right away but a little while later." Ben's heart raced in his chest, and for the next two hours he worked in a daze.

Ben watched as the blonde-haired girl made her way toward the woods. He waited what seemed like an eternity but it was no more than ten minutes before he started to look around, locating his brothers. He knew he could leave on some pretext or other, without arousing the suspicions of the other men but one of his brothers would notice his absence. He caught a glimpse of Issachar, but he had only eyes for his fiancée. All of his brothers, except Joseph, were in sight.

Ben descended the ladder he was working from and moved first to the wood pile and then to the water barrel. He lingered there just long enough to take a sip of cool water and then he turned and headed into the woods in a different direction then that taken by Giselle. He would circle back and meet her at the pool.

He made his way in a great circle, being cautious, almost as if he were hunting and did not want to alarm the game he pursued. As he approached the glade he had but a small portion of it in his view and what met his eyes stopped him in his tracks. Giselle stood, her back to him, naked save for her stockings. He could not believe the beauty of her slender figure. She was unbraiding her long hair, freeing it to hang down her back, touching nearly to her waist.

She turned halfway in Ben's direction exposing her full nakedness to him and bringing her hands up to her small breasts, she cupped them, smiling with some sort of self-satisfaction. One hand slowly made its way down across her flat belly and then between her legs. She bit her lower lip, and then smiled again. She let out a small laugh that both excited Ben and surprised him.

Ben was transfixed to the spot. Never in his wildest fantasies had he envisioned her so beautiful. He was afraid that if he moved in her direction she would be embarrassed and cover herself, mortified with the shame. But he wanted to touch her and was about to force one foot forward when Giselle reached out a hand in front of her. Ben moved some of the foliage that blocked his view of the glade and there standing before the girl was Joseph. Taking his hand in hers, she pulled Joseph toward her and they kissed, Joseph fondling her with his rough, callused hands.

Down they moved, onto the ground where she lay on her back in the cool grass. Joseph unbuttoned the front of his pants then crawled on top of her and nestled in between her legs. With the obvious delight of the girl, he began to move up and down with his hips.

Giselle let out small cries of delight and her legs moved with his motion. Her cries increased to deep moans as his thrusts intensified. Then, Joseph let out a sudden oath and collapsed on the girl, spent. Giselle still clung to him, her legs wrapped around him as if keeping him from getting up. She smiled in satisfaction and turned to gazed directly at Ben. Their eyes met, Ben's filled with horror, hers with delight. Her smile grew even broader, and she began to laugh.

Ben turned and began to run, he could hear her laughter behind him and his brother's voice asking her what amused her, but the sound of blood pumping in his head soon drowned out their voices Ben ran not caring where he went, or in what direction. He ran until he could run no more and then he collapsed to the ground and buried his face in his arms and cried.

He swore hatred for his brother, then for Giselle. How could she have done this to him? He contemplated going back to the glade and killing them both, but he knew that he couldn't do that. He wanted to get back at them in some way and contemplated telling his father, telling everyone in the small community what he had seen. Jacob would be furious, he would beat Joseph, and Giselle would be ostracized as the whore she was. These were the thoughts filling Ben's head as he sat and brooded alone and heart broken. He rose to his feet, and wiping the tears from his face with his shirt sleeve, he headed back to where the house was being built.

He worked the rest of the day with little thought or emotion, his head filled with the visions of the girl he loved and his brother. His thoughts broke only once when he saw Joseph emerge from the woods, a satisfying grin on his face. Giselle appeared some time later appearing at the same spot Joseph had left the trees. She looked about, and when she found Joseph and their eyes met, she licked her lips in a sensuous manner that made Joseph snicker and sickened Ben.

Working in silence, he brooded over what he had seen. He watched his brother and Giselle. Every time Joseph passed Giselle she smiled at him, sharing a secret Joseph thought only the two of them knew. But Ben knew, and it tore at his heart.

There would be one more meal served at the end of the day and the sun was dipping below the tree line in the west before Ben worked up enough courage to approach the girl. Tears welled in his eyes, his stomach churned, and there was a sour taste in his mouth. Giselle was setting food on a long table, helping prepare for the meal, when she looked up at Ben who had stopped in front of her.

"Hello, Benjamin." She cooed. "You didn't meet me in our special spot. Am I not still your favorite girl?" she laughed. Ben clenched his fists, rage and hurt welling up inside him. He felt a hand on his shoulder and whipped around to see Joseph standing behind him.

"You think you don't have to work like everyone else?" Joseph sneered. "I heard no call to quit work and eat. You don't have time to waste flirting with a girl that wants nothing to do with you."

Without warning, Ben sprang at his brother, hitting Joseph in the chest with all his weight.

Joseph, caught off guard was carried backwards to the ground, his brother on top of him. His superior size failed him as Ben's fists pounded into his face. Blows landed on his jaw and nose before Joseph could defend himself, but this consisted more of shielding his face with his arms than returning blows.

Several of the men reached them, pulling Ben off his brother. He struggled to free himself, kicking at Joseph. One of the men who held him was his brother Zebulun.

"Benjamin, stop!" Zeb ordered. "What has gotten into you?" Ben did not answer, but he did stop struggling to free himself.

"I'll kill you!" screamed Joseph, his hands held up to his face, blood making its way between his fingers.

"What is going on here?" It was Jacob demanding an explanation of the disturbance.

"He just went crazy," said Joseph. "I didn't do anything to him." He spat blood.

"Let me look at you," Reuben said as he turned Joseph's head to inspect his injuries. "It looks as if your nose is broken, and a split lip, that's about it."

Jacob looked from Joseph to Ben, his eyes filled with anger. "How can you shame your family in such a manner?" he asked, not really wanting an answer. "Go home, now! I'll deal with you when we are done here."

Zeb let Ben loose and Ben moved away. He looking neither left nor right, his eyes cold gray, the fire of his anger burnt out. As he passed Joseph he heard his brother hiss through a bloodied mouth, "I'll get you later."

Ben was drained of all emotions; he walked home, each step mechanical, one pace after another without thought, without care. He knew that when his father came home there would be a reckoning, at least in his father's mind, but it would be far from the end in Joseph's mind. One day prior these thoughts would have filled Ben with dread, with fear of his father and the older brother, but this day Ben didn't care. He was past fear, past caring what anyone thought of him, and this held him steady as he waited at home for his father and brothers.

The sun had set and it was well past dark when Zebulun entered the house, followed by Rosalinda. She placed a candle lantern on the table where Ben had sat in the dark. Her eyes were filled with tears as she started to speak, but was hushed by Zeb.

"Father is waiting in the barn," Zeb spoke softly, his words barely audible. Ben looked up at his brother, and Zeb repeated what he had said.

Ben moved slowly toward the door but Zeb reached out and stopped him.

"Why, Benjamin, why in God's name did you attack your brother?" Zeb almost pleaded for an answer. Ben looked into Zeb's face with blank eyes.

They moved out the door and toward the barn where their father and brothers waited for them. There was a single lantern illuminating the circle of Voss men when Ben walked in, and they parted so he could enter the center of this ring and face his father. Joseph's face was already showing signs of bruising, his lips were swollen and his nose was now bent to one side.

"Stand here boy!" his father ordered, pointing at a spot near one of the great beams that supported the barn roof. Ben stood looking into his father's face, emotionless, eyes like glass glazed over. He looked at his father's hands and saw the switch that was held tightly. Ben thought how new and green it looked. His father must have just cut it from a tree, on the way home. It was as big around as a grown man's thumb and about three feet long. Ben wondered if it would make a swishing noise as it was swung through the air.

"Let me have him, Father!" Joseph shouted as he

sprang for Ben, but was held back by his brothers.

"You and Benjamin may settle your differences another time," Jacob said, "This is a time for his repentance to the family." He motioned to Asher and Issachar. "Take your brothers arms and give his back to me." They turned Ben around and pulled his shirt up over his head and threw it to the side. Then, they each held an arm, not so much to keep Ben from running but in anticipation of supporting him when Jacob began to deliver the blows they knew were to be laid on Ben's back.

Jacob removed his coat, tossing it to Dan and then rolled up his sleeves. He stood slightly turned, feet apart, the switch in his left hand. Asher and Issachar felt Ben suck in a large breath as the shock of the first blow hit him. As the improvised whip swung through the air, it hissed, each time landing with a sickening slap against Ben's back. With each blow Jacob uttered a single word, shouted in his deep voice, "You...Will...Not...Shame...Me...Again!"

By the third blow, Ben's legs went out from under him and they had to support his weight, not knowing if the boy was still conscious or not. In truth, after that third blow Ben felt no more pain. Far off in the distance he heard his father's words, then a soft darkness enveloped him and he dreamt of cool water running in a brook. The trickling sound was like music as the water made its way around and over the rocks.

Ben awoke to the pain in his back. He lay face down on his bed and he could hear water being wrung from a rag as Rosalinda cleaned the cuts on his back. He turned his head and seeing the tears in her eyes could not hold back his own. He sobbed as she worked at the open welts, the blood still fresh. She applied a salve of lard and shepherd's purse on the cuts, and then laid a clean linen cloth across Ben's entire back.

She took the wet cloth and wiped the side of her brother's face. She shook her head as if to rid herself of what had happened. She knew her father could be cruel but had never dreamed he would hurt one of his own children so badly. She had resisted, but finally had to ask Ben what had prompted his actions.

"Why, Benjamin, did you strike Joseph so?"

"He had it comin'," Ben whispered.

"He'll be waiting for you. No worry just yet as father has told him to stay clear of you for now. As soon as you can leave your bed, he will want to get back at you for breaking his nose and taking out two of his teeth. He'll never look the same. He'll never smile with that gap in his upper jaw."

"He never smiled anyway." Ben surprised not only Rosalinda but himself with the remark, and they both gave in to a small smile of their own. She brushed his hair aside, and taking the bowl of water, started to leave the room.

"I'll come back in the morning after breakfast to check on you. Zebulun is waiting to see you. I'll tell him you're awake."

Zebulun entered the room just as Ben started to drift back to sleep but stirred him awake as he sat next to him on the bed. He gently lifted the cloth on Ben's back and whistled as he looked at the cuts then replaced the covering.

"How you doin'?" he asked.

"I'll be fine," Ben answered.

"I think I know what it was all about," he said. "I heard Joseph talking to Issachar. He said you were jealous that Giselle Wise was paying attention to him and not you."

"You could say it was something like that," Ben whispered.

"Well, if that's the truth of it, you should stay away from that girl." Zeb leaned closer to Ben's ear. "I'm not one to speak against a woman's reputation, but there is talk about her among some of the younger men that she is not pure." Ben let out a small breath with a knowing smile. Zeb went on, "They say she may have gotten the French sickness, and she has to use a medicine made from calomel. I don't hold much store in such talk, but if there is talk, there must be some truth, yes?"

Ben closed his eyes and wondered what everyone would say when Joseph came down with the pox. There was no vengeance better suited, he thought, then for Joseph's penis to rot and fall off.

"Father's temper has passed. Reuben and Simeon spoke with him and both of them would have you come to live in their homes, to separate you and Joseph for a time. Father has it in his mind that you are too willful and said as much, calling you a spoiled child. I know that's not true, Ben, you're just filled with too much thinking. You were never meant to be a farmer." He paused, "Father said he believes it best you were to leave for a time to learn what it is to be without family. He has written a letter to your mother's brother in Pittsburgh, asking him to take you in as hired help. He is a wainwright, a maker of wagons and he may take you on as an apprentice, even though you're a bit old for that form of service.

"I think it would be best for you, Benjamin. I hate to see you go, but it seems you'll not have peace here with Father or with Joseph." He placed a hand on Ben's shoulder. "I should not have told you this, but I wanted you to know what Father was planning. Know also that I am your brother, and always will be, no matter what. You needn't worry about Rosalinda. I promise I'll take care of her." He smiled and Ben knew that of all the men in the Voss family, Zebulun was the only one he could trust.

Ben slept little that night, the pain of his back mixed with anxiety of leaving the only home he had ever known. Before the sun rose, he left his bed and carefully dressed, pulling his shirt over his head. The cuts in his back stung from the movement, and from the cloth touching the tender flesh. He then made his way down to the kitchen where his sister was preparing to start the morning's fire. He moved over to her, taking the kindling from her. Forming the small pieces of wood into a pile he then took flint and steel to start the fire. Rosalinda stood behind her brother, her hand on his shoulder.

"I will miss you, Benjamin." She spoke softly, tears welling in her eyes. "I don't know what Joseph did, but I know you would not have struck him if he had not provoked you." Ben thought she may have been hinting she wanted an explanation but loved him too much to ask outright. He just stared as the flames in the fireplace grew to consume the small slivers of wood and he added larger pieces. He had decided during the night that he would keep what he had witnessed to himself. It would change nothing if the truth were known.

"I will miss you too, Sister," he finally said and he stood turning to faced her. He opened his arms and she moved into his embrace. They held each other for only a moment and Rosalinda pulled herself away. "Let me look at your back," she said, pulling out a chair from the table for him to sit down.

He removed his shirt, bringing more pain but held back uttering the least sound, not wanting his sister to know how much it hurt. She instructed him to sit backwards in the chair and lean forward against the chair's back. Tenderly she reapplied more lard and shepherd's purse to his wounds.

"Your back looks better, I don't believe there will be any infection, but you need to keep the cuts clean, and free of mortification. I'll put some salve in a pouch for you to take with you." Ben knew she meant well, but wondered how he would be able to apply the medicine himself. She helped her brother pull his shirt back on and she began preparing the morning meal.

"I will miss you so terribly," she said, the words choking in her throat as she fought back the tears.

"Zebulun will take care of you, Sister. As for me, I can't think of anything worse than having to stay here," Ben said. "I would hate for you to spend the rest of your life here under Father's hand. I will pray that someday William Hartmann will work up the courage to ask you to marry him." This surprised her. She had no idea that anyone knew that she and William had feelings for each other.

"How did..." she started to ask.

"Zeb noticed it a long time ago. Don't worry; your secret is safe with us. He only told me, he has said nothing to anyone else." Ben smiled. "Remember though Sister, if you stay here Father will work you into your grave like he did his wives. So if you have the chance, if William asks you to run away with him, please do so." Ben walked out the front door and moved to the porch where he watched the eastern sky begin to turn pale over the tree tops.

Jacob did not see fit to say goodbye to his youngest son. He would not even offer his presence when Ben left the farm, only Rosalinda stood in silence on the porch as her brother walked out of her life. Issachar and Zebulun would take Ben to his uncle in Pittsburgh. The journey would take three days down the Allegheny to where that river joined the Monongahela, forming the Ohio and the site where the first considerable settlement around Fort Pitt began to grow less than forty years ago. It was here that Whitney Blake built wagons, and hopefully, where Ben would begin a new life learning a trade as an wainwright.

CHAPTER 2
PITTSBURGH

Passing through the township of Elder, the three brothers followed Wolf Creek southeast to the Allegheny River and followed the river twenty-five miles downstream to Pittsburgh. The two older brothers, Issachar and Zebulun had both been to Pittsburgh five years earlier, but what lay at the junction of the Allegheny and Monongahela Rivers surprised them as much as it amazed Ben.

Pittsburgh had grown at a rate that seemed to burst from the forks of the Ohio. What had once been a small settlement of little more than 300 people, and a mere 100 houses along the banks of the Monongahela near the ramparts of old Fort Pitt, had grown to five times its size. After the Whiskey Rebellion of 1794, the main manufacturing had chiefly been in boat building with other industries such as a glass factory. When Issachar and Zebulun had visited in the spring of 1800, the commercial life of Pittsburgh revolved around sixty-three shops, half of these general stores, with four bakeries and four each shoe and hat shops.

Now there were over 300 different businesses ranging from the boat yards, paper and cotton mills and a brewery, to a stocking weaver and a comb maker. There were both saw and grist mills, oil, powder and salt works, but iron and textile manufacturing were the two largest industries in the town. All these businesses used the rivers as their life's blood for the shipment of goods of every sort, including coal, to as far away as Philadelphia via New Orleans.

What had at first seemed an easy task of finding their uncle became harder when the three brothers discovered that he was not the only wainwright in Pittsburgh, and Whitney Blake had moved into a new and larger location on Fifth Street. There were four other wagon yards in the town, producing everything from wheelbarrows to freight wagons, and it was late in the day when they made their way into the wagon yard of Ben's uncle. As they entered through the gate, they first saw three men working on a wagon wheel. Two of these came from the forge, holding a red-hot tire by long tongs, while the third, a tall, but burly brute, with broad shoulders and massive arms, waited near a tiring platform. This man was Whitney Ferguson.

The two men lowered the tire carefully onto the rim. As soon as the hot metal made contact with the wood it started to singe, sending up a gray smoke. With a flurry of hammering and levering, Whitney and one of his helpers positioned the hot metal evenly around the rim. When Whitney was satisfied the tire was in place, water was poured over the hot tire to start the quenching. When the tire cooled it contracted wooden parts of the wheel and there was the sound of the joints tightening. With a turn of the tiring platform clamp, Whitney allowed the nave to rise, adjusting what would be the final dish of the wheel. The wheel was then plunged into the tank of water under the platform for its final quenching.

"That will do for today, boys. A job well done and a good day's work," he said as he stood straight and wiped his hands together and then slapped the others on their shoulders. He smiled and turning noticed Benjamin, Issachar and Zebulun standing nearby.

"Uncle Whitney?" Issachar asked, not sure if this was truly Whitney Blake., and a bit uncomfortable calling the man Uncle.

"By gawd, is this a son of Jacob Voss?" Whitney

strode forward eyeing the three and holding out his hand, the smile still on his face.

"Yes Sir, I'm Issachar," he said, "And these are my brothers, Zebulun and Benjamin." He took the man's hand and shook it. Whitney's vise-like grip was strong and firm, but not in a show of power. It was the hand of someone who worked hard and had no need to prove his strength to others.

"Issachar? I would have taken you for your brother Dan, and you say this is Zebulun?" he took Zeb's hand.

"And this Sir, is our brother Benjamin," Zeb introduced Ben.

Whitney stood back and looked Ben up and down. This was the first time he had seen his sister's son. It had been years since he had seen the other two young men, and that was in the company of their older siblings Dan and Asher. These four had made the trip to Pittsburgh to purchase goods such as nails and glass that were needed on their farm and in the township of Elder. They had paid a visit to Whitney only out of courtesy to inform him that his sister Rebecca had died. They had called him "Uncle" at his insistence and out of respect for Rebecca and felt no discomfort due to Whitney's easy ways.

Whitney eyed Ben and then took the boy's hand and shook it, placing his other calloused paw on Ben's shoulder. "It is a pleasure to meet you Benjamin," he said.

"It's good to meet you Sir," Ben stammered.

"Well, what brings you lads to Pittsburgh?" he asked, but before they could speak he added, "We can speak of that later. The sun will be setting soon and you three will come home with me and have supper. You can stable your horses with the draft stock here but keep them separate. Those big Vermont drafters don't take kindly to farm stock."

When their horses were unsaddled, wiped down

and fed, Whitney was waiting for them at the yard gate. He had removed his leather apron and now wore a dark brown wool coat, cut in an older fashion, resembling a sleeved waistcoat. He placed a lock and chain on the gate to the wagon yard and turned down the road with the three young men following.

They had only to walk a short distance around the corner to the entrance where Whitney lived with his wife, Mairéad, but called Mary by most as the Celtic name was too hard to pronounce. The home was located on the second floor above wagon shop, and consisted of only two rooms, the kitchen and open dining area being the largest, and the other a bedroom for the couple. The Voss brothers would spend their night on the floor in front of the fireplace.

Mary was overjoyed to see the young men, and was not satisfied until she had seen them well fed. When the meal was over, she cleared the plates and resigned the men to sit around the fire and chat.

"Now then," Whitney began, "To what do we owe the pleasure of your visit?"

As the oldest, Issachar spoke, "We are here to beg a favor of you." He held his eyes down, almost embarrassed to continue. He felt shame for his younger half-brother.

"Uncle Whitney, if I may still call you that," Zebulun broke in, "There has been trouble at our farm and our father has sent us to you with a letter requesting your help." He looked over to Issachar who passed the letter to Whitney, who breaking the seal unfolded the paper and leaning toward the fire read its contents.

When he had finished, he looked from one brother to the other ending with Ben. Ben lifted his eyes from the floor to look into his uncle's face. A look of intensity had replaced the easygoing manner that had been there until now.

"Your father doesn't see much prospect for you,

Benjamin. He seems to think you are in need of breaking 'like a wild colt,' to use his words." Ben sat, not knowing if he was to make some form of reply to this accusation, or sit and listen.

"He says you are a willful and ungrateful child. Is this true?" Whitney asked.

"If that is what he states, Sir, then it must be true," Ben answered.

"We will see. He sends this note as a contract between him and me, bonding you to me as a servant. I am to do with you as I see fit."

"May I speak in my brother's defense?" Zebulun asked, and Whitney nodded in assent. "Since the passing of Benjamin's mother, your sister, our father has not been the most charitable toward Benjamin. I believe though Benjamin is not like me and our other brothers, the faults in him witnessed by our father are for the most part, in our father's eyes only. Benjamin is an intelligent and good hearted young man. I also believe, that with the proper hand, he could prosper."

Whitney sat for a short while and turning to Ben asked, "Benjamin, I will not accept you as a servant and will send this note back to your father stating as such. If you wish you may stay with me and if you work diligently, you will be treated with respect as a free man. The condition being that you treat me and mine with respect."

"I would be grateful, Sir," Ben said.

It was just before dawn the next morning when Ben said goodbye to his brothers, standing in the street outside the Ferguson house. There was a chill in the morning air, but Ben shook more from the feeling in his stomach than the cold.

"You do as you're told and don't add more shame to the family name," Issachar advised, his words flat and emotionless. Though he would miss Ben, he was attempting to be strong and set a good example for his young half-brother.

"Take care of yourself, Benjamin," Zebulun said, "Maybe in a few months Father will let you come home."

"I don't believe I'll ever return home Zeb." Ben shook his head. "I believe it would be best if I made my own way, as if I had no family back up the river."

"You'll always have family, Benjamin." Zebulun placed a hand on Ben's shoulder and gave a gentle squeeze. "Remember us Ben. Keep us in your thoughts. I will keep you in my prayers." He reached down and unbuckled his belt and removing his knife and sheath, handed it to Ben. "You keep this with you. It's a good knife and will service you well. I wish I had a good rifle to give you also."

Ben pulled the knife from the old leather and looked at it. The knife had come from Sheffield in England and had been Zeb's as long as Ben could remember. The blade was about seven inches long with the overall length just less than eleven inches. Attached by brass pins, the rounded, hardwood scales, were worn smooth and stained dark by his brother's hands. Zebulun had always kept a good edge on it and Ben knew this was a gift from the heart.

"I can't..." he started to say, but he choked on the rest of the words and tears welled up in his eyes. When he looked up, his brothers were mounted and riding up the street toward the river where they would cross on the ferry and then turn north for home.

Whitney Blake stood next to his nephew watching as the two young men rode away. As a friendly gesture, he slapped Benjamin on the back and was surprised when the boy flinched.

"Are you that frail that a simple touch makes you recoil?" he asked.

"No Sir," Ben replied, not wanting to complain about the whipping he had received. Whitney looked at the boys back and only then did he notice the cross-hatched stains on his shirt.

"Take off your shirt boy," he ordered, and Ben did as he was requested. Whitney stood back, a look of disgust on his face. It was not so much that he was opposed to the whipping of a man, but he wondered what the boy had done to deserve this from his own father.

"Put it back on son and tell me truthfully what you did to deserve these lashes." He paused, then added, "The whole truth, for I will know if you lie or leave out some detail."

Benjamin felt he had nothing to lose, and he told his uncle what had happened between himself and Joseph, including finding his brother with Giselle. Whitney shook his head, and motioned for Ben to follow him to the wagon yard.

As he unlocked the gate and swung it open he talking to Ben as they moved. "I am not in the habit of speaking ill of any man, but I will have you know that I was against my sister marrying that man. She had it in her head that his children needed a mother and that if she were a good wife she could make a good man out of Jacob Voss. I never thought he loved her, and I can see now that I do not believe he has given much love to her children either.

"I will ask you, Benjamin, is there more of your mother in you than your father?"

"Sir I believe there is none of my father in me," said Ben.

"Good, then make a pledge to me. I will give you a home and a means of making a living for yourself, I ask of you to treat me and your aunt with respect, be honest and give me a fair day's work for a fair day's wade." He held out his hand to his nephew, and Ben took it in his and they sealed the bargain.

"First thing we must do is let your aunt look at your back and determine when you can start to work in the yard."

"I can start now, Sir," said Ben.

29

"No, you cannot. You will pass the wife's inspection and will work only when she gives you release from her care."

Mary looked over Benjamin's back and was pleased with the medication her niece had prescribed for his care. She determined that in a few days he would be healed enough to take on some light chores, but Ben couldn't stand by idly and not earn his keep. He insisted that he do some form of work to repay his uncle and aunt. With this in mind, Whitney took him to the yard to show him around and to introduce him to the other men who worked there.

There were a total of eight employees at the Blake Wainwright; four from the eastern part of Pennsylvania, the others Germany by way of New York. Blake himself, had been trained as a wainwright in Ireland, but had left the Emerald Isle with his wife and sister, prior to the war with Britain.

They had made their way to Conestoga Township in Lancaster County, Pennsylvania, where Whitney's skill secured him work in a wagon shop. Though having little knowledge of the big freight wagons of the American west, his knowledge of Welsh Gambos, English Bow and Box Wagons, allowed him to master the complexities of these giants of commerce. He was soon a master of the craft and just after the war with Britain, Whitney moved to the area around what had been Fort Pitt.

Whitney led his nephew through the wagon yard to where a large wagon sat, and asked, "How much do you know about wagons, Benjamin?"

"Some, I guess," answered Ben.

Whitney smiled, and said, "I wager you do not know as much about wagons as you think. It is really of no matter. What you learned on the farm will do you no good here. We build wheeled vessels here as small as a barrow, and you will learn that craftsmanship is tested as severely there as with the wheels we make for these big freight wagons that carry 12,000 pounds of cargo.

"Look at her," Whitney said, placing a hand on the rear wheel. She is eighteen feet long, four foot wide. The floor has crosswise and lengthways sags in the middle and the front panel and rear door are slanted. This helps for when the wagon travels on steep inclines. This slope is carried on into the supports for the cover.

"Every point of strain is reinforced by iron, and all rubbing parts are given iron plates. The frame and the floor beams are of white oak and the boards of poplar. The hoops are made of hickory. The bed is only attached to the running gear at three points, one over the center of the front axle, where the axle swivels and two places over the back axle. The bed is not a simple box but is a basket which is able to take the strain imposed by the rough roads."

"She's a beauty, isn't she?" He took a step back, looking at the handiwork of his craftsmen.

Ben had never looked at a wagon as a thing of beauty, but as he listened to his uncle talk about the wagon, he could see the twinkle in the man's eyes, and the pride in what he had built. It was different from his father's pride of planting and harvesting a crop, his father saw no beauty, only labor, a chore to be done. Whitney's pride was not out of arrogance, it was almost a love of the art he practiced.

"It will be some time son before you have the skill of the least of the men that work here. This is not something to be ashamed of, it is ignorance, not stupidity, and ignorance can be defeated. You will start by learning the craft of building a wheel. Come with me." Whitney led Ben to the portion of the shop where the separate parts of wheel were produced.

"The first thing you must learn is that a wheel is not a simple thing. In fact, it is subtle and complex. It is built of wood and iron, without nail, bolt, or glue to hold it together. It can take the force of carrying two tons over rough ground.

"The ends of the axles that carry the wheels are not straight but inclined downwards. This causes the wheels to be slanted out at the top and in at the bottom. Wheelwrights call this inclination of the wheel the hollow, or the dip.

"Another most noticeable thing about the wheel is that it is dished–shaped like a saucer with hollow sides away from the wagon. This dishing counteracts the hollow of the wheel to bring the working spoke, the spoke that is carrying the weight, more or less vertical but not quite. The working spoke only becomes absolutely vertical when the wagon is running along the contour of a slope when the wheel will come under the greatest strain. The angle formed by the inclination of the spoke to the vertical on level ground is called strut. The combined effect of the hollow and dish strengthens the wagon wheel against lateral movement, especially the normal side to side movement of the drought beast. Flat, vertically- set wheels, such as those on a cart are not strong.

"Another subtlety of the wooden wheel is that the metal rim, the tire of the wheel, does not run at right angles to the spokes. If it did, the rim would only run on its inner edge. Nor does it run as right angles to an imaginary straight line between two opposite points on the rim of the wheel. If it did this, the rim would run on its outer edge. The rim of the wheel is in fact cut to a precise bevel so the whole width of the rim runs in contact with level ground. Every angle of a wheel has to be exact, and they must match those of the other wheels in the set. If any angle is wrong, the wheel will neither run nor stand up to heavy treatment.

"Learn the parts of a wheel; the tire, felloe, foot, spoke, tongue, nave, collet, foot, stopper pin," he said as he pointed to the parts, then added, "Don't worry too much about it right now, you'll catch on fast enough."

Within a week, Ben had learned his way around the wagon yard, and though he was assigned simple duties, such as cleaning out the stable area and sweeping up the shop floor, he gained a rudimentary knowledge of the flow of how the wagon yard functioned. He found the men who worked for Whitney Blake acted as a well-trained team, each man knowing his particular part of the trade, and their individual skills reflected in the finished product.

Not only did their craftsmanship add to what was made in the yard, they seemed to get along as a type of family and genuinely seemed to like each other. It was not long before Ben was taken into the fold and made to feel as if he were part of the group.

Another change was made in Ben's sleeping arrangements. As space was small in the apartment of the Blake's, Whitney gave Ben his own room above the work shop. Located close enough to the forge below, the space would be warm in the winter. To cool the room during the rest of the year, a window could be cut through into the wall looking out onto the street below. The area had been little used, housing odd planks of wood found unsuitable for the construction of wagons. These were more than adequate for creating walls, a door and a comfortable bed for Ben's quarters. It was the first time in his life that Ben had a place he could call his own, and he soon began to think of it as home.

*

As days and weeks passed, Ben gained the confidence of his uncle and the other men in the shop. He was enthusiastic to perform any task assigned him, and his knowledge of the wainwrights craft increased by leaps and bounds. Though he still performed the most menial duties, he also lent a hand at the forge and at the tiring platform where the hot iron tire was placed on the assembled wooden wheels.

His relationship with his uncle and aunt also blossomed. Mary treated Ben like the son the childless couple had always wanted. She would dote on him, mending his clothing, and making sure he was fed properly. In Ben's mind, she had taken the place of the mother he had lost many years ago.

In the wagon yard, Whitney treated Ben as he did all his employees, fairly but sternly. He showed no favoritism, giving Ben praise where it was due, and reprimanding him when needed. This treatment changed outside of work. When Whitney found out that Ben enjoyed hunting and had good skills as a woodsman, he made a bargain with his nephew. Whitney paid Ben a more than fair wage of 40¢ a day, and from this he deducted 5¢. This was to pay for an old rifle made by John Beck of Lebanon County. The long curly maple stock bore evidence of its use of over thirty years in the woods. Its relief-carvings were worn smooth by handling and the sliding wood patch box cover was missing, but the rifle's 41 inch barrel delivered a .42cal round ball with deadly accuracy. As a personal gift, Whitney had given Ben a sturdy hunting pouch and good powder horn. As an extra surprise, Whitney had scrimshawed, "Benj. Voss ~ His Horn ~ 1804," on the horn in an intricate script. On the opposite side of the horn, Whitney had placed the figure of a catamount, crouching as if to spring on its prey.

Ben could not have received a better rifle, at twice the price, even though Ben knew that there would come a day when the rifle would need to be bored out. A gunsmith would run a rifling tool down the barrel, cleaning the lands and grooves, of the barrel. This would increase the accuracy of the rifle, and also enlarge the caliber. Bu this would not be necessary for some time.

Sunday, the one day of the week free of labor, Whitney and Ben were like father and son, hunting together in the woods outside of the town. More than often, they came home empty handed but the time they spent together allowed them to truly get to know each other.

By Christmas, Ben had all but forgotten his life on the Voss farm. He had written two letters to his sister, and both had been answered by her. Her second post let Ben know that she and William Hartmann had planned on marrying, with or without Jacob's permission. If the patriarch of the Voss family would not agree, they intended to run away together. She promised she would let Ben know where they settled, hoping it would be as far from Jacob Voss as possible. Now that Ben knew that his sister was also free of their father's grip, he gained a real feeling of independence from the past and he could look to his future. He was truly happy.

SAM J. PISCIOTTA

CHAPTER 3
THE WHITEMEN

Captain Lewis gazed eastward out across the vast reaches of the plains, void of trees or shrubs, yet lush in midsummer grass fed by the recent rains. His blue eyes took in the rolling vista, scarred only by the course of Cut Bank Creek, flowing from mountains in the southwest, then turning and heading southeast to the Marias River and the direction he and his small party had traveled from.

Though his belly was full from the fresh game he and his party had found the past weeks, he was uneasy and disappointed that the last three days had been overcast, making it impossible for him to take celestial readings. Without making a sextant measurement of the daytime sun to moon distance, he could not set his chronometer at noon, which gave him the information needed to determine his latitude on the face of the globe. He was meticulous in his readings and in his journal entries and this lack of knowledge irritated him. He wanted to know exactly where he was.

To compound the disappointment of not being able to take his readings, he was apprehensive as to the safety of his small party. He was accompanied by only three men; the half-breed, George Drouillard and the brothers, Reuben and Joseph Fields. To explore the Marias River, Lewis had separated from his friend, William Clark and the main party, taking only eight of thirty-three men with him and then left four to portage baggage and canoes around the Great Falls of the Missouri. His original desire to meet the *Piikáni*, or Blackfoot Indians, had turned to doubt and he hoped

37

that he would not encounter them.

This uneasiness had grown over the past two weeks when he had lost seven of his horses to Indians. Drouillard had tracked the thieves for two days, returning empty-handed and with the news that whatever tribe of Indians had stolen the horses had left a large camp site, possibly fifteen lodges in size. By having his horse herd cut almost in half, Lewis then decided by necessity to leave the four men behind for the portage and take only three with him up river. He had made many choices during the expedition over the course of the past two years that were not easy ones, and this was one of those times. He was compelled to seek the source of the Marias River and calculated the chance was worth taking. He still held the welfare of his men as a priority, and almost as important, the safety of the records and specimens that he had collected.

Coupled with the diminished strength of his party, and the loss of the horses, were the warnings he had been given by the Nez Percè. These Indians, who had befriended Lewis and his company, said the Blackfoot were not to be trusted for they were a vicious and warlike people with no laws. Lewis was convinced that if he encountered a sizable number of Blackfoot he and his men were lost.

By midmorning, it was evident that cloud cover would not dissipate. Lewis, deciding to reduce the chance of being caught by the Blackfoot and waste no further time, descended from the bluff overlooking their small campsite in a grove of cottonwoods and ordered the horses saddled and the baggage packed. The four men headed south in the direction of Two Medicine River, reaching there by noon.

In the river bottom they found the site of what appeared to have been an Indian winter camp. Both sides of the river was covered in cottonwoods, honeysuckle and berry bushes. Rubin Fields killed a young deer and the four men settled down to eat fresh venison and allow their horses to graze. As they ate, they noticed a small group of antelope at a slight distance. They grazed on the rich grass on the river bottom until they were alarmed by the presence of wolves and took to flight, the large predators at their heels.

Drouillard pointed out two, reddish-brown swift fox playing on the opposite bank of the river and the party watched the small animals' antics until their meal was finished. Their short rest over, they followed the Two Medicine River southeast, with Drouillard traveling along the river bottom hunting more game as he proceeded, and Clark with the Fields brothers moving through the low hills, then on up to the open plain above.

They had no sooner reached a point where their view was unobstructed for endless miles when Reuben Fields pointed out what appeared to be a small herd of buffalo moving slowly in their direction. Lewis pulled out his telescope and confirmed his worse fears, what approached was a band of Indians not a mile away. A rough count gave him the number of over two dozen horses, but it was hard to discern how many were being ridden by Indians. Lewis was certain that these were Blackfoot. He was also certain they had not yet spotted him and the Fields brothers, as their attention seemed to be drawn toward the river bottom, possibly in the direction of Drouillard. His first impulse was to pull back in hopes that the band would pass them by, but if Drouillard was the object of their attention, this move would leave him prey to them and the loss of such a good man was not a consideration.

"Unfurl the flag," the Captain ordered Joseph Fields. The banner fluttered in the slight breeze and this drew the attention of the Indians, who when spying the pendant, began to mill around as if alarmed. They still maintained their course, approaching with caution. When a quarter of a mile away, one of the Indians made a break from the group and headed straight toward the white men. A cry from his lips pierced the cool summer air and sent a chill through the three men.

The warrior came to a skidding halt not a hundred yards away, his pony's hooves kicking up sod. Others in the Indian group howled their approval at their companions act, encouraging him. He spun the little horse around twice, whooping and calling out either taunts to an enemy or bragging to his friends of his bravery. He then wheeled his mount around and with a flick of his quirt sped back to his waiting companions.

Closer now, Lewis counted only eight Indians, mostly young men and boys, driving the riderless horses, some of which were saddled. Eight warriors made the odds two to one, and the Captain wondered if there were more Indians hiding close by behind the bluff.

"These may be Minnetare of Fort de Prarie, and from their known character, I expect that we might have some difficulty with them. If they believe themselves sufficiently strong, I am convinced they will attempt to rob us. Be ready for any treachery." Lewis told his men. "Keep back and I shall attempt to talk with them." He moved slowly toward the waiting Indians who had halted to watch the antics of the single brave on his brag ride. The thought that this may be a war party of young men out to make a name for themselves crossed his mind. The heated blood in a young man's veins could cause him to do rash things, and at this moment, Lewis wanted nothing to happen that wasn't thought through by cool heads. Holding up an open hand in a sign of peace, the Captain moved ahead of the two brothers. A single rider, different from the first, did likewise from the other side. He wore several raven feathers attached to the scalp lock on his head.

At a hundred paces, the two men meet and shook hands. The Indian was in his mid-twenties, as best as Lewis could guess, but had the look of a seasoned warrior and most likely the leader of this small party. Across his lap lay an English trade gun. The 20 gauge smooth bore could be loaded easily with either a round ball or lead shot, both devastating at a close range.

He passed Lewis and moved to the Fields brothers and shook their hands. While this transpired, the remaining Indians dismounted and advanced to Lewis and each shook his hand. One or two actually smiled at him.

The apparent leader came back to Lewis and made gestures in hand sign. Lewis wished Drouillard were present, for he was the master in speaking the hand language of the natives. Lewis understood the sign of "pipe" and "smoke". He replied in his limited use of signs, saying that the pipe was with another of his party down along the river. He suggested that as the Indians had seen the way this man had gone, one of them could accompany Reubin Fields, ride down and find Drouillard, and then they could all sit and smoke.

While they waited, the Captain then asked if they were Minnetares, of the Hidatsa nation. The one with the feathers in his hair answered that they were, but in a manner as if dismissing the question with the movement of his hand in sign language, saying yes. Lewis was now sure they were not Minnetares, but possibly Blackfoot.

He then asked if there was a chief among them. The group pointed out the young man with the feathers and two more. Certain that all there were too young to be chiefs; Lewis decided to give each a small gift. He instructed Joseph Fields to fetch presents from the packs. The Captain then gave an American

Flag to the warrior with the feathers, to the next a bright red handkerchief and to the third, one of the peace medals with President Jefferson's portrait on it. This seemed to please the three.

The afternoon sun was edging the western horizon and Lewis suggested that they camp together for the night. In this way, they would be able to talk, as he had much to tell them. Together they moved toward the river and were met by Ruebin, Drouillard and the Indian. Three aged cottonwoods stood in the river bottom and amidst these the Blackfoot threw up a domed shelter of tree branches covered with buffalo skins. Though open on one side, the half round tent had more than enough room for the eight Indians and they offered space to the Captain and his men. Lewis and Drouillard accepted, but both the Fields brothers chose to sleep in the open near the fire in front.

George Drouillard was a half-breed, French on his father's side. He was tall, straight, and had the black hair and dark eyes of his Shawnee mother. He was adept in the Indian sign language and Lewis now knew that there would be a better chance to communicate with the Blackfoot. For the past three years, George had always been with either Captain Lewis or Clark. He could be counted on in times of emergencies or danger, when his iron nerve, and coolheaded judgment had made the difference in the survival of the entire expedition.

While they sat and smoked the tobacco offered by the whites, the Blackfoot listened intently to what the White Chief had to say. They also answered his questions with what seemed to be sincere honesty. Through Drouillard, Lewis learned that they were part of a large band, less than two days march to the west, and there was a second larger band hunting buffalo near the broken mountains. He also found out that there was a white trader with one of the bands. This could only be a representative of the British for they said he had come down from the trading house on the Suskasawan River, only six days away. There, they traded wolf and beaver pelts for guns, powder and lead as well as liquor and blankets.

The Trading house they spoke of belonged to the British North West Company, and Clark wanted to win over the Blackfoot trade from the British. Lewis spoke to them through Drouillard, "I am a chief of a great Nation from where the sun rises. I have come a great way from the East up the large river which runs towards the rising sun. I have been to the great waters where the sun sets and have seen a great many nations all of whom I have invited to come and trade with me on the rivers on this side of the mountains. I have found most of them at war with their neighbors, and have succeeded in restoring peace among them. I have come in search of your Nation in order to prevail upon you to be at peace with your neighbors particularly those on the West side of the mountains. I wish you and your neighbors to come and trade with me when an establishment is made at the entrance to this river."

They seemed to follow the words as they flowed from the hands of Drouillard. Some nodding their head, others signify by the utterance of a slight "Ah huh." The Captain was pleased that the conversation was moving smoother with his friend Drouillard translating.

Lewis continued, "I am now on my way home and have left my party at the Great Falls of the Missouri with orders to descend that river to the entrance of Marias River and there await my arrival. Send some of your young men to your band and invite your chiefs and warriors to come down and council with me at the mouth of the Marias River. Tell them also to bring the white men you trade with.

"I am anxious to meet my men for I have been absent from them some time and I know they will be uneasy until I return. The rest of your group can travel there with us."

He paused, waiting to see if they would agree to his request. When they offered no reply, he added, "If you will accompany me, I will give you ten horses and some tobacco." There was still no answer to his proposition. The Blackfoot began to play a hand game with a stone and the Captain took this to mean the conversation had ended.

The Fields brothers watched as the Indians played their game and once in a while the Indians would attempt to draw them into the game. Both men declined using gestures as neither of them spoke the language of their guests nor the hand signs.

Lewis decided to take the first watch himself. He would rouse Ruebin before midnight and then lay down for an uneasy but needed rest.

*

This was the moon the Blackfeet called "When Birds Lay Their Eggs," and Walks Long lay on his side, his eyes wide open in the darkness. He loved this time of the year, the grass was still green, and there would be at least three or four more moons before the snows would start. He was far too excited to go to sleep, the events of the past days whirling in his head. Not four sleeps back, he and his companions had made a successful horse raid on their enemies, the Shoshone. The horse stealing raid had been his first and he was moving into manhood with pride and the wealth of horses. Now they had encountered these white men who camped with them. All of this had only been made better in that he had shared the adventure with his best friend, Calf Standing. The two were of the same age, born the same night, sixteen winters back. They were inseparable, and some in their band said they were of the same father. It did not matter to them for they thought of each other as brothers.

Walks and Looks at the Calf were accompanied

by six other Pikuni Blackfoot, of the Skunk Band, and were returning to their main camp with thirty horses. The leaders of this little party were Black Feather, the oldest among them at nineteen winters, Bear Head and He that Looks at the Calf. They each would receive four horses of their choice from the small herd. Walks Long, Wolf Calf, Calf Standing, Broken Horn and White Antelope would each receive three horses. Walks had chosen two fleet-looking mares with many colors in their coats and a young colt whose coat was almost blood red. This one, Walks thought, would make a great warhorse.

He listened to the crackling of the fire behind him and the snoring of the white men. Two of them looked very much alike and White Antelope guessed they may be brothers. The Whiteman with hair the color of dry grass, seemed to be their leader, and had just entered his bedding. One of the brothers now walked back and forth outside, constantly going from the fire to where the horses were picketed. The other man with the whites slept not an arm's length away from Walks Long. He was tall and dark-skinned like Walks and his friends, but he was not *sopokíítsitapiikoan,* a full blood, but a half breed of some tribe unknown to Walks. This one spoke the hands signs well, but like his companions could not understand the language of the People.

It was the tall one that had been noticed first in the afternoon. He was making his way along the river and had attracted their attention until they spied the other three and the medicine flag fluttering in the breeze. They quickly brought the horses into a closer group, for there was no telling how many more of these riders there may be close by. At first it was thought that the Raven People, the Crow, had caught up to them and that they may have to fight to keep the horses. Walks thought of this with mixed emotions as only two of their number had the

Whiteman's firearms and the other were armed with bows.

When they came up on the three riders, Walks could see they were white men, but not from the trading house in the north. These men were different, their clothing was a mixture of white and Indian but somehow nondescript. The moccasins on two of them seemed to be of the pattern worn by the Nez Percè, who use the bluish-black paint and pierced their noses. After the initial meeting it was agreed to camp with these men, they had offered tobacco and the opportunity for more gifts seemed possible. Black Feather had offered to share their shelter with the white men. Their chief and the half-blood had placed their bedding inside but the other two slept outside. This seemed foolish for there was more than enough room under the arbor and there was a chance of rain.

There had been much talk among Walks companions through the evening about these men. They all spoke openly for they knew their words could not be understood by the White men.

"These men do not know how to play this game very well!" Looks at the Calf said to his friends as he moved the small polished stone from one had to the other.

"Do you believe they know that they have each lost a horse in betting against you?" White Antelope asked.

"How can they not?" answered Looks at the Calf. *"I am now going to take their firearms as well. I may even let them gamble away their moccasins."* He let out a small laugh.

"I would not be too greedy, Calf," warned Black Feather. *"We do not know if they will honor their losses. Both you and White Antelope may be right in thinking they do not know how to play this game and possibly they do not understand that they have wagered away their horses and guns."*

"That is no concern of mine," Looks at the Calf

quipped. *"If they are too ignorant to understand the language of a human being they deserve to lose everything."*

"They do not even know we are Pikuni, of the Skunk Band." White Antelope said. *"Did you not tell them that we were Minnetares? They cannot tell one of the Real People from those dog eaters!"*

"They are smart enough that they wish to trade with us," Wolf Calf said.

"This is true, but their chief said they also wish to trade with other tribes," added Calf Standing. *"Do you want them giving firearms to our enemies the Crow, or Shoshone?"*

"I am uneasy here among these men," said Bear Head. *"They are generous with their gifts though."*

"They gave us plenty of tobacco," said Looks at the Calf.

"You say this only because they gave you the amulet that hangs from your belt." Bear Head pointed at the Peace medal that Lewis had given Looks.

"Would it not be better to leave early in the morning?" asked Broken Horn. *"They may sleep late and we would then be able to take the guns and horses before they can protest."*

"This would be best," Bear Head agreed.

"It is settled," Black Feather said. *"When the sun has not yet risen, we will leave. We will divide in to two groups. I will take part of the horses with Bear Head. We will go upstream and cross the river in that direction.*

"I will hold back and cover our retreat with my gun. Calf Standing, Broken Horn, will follow us after taking the guns from the two who sleep outside. Looks at the Calf and Wolf Calf, you will take the other half of the horses and go in that direction, up the river bank. Looks at the Calf, make sure your gun is ready to use so you may cover Walks Long and White Antelope as they take the guns from the chief and the half blood."

To Walks Long it seemed he had just closed his eyes when Black Feather touched his shoulder to wake him. In the early dawn he could see Looks at the Calf and the other two chosen horse thieves moving away from the fire light. Looks glanced back and smiled at Walks. When Black Feather was certain Walks was awake, he too moved off toward the horses. As he disappeared in the morning mist, one of the white brothers came over to where his sibling slept and lay down his rifle. He then turned toward the fire to add more wood, his back away from his firearm and everyone left in camp.

Walks glanced around the half shelter and could see his remaining three companions were slowly moving out, Calf Standing and Broken Horn edged toward the fire and stood there next to the lone Whiteman who was awake. White Antelope was positioning himself to take the half breed's gun and now it was Walks turn to move in and take the gun that lay next to the white chief.

He moved out from under his buffalo robe and while still on his hands and knees placed his trembling hand on the rifle. As one, all four moved to take the firearms from the whites. Walks Long stumbled and as he was getting to his feet he heard the half breed yell an alarm. Looking over his shoulder he saw White Antelope wrestling with the big man and turning spied Calf Standing and Broken Horn running away with the two brothers close to their heels.

Walks waited no longer, but ran as fast as he could with the chief's gun in his hands. The chief pursued him, yelling in his own tongue and fear welled up inside Walks. He thought of turning and using the rifle he held but had never fired a gun before and didn't know how to use it.

Over the sound of his own breathing, Walks heard the crack of a gunshot. At the same instant, he felt more than heard a buzzing go past his head like the sound of an angry wasp. He realized that he had been shot at and turning he found the chief still after him, a small gun in his hand. Walks came to a halt. The ownership of one of the Whiteman's guns was not worth dieing for this day. He dropped it in the grass and stood transfixed to the spot, unable to move.

The two white brothers now approached at a run and raised their gun, pointing in Walks direction. Before either could fire, the white chief spoke words and they lowered their weapons. Walks found the nerve to turn and moved away, first with a few hesitant steps then he broke into a dead run. He knew now that the whites had been able to retrieve at least three of their weapons. He hoped that White Antelope had been successful in taking the gun from the half breed.

He was now among the milling horses, both those of the whites and their own when ahead of him he saw Looks at the Calf, musket in hand. He motioned Walks to move to one side and raised the smooth-bore English gun to his shoulder and fired. Again there was the sound of lead flying through the air, like an angry wasp, and Walks ducked involuntarily. When his gaze came back up he saw Looks at the Calf holding his stomach and blood pouring out from between his fingers. Looks fell to his knees and then to the ground. Rising up on one elbow, he took aim and fired back at the White men. Walks ran to him but found he was now dead.

The gun fire had startled the horses and they broke into a run. Walks vaulted to the back of the first horse available and using the other horses as cover, managed to make his escape, across the river and then up the other bank. There he found the others waiting for him. As soon as Walks joined them they turned, and driving the horses before them, moved westward.

After a few hundred yards they crossed back to the northern bank of the river and turned north. Walks took a quick count of the horses finding that they had taken one of the Whiteman's but had lost almost ten of their own. This was a poor trade. He was now sorry that Calf Standing and he had come on this raid. He glanced to see where his friend was and found him slumped in his saddle as he rode. His chest was crimson with blood and it flowed out onto his stomach. Within a few paces, he slid forward and fell from his horse.

"Stop!" Walks called to the others as he pulled up hard on the reins, tightening the loop around the jaw of his mount. He vaulted from horse before it had a chance to stop and ran back to where Calf Standing lay in the grass, face down.

Turning Calf over he saw the gaping wound in the boy's chest, dark blood pumping out in spurts. His friend's breathing was labored and his skin was growing pale. Black Feather and Bear Head dropped from their horses and walked over. Bear Head knelt and inspected the wound.

"We must help him!" Walks pleaded.

"It is too late," said Bear Head. *"The light can no longer travel from his eyes to his heart."* Almost as to confirm what Bear had said, Calf Standing exhaled one long breath and breathed no more.

"This cannot be!" cried Walks. *"How did this happen?"*

"The two who looked like brothers chased us and one of them caught Calf Standing by the arm," said Bear Head. *"They struggled and the Whiteman took out his long knife stabbing Calf Standing in the chest.*

Black Feather stood looking back in the direction they had just come from. He was the leader of this small band and he felt he was responsible for the death of the boy lying in the grass. He looked back at the others and noticed that there was one more young man missing.

"*Where is Looks at the Calf?*" asked Black Feather.

"*He was killed by the white chief with his gun,*" Walks answered.

"*What do we do now?*" asked Bear Head.

"*We cannot go home without Looks at the Calf. I will go back for him.*"

"*I will go with you,*" said Walks. "*I wish to kill the white chief.*"

"*That may not be possible,*" cautioned Black Feather. "*We only had two firearms and we have lost one of those with Looks at the Calf. You do not even have your bow and arrows.*"

"*I must have lost them in the camp.*" Walks shook his head, then looking up at the others he said, "*Give me one of your bows, or if not I will go with only my knife.*"

"*We will go back only for Looks at the Calf,*" said Black Feather. "*We are not strong enough to fight these men.*"

"*I will go with you also,*" offered Bear Head.

"*This is good. The others will take Calf Standing toward our village and drive the horses. We three will ride back.*" He looked older than his nineteen years as did the boys with him who had now become men.

*

Crawling on their bellies to peer down onto the camp site, they spied dark smoke rising from what had been the fire. The White men had left, but before abandoning the area they had burned what belongings the Pikuni had left behind. In the dying flame were the remnants of shields, bedding and Walks bow and quiver of arrows.

They found the body of He that Looks at the Calf lying on his back. His English Trade Gun was missing, but around his neck was the metal amulet given to him by the chief not a day before. Walks bent down, and removed the medallion and inspected it.

One side had the profile of a Whiteman and the other the representation of two hands clasped.

"Why did they leave this?" Walks asked Black Feather.

"I would think it is to insult him." Black Feather pointed at the body.

"They did not scalp him or cut his body in any manner," Bear commented.

"It is possible that they do not know our ways and were afraid to touch the body."

"Is it not possible that they feared his spirit would..." Black Feather stopped Bear from speaking by placing his fingers on the young man's lips.

"We must not speak more of this. The medicine of this place is already bad."

They found that the White men had left nine horses behind, taking only what they needed to ride and carry their possessions. They placed the body of their friend on one of these and driving the horses before them moved up onto the plain. Black Feather thought it would be the right thing to do by giving all his horses to the families of Looks at the Calf and Calf Standing. He thought about this and wondered what kind of people these White men from below the great river were. He turned to look back and saw that Stands Alone was not following. The boy sat motionless on his horse looking in the direction the whites had gone. Black Feather rode back to him.

"Come little brother. We must take our friends home to their families."

"I will follow these men," said Stands. *"I will find where they go and leave signs for you to follow. Take our friends home and then come back with a war party. I will lead you to them and we will kill them."*

"Take my bow and arrows," said Black Feather. *"I have my gun and do not need them. We will be no more than three sleeps behind you. Do not attempt to revenge the deaths of our friends until we arrive."*

"I will only follow the whites," said Walks Alone. As he spoke, he reached to his waist and drew out his knife. With the sharp flint blade he cut away the long locks of his black hair to show mourning for his lost brother and friend.

Walks Long followed the tracks of seven horses, three were those that had belonged to the whites, and four were ponies the Pikuni boys had taken from the Shoshone on their horse raid. The men he followed took no action to hide their tracks, but seemed to be moving fast. By midday he knew he was close for he found a place where they had rested and grazed their mounts. Their course took them back down along the river and then again up onto the plains where the traveling was easier.

He hoped that the sky would not cloud over and he could follow by the light of the moon. Out on the open plain the grass lay flat where the horses of those he pursued had trod flat. He was satisfied that he would have no trouble following these men until in the distance he saw a large herd of buffalo slow making their way across the grassland. In doing so, they destroying the tracks of the men he followed. Walks decided that he would kept his course in the direction of the Great River, for it was there, he remembered the white chief said he was headed to meet with more of his kind.

Just at dusk, the sound of a distant gunshot reached Walks ears. He stood on the back of his horse to try and gain a better look around thinking he knew where the sound had originated, but was not sure. He stood on the little horses back long after it became dark and then in the distance he spied a soft glow. The whites had stopped to camp and were making a fire. Stands moved toward the light. There were no landmarks to use as reference on the flat grassland and the camp fire was but a small speck to the south. The moon shone bright though heavy thunderstorms obscured the rest of the sky.

Walks knew that the moon would reach its fullest point in one or two more sleeps and that the night light would be good for tracking. The raid on the Crow was made while the moon was small in the night sky and harder for someone to follow the horse thieves at night. Now it was Walks that followed using the small fire as his beacon, flickering from time to time and then growing dim. He was almost on top of the camp site before he realized it. A large dark shape seemed to swell up from the ground as he approached, the orange coals glowing in a small circle on the ground. Small shapes moved back and forth around the mound and the sound of growls meet Walks ears.

"Wolves," thought Walks as he dropped to his hand and knees, crawling forward. The squabbling among four large prairie wolves grew louder as Stands moved to within yards of them. In their gluttony they had no knowledge of his presence as they feasted on the fresh meat of a large buffalo cow. There were no White men in view and Walks surmised they had killed the cow, cooked some of the meat and then left. This meant that though they were not making an effort to conceal their tracks, they had rested only a short time and then moved on.

They feared they were being pursued. Walks felt a tinge of pride, thinking these whites were afraid that the Pikuni Blackfoot would catch them and take revenge for the killing of two from their band. Walks rose to upright position and let out a war whoop, frightening the wolves, scattering them. He walked over to the buffalo and cut meat away from the back strap. He blew on the hot coals and brought the fire back to life. Placing the meat on the fire he turned back to the cow.

The wolves had pulled at the soft belly flesh, exposing the entrails. These they had half devoured. Walks reached around in the mass of organs and found what he was looking for. His four legged brother had not gotten to the liver. As the piece of back strap cooked on the fire, he sat and cut small slices of the raw liver and ate them with relish.

This was the first he had eaten since the night before when he had camped with the whites. As he slowly chewed each bite, he contemplated the events of the past two days. He had always thought of other tribes with a mixture of contempt and to some degree respect. This included the Englishmen and what the Pikuni called the Real Whiteman, the French. These, he and his people had tolerated because they offered weapons that the People could use against their enemies. Now had come new White men from below the Big River who wanted to give guns to the enemies of Stands' people and had killed two young men of the People.

Walks thoughts were consumed by the notion that he must do everything in his power to keep these men from the land of the Pikuni and their brothers, the Siksika and Akainawa. These three bands made up the nation of the Blackfoot People. He was determined that he would take revenge on these men for the death of Calf Standing. With this resignation he allowed himself to rest, and slept until the sun's light shone on the horizon, turning the underbelly of the thunder clouds to orange and pale blue.

Walks Alone had never traveled so far by himself. He knew that the river he followed flowed into the Big River not far from his present position and it appeared that those he trailed were headed directly to the Big River above that point.

The sun was almost directly over his head when the sound of what could be thunder reached his ears. He was puzzled though as it seemed muffled, not quite clear. He hurried on and soon the sound of gunfire was clear to him. He was certain that he was almost upon the whites.

The Big River was ahead and Walks dropped from his horse and crawled the last few yards to look down from the bank. The whites were there below him and with the four he had trailed were more. He counted, five, eight, ten, and twelve. There were now sixteen of these men. Still this was of no great number if Black Feather arrived with a fair size war party.

The whites had unpacked their horses and set them loose. They loaded all their belongings in to canoes and set off downstream followed by Stand Alone. They went only as short distance when they pulled up onto the opposite bank and disembarking, began to search as if looking for something lost. One of them called out and they began to dig, revealing a hiding place where many goods had been secured in a hole in the ground. Some of the items they loaded into their canoes and others they discarded.

While Walks watched from the opposite shore, more whites rode up to join the group. This made the total of enemies three times ten. Stands hoped that Black Feather would bring a large war party. He also wondered what damage so many rifles would make in a battle.

When they had finished loading the canoes they set off again downstream to where the Marias emptied into the Big River, there they landed on an island in midstream. They spent some time there and emerged with a large canoe, one like Walks had never seen before. It was white in color, as wide as a man was tall and better than ten paces in length. From its center rose what appeared to be a lodge pole and hung from it was a large white skin or blanket that caught the wind.

It was not long before all the White men were either in one of the five canoes or the large one and quickly moved down river. Walks could not keep up, and watched as they disappeared down the Big River. He sat staring at the water as it flowed toward the east until the sun dropped behind him, then he slept.

His dreams were filled with many images and as one point Calf Standing stood over him. His skin was pale like the belly of a fish. His eyes were black as dead coals. No blood flowed from the gaping wound in his chest and from his lips there came the sound of rushing wind and then thunder. Rain fell in sheets about him causing Walks to shiver with cold and fright.

Walks Long woke, startled by the vision of a ghost. Around him a storm raged, just as in his dream and he was not sure if it had been a dream or a vision. This ghost was real and there was no rest for a spirit when the light was cut off for its heart. Stand wondered if he would live with this specter as his companion in the same manner he had lived with Calf Standing in life.

SAM J. PISCIOTTA

CHAPTER 4
FROM THE FORGE TO THE FIRE

Sparks flew as the hammer struck the hot metal Ben held on the anvil with a long set of tongs. Though his arms ached, and sweat rolled down his face stinging his eyes, Ben concentrated at the task at hand. He was attempting to weld links of a chain, and though he had only been working in his uncle's shop for three years, he intended to master this one skill that most apprentices didn't attempt until after twice that many years. The process required the welding, or forging of two identical links, then joining these two with a third un-welded link. After producing several sets of three, each of those was joined together with a seventh link weld, as so on.

Ben was frustrated. Either some of his welds were weak and rough, or one link here or there, was not identical to its mates. He was tempted to vent his frustration by throwing the hammer he held in his hand, but thought better. Under his uncle's tutelage he had been taught patience. Whitney Blake was an exceptional man. He was a hard taskmaster, demanding only the best quality from his employees, but he treated these men fairly and rewarded them generously for their labor. This generosity included such acts of kindness such as seeing that the family of an injured employee had food on their table when that man could not work for over a week. Whitney was loyal to his employees and they, to him.

"You're trying too hard," his uncle said, as his came up from behind. He patted Ben on the shoulder, as he spoke.

"I'm sorry, Uncle Whitney," Ben said shaking his head. "I just can't get it right."

"It takes time. Most apprentices start at a much younger age than you did. And even then, you know they don't master something like this after a few years." He turned and spoke as he was walking away, "Put your tools away and clean up, supper is ready and your aunt will be putting it on the table."

Ben looked down on the chain links, shook his head again in frustration, and turning away from the anvil left the forge. He knew his uncle was right, there would be plenty of time to master the craft of turning iron into what he willed it to be.

It was the first week in April of 1807, and the weather had turned warmer, with the daytime temperatures increasing daily. The nights were still cold but it seldom made it to freezing. What lite snow or rain that fell, left the ground muddy. As the sun dropped in the western sky, the chill in the air was intensified by a wind that blew in from the rivers on either side of Pittsburgh. Ben's shoulders, arms and neck started to stiffen as they cooled down after working in the wagon yard. He would wash his face and hands before he went into his uncle and aunt's living quarters adjacent to the wagon yard. It had been a long week and the next day was Sunday, a day of rest, and he would have to wait until Monday to try his hand at welding the chain links again.

Mary had waited until her husband and nephew were seated at the table before she placed the evening's meal before them. After a short prayer of thanks, they shared the meal of roasted beef, potatoes and bread, Whitney and Ben washing it down with beer while Mary abstained from the brew, preferring to have a cup of tea.

This time of the day was special to Ben. At the end of the meal, his uncle and he would talk, discussing the local news and the world outside of Pittsburgh. They compared the newspapers of Pittsburgh, The Pittsburgh-Gazette, The Tree of Liberty and the newest publication, The Commonwealth. Each had its own agenda, from conservative, to the more the Democratic-Republican principles expressed by Thomas Jefferson. Whitney tended to be more moderate in his views, but leaned a bit toward the newer views expressed by the President.

Though Whitney shared his general knowledge of the outside world's history, Ben was more interested in recent news. In September of the previous year, Captains Meriwether Lewis and William Clark had returned to St. Louis, from an overland journey to the Pacific coast and back. The Corps of Discovery, as it was called, had set off more than two years before to explore the territory of the Louisiana Purchase. Two of the boats the Corps used were made just down the river from Pittsburgh. Boats similar to these, were used up and down the Ohio river to haul freight as far as St. Louis, and beyond, to New Orleans on the Mississippi.

"What do you think it is like, out there in the Stoney Mountains?" Ben asked his uncle.

"I have no idea, Benjamin. I lost all wanderlust years ago when I found your Aunt Mary." He chuckled, and added, "She has been more excitement than I could ever hope for."

"Your uncle is lying" Mary interjected, "If he was a bit younger, the truth be known, he'd be off down river and out with those wild savages in the west, married to me or not."

"Now, Mary, you know that's not true, at least not wholly." He winked at Ben.

"Why do you think he tags along with you into the woods to hunt, every chance he gets?" Mary asked, not expecting an answer.

"I thought he just liked to hunt," said Ben, smiling at his aunt.

"Then, it is a good thing that our situation does not rely on his hands to put meat on the table, rather than his skill as a builder of wagons!"

"You cut me woman," Whitney feigned hurt feelings, "Have I been that derelict in providing for you?"

"You my love, have never, ever disappointed me," she said as she moved over to her husband and placed a hand on his shoulder. Leaning down she kissed his forehead, and added, "And, who else would put up with you?"

Even after living with his aunt and uncle for the past three years, Ben was always amazed at the difference between their marriage and that of his father's. There was never a harsh or bitter word passed between Whitney and Mary. Though they had been married for almost thirty years, they acted as if they were still courting. Their love was as fresh now as it had been when they first married. Ben wondered if he would ever find someone who he would feel that way about, and they him.

It was not that Ben hadn't met and been with some of the young girls in Pittsburgh, it was that they seemed perplexing in their behavior. They would either be overly coy, or worse, coquettish, endeavoring to gain the attention and admiration of men without sincere affection. He found them either boring, or childish. After his experience with Giselle, he dared not give his heart to any girl, at least none he had met yet.

Their conversation was interrupted by a knock at the door. Whitney asked Ben to see who it was and when Ben opened the door, his friend Dob Bergmann pushed in from the cold outside.

"Are you ready, Ben my boy?" he asked.

"Dob, I plum forgot," Ben said. Then turning to his uncle he explained, "Uncle Whitney, I forgot that I had promised Dob I'd go with him for an ale or two."

"As tomorrow is not a work day, I see no harm in it," Whitney replied.

"It is the Sabbath, though," commented Ben's aunt. "It would be nice to have you at services," she added.

"I won't be out too late Aunt Mary," Ben promised, as he reached for his coat and hat, hung by the doorway.

"Keep warm," his aunt reminded him.

Dob's real name Robert Bergmann, Dob was short for Robert and seemed to fit the young man better Bob or Robby. Ben took an instant liking to him when they first met. Though he was smaller than Ben, he was just as muscular from his hard work in the boat yard owned by Joshua Tanner. Dob had a head of black hair, and pale blue eyes that showed a hint of trouble. With most men, these two physical traits would be enough to set them apart, but Dob had a birthmark on his left check, extending down to the jawline. Shaped like a small three fingered claw, it was the subject of conjecture as to its meaning on the boy's face. There was a rumor that Dob had been abandoned as a child because his mother believed it to be the mark of Cain, and he had been touched by the Devil's hand at birth. No matter, the mark in some instances drew the attention of some of the young ladies of Pittsburgh, and Dob knew how to take advantage of it.

It wasn't long after Ben's 17th birthday that Dob convinced him into visiting one of Pittsburgh's many taverns, Dob's favorite being Shawan's Tavern, on the other side of the Monongahela River. Crossing the river required paying a ferry fee, and most times, Dob depended on Ben's generosity to supply this fee, stating that he would treat Ben to the first drink. This happened seldom as it seemed Dob was in constant need of money.

The patrons of Shawan's Tavern were a rough lot. From the first time, and each succeeding visit by the young men, fights inevitably broke out, ending down the lane near the glass works or in the coal pits. Ben's only apprehension in a confrontation was avoiding physically getting involved himself. He would exert enough of his own strength as needed only to get Dob out of a predicament. And though he had learned to wrestle with his brothers, Zebulun being his best teacher, if for nothing else to help Ben avoid being bested by their brother Joseph, Ben found out early that the men who frequented the taverns, didn't wrestle for fun.

So for his part, Ben would whisk Dob away, time after time to avoid the anger of an older and bigger adversary, infuriated by Dob's attentions to one of the barmaids, or when Dob cheated or welched on a bet while playing the game of Hazards.

Hazards, or Crebs as it was also known by some, arrived up river from New Orleans. It was played with a set of dice, and the players made their bets, wagering on whether the caster of the dice would win or lose, compared to a certain number established by his first throw of the dice.

It soon became obvious that Dob had learned how to manipulate the dice in his favor, and suspicions rose as well as tempers, placing not only Dob but Ben in jeopardy. Though they became the best of friends it was obvious that Dob gave little thought to Ben's safety, and compromised him often.

For his part, Ben accepted Dob for what he was, a careless, but good hearted friend. To him, Dob couldn't be any other way. If Dob had a dollar, he spent a dollar plus. If Dob had a loaf of bread, or a bottle of rum, he shared it with Ben. If Ben had the same, Dob expected him to do likewise.

During the winter months Ben and Dob looked for entertainment closer to home, avoiding the need to cross the river. This caused the trouble to come closer to home as well. But, with a good heart, Ben always seemed to help Dob out of his current predicament, and save him from physical harm and their friendship grew stronger as the months turned into years.

With the energy of young men turned loose, Ben and Dob headed into the cold evening air, Dob almost dancing down the street.

"Ben, my friend," Dob started his sentence in a way that warned Ben that Dob was about to ask for something. "I was hoping you might be in a position to loan me a bit of silver, possibly a dollar or two?"

"Dob, I don't have that kind of money to loan," Ben started, "I'll buy you a beer, but I have to watch where my wages go. My rifle is still in Coll McAllister's shop, and I have to pay him for the repairs to the patch box and re-bore of the barrel."

"Your Uncle owns the wagon yard," Dob said, "Are you saying he wouldn't let you have an extra levy or two? What is a half of a dollar to a man like him?"

"Dob, you know it isn't that way with my uncle. He has what he does because he works hard and he is frugal. He pays me a fare wage for my work. He doesn't 'give' me anything except a place to live." Ben could see his friend couldn't understand.

They made their way down to Water Street and then up river to Wood Street where the ferry for the middle crossing over the Monongahela River was located. Ben paid the ferry fee for the two of them without Dob asking, and Dob acted as if it was only natural. After dodging bits of floating ice on the black river's surface, the ferry landed them near Shawan's Tavern, and before entering Dob again asked Ben if he could spare at least some money.

"I tell you what," Ben said, "I'll loan you the half dollar, but you have to make that last." Ben knew that a half dollar could buy ten pounds of bacon, or twenty-five pounds of beef, but he also knew a gallon and a half of whiskey cost the same. He also knew Dob wasn't about to buy beef or bacon, and he would more than likely buy only one or two drinks. His friend would gamble away the silver, and at the end of the night, be broke again.

They found a corner table to sit at, and enjoyed a cup of beer while they watched the growing crowd of customers. Ben looked for nothing in particular, but Dob had his eye open for those men who he knew would want to gamble. It wasn't long before his vigilance was rewarded. A lanky fellow wearing a flowery waistcoat and a linen cut-a-way jacket entered Shawn's.

Dob waited until the man ordered a drink and found himself a table with a few other patrons. He watched for a short while as they chatted, and then the man in the fancy waistcoat pulled a pair of dice from his pocket. The others around the man's table positioned themselves around an open space next to the wall and started a game of hazards. This was what Dob had truly been waiting for. He rose and slowly made his way over to the group of men huddled around the "playing field." He stood on the outside of the circle, and sized up the players and what his odds might be of coming away with a few of the coins he saw tossed onto the floor during the betting. More important, Dob inspected the dice. He knew the man in the fancy waistcoat, and he knew that his dice were made of bone, and this pleased Dob. Dob had spent many hours making a set of dice that looked exactly like those being used, the difference was that Dob had imbedded a very small amount of lead near one corner of each dice. This weight, though small, made the dice heaver on one side and increased the odds of the same number coming up. Dob had practiced, and his dexterity with switching the sets of dice was unnoticeable

When the time was right, Dob made a few side bets, then he worked his way into the game. His first time at being the tosser, he lost what he had bet. This was not a worry, for on his second chance he switched the dice and he started to win. Throw after throw brought more money his way until there was better than twenty dollars in his possession. He calmly switched back the dice and lost his next throw, losing but a half dollar. With this loss, he bowed out of the game, stating he had to go outside to pee, and would return. To the protest of some and the relief of others, Dob headed out into the darkness outside the tavern.

He made his way behind the tavern and unbuttoned his fly. As he urinated on the snow covered ground, a man came to stand beside him, and proceeded to pee also.

"You were pretty lucky in there," the man said.

"Yep, I was lucky," Dob answered, as he buttoned back up his pants, and tucking his shirt in.

"A fellow might just think you had a bit of help," the man said turning to face Dob.

"No, just lady luck is all," Dob started to walk away, but was stopped by the man's hand on his shoulder. With the reflexes of a cat, Dob spun around to face the man, pulling a knife from its hiding place beneath his coat. "I don't want no trouble, friend," he said.

"Oh there's not gonna' be any trouble," the man pointed behind Dob. There, standing a few feet away were two other men, one holding a horse pistol. "There ain't gonna" be any trouble at all." He reached out and took the knife from Dob with one hand and swung the other catching Dob in the stomach. Dob fell to the ground, the wind knocked out of him. He lay there gasping for air.

"Shit," he gasped, between clenched teeth, more furious than afraid. All the hard work he had gone through, and now he was going to be robbed while taking a piss.

"Yes, you're lucky tonight," the man said. "My name is Griffin, and I work for Mr. Muller. Mr. Muller figured you'd be here tonight and he wanted me to collect the money you owe him. You have it?"

"Yea, let me get up and I'll give it to you." Dob made it to his hands and knees then onto unsteady feet. He reached into his coat pocket and pulled out the coins. He counted out eighteen dollars and placed it in the Griffin's hand.

"There, eighteen dollars," Dob said.

"No, you seem to be missing a few dollars," Griffin said flatly. "It was eighteen dollars a month ago. Now it's twenty-five."

"Twenty-five? You're wrong, it was only eighteen!" Dob protested.

"You don't seem to understand. It was eighteen then, now it's twenty-five."

Dob looked at the few coins he had left and could only come up with another three dollars. "That's all I have," he said.

"Tisk, tisk," said Griffin, "Mr. Muller has been a patient man, and he said he has let you go for weeks at a time, owing him money. He says to me, that if you didn't have the whole twenty-five, I was to break a hand or maybe both your hands, then you couldn't throw those dice anymore."

"I'll get the rest. Give me another week," Dob pleaded.

"You know something? Unlike Mr. Muller I'm a tolerant man, and I'm gonna" give you two days to come up with another five. That will compensate me for speakin' on your behalf to Mr. Muller."

"I appreciate that," said Dob, as he backed away for Griffin and his companions. "Maybe you'd see fit to leave me with a shilling or two so's I can get back in the game. Maybe win enough to pay you off?" he asked.

"Not likely, seems them boys were sayin' maybe you ought to be watched a bit more carefully. I do believe they think you might be cheatin' them, and I don't want anything to happen to you while you owe money to both Mr. Muller and me."

"Sure," said Dob, "Can I go now?"

"I reckon so," said Griffin.

Dob turned and walked back to the tavern. He had expected to dodge paying back Diederijk Muller as long as possible, but Muller was a short tempered man with a reputation of extracting what was owed him by the use of a heavy hand. Now Dob was backed into a corner with no idea where to acquire another five dollars, and his first thought was going back to Ben for help.

Ben was still sitting at the same table, but was now chatting to the barmaid, and it was evident that he had not even missed Dob's presence.

"Ben," Dob interrupted his friend's conversation, "we need to go, now."

Ben knew what that meant. Dob had overstayed his welcome, and to stay longer was to invite trouble.

As soon as they cleared the front door, Dob placed a hand on Ben's shoulder, and spoke with an intensity he rarely showed. "Ben, I need to come up with five dollars, now."

"Five dollars? Dob that's half a month's wages. You already lost what I gave you earlier?"

"No, had it taken away from me."

"You been robbed?" Ben stopped and turned to face Dob.

"Not exactly, I owe Diederijk Muller and I can't pay him back everything I owe him."

"How much were you into him for?"

"At first it was only a few dollars, but I kept gettin' in deeper and deeper, till he sent someone to collect."

"Maybe we can go talk to him and get you some time to pay."

"The time for paying is long past. I need that money now, or I got to leave Pittsburgh."

"Damn, Dob, I've got a bit saved up, but not five dollars," Ben almost apologized.

"No, you've done enough for me already. I got to

get the whole amount."

"Maybe you could talk to Joshua Tanner, and ask him to advance you the money."

"Yea, I'll do just that," Dob said and he turned back toward the ferry crossing with Ben at his side. Dob knew there was no need to ask his employer for an advance, as the man was constantly on the verge of firing Dob as it was.

*

Sunday passed, Monday's work day was almost over, and Dob was nowhere near figuring out how to find the money he needed to pay off his debt. He had watched his employer all through the day and as usual the man was never far from the office where he kept a small locked box containing the boatyard's cash. Dob had tried his best to come up with a way to ask for the money, but knew it would be fruitless. It was then that he decided to come back after work and break in to the office and steal the money, but fortune smiled on him. Joshua Tanner came out into the yard, and speaking to Elijah Becker, his foreman, said that he would be leaving early and that he expected the yard to be locked up at the proper close of day. Dob knew that as soon as Tanner was gone, the foreman would break out a bottle of rum and along with a few of the others, find a quiet and warm place in the boatyard to drink.

As he had thought, no sooner had Tanner closed the gate behind him than the foreman and three of the other men disappeared into a secluded corner of the yard. Dob made his way to the office and had little trouble prying open the cash box with his knife. As the tin box yielded to his efforts, what was revealed disappointed Dob. Inside the box were only a handful of papers, and a few banknotes, but no silver. Dob knew he couldn't transfer the banknotes, there would be too many questions.

He looked around the office, and hanging on the

wall he spied Tanner's fowler and shooting bag. The double barreled gun was made by William Westley Richards of England, and worth over twenty dollars. He grabbed the shotgun and slipped out the office and then made his way to the front gate and out onto Water Street. He dared not run, but moved as fast has he could walk, putting the boatyard far behind him. He had acted without much thought, as the shotgun would be just as hard to sell, as the banknote would be to turn into silver. He could give it to Muller's man Bob, but the gun was worth far more than what Dob owed and he decided to keep it. Rather than go to his own lodging, Dob headed for Whitney's wagon yard. He thought he could hide the gun in Ben's quarters, and retrieve it later.

The stairway that lead up to Ben's room was just outside the gate to the wagon yard, and Dob had no problem reaching the top without being noticed. Once there, he entered Ben's room and slid the shotgun under the bed. When he was satisfied the gun was well hidden, he went back down to the yard and looked for Ben.

He found his friend talking with his uncle in the office, and entered unnoticed until he stood next to Ben. When Whitney Blake looked over to Dob, he smiled, receiving a nod of the head from the young man. Ben turned and seeing his friend smiled and said, "Hey Dob."

"Hey yourself," Dob replied.

"You're just in time ta walk with me down to Coll McAllister's," Ben said.

"Oh?"

"Yep, Uncle Whitney just gave me my pay and an extra bonus. I have enough to pay off the repairs on my rifle."

Dob looked over and could see a drawer open in the large upright desk sitting on the bench top in front of Whitney. Whitney placed silver coins into a small leather bag, and then deposited the bag into the drawer, locking it with a key which he placed in his waistcoat pocket.

"You hear me, Dob," Ben broke into Dob's thoughts. "I'm going to get my rifle."

"That's just some, it is," said Dob.

"Come on, let's go," Ben urged Dob.

"It seems like it's been forever since I left my rifle with McAllister," Ben said. As they made their way to 3rd Street, the excitement was evident in Ben's voice. He looked over at his friend and then the realization came to him that his own stroke of good luck couldn't be shared by Dob. "Hell Dob, I forgot about the fix you're in. Here, you take the extra dollar I have if it will help." He held out the coin for Dob, who looked down at it then into Ben's eyes.

"Na, you keep it. I got it all worked out. You just go get that rifle of yours and don't you worry about ol' Dob Bergmann. I got it all figured out," he paused then added, "As a fact, I can't go with ya, I need to meet with a fellow and settle up my affairs." He turned and walked back in the direction they had just come. Puzzled a bit, Ben continued to 3rd Street, then down to Redoubt Alley and to Coll McAllister's gun shop.

Dob wasn't sure if he was angry with Ben, or jealous. Ben was always so damned self-righteous, he thought. He had almost considered the offer of a single dollar an insult and he knew what he'd do about his predicament with Muller. With each step he took, his anger turned into resentment, and his plans changed to getting out of debt, to getting out of Pittsburgh.

Whitney Blake was just getting ready to lock the wagon yard when Dob reached the gate, and stopped him.

"Ho, Mr. Blake, I lost my belt knife and wonder if it dropped back in the yard?"

"You're lucky you caught me Dob," Whitney said. "Let's go back in and we'll look." He swung the gate back open and they entered going to the office.

Dob pretended to look along the ground as they walked, and as soon as they entered the office he pulled the knife from under his coat, moving closer to Whitney. The older man turned to speak, and was surprised to see Dob with a knife in his hand.

"I see you found it," he said, only to realize that Dob was coming at him with the knife.

With reflexes, uncharacteristic of a man his age, Whitney swung his left arm, deflecting the swing of Dob's knife, and with his right fist landed a glancing blow to Dob's the chin. He then turned to reach a pistol he kept in one of the drawers. Dob lost his grip on the knife, and it dropped to the floor. Quickly, Dob reached for the first item handy and taking up a wagon spoke, struck Whitney across the back of the head. The older man sank to the floor, unconscious.

Dob rubbed his jaw where Whitney had hit him and cursed under his breath. He retrieved his knife and using it, pried open the drawer that held money. The leather bag was heavy and Dob opened it, pouring the contents onto the countertop. There were at least fifty whole silver coins as well as a few pie shaped bits.

He left the office and went up the stairs to Ben's room. There he retrieved the shotgun and shooting bag he had stolen. He looked around Ben's quarters and noticed how tidy Ben kept, and this irritated him. Things came too easy for Ben's he thought. Ben had a nice place to live, he was good at his job, he had a family who took carc of him and, the more Dob thought about it, the more he decided he hated Ben. He found a tinder box next to a candle near Ben's bed. Drawing out tinder, flint and steel, Dob lit the candle. He looked around and decided the bedding was the perfect place to start a fire. He figured that the fire would spread through the room and then down into the smith and wagon yard. He closed the door behind him and calmly walked toward the ferry crossing over the Allegheny near St Clair Street.

This time Dob would pay his own way across the river, and once on the opposite bank he would make his way down the Ohio to the Mississippi River and on to New Orleans. As his feet hit the opposite shore he never looked back toward Pittsburgh.

*

The stock on Ben's rifle gleamed with a deep, rich luster under a new coat of gun wax. The tiger stripping of curly maple stood out, and with the new finish on the barrel and other hardware, the firearm looked as good as new. Coll McAllister had taken the time to give Ben's rifle a complete makeover. Not only had he re-bored the barrel to a respectable .45 caliber, but had replaced the missing wooden patch box cover. The new one, matching the grain and stain of the stock, looked as if it were the original. He had also buffed out many of the scratches on the rifle. Lastly, he made Ben a new bullet mold for the larger size lead balls the rifle would now shoot. Ben could not have been happier as he walked down the street. Somewhere in his mind he fancied himself the image of a frontiersman, or a long hunter. He thought with a rifle like his, he could be a match for any game, or even a wild Indian.

As he turned the corner off of 3rd Street, he spotted the glow of a fire and smoke rising into the sky above the roof tops. It brought to mind his first summer in Pittsburgh, when a fire had broken out in a bake house on Market Street. The fire had quickly spread, and soon twenty building were engulfed in flames. Since that day, the inhabitants of Pittsburgh had been cautious when it came to fire, and large destruction by it had been avoided.

As he neared home he could see people rushing in the same direction, buckets in hand, and a knot grew in his stomach. He turned the final corner and saw the wagon yard on fire, and the crowd of people fighting the flames to get it under control. His first urge was to fight his way in and look for his aunt and uncle. When he made it to the walk outside their home, he found Mary sitting on the ground, cradling Whitney in her arms.

"Aunt Mary," he said, "Are you alright? Is Uncle Whitney hurt?"

"They found him in the yard and drug him out here," she answered, "I don't know, I don't know," she sobbed.

"I'll be right back," Ben said and leaving his rifle by his aunt, he went to help fight the fire.

It was several hours, and way into the darkness of night before all the flames had been extinguished, and any fear of a flare up put to rest. Those who had battled the blaze congratulated each other in succeeding to save most of the wagon yard, and the adjacent buildings, including the Blake home. Ben thanked as many of these men as he could and then turned his thoughts to his uncle and aunt. They had been moved one street down, to the home of Major Ebenezer Denny on Market Street between 2nd and 3rd Streets. Dr. Bedford had been sent for and was leaving Denny's house as Ben arrived.

"Dr. Bedford, is my uncle alright?" Ben asked.

"I believe he will live," the doctor said, "He took a good blow to the head. He hasn't regained consciousness yet, but hopefully he will by morning. If not, send someone for me and we'll decide if we must relieve the pressure on his skull by surgery." He smiled and placed a hand on Ben's shoulder to reassure him. "He is a tough one, your uncle, and I think it will take more than a knock on the head to kill him. Go in now and see your aunt."

Ben knocked on the door of the brick house and was admitted by the house keeper. Ebenezer Denny was a distinguished veteran of the War with Britton and choose to settle in Pittsburgh, first starting as a farmer and then investing in the glass works in 1801. This opened up other opportunities for him in the banking business and it was through the Allegheny Bank he had made many friends and business acquaintances. One of these was Whitney Blake and they had become close over the past year. The Major had intended to relocate to Louisiana for the sake of his young wife's health, but she died in May of 1806 at the age of thirty-one, and he remained in the house on Market Street, with Whitney a frequent visitor and a source of support.

Now it was the Major who would be support for Whitney and his wife. He was with Ben's uncle and aunt when the young man entered the room, Whitney lay in a bed, his head wrapped in a white bandage. Mary sat at her husband's side, holding his hand in hers. She looked up at Ben, and he could see she had been crying. He moved over to her and knelt next to the bed.

"His breathing has eased up some," Mary said, "We almost lost him Benjamin."

"He's pretty tough Aunt Mary," Ben tried to assure her. He stood and turning to the Major, asked, "Do you know what happened?"

"It would appear that the fire started above the smithy, and spread across that portion of the building. Most of the damage was there and to the roof."

"Above the smithy?" Ben asked himself, thinking that was where his room was located. "How was my uncle hurt?" he asked the Major.

"That's a cussed question. He was below on the floor of his office, unconscious, a result of that crack on the side of his skull I would surmise."

"I had best get back to the house and the wagon yard," Ben said. "I need to figure out what happened, and how the fire started."

Ben walked back down the street mulling over the questions in his mind. Was it a possibility that he had left a candle burning and it had started the fire? No, a candle wouldn't have lasted all day long, and then it would have just burned out. Could an errant spark from someplace such as the smithy floated in the air and started the fire? That was unlikely, as this everyone in the yard was careful about the way fires were handled. There had to be another explanation.

When Ben arrived back at the wagon yard, Albert O'Connell, the foreman already had the other employees looking for other potential places a fire might start, and assessing the damage.

"Ben, how is Master Blake?" he asked.

"We're not sure yet, "Ben answered.

"Well, you tell him we have it all under control, and not to worry. It don't look like there is too much damage, and we can be back in business come Monday."

"They said the fire started upstairs?" Ben questioned.

"It appears so," Albert commented, "Most of the damage is up there, in your sleeping quarters. Floor still looks stable, like I said no real damage." Ben wondered if Albert was insinuating that the fire could have been his fault.

Ben walked up the steps to his room. He couldn't understand what could have caused the fire to start there. He then noticed the brass candle stick holder lying among the remnants of his bed. "How did it get from the table to over here?" Ben said aloud. It was now obvious that the fire had been set intentionally, but who would do such a thing? He went back down into the yard where Albert waited.

"I think the fire was set on purpose," he told the foreman. "A candle was set under the bed, I found the holder there. I believe someone hit my uncle and then started the fire."

"Why start the fire up there if they wanted to cover up attacking Master Blake?" Albert questioned. "Don't make sense."

"Could have been my fault," Ben said. "Could have been meant to get back at me for something."

"What could you have done to make someone hurt your uncle and try to burn down the Wagon yard?"

"I don't know, but maybe we'll find out when Uncle Whitney comes around."

*

For the next three days Whitney Blake drifted just beyond consciousness. Mary barely left his bedside, leaving only when forced. It was her, that Whitney first saw when he did finally open his eyes. Through parched lips he whispered her name, and smiled and she turned and took his hands in hers.

"Whitney Blake, don't you ever scare me like that again," she scolded as tears of joy welled up in her eyes and flowed down her cheeks. She then bent over and kissed him, again and again.

Ben entered the room just as Mary was holding a cup of water to her husband's lips. Whitney looked over the rim of the cup and it was evident that he was glad to see his nephew. He drank, the cool water refreshing his dry mouth and throat. When he had finished he motioned for Ben to come close to the bed.

Ben knelt next to his uncle and the man reached out to take his hand as he spoke, in hesitant words, "Did you find him?" he asked.

"Find who, Uncle?"

"Dod," Whitney closed his eyes as if trying to clear his head and form more words.

"Dod? Why would I need to find him?"

"He...he...was the one who hit me," Whitney finally put the words together.

"Why?"

"Don't know. He said he had lost his knife...then he hit me...from behind."

"You rest, Uncle, I'll go find him, and get to the bottom of it all."

Ben was both puzzled and angry as he left the Major Denny's house and headed down to Water Street. At a dog trot he moved down the street to the boatyard where Dob worked. With no hesitation, he searched the yard looking for his friend.

"Hey there," called Elijah Becker, "What do you want here?"

"I'm lookin' for Dob Bergmann," Ben said.

"Well sir, you are not the only one looking for him." He then pointed to the office where Joshua Tanner, the owner of the boat yard stood. Ben headed over to the man who turned as he approached. Tanner was a short, square built man, with a large barrel–like chest, and large round head that sat on his shoulders with hardly any neck visible between the two.

"Mr. Tanner," Ben spoke as soon as he was close enough for the man to hear him, "I'm lookin' for Dob Bergmann."

"You are, are you?" Tanner's small round eyes blazed with anger and his fleshy jowls reddened as he spoke. "You're not he only one looking for the little bastard. You'll have to stand behind others that have first call on his hide."

"You don't understand Sir, he has done injury to my Uncle Whitney, stole what silver he had, and set fire to his wagon yard."

"You mean Whitney Blake's business?" Tanner asked.

"Yes, Sir," Ben answered.

"We can add those crimes to his thieving, and violation of contract." Spit flew from his mouth as Tanner spoke. "I'll be placing an advertisement offering a reward for his return. He was indentured to me, though out of the kindness of my heart I did give him a stipend and a place to sleep. He then repays my good heart by emptying my cash box of $70 in bank notes, and relieved me of my fine English fowler and hunting bag. He'll not be able to draw silver on the notes, as they are made out to me personally."

"Then you have no idea where he may be?" Ben said this more in resignation than as a question.

"I'll tell you the same as I did the others that came looking for that scalawag, Dob Bergmann, I have on good authority that he has gone down river. It is there that I will post notice for the reward of his capture and return of my gun."

"You say that there were others looking for Dob?"

"Yea, and they looked a rough sort too. I only hope if they find him, they leave enough for me to get a piece of his hide."

"Thank you, Mr. Tanner. I 'spect I'll be headin' down river after him," Ben said as he turned and left the boat yard.

Ben returned to Major Denny's home. His uncle had fallen into a peaceful sleep and his aunt was also taking some rest, assured that her husband would recover. The Major took Ben aside to learn what Ben had discovered about Dob.

"I intend to go down river after him," Ben told Denny.

"Don't be too rash, Benjamin. We can send word down river and have him apprehended. I know Jean Baptiste Lucas, the Superior Judge, and Territorial Secretary Frederick Bates, acting Governor for Louisiana Territory. I will draft letters to both men and we shall have some real action when it comes to finding your Mr. Bergman."

"I appreciate your offer, but I feel that I must go after him. It isn't that I don't trust the way of the law, it is just I want to bring him back myself."

"I understand that you feel compelled to act on your own, but let me place letters in your hand as a means of introduction, to aid you."

CHAPTER 5
THE OHIO RIVER

It took Ben little time to find that Dob had used the ferry crossing near St. Clair Street, and less time to discover that Dob had paid $1.00 for passage on a keelboat downstream. Though Ben had a pouch with twenty silver dollars hanging by a leather strap around his neck, and hidden beneath his shirt, he choose saving his money, and easily found a place on a flatboat heading down river with various goods to trade. He knew this would make his journey a bit slower, but the frequent stops made by the flatboat for trading, would gave him the opportunity to ask about Dob. In return for his passage, Ben had only to work as part of the boat's crew.

The flatboats that plied their trade up and down the Ohio, and Mississippi were built especially for navigating big rivers. They were used by freighters, traders, and sometimes by two or more families traveling with their farm animals. Some flatboats transporting larger cargos, could be 100ft long by 20ft wide or more, and were normally covered throughout their entire length. These required a crew of at least, four men and a pilot, who were contracted for a four-to-six week period; some professional flatboatmen made three or four trips yearly down river.

Ben's flatboat was 55ft long and 16ft wide. At the rear was a pen containing four cattle, and forward there was a cabin that served as living quarters and storage. Built like floating forts, the cabin had only one door, and four small windows, with sliding shutters. The walls were pierced with loopholes through which guns could be fired. For navigation, the flatboat was rigged with 40 foot long sweeps on the sides, a combination rudder and steering-oar at the rear, and a short front sweep called a "gouger". The side sweeps, resembling horns from a distance, gave rise on the river to call these crafts Broadhorns. The side sweeps were used for directing the flatboat into the current, or for pulling into slack water when landing, rather than for propulsion. Ben's craft also had had a rope hawsers mounted to a reel. This could be attached to a tree or stump and wound in to warp the boat off a sandbar, or to assist in landing.

It was 60 miles downstream, at Stuebenville on the Ohio bank of the river, that Ben got his first news of Dob. After unloading the cattle brought down from Pittsburgh, Ben went into the store and its proprietor easily remembered the young man with a red mark on his face, and readily admitted that he had sold Dob a jug of corn whiskey, and traded him an older Wheeler rifle for the shotgun. He even admitted that he thought he had gotten one over on Dob as the Wheeler was no were near the worth of the fine English fowler. Ben thought better than to tell the merchant the shotgun was stolen, but he did post a short letter to his Uncle, in care of Major Denny, advising that he had found word of Dob and that Joshua Tanner's gun was at the store in Stuebenville.

Ben also learned that Dob had stayed on the keelboat and was still headed down river, toward the Mississippi. He also found that someone else had been looking for Dob. Three men, one named Griffin, had asked about Dob, offering a reward of $10 in silver. The merchant was more than happy to supply the same information to them as he had Ben.

Ben was now at least a week behind Dob. He worried that the slow pace of the flatboat would put Dob further and further out of reach, but his fear was relieved when the pilot of the boat told him that there would be fewer stops as they had taken on all the goods they could carry, and the intent was to get down to the Mississippi as soon as possible.

Ben knew that sooner or later he would find Dob. His one hope was that he found him before Diederijk Muller's men. He knew who Griffin was, and figured Dob must have somehow gotten cross ways with Muller and sent his minions after him.

The remainder of the trip along the Ohio River was eventless, and at what few stops that were made, Ben was reassured by news that Dob was still headed down stream. At Cincinnati, he found that the gap between the two of them had narrowed to only four days.

Four weeks later, after maneuvering the Falls of The Ohio River, the flatboat pulled in at Clarksville. As at other stops, Ben asked around about Dob, and was surprised to find out that a young man with a red mark on his face had not only stopped there, but might still be in either Clarksville or on the southern bank, in Louisville. Knowing his friend, Ben was in no doubt where Dob would be found, either a place where there was liquor, women or both.

He started with the obvious first, a tavern where, as he approached he heard what seemed to be a fight inside. He no more reached the front steps then the tavern's door flew open and Dob burst out. Dob couldn't stop, and Ben couldn't avoid being bowled over by him. As they hit the ground in a dusty heap, three men exited the tavern in pursuit and where on top of Dob, each attempting to land blows with fists, well aimed kicks, or in one man's case, a wooden club.

Ben dodged the flying fists and kicks, rolling away from the melee and gaining his feet. It was obvious that the men were going to beat Dob to death if Ben didn't stop them. He retrieved his rifle and standing a few yards off yelled for the men's attention.

"Hold there," he yelled, "Or I'll fire on you." This stopped two of the men, but the biggest of the three kept striking Dob.

"I said stop!" Ben cried out, and pointing his rifle at the man took one step forward. His hands were sweating, but steady as he centered the rifle's front site on the man's chest.

"This is none of your business," the big man said, "You best lower your peace, turn and walk away."

"I'm afraid I can't do that," Ben said, a small bit of his frayed nerves reflected in his voice.

"This son-of-bitch a friend of yours?"

"He was, but I come to take him back to answer for what he done up in Pittsburgh," Ben said, his voice becoming steadier.

"Well, my name is Seth Griffin, I work for Diederijk Muller of Pittsburgh, and I do believe I have first claim on this peace of shit," he paused and took a step closer to Ben. "You can have what's left of him when I'm done, and that won't be much."

As Griffin spoke, his companions started to move further apart, one to each side of him, spreading out making harder for Ben to cover all three with his rifle. If they rushed him, he had only the one shot and the other two would be on him, then he would surely get the same beating they had in mind for Dob, or worse.

"You look as if you intend on killing him, I can't let that happen," Ben said as he took a step back, but keeping his rifle pointed at Griffin.

By this time a crowd had gathered to watch as the men faced each other, and it seemed that no one noticed Dob rise to his feet, retrieve his rifle and slip away toward the river.

"You know you can't shot but one of us," Griffin said as he smiled. "It would be a shame for you ta' die over the likes of Dob Bergmann. What do you want to take him back for?"

"He stole from my Uncle, hurt him pretty bad too."

"It would seem you and me have come to an impasse. No needs for that, as we both want the same thing. You want him to go back and to pay for his crime, me I just want my money or a pound of flesh. The way I see it, you leave him to me and I'll save you the trouble of having to haul him all the way back up river.

By this time one of the trio had moved far enough to one side that he made a move for Ben, who sung his rifle in the man's direction, but not soon enough. The man on the opposite side also moved toward Ben and landed a blow to the side of Ben's head with the short club.

Ben went to the ground, knocked senseless, and slipped into unconsciousness. When he awoke, he was propped up on the porch of the tavern, an older man standing over him, with a watchful eye. Ben blinked his eyes into focus, the back of his head felt as if it had been cracked open like a ripe melon. He lifted a hand and felt the back of his skull. Thought not as bad as he feared, there was a sticky wetness in his hair, and he brought away fingers with blood on them.

"You seem to have gained your senses. It would appear you got yourself rowed up Salt River," the man said, meaning Ben had been beaten. "No offence meant, you seem to be capable of handling any one of those fellows one on one, but with the odds three to one, you didn't have much chance. I don't cotton to three big men tearing into a single man."

"Thank you. Not sure what happened." Ben looked around and found his rifle and belongings leaning against the wall next to him.

"My name is Clark, I own the grist mill here," the man said. Can you stand?"

"I think so," Ben replied, rising on unsteady legs. The movement brought new pain, especially in his ribs. Ben felt them gingerly.

"Easy now," the man said, putting out an arm to help Ben up. "You took some good kicks before we could separate you from those fellows. I take it they weren't friends of yours?"

"No Sir, just tryin' to stop them from killin' Dob is all."

"You mean the scoundrel that took off and left you to fend off those three by yourself?"

"Yep, do you know what happened to him?"

Last I saw of him, he was headed that way," his pointed over his shoulder in a general direction with his thumb.

"Thank you," Ben said. Steadying himself, against the rough log wall of the tavern, Ben felt not so much better, but satisfied he wasn't hurt too bad.

"You headin' after this friend of yours?" ask Clark.

"Yep, though he isn't a friend, he's a thief and worse. His name is Bergmann, His given name is Robert, but most everybody call him Dob. I aim to take him back up river to Pittsburgh."

"Well I admire your tenacity, but it doesn't appear he wants to go back up river, now dose it?"

"No, I 'spect not," Ben said.

"Then what do you intend to do?"

"I guess I'll figure that out when I catch him. Right now I just want to get to him before they do," he said referring to Griffin and his mates.

"Come I'll walk a ways with you and we'll see if we can determine where your quarry is headed."

They moved toward the river front, and as they walked some they passed tipped their hats, saying, "Afternoon, General" or "Good day, General." and Ben took a better look at the older man walking next to him. He was possibly the same age as his father, Jacob, standing slightly taller than Ben, and Ben could tell age must have taken away some of the man's height, making his well over six feet tall when he was younger. His head was bare of hair on top, though the sides and back held thick strands of gray that hang down to his shoulder, and pulled back behind his ears. He walked erect, with a military bearing, but it was clear that years of hard living had taken its toll on him, and though not evident at a glance, a close look showed a man who's movements were not as fluid as they were at one time. There was a slight limp signifying a posable injury or the affliction of rheumatism in his left hip.

"Do you have any idea where your friend might go?" Clark asked.

"Until now, he has been going down river, I figure all the way to New Orleans."

"That's one option," said Clark, "From here, he could also take to the Old Indian Trace. It leads west toward Vincennes on Wabash River. There's east also. He could cross over to Lexington on the other side of the river. Then again, a lot of folks are headed up the Mississippi to St. Louis and the Rocky Mountains."

"The Rocky Mountain? You mean the Stoney's?" Ben showed a bit of excitement.

"Yes, some call them that," added Clark. "As near as I can remember, the Spanish have called those mountains the Rockies for some time. They are in a part of the new territory that has been added to the States."

"Part of the land purchased from France," Ben said, in an attempt to show he wasn't ignorant of the world.

"Yes," said Clark, "so you know about the Corps of Discovery?"

"Yes Sir, my Uncle Whitney and I talked about it. He told me he would have gone west with them fellows if he'd been younger and not a husband."

"I would have like to have gone myself," said Clark, "but I had to be satisfied that my younger brother, William was part of that enterprise."

It was at this moment that Ben realized who the man he walked beside was. His steps hesitated and then he spoke, "Sir I heard those fellows back there call you 'General.' Are you General Clark? General George Rodger's Clark"

"Yes, but for now I am only the owner and operator of a grist mill," he said, "and, my days exploring and fighting Indians are over. That doesn't mean I cannot help you find your Mr. Bergmann."

Once they reached the river there was little information to be gained about Dob. Several people had seen the dark-haired young man with the mark on his face, but no one could agree on which direction he had taken.

"I seen someone kind'a like that headed up toward the old Indian Trail, the Trace, Gen'ral," a boatman offered, adding, "that's what I tol' them other fellows, 'bout an hour past."

"Was one of those fellows a big man, had the look of a feral hound about him?" asked Clark.

"Yea Sir, ugly brute, he was."

"I guess I'll head that way after them," Ben said. "He isn't that hard to track with that mark on his face."

"What mark is that?" asked the boatman.

"A red mark down the left side of his face, all the way to his jaw," Ben said, making a claw-like motion down the left side of his face with his hand.

"Oh then I told those others fellows wrong, I don't think the rascal I seen headed toward the Trace, had a mark on his face."

"Did you see anyone who did?" Ben asked.

"Sorry, not many people around these parts with a mark like that."

Ben had no idea what to do next. It seemed that he had Dob in his hands and let him slip away. For a brief moment he was sorry he stopped Muller's men from taking care of Dob, but he knew it wasn't the right way to bring about justice for his uncle.

"Looks like you have some decisions to make, young man," said Clark.

"I 'spect I do," Ben said with his head down.

"Why don't you come up to my cabin and spend the night? In the morning, with a new look on things; you can get a fresh start. In the meantime, I'll spread word to see what information we can get on the whereabouts of Mr. Dob Bergmann."

The sun had risen above the trees across the Ohio River and Louisville was lost in the morning haze, the mist that clinging to the river. Clarksville, on the opposite side of the river, was starting to glow with the red of dawn. Ben, sat on the front porch of George Clark's cabin, a cup of hot tea in his hands looked out across the river, letting the new sun and the tea's warmth seep into his body. He was sore from the blows he had received the previous day, but not hurting so bad as to dampen the beauty of the view in front of him.

The General had moved to this site, on a rocky point overlooking both the town and the Falls of the Ohio River, only four years ago, built the cabin, and situated the grist mill at the upper end of the falls, near the lower rapids. Until that time he had lived across the river at his sister, Lucy Clark Croghan's home, in Locus Grove, Louisville. Though not a spacious as the brick, Georgian style house of his sister, the two room cabin was as comfortable and roomy as he could want. His only fear was that his years spent exposed to the element of nature, had now manifested itself in the weakness of his limbs. His left hip in particular had shown signs of be rheumatic, and at times he was unsteady, teetering as he walked. It was frustrating to admit that his strong will and character would be defeated by a body that had grown weak.

Ben liked and admired the man. Though grown old, and to some point infirmed, he was what Ben pictured as a hero. He had been a soldier, and an explorer. They had spent the previous evening

chatting, the General telling Ben about the war with
Britton here in the West, and Ben letting him know
about himself, his life on the farm and in Pittsburgh.
Ben also explained what Dob had done and why he felt
responsible to bring him back to face the law for his
crimes.

"Retribution is not always achieved through the
courts," the General said. "At times right and wrong
just have a way of working things out," he paused,
"Not that fate doesn't need a helping hand now and
then, mind you."

"I guess that's kind of what my Aunt Mary would
say. She'd tell me that God will take care of Dob, but
Uncle Whitney would agree with you on that part
about the helping hand," Ben said.

"How old are you Ben?"

"I just turned twenty, Sir."

"Hum, when I was about your age, I left my home
for the west. I lived with my grandfather so I could
attend school and he taught me how to survey land. I
went to survey in western Virginia and then up to
Pittsburgh, and down the Ohio into Kentucky. I would
say you're ready to head out and see what the world
has to offer, even if you don't find this friend of yours."

Ben gained confidence from the General's words
as he fell asleep that night, but now in the lite of day
his concerns didn't seem to weigh as heavy. He sipped
his tea wondering what to do next.

He heard foot steps behind his as the General
came out on to the porch to stand beside him. He
stood out of respect not only for the man who was hero
in the war against the British, but for the man who
had taken him in as a guest.

"Good Morning, Sir," Ben said.

"Good Moring, Master Voss," replied the General,
"it sure is a beautiful site, isn't it?"

"Yes it is."

"You sure you want to go traipsing off after this Dob fellow? Is he really worth the effort?"

"I think so, Sir," Ben paused, trying to find the words to express how he felt. "I guess it's a matter of honor. He took advantage of my friendship, and that I could let go, but he hurt the people I think most of in this world. I can't let that go."

"I can understand that. Set your cup there and we'll go back into the town and see if we can find more information about him."

They walked the short distance back into the town and with the company of the General, people willingly offered any information they had. Most was of little help until they heard what a black slave had experienced the previous night. His master having lost a canoe, blaming his servant's lack of vigilance.

"Tell your story to the General," his master ordered.

"Yes Sir," the salve said, "I seen the devil! I swear!" His master scowled at him, of course not believing the story.

"You saw the Devil?" asked Clark, "Can you tell us what he looked like?"

"Yes Sir, he had the mark of Cain on his face, all down one side."

"This side of his face?" Ben asked, pointing to his own check.

"Yes Sir," the salve shook his head. "He done climb into the canoe and shoved off."

"That has to be Dob," said Ben, "It means he either crossed over to Louisville or headed down river."

"Easy enough to find out if he went over," remarked Clark, "We cross over and see if there has been any sign of him. Possibly find the canoe there."

The General sent word back up to the grist mill and soon one of his slaves appeared, carrying the General's rifle and shooting bag. The three borrowed a batteau and with two other men, Ben and the slave rowing, the flat-bottomed boat, quickly crossed over to the opposite shore.

It was clear that George R. Clark was equally respected on both side of the Ohio, for his quarries were taken serious and quickly answered. There had been no site of anyone answering Dob's description, and no discovery of a unclaimed canoe.

Slightly dejected Ben made no comment. He ran things over in his mind as he helped row back across the river. Should he give up and return home? What would his uncle and everyone else think of him if he did? Or, should he take advice form the General's own life and head off into the unknown? If he found Dob, so be it. If not, what difference would it make?

By the time they reached the opposite bank Ben had decided that he must try to find Dob, if nothing else, to lend fate that helping hand. He had no intention of killing him, but he would make sure Dob never forgot that he hadn't gotten away with anything.

As they stood on the dock, Ben weighed his options on how to follow Dob downstream. The flatboat he had arrived on had departed earlier in the day, taking with it his haversack and blanket. Now, he was not only without transportation, he had lost most of his personal possessions. He was grateful that he still had his knife, rifle and shooting bag, as well as what little money he possessed in a leather pouch hung by a leather thong suspended around his neck. General Clark could see some distress in his new friend's eyes.

"Young Master Voss, I won't give you advice other than what remarks have passed between us already, but I can see you are determined to follow Dob Bergmann. I would like to aid you in this venture. I'll help you acquire passage down river," he reached inside his coat pocket and withdrew a folded piece of paper and handed it to Ben. "And, I have written a letter of introduction for you. It may open doors for you that might otherwise be closed."

"Thank you, Sir," Ben said, taking the letter and placing it inside his shirt.

"We have other business to attend to before you set off," said the General. He turned motioning for Ben to follow him, and they walked to a small store near the river front.

As the General entered, he was greeted by the proprietor, "Good morning, General."

"Good Day to you, Mr. Amos," he replied. "I am in need of a few items and would like them add to my account."

"Not a problem, Sir. What can I supply you?"

Clark looked around and selected a used, but stout haversack made of tanned deer hide. He also pointed to a stack of wool blankets saying, "One of those point blankets, I believe a white one, with the indigo strips, a four point in size." He paused, then added, "Add some jerked meat, some ship biscuits, salt, a pound of coffee beans and one of those pint tin cups." The storekeeper collected the dry goods from behind the counter, the hardtack from a box labeled "G. H. Bent Company, Water Crackers, Milton Mass."

The General eyed each item as it was placed on the counter and turning to Ben asked, "Do you take sugar with your coffee young man?"

"Yes, Sir," Ben said, only then realizing that the goods the General was purchasing were intended for him.

"A cone of sugar also, Mr. Amos," Clark said with a smile.

"Will that be all?" Mr. Amos asked, as he placed each of the small items inside the haversack.

"I believe so, just enough to keep a body fed for a few days." Clark turned back to Ben. "I cannot send you off without sustenance and a good blanket. The English make damn fine blankets, and a four point is a good size to keep you warm without being too heavy to carry."

"General Clark, I can't afford these things," Ben said, looking at the goods in front of him.

"If I felt payment was necessary, I would have broached the subject before we entered the store."

"Sir, I can't accept such kindness, it is way too generous," Ben began to protest, feeling uncomfortable.

"Ben, I took men into the wilderness, asking them to trust me, and they suffered greatly from starvation. I will not send you off without a bit of dried meat and some hard bread."

"Thank you, Sir."

"I would also like to give you a personal gift." From a sheath attached to the back of his own shooting bag, he pulled out a tomahawk. "I have had this for many years and I would like to see it go west with you." He handed over the long handled belt axe, and Ben's eyes welled up with gratitude.

The axe was typical of the type carried by both soldier and militia long before the French Indian War. Its head was formidable measuring six inches with a blade edge of almost four inches. The back was poled, with a flat surface that could be used like a hammer. This was all at the end of a dark hickory handle nearly sixteen inches in length.

"I don't know how to thank you, Sir," Ben stammered out.

"You thank me by coming back here some day and telling me about what adventures you have had!"
*

Dob had headed toward the falls on the river and then took to the Trace. The Trace was a major trackway crossing the Ohio River near the Falls of the Ohio and continued northwest to the Wabash River. It was known by various names, including Buffalo Trace, Louisville Trace, Clarksville Trace, Vincennes Trace, as well as the Old Indian Road. Well known and used by Indians, the Trace was originally a buffalo migration route, twelve to twenty feet wide in places. Later, traders and American settlers learned of it, and many used it as a land route to travel west into Indiana Territory.

In 1802 William Henry Harrison, governor of the Indiana Territory, recommended that the Trace be improved as a road suitable for wagon travel, with inns developed for travelers every thirty to forty miles. By 1804 the Trace was so well known that Harrison used it as a treaty boundary with Indians. The Vincennes treaty of 1804 gave the U.S. government possession of Indiana land from south of the Trace to the Ohio River, including the Trace itself.

Dob knew by the traffic on the road that he could easily lose his pursuers. After fleeing from them at the tavern, he followed the Trace until just before dark. He then left the trail, and from a hiding place that gave him a good view of the trail, he waited. Within an hour, Griffin and his men came up the road and passed him by. Waiting for the sun to set in the west, Dob returned to the trail and headed back toward the Ohio River. Once there, he went to the river front, found the canoe and slipped into the river to drift down stream in the dark of night.

Dob had not expected the appearance of Diederijk Muller's men, but Ben showing up as he had, took him by more surprise. He was somewhat afraid of Griffin and his two goons, but the thought of Ben so close shook him physically as well as mentally. Even now, the next day, he quivered a bit at the thought of Ben somewhere behind him. His escape was not the best planned but he was pleased with himself that he had outwitted Griffin and possibly Ben too.

He had made up his mind. New Orleans was not the place to go, as there were too many people in that big city. Instead, once he reached the mouth of the

Ohio, he would go up the Mississippi to St Louis. He had heard that there were no laws in this frontier town, that whiskey flowed like water, and women threw themselves at you. He also understood that it was the gateway to the west and offered limitless opportunities to get rich, the streams so thick with beaver you could walk up and club them with a stick. Yes, St. Louis was the place for him.

CHAPTER 6
THE GATEWAY

Once again, Ben traveled down river on a keelboat. Dob was at least a full day ahead of him and Ben had no way of knowing how far the canoe could out distance the larger, heavier water craft he was on. He felt in his gut, that the distance between Dob and himself would increase as each day passed, but that wasn't worth worrying about until later. For now, his only fear was that once Dob reached the Mississippi, he would go down river, to New Orleans, while the destination of the keelboat Ben was on would travel in the opposite direction, up river to St. Louis.

The keelboat made fewer stops as it moved down the Ohio River to the southwest, but at what stops it did make, Ben found word of Dob. Dob had stopped, at almost every landing there was, and in his wake, had left hard feelings. A chicken stolen here, a man cheated at dice there, and more than once, the father or brother of some young girl that was interested in the where-a-bouts of Dob Bergmann.

What was evident though, was that Dob was increasing his distance between himself and Ben. Sixteen days after leaving Clarksville, Ben reached Fort Massiac, on the Illinois' Bank of the Ohio, and word had it that Dob was now more than a week ahead. From Fort Massiac, it was a mere thirty-five miles to the Mississippi, and Dob would have already made his decision whether to go up or down stream. In his own thoughts, Ben wondered that due to Dob's laziness, he wouldn't prefer to drift down stream rather than work to paddle up to St. Louis.

A week later the boat was within a day's travel

from the end of the Ohio. It was here that they landed and the crew found an illegal trading post with whiskey as the main trade item, and the boat's captain had a hard time in keeping the crew from an extended leave. Ben had no wish to linger either, but the stop was rewarded with a bit of information about Dob.

As Ben waited near the trading post, he was approached by a girl that appeared to be no more than thirteen or fourteen years old. In her hand she carried a crockery jug of what Ben supposed was whiskey. She walked in a way that reminded Ben of a cat as it moved closer to a mouse trapped in a corner. Her thin cotton dress barely covered her willowy frame, and revealed far more of her "charms" than Ben had the inclination to see. She was barefoot and it was obvious she hadn't been acquainted with bathing for some time.

"Hey there," she cooed, in her best seductive voice. "You want a pull on this here jug?"

"No, thank you," Ben replied

"How about something else?" she asked, pulling the tattered dress up her pale legs, and above her waist, to expose more bare flesh. This was as filthy as rest of her, and rather than excite Ben, it made his stomach a bit queasy.

"I do appreciate the offer, but I don't have a coin to spare," he replied to her offer.

"You have to give me somethin'," she demanded, her voice changing becoming somewhat threatening. "If'n I go back up there, without somethin'," she pointed with a nod of her head toward the trading post, "I'll get a whuppin', and I ain't gonna' get that. I'll tell my Pa, you done took what you wanted and then didn't pay me none. He wouldn't like that one bit. Might have to come after you." She smiled a broad, green-toothed grin.

"You're some, you are," Ben said. He knew he had to give the girl something, but had no intention of reaching inside his shirt to reveal the location of his coin pouch. He reached into his haversack and pulled out the cone of sugar, unwrapped it, and then cut off a small piece with his knife. "I'll give you a bit of sugar if you leave me alone."

At the sight of the sugar, her eyes lit up, and she shook her head yes. Ben offered her the large chunk of the rich, brown sweetness.

She popped the chunk of sugar into her mouth and chewed on it, closing her eyes and smiling in delight. "That was just about the finest thing! I don' 'member when the last time it was I had me some sugar."

"You're pa really beat you if you don't come back with somethin'?" Ben asked.

"Yep, but I 'spect I can get by this time. Not like when that some-bitch with the devil's mark poked me and then stole a full jug of Pa's whiskey. Pa gave me a blinker," she pointed to her eye where the last purple-green, remnants of a bruise still lingered.

"A devil's mark?" Ben asked.

"Yep, real sweet talker, but had the Devil's mark all down one side of his face. Kinda' shaped like a small claw." She frowned, and with a slight pout, added, "He done promised me he'd take me with 'em. Said he was goin' all the way to St. Louie. Said he was gonna' make me a real lady. I should never have let him have a poke without givin' me a penny first."

"You sure he was headed to St. Louis?"

"That's what he tol' me," she insisted.

Ben felt a bit better about Dob's direction of travel. Though Dob most likely lied every chance he got, there was always some bit of truth in what he said.

The keelboat's captain was finally able to persuade his crew into returning to the boat with threats of reduced pay for the voyage. And so by the end of the following day, they had reached the junction of the Ohio and Mississippi Rivers. It was at this point that Ben's education about working on a keelboat truly began.

So far, the labor of poling had mostly been to fend off debris or to drag or maneuver over shoals and sand bars, and the flow of the river had done a great deal of the work. It was a completely different story when they turned up the Mississippi River against the current.

This keelboat was larger than the first he had been on when he left Pittsburgh. It was seventy feet long, had an eighteen feet breadth of beam with a depth of hold four feet, carrying twenty-eight tons of cargo. There was a crew of thirty men as well as the captain, and the task of going up stream against the current seemed impossible to Ben.

While poling was still used, the main means of propulsion up-stream was the use of a cordelle, a rope line about 900 feet long, pulled by men walking on bank. The cordelle was fastened to the top of the keelboat's thirty foot mast. From there it was connected to the bow of the boat and then a through ring. The object in having so long a line was to lessen the tendency to draw the boat toward the shore; and the object in having it fastened to the top of the mast was to keep the cordelle from dragging in the water, and to allow it to clear the brush along the bank.

It required almost the entire crew to cordelle the keelboat up the river. For the most part there were no established towpaths, as the flow of the river constantly eroded the banks, and changed the bends, thus preventing the development of any form of a path. It was necessary for the men to struggle through underbrush, climb up and down steep bluffs and wade through the muddy shallows. When the undergrowth was too dense, and it was impossible to walk and use the cordelle at the same time, the end of the line would be taken past the obstruction, tied fast, and the boat was pulled by drawing in the line.

Ben spent most of his days pulling at the cordelle, cutting brush or setting a pole and pushing along the walkway to force the keelboat along. Overcome by exhaustion he had no trouble falling into a dreamless sleep each night, the muscles in his arms, legs and back aching. It seemed as if he had just lay down to sleep and it was time to wake and start the day over again. During each day, his thoughts were filled with the task at hand; make it to St. Louis and find Dob. Pushing at the pole or pulling at the cordelle, each step brought him closer to Dob.

They left the junction for St. Louis and were compelled to cross the river east to west, west to east at every bend, ten to fifteen miles per day, and the best they could manage, seldom making more than one mile per hour. It took five days to reach Cape Girardot, with St. Louis still over one hundred miles away. Here, on a promontory rock overlooking the Mississippi River, an ex-French Soldier, Jean Giradot, had established a trading post. Giradot moved on, and a French-Canadian named Louis Lorimier moved to the area as an official of the Spanish Government to trade with the local native tribes.

Although Lorimier had renamed the trading post Lorimont, the name Cape Girardot was already in common use by the locals and the city itself inherited that name. Under Lorimier's government, the settlement thrived, and in 1803, with the purchase of upper Louisiana by the U. S., Lorimier embraced his new role as a U. S. citizen. He donated four acres of land for the establishment of a seat of justice, and in 1806, the city was platted and plans were underway to have it incorporated.

This would be the last stop along the River before St. Louis and Ben took advantage of the short stay to inquire about Dob. He first questioned those he met along the river front and made his way to the public square. His inquiries were again successful as Dob seemed to leave a well beaten path behind him. As in other towns along the Ohio River, Dob had made no attempt to hide his name or his final destination. The young man with a claw-like birthmark on his face was easy to remember and easy to follow.

Six days later, the keelboat that Ben was on, sighted St. Louis on the bluff above the flood plain. Just over four decades old, and a short three years as part American territory, the city had become an important place in the West. It sprawled out along the Missouri River, its buildings perched atop a natural levee. The white lime wash on the mud bricks and rough-cut stones made the buildings stand out from a distance, shining like a beacon on the Mississippi. The numerous shops, warehouses and businesses were bent on one sole purpose, the fur trade. St. Louis was the gateway to the region drained by the Missouri River, and the Rocky Mountains with their beaver rich steams.

Due to an exclusive trade license, the local aristocracy had already made their fortunes in land and sales of trade goods to the natives. The "founding families" were the French fur traders; Auguste Chouteau, Sr., his half-brother Pierre Chouteau and their brother-in-law Charles Gratiot.

Most of the trade goods that came to St. Louis were imported from Europe. Items such as blankets, firearms, glass beads, tea, wine and ironwork, came from faraway places like England, France, China and Germany. Goods manufactured in the States were also a valuable commodity, such as the glass and coal that Ben's flatboat had brought down from Pittsburgh.

Not only were the natives a source of income, but for years American pioneers had been slipping across to the Spanish side of the river, clearing land and making farms. When the transfer of Louisiana from

France to the United States took place, the trickle of Americas into the territory had increased creating more new customers.

The monopoly held by the Chouteaus in St. Louis was solid until the Spanish Creole, Manuel Lisa, came up from New Orleans. Lisa muscled his way into the trade, and after applying pressure, he eventually gained a trading license from the Spanish, if only to quiet him. Now that the Americans were in control, Lisa turned his eyes to the upper Missouri. In his own words, he put great effort into his operation, and went a great distance, while others were still considering whether they would start today or tomorrow.

Early in 1806, Lisa had joined in a partnership with a local businessman named Jacques Clamorgan, and the two were looking toward Santa Fe, located in the northern frontier of Nueva España. However this idea paled in comparison to the riches that were promised in the upper Missouri, and Lisa was lured into a new partnership with two successful Kaskaskia merchants, Pierre Menard and William Morrison.

This was the St. Louis that Ben found himself in at the end of May. He received his meager wages and bid farewell to the keelboat's captain, then walked up into the city. With his two letters of introduction, one form Major Ebenezer Denny and the other from Gen. George Rodgers Clark, tucked inside his haversack, he sought out the Government house, and presented the letters asking to see Jean Baptiste Lucas, the Superior Judge for Louisiana Territory, or Frederick Bates, the Governor for Louisiana Territory. To Ben's consternation, he found that the government was in a flux of change. Meriwether Lewis had been appointed governor, and William Clark was the new Indian Agent. Of these two men, neither was in St Louis. Frederick Bates was now Secretary of Records, but retained his post as acting governor until Lewis would arrive. Ben was allowed in to see him and stood a respectful distance from the man's desk as the governor read both letters.

Placing the papers on his desk, Bates addressed Ben, in a kind but somewhat condescending manner. "Mr. Voss, I admire your tenacity at perusing this Robert Bergmann, but I am not sure there is a way for me to help you. St. Louis has yet to establish a permanent presence for law enforcement, though we are considering it, possibly two or three militiamen. If you apprehend this Mr. Bergmann you are more than welcome to bring him before the court here, or take him back to Pittsburgh on your own." He paused when he could see the effect his words had on Ben. "Again, I admire your tenacity, but the population of St. Louis has doubled in the last few years, and many people come here and then leave for the frontier. I cannot help you search for your man, as I believe you will have a hard time in finding him at all. I will give you a note that you may show as a sign of my support, but I doubt this will be of much help."

Ben asked Bates if he would help get a letter to his uncle and aunt, advising them of the situation.

"With your permission, Sir, I'll return tomorrow with the letter. I have to decide what I intend to do."

"It would be my pleasure, Mr. Voss," Bates assured Ben, and then asked, "Have you made arrangements for lodging?"

"No, Sir. I have just arrived and came straight here."

"I would be careful as to where you lodge," Bates said, "Look for the establishment of Joseph Drury. He offers a clean bed and good meals at a fair price."

"Thank you, Sir," Ben said and he turned and left.

Ben made his way in search of Joseph Drury's to spend the night. With the remains of his original twenty silver dollars, and the fifteen days wages from his labor on the keelboat, Ben had eighteen dollars, the equivalent of two months wages. He would spend as little as possible for a meal and a place to sleep this one evening, and then decide what his next move would be.

The Tavern was not hard to find, being a substantial, two-story building set back from the street a bit. It was originally the Drury home, and had been converted into a business. A spacious, covered porch ran across the front, and there sat a few men the likes of which Ben had never seen.

One looked somewhat like the French Canadians Ben had met on the river, but he like his companions, he was dressed more like an Indian than a Whiteman. He wore a bright blue silk scarf tied around his head and a fringed buckskin jacket over a red flannel shirt. Around his waist was a wide belt with a large hunting knife and sheath tucked into it, and on his legs he wore fringed leggings. Finishing off his appearance, and that of his companions, were feet shod in moccasins.

Ben tried not to look at these men as he passed them, but could not help himself. This did not go unnoticed by the stout little French Canadian in the blue scarf.

"Have you never seen a wild *savage?*" he joked half in French and half in broken English, letting out a growl and then a hearty laugh. His companions joined in on the laughter, and Ben turned his eyes toward the tavern door and entered.

Ben moved into the darkness and let his eyes become accustomed to the change in light. Somehow, the tavern reminded him of the Voss house. It was not that much bigger, and the large common room matched that of where Jacob Voss held "court" at the dinner table. Ben let a small smile cross his lips. He hadn't thought about his father in years, and now so far from the farm, he let the man creep into his thoughts. But there was no fear in these memories, only the vague recollection of a man large in stature but small in character.

Joseph Drury had come down to St. Louis from Montreal, and like so many others, he had dreams of making his fortune in the Indian trade. His wondering days were limited though when he met and married a Shawnee woman. They settled in St. Louis and raised their family. The sons had all drifted away and the single daughter, Jean, a dark-haired beauty, helped with the tavern.

Joseph kept a close eye on his daughter and there was no doubt that she was not one of the items for sale in the tavern, though not a day went by that some misguided guest didn't attempt a proposition of one sort or another. Jean herself, though of good character, was neither naive nor stupid. Unknown to her father, she had been down that road and had lost her virtue some years back to the winning smile and empty promises of a man from New Orleans. She had also learned how far she could tease the patrons without getting herself in to trouble.

It was this doe-eyed, young woman that caught the first glimpse of Ben as he entered the tavern. Looking him up and down, she noticed the strong and muscular body under his homespun clothes, and lastly the well-worn brogans. She smiled as she moved to Ben who stood just inside the door.

"Good day, how may I be of service?" she said in French, and then seeing he didn't understand, she switched to Spanish and repeated her greeting. This too, brought no response, so she reverted to English, "Good day, how may I help you?"

"Ah," Ben stuttered, "I was told that I might find a room here for the night, and maybe a meal."

"Yes, we can accommodate you," she cooed, her voice unsettling Ben slightly, but for a reason he couldn't understand.

"How much?" he asked.

"Do you have silver?"

"Yes ma'am," Ben assured her.

"A room and a meal will cost you four bits."

"Bits?" Ben questioned.

"Where are you from?" she asked.

"Pittsburgh," Ben replied, becoming a bit annoyed with the feeling he was being made fun of.

"I see, then the cost is two levys, or shillings if you see it that way."

"I have American silver," now Ben was sure she was making fun of him.

"One half of a dollar will get you a meal and a room here. You must share the room with others though; we do not have private accommodations. I'm sure a gentleman such as you won't mind though." She smiled broadly and Ben realized that she was teasing him but it was not meant maliciously, and his hurt feeling turned to slight embarrassment as his face reddened.

This made Jean smile that much more and she asked him to follow her to a where a large ledger was kept so that she might record his name and take his payment.

"Your name?" she asked as she dipped the pen into the ink well.

"Benjamin Voss," he replied.

"And you said you were of Pittsburg?" she asked, not expecting an answer but writing this down next to his name.

"Yes," he answered even though he now knew it wasn't necessary.

"And you are staying for just one night?" she looked up and into his eyes.

"Yes, Ma'am, just one night, maybe two, I'm not sure just yet," Ben's embarrassment was starting to turn into something else as he looked back into her eyes, so dark brown that her iris' hardly showed in contrast between them and her pupils. A fellow could get lost real easy there, Ben thought to himself.

"You can stay upstairs, last room on the right hand side," Jean broke into his thoughts.

Again he said, "Yes Ma'am."

He headed toward the stairs and heard her call after him, "We serve one meal, and that will be soon. Don't be late as when the pot is empty, there is no more."

As he ascended the steps he thought about the girl. He intrigued him, her brown eyes dark and mysterious, her skin the color of honey, and her black hair shining like a raven's wing even in the dim light of the tavern. He wondered if she was more French or more Indian. Either way, Ben felt something stir inside that warmed him.

He found the room spacious and containing four beds, two being of a fairly large size. It was evident now that not only would he share the room, he might have to share a bed as well. He placed his rolled blanket on one of the smaller beds and stowed his haversack underneath it, as far back as possible and against the wall. He thought better about leaving his rifle, so decided to take it back down with him. He then retraced his steps down stairs to see about the meal the girl with the deep brown eyes had mentioned.

The common area of the tavern accommodated two long tables with benches along each side. Several men were already seated, including the men Ben had seen outside when he arrived. The girl was laying down tin plates in front of them and placed a handful of spoons at each table. The men each grabbed a spoon and Ben, seating himself at the end of one bench, was lucky to place his hand on one before they were all gone.

Across from Ben sat the French Canadian who had spoken to him earlier. He eyed Ben, and Ben had the uneasy feeling that this man would be trouble. Looking back at him, Ben sized him up. He was smaller than Ben by at least a half a foot in height, but broad shouldered and he looked as stout as the men Ben had worked alongside coming up river. Ben figured he might have a chance of beating this man if it came to a fight, but didn't want to find out.

Jean came along with a large black pot of stew and ladled it out onto each man's plate. Ben looked up at her as she spooned out his portion and she smiled at him; and as an unmistaken sign of preference, she placed a second portion of the stew on his plate. This did not go unnoticed by those sitting closest to Ben, especially the Canadian, whose gaze became more intense.

When Jean had dished out the stew, she returned with loaves of bread and placed several on each table. The men took hold of the loaves and tore off a chunk, and returned the remainder to the table or handed it the man next to them. Ben reached out for a piece of bread that had just been placed in front of him and like the strike of a snake, a knife came down, its blade sinking into the bread and table top a fraction of an inch from Ben's outstretched hand. Ben instinctively pulled his hand back, and for a moment was frozen with surprise.

The Canadian, his eyes fixed on Ben, spoke in French, low, but steady, "Tu me fais chier. *You are a pain in the ass.*"

"Calm down Estienne," a bearded man next to the Canadian said, placing a hand on that of the Canadian which held the knife.

"T'as vu ce cul? *Did you see that ass?*" the Canadian said to his friend.

"Yes I did," he paused, and then added in French himself, "Tu l'as dans le cul. *Suck it up.*"

"Cet homme pauvre naze. *He is a useless person, probably stupid as well.*"

"You're only jealous that Jean gave him more stew. Now share the bread with him and don't be rude, introduce yourself."

"C'est vraiment des conneries! *That is really bullshit!*" said Estienne. Then he pulled the knife up from the table, took the bread from its blade and tearing the bread in half offered it to Ben.

"What did I say about being rude?" the bearded man said.

"Ah, I am Estienne Lapin," he said in English, "and thes' pain in my ass, and your ange gardien, *guardian angel,* es Silas Scott."

Ben, still taken aback, cautiously extended his hand across the table in a sign of peace, and the Lapin accepted it, with an overly strong shake.

"Ben Voss," Ben offered.

Then the man, Scott, extended his hand to Ben and though his grip was also strong, there was no intent to prove his strength to Ben.

"Now, we are all friends," Silas said.

"Putain! Whore!" said Estienne.

"You must excuse my excitable and vulgar friend," Silas said, "he has been mooning over Jean Drury since we arrived here three months ago, no matter that she will have nothing to do with him and that he probably has a wife somewhere, maybe two."

"No problem then?" Ben asked.

"No, I think not, buy him a pint and he will be your friend for life." Silas let out a soft chuckle.

When the meal was over and Jean had cleared the plates, most of the men sat and share stories while they drank. As he was advised, Ben bought Estienne a pint of rum, and thinking it a good idea bought one for Silas Scott and a third companion of theirs, Caleb Thompson.

As the warmth of the fire in the hearth and the rum warmed them up, Ben learned more about the three men and even started to like Estienne, as the Canadian seemed to become friendlier as he downed pint after pint. Silas seemed to keep an even keel, no matter how much he drank and Caleb sat quiet but amused by the stories and the joking of his friends.

Ben learned that the three of them along with three others were biding their time waiting for important government papers, and a few last minute trade goods that they were taking up the Missouri River into the Rocky Mountains for Manuel Lisa. Lisa had left almost three weeks earlier with sixty men and two keelboats loaded with trade goods and supplies. This brigade of men were to trade with the Indians of the upper Missouri, and trap beaver and other fur bearing animals that would bring in cash when brought back to St. Louis.

Ben opened up to his new acquaintances and told them about himself and his mission to find Dob. He also confessed that he had no idea what to do next.

Estienne, in his drunken stupor, suggested that Ben abandon his hunt for Dob, and accompany them. Silas reminded him that there was only so much room in their pirogue, and adding another man to the boat would not be possible.

"But, mon ami, he es strong, and he could row for me, no?"

"You'll do your own rowing!" Silas said. "I have no doubt that Ben will find his prey."

"Yep," said Ben, "with that face of his he hasn't been that hard to track."

"What is wrong with his face?" asked Caleb.

"He has a red mark that goes down one side, looks kind of like he had been clawed by something."

"On his left check?" asked Silas.

"Yes," Ben became excited. "Have you seen him?"

"Sure have," Caleb interjected, "he's on his way to the Stoneys with Manuel Lisa."

"You mean where you're headed?"

"Yep," said Caleb.

Ben looked over to Silas, pleading as he spoke, "Please Mr. Scott, let me go with you. I'll pull my weight, and more!"

"I sympathize with you Ben, but I just can't see making room for you, we're over packed as is, and I'm not sure those mountains are a place for someone like you."

"I've come this far, I can handle myself."

"I have no doubt of that, but we are all experienced and seasoned trappers and I can't just sign you up, I don't have that authority."

"I understand," Ben said dejected, "but that don't mean I can't find my own way up the Missouri and track down Dob."

"Son," said Silas, "I don't think you'd last long out there on your own. Go home to Pittsburgh, go home to your family and be grateful you have them."

They sat in quiet, the pleasant mood broken and sullen. As if to emphasize the despair Ben felt, the door to the tavern opened and in walked Griffin and his two associates.

The big man surveyed the room, and almost as if his internal compass pointed to Ben, he headed straight for him. He was deprived of Dob, so he was intent getting at Ben.

"You son-of-a-bitch! You made me loose that little piss-wipe, Bergmann, and cost me time back in Clarksville, now you're goanna pay for it." Before Ben could gain his feet, Silas Scott was up and between him and the big man.

"I'd be careful, if I were you friend," Silas warned.

"Well, you aint' me, an' I got business with this bastard." By this time, Ben as well as others had reached their feet.

"There's to be no trouble in here!" the voice came from behind the group of men. It was Joseph Drury, and in his hands was a blunderbuss. The huge bore of the short gun was threatening enough, but the promise of the gun going off would mean no one in front of the muzzle would go unscathed.

"Take it outside," Drury demanded, and slowly

Griffin and his men retreated, backing away toward the door.

"I'll get with you sooner or later," Griffin pointed a stubby finger in Ben's direction. "And don't think I won't remember you either," he said to Silas.

When they had left, Silas turned to Ben and said, "You sure do have a way of attracting the wrong kind of people, don't you?"

Ben spent a restless night, sleep evading him as worries crossed thought his mind. He knew now where Dob had gone, and with the threat of Griffin also following, Ben felt that possibly Silas Scott was right.

With the rising of the sun, Ben ventured out with the intent to revisit Frederick Bates. He moved along the street lined with warehouses, these filled with either trade goods bound for the wilderness, or furs bound for the east. As he passed an alleyway between two buildings, he was pulled into the confines by force.

Griffin landed a blow to Ben's face before Ben had time to react, and as Ben fell back against the rough timbers of the building, the three men hemmed him in cutting off any escape.

"Now, you little shit, you and me are going to have a discussion about Dob Bergmann," Griffin hissed through his teeth.

"I was afraid it was going to come down to this," Silas Scott's voice echoed in the alleyway. With Silas were Estienne and Caleb.

Griffin turned from Ben and lunged at Scott. With this movement, Estienne and Caleb launched themselves into the alleyway at Griffin's two men. Griffin's man with the cudgel brought the weapon down with surprising speed and caught Caleb on the right shoulder, bringing him down to the ground, and was in the attempt of raining down another blow when Ben stopped him with a blow of his fist. The man turned, dazed and this gave Ben the opportunity to land more blows to his face and midsection. Unable to mount any defense, the man fell to the street near Caleb who was holding a useless arm close to his chest. The cudgel had fallen and Caleb reached for it with his one good arm bringing the short club down on the fallen man's head.

"Some-bitch won't get up for a while," Caleb said, wincing with his own pain.

Ben, saw Silas standing over the prone figure of Griffin while Estienne was tossing a rock at the fleeing last member of the trio.

"Damn, Silas, how'd you beat him so easy?" Ben asked.

"It isn't always about size, Ben, in a fight, never forget, a bigger man has the advantage and all the speed and brains a fellow has don't always mean he can prevail against those odds. That big son-of-a-bitch came close to killing me." He looked down and the open front of his buckskin jacket revealed where his shirt had been cut by Griffin's knife, the blade passing his flesh harmlessly. Ben looked down and could see the big man's own knife protruding from his chest.

Ben then looked to where Estienne was helping Caleb up. Griffin's man was also dead; the blow from the cudgel had cracked his skull.

"What do we do now?" Estienne asked Silas.

"We drag this carrion over to the river and toss em' in," Silas said with little more emotion than if he were talking about a dead dog.

"Don't we have to contact someone?" Ben asked.

"Not unless you want to be arrested," Silas said, "You'll be stuck here waiting trial, and with little defense and no witnesses you could very well hang."

"But I didn't kill them, and you can tell what happened."

"We aren't sticking around that long, I told you we need to get up river as soon as possible." Then Silas looked over to Caleb. "And I see you might have cocked things up for us there. Come on, let's get back to the tavern and sort this out. First though, let's do away with this lot.

They drug the two bodies toward the river, down the bank across the tow path and slid them into the muddy water. The bodies drifted for a short bit then rolled under the brown water to disappear.

Back at the tavern they determined that Caleb's shoulder was broken and he would be of no use in rowing the batteau, and he would only burden the small group until he healed.

"Shit!" Caleb said, "Just my luck."

"What is next?" questioned Estienne.

"I would say that Ben has found himself a place at the oars in the pirogue. But that puts Caleb in a fix," said Silas. His gaze turned to Ben. "Caleb was contracted out and was guaranteed to make a good sum of money in the next year. Now he won't be able to work for at least three or four months. What you gonna' do about that?"

Ben reached inside his shirt and pulled out the leather pouch containing the eighteen dollars in silver, and handed it over to Caleb.

"I don't rightly think there is enough in there to make up for you bustin' a shoulder, but you're welcome to it. I just need enough to pay for my room at the tavern," Ben said apologetically.

"The company will settle your account at the tavern," Silas said. "You good with what's in that pouch Caleb?"

"Sure," said Caleb as he looked at the contents of the pouch.

"Good, then. We'll leave as soon as the last of the cargo is available and the papers come through."

SAM J. PISCIOTTA

CHAPTER 7
UP THE MISSOURI

The pirogue rocked gently in the late evening darkness, as the water of the Mississippi River flowed past. Tied to the dock, the boat's thirty-five foot length seemed to let the waves flow gently under its flat bottom, and pass on downstream, each lifting the boat and gently letting it settle down, only to be lifted again. Ben sat on the cargo that had already been loaded, the last remnants of goods that were to be taken up to the trading post that Manuel Lisa planned to build on the upper Missouri.

In the past few days, he and his new companions had been waiting for the last items promised by Chouteau & Co., and the papers signed by the new governor, Meriwether Lewis. What goods that were already available had been loaded onto the pirogue, almost six tons, with another five or six hundred pounds expected from Chouteau. With the valuable cargo sitting on the pirogue, someone was required to be with the boat at all times. This night was Ben's turn to stand the first watch, until midnight, and this he didn't mind. He had slept little each night since the fight with Griffin. Those few fleeting hours he did rest were filled with guilt and doubt.

Ben had written a letter to his aunt and uncle, explaining that he was bound for the west in search of Dob. He explained that he was now in the company of good men whom he trusted, and he promised that he would write as time and circumstance allowed. He closed his letter asking them to forgive him for being away so long and that he hoped they would keep him in their prayers.

The coolness of the evening had driven away the mosquitos, which seemed to hunt only in the hours just before dark, and Ben was relieved that at least that nuisance was out of mind. In his melancholy, he allowed the warm thoughts of the girl Jean to drift in and push away everything else.

These past few days, he and others at the tavern had noticed that she was paying a bit more attention to him, and she had made no attempt to hide it. She was so different from the girls he had known in Pittsburgh. Though there were girls with Indian blood in them, they couldn't compare to this girl with the hypnotizing eyes and the quick smile. He wondered what her honey colored skin would feel like under his touch, but this embarrassed him and he chided himself for even thinking she would really be attracted to someone like him.

As if his wondering mind was playing tricks on him, Ben heard her voice calling his name from out of the darkness, "Benjamin Voss, where are you?"

He stood, steadying himself as the waves moved the pirogue under his feet. He looked in the direction her voice had come from and there she was, a candle lantern in her hand to light her way. Ben stepped onto the dock and called out to her, "Here. I'm over here."

She peered past the light in her hand and Ben could see her smile. She moved now toward him and Ben could see she was wrapped in a dark, hooded cloak, and in her other hand she carried a cane basket.

"What are you doing out here this time of night?" he asked.

"That isn't a very nice tone to take with someone who has brought you supper." She pretended to be hurt.

"No, I...I mean you surprised me, and it probably isn't safe for you to be by yourself."

"I'm not by myself," she said impishly, "You're

here."

"That's not what I meant." Ben had no idea what he really meant. Her showing up just as he was thinking of her had surprised him so much.

"You walk here all by yourself?" he asked.

"No, I had an escort, your friend, Rabbit, Estienne," she said again smiling at Ben. Ben looked back up toward the buildings on the bluff and saw a figure wave, and then turn and walk away. "You see, he made sure I found my way to you," Jean added.

"Why did you take such a chance to come out here?"

"I told you, I brought you some supper." She raised a cloth cover on the basket and revealed its contents. "Are you going to invite me to come aboard so we can eat together?"

"Sure," he said stepping back onto the boat and extending a hand to help her climb on board.

She sat the lantern on one of the boxes and the basket next to it. She laid out the basket cover as a makeshift table cloth and pulled out the contents setting them down. There was a loaf of bread, some cheese, a few slices of cold beef and a long necked glass bottle with a cork in the end. She then produced two small tin cups and set those near the food.

"Sit now and we'll enjoy some food and a bit of my father's Madera," she said. Ben had no idea what Madera was, but at this point he didn't care. He was excited by her presence, by the mere fact that the two of them were alone, and he had no idea how to react.

She sat next to Ben and began to work on the cork in the bottle's neck. As it pulled free, she tossed it over the side of the boat remarking, "We won't need the cork, we'll finish what is inside the bottle."

She poured the fortified wine into the cups and handed one to Ben. He brought it up to his lips and the faint aroma of burnt sugar was evident. He sipped the sweet wine and found it to his liking.

"What do you think?" she asked.

"First time I have ever tried...what did you call this?"

"Madera. It's from my father's private keg. He never shares this with anyone."

"Will you get in trouble with him for taking some?"

"No, he'll never know. Anyway, this is a special night, your last night here in St. Louis." This took Ben off guard.

"What do you mean, my last night?"

"I heard Silas Scott tell my father that he would settle up on the bill in the morning and you all would be leaving."

"Oh." The sound of disappointment in his voice was evident.

"Aren't you happy to be leaving?" she asked.

"Yes Ma'am, but I was kind of getting used to being around..." he stopped himself from saying, "Around you."

"Ma'am?" she broke in. "Don't you think you should call me Jean?"

"Yes, I like that," he admitted.

"Good, now eat and drink, while we talk."

Ben relaxed a bit and enjoyed her presence, her laughter at small things, and the sound of her voice. He wondered if this is what love felt like, not the feelings he had so many years ago for the girl Giselle Wise, and certainly not for those perplexing girls he had meet while living in Pittsburgh. Jean was different, open and genuine.

They sat, talked and finished the entire bottle of wine long after the food was gone. Ben found her easy to talk to, and he opened up to her about his past and why he was in St. Louis. The one thing he did not share was the killing of Griffin and his partner. This was something he knew he couldn't expect her to understand, as he himself didn't understand.

Ben felt lightheaded and a bit giddy. The world

seemed perfect there and then with Jean. They lay back on the boxes and looked up at the stars making their way across the sky. For a few minutes neither of them said anything at all, then Jean broke the silence.

"I am very happy at the tavern, living and working with my father." She paused, and then added, "I wouldn't change anything about it. Sometimes I get a bit lonely, and I feel that I need the company of someone else. Ben, I like you and I want you to know that."

"I like you too," Ben said, his thoughts still a bit fuzzy with the effects of the wine.

"What I am trying to say is that I want to stay with you tonight," she said, turning her head to look at him, her hand reaching over to take his.

"I'd like that," Ben said, feeling the warmth of her hand in his.

"You don't understand, do you?" She let out a small laugh. "I want to spend only this one night with you, I am not looking for anything more, I don't want empty promises, I don't want to have a hold on you, and I don't want you to think you have one on me either."

Ben, in his wine induced thoughts wasn't sure he understood what she was saying; and then she eased her way from next to him, to on top of him. Her lips were close to his and she held herself there for the briefest of moments, and then pressed her lips against his mouth, gently, but long and with an eagerness that made her tremble. Ben, his arms now around her, found it easy to lose himself in the kiss. Her lips brought back the taste of the wine, and something else, the flavor of her, and this excited him, and he too trembled slightly.

As the waves of the river gently rocked the boat, Jean and Ben found comfort in each other. First tenderly and soothing, and then abandoning of their shyness, they enjoyed one another with a passion that quenched their desires, needs, and hunger.

At midnight, Estienne reappeared on the dock to relieve Ben, and Ben walked Jean back to the tavern. They walked in silence, overcome by the afterglow of their intimacy. They had almost reached the tavern when Ben started to speak, "Jean..." But Jean stopped him, placing her hand over his mouth.

"We will not talk about tonight. We will remember, and we will smile, but we will never talk about it." She looked at him, seeking some sign of agreement. Ben shook his head in consent, and they walked the rest of the way to the tavern. Stopping just outside, Jean rose up on her toes and gave Ben one last kiss on the check. She turned, gained the front steps and went inside.

Just past sunup, the entire crew was loading the final cargo onto the pirogue, and by midmorning, Silas had returned from the Government House with the last papers of license for Manuel Lisa. With Silas at the tiller, and the other five men at the oars, they shoved off from the shore and headed up stream to the mouth of the Missouri River, some eighteen miles away.

As he rowed, Ben's thoughts were on Jean and he wondered if she would be waiting for him when he returned the following year. Then, he chided himself, recalling what she had said; they would have no hold on each other. But, Ben could not help but feel she had taken a part of his heart and thought he may very well be in love with her. Then he wondered, "Do I know what love really is?"

As the miles slipped behind him, Ben finally understood. She intended that what they had shared was to be only a memory, and he smiled with the thought of her. And as she had wished, he would never forget her.

They made little progress that first day and used the first leg of the journey up the Mississippi as a shakedown to make sure the cargo was stored properly, and to get the small crew in synchronization with one another. By the second day they had reached the Missouri, and once past the first large bend in that river, were headed north, a slight northwest breeze helping move the boat with the use of the sail. Ben was on his way into the west, to the Stoney Mountains.

*

The very character of the Missouri River seemed to be against Dob. He felt deep down that the river hated him, and in return, he hated the river and he took every moment of discomfort; every ache of his muscles, every blister on his hands and feet, as personal.

When Dob had signed his contract with the Spanish Creole, Manuel Lisa, he had no idea that he would be required to work as hard as what was expected of him now. He had thought the journey up the Missouri would be no harder than that up the Mississippi river from its confluence with the Ohio to St. Louis. But for that leg of his journey, he had paddled the stolen canoe and it was no comparison to the keelboat he now labored on.

To add to his personal hatreds, were the French boatmen, the voyageurs, and especially the patron, or master of the boat. This was the man who stood at the rudder on the rear end of the cargo box. Here he had an elevated point of view from which he could overlook everything and give commands as needed.

Dob had worked hard in the Pittsburgh boatyard, but nothing like the poling, cordelling or rowing required to move the heavy craft upstream. Dob's entire body ached, he dreaded pulling on the cordelle, but there were times when this was not possible and he was required to use a pole or man the ores. He had no idea which he hated more, cordelling, poling, rowing or the kellboat's patron, who shouted the orders from his position at the tiller. With each step

Dob took, whether the cordelle or pole in hand, his hatred grew.

To move the keelboat by poling, the crew manned long poles, with a knob of wood on one end that rested in the hollow of their shoulder, the other end an iron tip or "shoe." Eight of the crew would man each side of the keelboats' catwalk, or passe avant as it was called, that ran along each side of the cargo box. Facing the stern, they would line up near the bow, pole in hand, one in front of the other, as close together as they could walk.

At the patron's command, "A bas les perches," the crew along the passe avant thrust the lower end of the poles into the river close to the boat and placed the knob ends against their shoulders so that the poles inclined downstream. They would all push together, forcing the boat ahead as they walked along the passe avant toward the stern until they reached the back of the keelboat. At this point the patron would call out, "Levez les perches," and they would withdraw the poles from the muddy bottom, and walk quickly back to the bow and repeat the operation. The passe avant had cleats nailed to it to keep the men's feet from slipping, and when pushing hard, they sometimes were required to lean over far enough to catch hold of the cleats with their hands almost crawling on all-fours.

In places where the water was too deep, and it was impracticable to either pole or cordelle, Dob was required to man one of the twelve oars each keelboat carried. The only relief from these labors was when the wind blew sufficiently enough for the large canvas sail to be of assistance, but this did not happen often enough to suit Dob.

It seemed also that the river was not content with Dob suffering only this tedious and back-breaking work. It did everything in its power to stop travel upstream, and, if failing that, it made attempts to harass the crew or even sink the boats.

And here, in Dob's opinion, was where the river showed its personal hatred for him. When he would retreat to his bed for the night along a relatively quiet stretch of water, the river would change its mood and send heavy waves to splash over the sides of the keelboat soaking him. If depriving him of sleep was not enough, the river "grew" obstacles such as rocks just below the surface, or large trees branches that hung low over the river. The bank would erode, pulling the men at the cordelle into the water, or tumbling an entire tree off its roots to either smash whatever it hit, or sometimes float, bobbing in the current, sometimes submerged, sometimes on the surface, or anchoring itself in the bed of the river to tear at the bottom of the boats. Every manner of flotsam was a possible threat, especially when combined into what was called an embarras. These were a mixture of trees, dead animals, and anything else that floated from up stream. Some could even contain the carcass of an entire buffalo.

Of all the miseries the river hurled at Dob in its hatred the hordes of mosquitoes were the worst. They not only bite with a vengeance, sucking Dob's blood, they flew into his eyes, mouth, ears and nose, driving him to the point of near madness. When the boats tied up to the shore of either the river bank or some island and fires were built, Dob and his fellows stood close to the fire, drenching themselves in the smoke to ward off these tiny, winged enemies. Another deterrent was the use of what was called voyageurs grease, a horrid mixture that Dob felt rather than repel the mosquitos, attracted them.

Yes, Dob was sure the river hated him, and he was determined to desert the first chance he had. But, this was not as easy as he had first thought. Each night he was totally exhausted and what sleep he did get was not enough. When he was tasked to stand guard at night there was no way to get past the others who also stood watch. During the day, when the boats were not moving and anchored close to shore, he was never out of sight from at least someone who would notice his absence.

It had been almost a month since he had left St. Louis, and he had bide his time to make his getaway, but he was now four-hundred miles upstream, at the mouth of the Kansas River, and the night watch had increased due to desertions that had already occurred it would not be easy. Soon he would be deep into Indian Territory, the land of Sioux, and Dob had no wish to encounter any Indians, especially alone.

Dob had plenty of time to hear the stories about the temperament of the natives from the voyagers and the Americans in the group. These Americans included several who had spent the past few years in the West with Lewis and Clark. Dob remembered how Ben had yammered on and on, about the two captains and their trek across the continent. It had bored him then and now he was forced to hear the stories again and again from these men.

There were five of these men from the Corps of Discovery; John Potts, George Drouillard, Jean-Baptiste Lepage, Richard Windsor and Peter Weiser. Of these, he disliked the half-breed Drouillard the most. Dob wasn't sure if it was because of the man's Indian blood, or that it seemed everyone else respected him to such a high degree. It also appeared there was nothing that Drouillard wasn't capable of doing, and doing better than anyone else.

Dob, for his part, didn't go out of his way to make friends, and the other engagees were not as easily swayed by his charm and slick talk. These men had too much experience in life to be taken in by a golden tongue. They had pegged Dob right from the start and gave him no quarter when it came to the worst end of things. There was only one man, Obadiah Cash, who took the time to talk to Dob, and even attempted to instruct him in the ways of the woodsman.

Obadiah was from Georgia and had grown up pretty much on his own, among the Cherokee Indians. He attempted to pass on his knowledge about hunting and trapping on to Dob, even though Dob seemed to pay little attention. Diah, as he was called by some of the others, saw potential in Dob that no one else did; and to everyone else except Diah, it was obvious that Dob wouldn't last in the Rockies.

*

Silas Scott pushed his small group as hard as possible. They were three weeks behind the two keelboats, and the start of the expedition had been late in the year as it was. The intent was to reach the Yellowstone River in the mountains and build a trading post. Once the post was complete, men would be sent out to spread word among the friendly tribes that the Americans were there and ready to trade. The remainder of the engagees, would be split up with some maintaining the post and the other divided into small groups to go out and trap. As it was late in the year, it might possibly too late to send out men to trap, the weather in the high country would decide that for them.

It was in this capacity, engaged either as a trapper or at the forge in the post, that Ben would be employed. On the journey up stream, Silas would judge his skills as a woodsman and if he seemed lacking, his knowledge as a wheelwright would be put to use as a blacksmith at the trading post.

Silas had explained this to Ben, and Ben tried his best to demonstrate his abilities as a hunter. When time allowed, the men would supplement their diet with fresh game; and as Ben's turn to hunt came around, he never returned to the boat empty handed, and better still never lost his way when venturing out away from the river.

Ben's knowledge also increased from his

companions each day. Not only did he get to know them better, but it seemed that each of them had something worth teaching him and he was eager to learn.

To Ben, Silas had become somewhat like his brother Zebulun. He took the time to explain the methods of trapping beaver and how trade with the Indians would work. He answered any questions Ben had as honestly as possible and was straight forward with his opinions as to any shortcomings Ben exhibited, helping Ben correct or improve his actions. Silas was inherently a good man, and the more Ben learned about his past, it became easier to place the killing of Griffin in a different light. They had even come to a point where they discussed it.

"You're a good sized young man," Silas said, referring to Ben's height of over six feet, "But there are bigger men out there. With time and experience, you could be a match for most men in a tussle. As I told you before, when it comes to a fight, a large, confident, athletic person may well prevail. Coordination and sheer size both matter. So, while you may be experienced, know how things should work. There's no revelation like facing a big, strong opponent with good reflexes and no reservations about hurting you," Silas told him. "When you get into a fix, you don't have time to decide how far you'll have to go. Push on until you've seen the outcome will be in your favor." He paused to let these words sink in, then continued, "I do not see the taking of another human life as something to be held lightly. I find it abhorring, and do it only as a last resort."

Ben asked, "Have you killed many men?" As soon as the words had left his mouth, Ben regretted it, and added "I'm sorry, I shouldn't have asked."

"No, that's alright. It's just not what a gentleman would ask, nor answer."

Ben had never thought of himself as a

gentleman, and until now, he would never have thought Silas was one.

"A gentleman?" he asked, and Silas laughed.

"Yes. You will learn that you can find them in the most unlikely places."

Silas never ceased to amaze Ben. Though he spoke a better educated form of English than his companions, there was still a hint of his Scottish upbringing in his words. At times, he would sound exactly like the voyagers or the river men, copying their slang, butchering the English language, and adding the words only they used. At other times he would display his knowledge of French, Spanish or a spattering of Native tongues.

The others in the small party each had their own story also. Estienne was, contrary to Ben's first experience, a joker and the most light hearted of the group. He had been born in Québec and was about the same age as Silas. And like his namesake, he was as quick as a rabbit.

Antoine Martin, and Bernard Laurent were also from Canada, and like Estienne, were for the most part easy going, but hard working. The last man Jack Cox, had come west from Georgia with Silas. Like Silas, he had lived among the Cherokee and had learned his woodcraft there among those people.

Ben liked each of them and over the following weeks he grew attached to them and almost considered them family. He was looking forward to spending the next year of his life with these men. It seemed that Dob Bergman had slipped from his mind, or at least was now placed where he no longer was the center of Ben's life.

By the time they reached the Kansas River in the last week of July, the little crew had become one cohesive unit, each man acting and reacting to the tasks at hand in the daily travel and progress of the pirogue upstream. They developed a bond that could not have been possible if they had been with the larger group of sixty men that had gone before them. Silas was the unquestioned leader, even though he had been placed in that respect by Lisa.

The three Canadians: Martin, Laurent, and Lapin, were familiar with the Missouri River and they informed the others that they were half way to the Platte. This would put them in the territory of the Poncas and Pawnee Indians. They were not overly worried about either of these tribes, for as long as the three remembered, the Poncas and Pawnee, had been a source of slaves to New France, obtained from the Algonquian tribes of the great lakes.

Estienne pronounced the word Pawnee "Panis" which was synonymous with Pawnee and meant slave. As a quirk of fate, and probably self-preservation, the Pawnee themselves had gained a reputation of providing slaves from other plains tribes.

"I have never seen the villages of the Panis," said Estienne, "but I am told that they live like the Mandan, and the Rees in mud houses."

"I understand that their villages can be found if we were to go up the Kansas," added Martin. "The ones we will have to look out for are the Rees or maybe the Yankton, no?" He referred to the Arikara and the Nakota Sioux tribes.

"As I see it, it's best if we don't run into any Indians at all," said Silas.

"Ah," said Laurent, "I have been with some of the Ree women, I lived with them for a time. The women, they are, *très belle*! Very pretty, no. The 'usbonds sometime encourage their *épouses*, to *foutre* to me, 'opeing that some of the power of my blood would be transmitted to them through their wives. One warrior even guarded the entrance while I was mounting his *épouses*." He let out a laugh and grabbed at his crotch, making thrusting motions with his hips.

"Oui, and those Ree women, can give you more than their charms," Estienne quipped. "You are lucky they did not give you the love sickness!"

"It would take more than the pox to make that little bastard's pecker fall off!" Jack interjected, "and even if that happened, he'd still find a way to service them Ree women!"

The talk about the Arikara women brought thoughts of Jean back into Ben's mind. It seemed that the thoughts of her decreased in proportion to the distance he traveled away from her, but now, she was back in his mind, and a warmth surged thought him and he blushed.

Estienne saw the change in Ben's complexion, and quipped, "All this talk about *pachole* has made our young friend *mal à l'aise, no!*" He laughed and the others joined in, causing Ben's face to redden that much more.

When Ben rolled into his blanket to sleep that night, Jean worked her way back into his thoughts and he fell asleep with the memory of her lips on his, her arms around him.

SAM J. PISCIOTTA

CHPATER 8
THE ARIKARA

Smoke from the dying fire curled up from the fire pit situated in the middle of the medicine lodge causing the already stifling air inside the structure to become even more suffocating to Manuel Lisa and his companions. The diameter of over fifty feet made it larger than the other mud houses in the villages of the Sahnish or Arikara, but this size only made the closeness of so many people packed into it more evident. This one, occupied by one of the three chiefs, Little Raven, served as not only as his residence but also as the council house for village meetings. The mixture of various odors, old and stale to the noses of the White men, made them uneasy and what appetite they might have had before entering the subterranean abode was washed away by a slight sense of nausea and claustrophobia. Lisa thought about the clean September air that was just outside the lodge, and he couldn't wait to be done with the formalities of appeasing the chiefs of the three villages. And, he had to consider the odds of almost 2000 Arikara to his five dozen men.

The first village, where Lisa was now, containing about sixty lodges, sitting on an island in the middle of the Missouri, at Oak Creek, a tributary to the Missouri just two miles above the Grand River. The other two villages were on either side of the creek, just past the island.

From the exterior, the mound houses of these three villages appeared round but were actually squares with rounded corners. The houses were constructed by first excavating a pit about twelve to twenty-four inches deep, and between twenty-five and forty feet in diameter. Cut timbers were then inserted into the ground to form an inner square and an outer ring of shorter timber posts with cross beams. Next, a dense mat of small saplings and reeds in a radial pattern were laid across the timber cross beams. Clay or earth was packed against the sapling mat at least six to eight feet high. To finish the structure, sections of sod were placed on both the roof and the earth berm to create a living façade material which protected the interior of the house from extreme temperatures and severe rain damage. A hearth was constructed in the center of the floor, and a hole was left in the top of the roof to allow smoke to escape. A bullboat made from buffalo skin was placed over the smoke hole during heavy rains or snow. The interior was sectioned off to create partitions which separated living, sleeping and storage spaces. The sleep spaces were often insulated with buffalo or other tanned animal skins.

The villages themselves were each surrounded by a makeshift palisade, the houses clustered around a public plaza where large gatherings were held. At this time, the plaza was filled with people from all three villages, interested in the White men counseling with their three chiefs; Little Raven, Buffalo Rib and Crow Killer. These White men were not the first to visit the Arikara. They had been visited by the French voyageurs out of Canada for several decades. Only last year the Americans, Lewis and Clark, had made their second appearance when they returned from their trip up the river.

The Arikara were uneasy about the Americans, as Lewis and Clark had spent the winter before last with the Arikara's enemies, the Mandan. It seemed these men from down river could not understand the dynamics of the people who called the lands along the Great River their home. For as long as their memories could recall, the two tribes had been adversaries, and trade goods coming from the Canada had made their way to the Arikara and Mandan through the Sioux. Now, there was a chance of obtaining trade goods from these Americans. But not only did the White men want the Arikara to stop their war against the Mandan; these whites said that they intended trade not only with the Mandan, but with their other enemies, the Crow, and Hidatsa. Of all these goods the Americans had to offer, the Arikara wanted guns, powder and lead.

Lisa had brought goods especially to give as presents to the Arikara chiefs. A wooden box containing; butcher knives, mirrors, red flannel cloth, steel awls, brass kettles, glass beads, and packets of vermillion, sat between Lisa and George Drouillard. With them was Lisa's interpreter, one of the voyageurs called Petit Hugo who spoke the language of the Rees, and a new addition to the company, John Colter.

Colter was another Lewis and Clark alumni, but unlike the others, he had spent the past year trapping in the Rockies and possessed a better knowledge of the country than anyone else. Colter was making his way alone down river in a canoe when he ran into Lisa near the Platte River. It took little to persuade Colter into turning around and joining the expedition headed up stream. The presence of old companions Drouillard, Potts and Weiser were an added incentive.

Manuel Lisa found the delay irritating, especially with the knowledge that he would have to make the same type of stop in approximately two weeks at the Mandan village between the Knife River and the Little Missouri. It was the middle of September and time was short. At the rate they were traveling it could be another two months before they reached the territory of the Crow Indians where Lisa intended to build his trading post.

"Give us guns so that we may fight our enemies,"

Little Raven asked.

"*We will trade for the fur of the beaver,*" Hugo said speaking in Arikara and using hand signs, "*or if you have them, dressed buffalo robes.*"

"*We have no skins of the beave or those of the buffalo to trade, they are few among us, and those we have, we will need for the coming cold days,*" said Little Raven, disappointed.

"*We will return down the Great River when the grass turns green, maybe you will have more furs to trade then?*"

"*We will see,*" Little Raven replied.

"Tell the Chief that Silas Scott and the pirogue will be coming up river soon and that we do not what them molested or bothered in any manner," Lisa spoke to Hugo. Hugo translated this information to Little Raven and the others present.

"*Will this canoe have gifts for us also?*" asked Little Raven.

"*Yes, there will be gifts,*" spoke Hugo.

"*We will treat them with respect,*" Little Raven assured. With this, the parley was complete and the White men left the Medicine Lodge headed back to the keelboats. Several of the men would be allowed to remain in the village for a short while to take advantage of the Arikara women's hospitality. Lisa knew that it would be a long winter and the absence of women would make it that much harder to endure. As for himself, he did not seem to find the offers of the Arikara maidens enticing.

Dob watched the village from where he sat on the keelboat. Along with more than half of the crew, he had been posted to stand guard while Lisa and the others went up into the villages. He had heard about the Arikara women from some of the voyageurs and his imagination fueled fantasies that made him ache with an insatiable hunger. His distorted idea of what sex with a woman should be like, and his predatory approaches to women, only made his frustration that much worse. He found himself aroused at the mere thought of the Indian women just a stone's throw away, and was determined that no amount of self-gratification would sate his appetite.

It was in this state of mind that just after nightfall, Dob made his way along the outskirts of the lower village, in a hunt for relief of his mental and physical desires. Some of the men returning from the village had boasted of their prowess, and the rewards offered by the Arikara in return for their bedding of these willing maidens. With this in mind, Dob searched for one of these dusky damsels, a hank of blue glass beads in his hand. He was told that no Indian girl could pass up the Venetian beads and would offer herself up easily for such a prize.

It took little to find a young girl walking down the path to the river, a brass kettle in her hand, with the intent to fetch water. Dob stepped in front of her blocking her path and she stepped back in shock at his sudden appearance. Her apprehension was relieved when Dob held up the handful of sky colored beads, and a smile crossed her face. Dob smiled back and as her eyes went from the beads in his hand to his face she saw the birth mark.

She was puzzled at first, thinking it was paint, and then saw that it was some sort of permanent marking, not a tattoo, but something she perceived as an evil omen. Her smile faded and she started to turn away and retreat back to the safety of the village, but Dob reached out and took ahold of her arm, stopping her.

The girl let out a cry for help, "ut iŝtatata'uuhak!" Dob pulled her close and clamped his free hand over her mouth. The slender girl was no match for his superior strength and he dragged her into the concealment of the foliage along the river bank.

She managed to wiggle her mouth free long

enough to clamp down on his hand with strong teeth. "Bitch!" Dob hissed and swinging the injured hand in a fist, struck her hard in the face, and then again. The girl went limp and Dob let her fall to the ground, his attention now on his wound.

"Bitch," he said again. He looked down at the girl and decided that fate had offered him an opportunity with little expense, other than a sore hand, and he proceeded to vent his lust, anger and self-loathing on the helpless girl.
*

Little Raven and the other chiefs of the Arikara watched as the two large boats moved slowly away from the island, upstream. They were disappointed that the Whites didn't stay to trade with them, but then again these men from down river wanted beaver skins, not the corn, and vegetables the Arikara had to offer. Now these men would build a trading post in the land of their enemy, the "tUhkaáka," the Crows. In the time of Little Raven's father, there were thirty-two villages of the Arikara, now there were but three. Their enemies were many, and what the Arikara needed was guns. Little Raven did not trust these pale-skinned men, and believed they would bring his people nothing but evil.

It was well into the evening that same day that the body of Little Corn Woman, was found lying in the bushes near the water. The bruising around her neck, and the broken blood vessels in her once bright eyes, proved that she had been strangled, and the condition of her buckskin dress made it evident that she had been defiled. Near the body was found a hank of sky blue beads, like those the Americans had offered.
*

In their pirogue, Ben and his companions had made an unbelievable amount of progress up the Missouri compared to that of the keelboats of the main party. Unknown by them, their herculean efforts had reduced the distance between them drastically and they were only a mere ten days apart. By Silas' reckoning, he had hoped to make it to the proposed location where the trading post would be built not too long after Lisa arrived there.

There had been no contact with any Indians since a small encounter with some Otos near the Kansas River, and Silas had offered them some glass beads, half a dozen small mirrors and three butcher knives. In gratitude, the Otos had provided news from up river. They had noted the passing of the two keel boats, some two weeks prior. This news had assured Silas that they were closing the gap between them and Lisa.

Now they were approaching the Grand River, an area that both Antoine Martin, and Bernard Laurent were familiar with. It had been only a few years since the two had wintered with the Arikara, and they were looking forward to stopping at the site of the three villages, if only for a single night.

The pirogue passed the Grand River and within a few miles the Arikara villages came into site.

"There they are," called out Silas from his position at the tiller. "We'll go to the offshore side, and find a place where we can have some security." He moved the tiller and the boat slid across the muddy water toward the shore opposite the villages.

It was not long before they were discovered and several bullboats were placed in the river by the Rees and headed toward the White men. The bullboats were not very steady because they were hard to handle and bobbed around like a cork in the water. Most of them were manned by women though, who seemed much more adept then the men at navigating them in the direction they wanted to go. They were a simple craft made from a framework of willow branches bent in a huge bowl shape about four feet across the top and about one and one-half feet deep.

A green, bull buffalo hide was then stretched around this framework and allowed to dry naturally, creating a tight fit. The hair was left on the hide as well as the tails, the tails used to tie the boats together. They were light, weighing not more than thirty of forty pounds.

It was with difficulty that the men on the pirogue kept the Indians from swamping their boat. With the aid of the three voyageurs, who each spoke at least some of the language, the natives were made to understand, they must back off. This most of them did, one man held fast to the gunwale and made it clear that he would not let go. He finally made himself understood, in conveying a message from the chief of the village on the island. They wanted to parlay.

"Tell them that we will set up a camp here on this side of the river and that the Chief and only a few of his people may come across. Then we will talk." Silas spoke to Martin who passed this on to the man.

"We damn near capsized," Cox exclaimed, as the bullboats pulled away and made their unsteady way back across the river.

"Yes, we are lucky," said Silas. "Now, we need to prepare for our guests."

It took little time to set up a canvas arbor and throw down some blankets for the Indian guests to set on. Silas had a box set aside with gifts meant to be doled out to the Indians as gifts. Once these were handed out, and the formalities of smoking a pipe passed, Silas asked about Lisa and his men. He was very pleased to learn the gap had narrowed between Lisa's main party and his small group. He was sure that they would reach the Yellowstone at about the same time as Lisa.

The parlay went well and the three chiefs from the villages seemed to be satisfied, though not very enthusiastic with their meager presents. As they departed they invited the White men to come across the river to enjoy their hospitality.

Numbering only six to the thousands across the water, Silas thought better of leaving the trade goods unattended and thanked the chiefs for their offer, but said he had to decline. One of the headmen named Red Dog, seemed offended and made it clear that this might create bad blood between his people and the whites.

After a brief conference amongst themselves, it was decided that Bernard Laurent and Jack Cox would cross over the water and accept the honors offered. As a precaution though, the pirogue would be moved to mid-stream and anchored there for safety and within reach of Laurent and Cox, if needed

"You two keep your wits about you," Silas warned, "Best not trust them too much."

"Do not worry mon ami," said Laurent, "We will be careful, and return before it is too late."

"You had better, because we leave before sunup. We can't waste any more time than we have to."

"Make a baby for me," Antoine Martin said to Bernard, slapping him on the shoulder. Antoine was disappointed that he was not the one paying a visit to the Arikara camp, but happy for his friend.

The time for mourning had passed but Red Dog's heart still ached for his daughter, Little Corn Woman, and what hurt more than her loss, was that he would no longer be able to utter her name outload. He saw no way to ease the pain he felt and was determined that the only cure for his torment was to have blood for blood.

As the sun set the temperature quickly dropped in the early November evening. The White men waited, their rifles at the ready, watching the river shore for the return of Cox and Laurent. Silas would stand, peer into the darkening night, then sit back down for only a brief while, then regain his feet his gaze toward the light of the bonfire in the village.

"Aidez-moi à mes amis !" A cry came out of the darkness, the voice was Laurent's. "Aidez-moi! J'ai été blessé! *Help me! I have been injured!*" he shouted from the shore.

The men on the boat strained their eyes and in the light of the three-quarter moon, they could see the voyageur running toward the water. He dove in and struggled to swim to safety. He reached the boat where he was pulled aboard. From his back protruded several arrows.

"MAIR-duuuhhhh!" he hissed as they lay him down to inspect his wounds.

"Where's Cox?" Silas asked.

"Back there, I think 'e has gone under!" Laurent gasped.

Their attention was drawn back to the river bank, the quiet of the night broken by the shrill cries of the Arikara. With torches, they had come down from the village and before them they drove a lone figure, Jack Cox.

In the light of the torches, Jack's naked body glistened with the blood that flowed from uncountable wounds, his face crimson where it had streamed down from his scalped crown. He staggered, and then fell face down to the sandy soil. With the rage of demons, the screaming Arikara fell on him and with stone-headed clubs and tomahawks, they ended his torment.

"Fire," Silas ordered, and without hesitation, the four men on the boat each threw a shot into the crowd on the beach. New screams erupted in response and a few shots from trade guns and arrows flew at the boat. Several of the Indians hurried toward bullboats on the shore and started to paddle out toward the White men trapped on their boat.

While the whites were reloading their rifles, Silas yelled, "Fire another round and then man the oars.

Turn her in the water downstream." He then cut the rope that had anchored them stationary. The boat swung in the current and floating freely down river. Each of the men in the boat fired parting shots before manning the ores, each shot taking with it one of the enraged Arikara. The paddling, aided by the downward flow of the river soon swept them to safety, but in the opposite direction of their intended destination.

SAM J. PISCIOTTA

CHAPTER 9
THE GRAND RIVER

The river was treacherous in itself during the daylight hours, floating down it in the dark of night was almost foolhardy, but Ben and his companions had little choice. Once they felt they had left the immediate threat of the Arikara, Silas took to the tiller and steered the pirogue as close to the center of the Missouri as best he could by the light of the moon.

None of the men spoke, and the only sound save for oars splashing in the water and the lapping of the current against the gunwales of the boat, was the moans of Bernard Laurent suffering from his wounds. There had not been time to stop and tend to him. This would have to wait until someplace safe was found.

Downstream was the mouth of the Grand River and Silas swung the tiller pointing the pirogue into it. As the boat hit the flow of the Grand, its speed dropped. Once they adjusted to the push of the current against the boat, they maintained a steady rate of travel and rowed through the rest of the night. When the eastern sky started to show a reddish-orange glow, Silas edged the boat over to the shore, and under the cover of the cottonwoods, they took their first rest.

"Estienne, climb the bank and keep your eyes on the sky line for them damned Ress. *Allez vite!*" Silas ordered, and the little voyageur, rifle in hand scrambled across the river bottom, up the bank and disappeared.

"Now, let us tend to Bernard," Silas said.

They moved the man for the first time since he had been pulled aboard, seeing the number of arrows that had penetrated his back. Half a dozen of the feathered shafts protruded from his shoulders down to his hips. He moaned with pain as they laid him flat on the cargo, and Antoine began to cut away his friend's buckskin hunting jacket and cotton shirt. Pulling back the canvas that covered the cargo, Silas lifted up a five gallon keg of alcohol. Knocking loose the cork, he tipped the keg to pour the liquor across Bernard's back. This caused Bernard to scream in pain, and then he passed out.

Antoine examined each of the arrows and found that four of the six could be removed by slightly cutting the skin near the entry point. The remaining two posed a problem.

"This one here, it is very deep and maybe it has gone into his lung," he told Silas and Ben, "The other one is also deep, close to his *vertébrale*, and from the angle it maybe by 'his *coueur*. I am afraid to either pull them out or to push them through."

"Let's roll him onto his side, and see if the point might be sticking out there or at least close to the surface," said Silas, "Then we can decide if we pull them out or push them through." They gently rolled Bernard onto his right side, and before they examined his chest, noticed frothy pink blood around his mouth.

"Yep, one of them went through his lights," Silas said using the slang for lungs. "Take his shirt away and let's have a look," he added.

As they had hoped, the point of one arrow had went through Bernard's chest and it could be pushed through causing less damage than if they pulled it out from his back. Taking his knife, Antoine cut the arrow shaft at the base of the feather fletching. When Silas gave a nod of his head signaling he was ready, Antoine placed the flat of his knife against the shaft's end and with a sharp blow drove the arrowhead out through Bernard's chest. Silas then took hold of it and pulled the rest of the shaft out. Deep red blood flowed from the wound and then more of the frothy pink liquid.

With this done, they turned their attention to searching for the point where the last arrow might be. Their search was fruitless, and they had to leave the arrow as it was. They cut the arrow shaft where it protruded from Bernard's back leaving only a short stub. They then decided the best they could do for the present, was to apply a salve of bear grease and Shepherd's Purse to the wounds and dress them with clean bandages.

They propped their companion in as comfortable a position as possible, taking care not to put more pressure on the remaining arrow shaft. He gained consciousness, and moved causing pain to radiate through his body. He winced and through clenched teeth cursed, "Merde, qui fait mal! *Shit, that hurts!*"

"Bernard, you are still with us, No?" said Antoine, forcing a smile.

"It will take more than a stinking Ree arrow to put me under," Bernard said, the action bringing about a cough that pulled more blood from his punctured lung. This he spat out, in disgust. "Give me a drink," he asked. Antoine, put a cup of water to his lips and Bernard turned away.

"Not that piss! Give me something better."

Silas took the cup from Antoine, tossed out the water, picked up the liquor keg and filled the cup half full. He then handed it back to Antoine who held it to Bernard's lips. The injured man took a sip which made him cough again and brought up more blood.

"Facile, mon ami. Take it slow," Antoine cautioned.

"Another," demanded Bernard. This time he sipped the alcohol, and licking his lips smiled. "That is better." He took a few labored breaths then asked, "Did Jacques go under?"

"Oui, il est mort," Antoine said, "There was no way to save him."

"What happened back there?" Silas asked.

"I am not sure," said Bernard, "We went to the lodge of one of the chiefs and they fed us. Jacques he has his eye on this Ree woman, and her husband sees he is interested. I know this man from when I wintered with the Rees, he is called Le Chien Rouge, Red Dog. The woman is his femme, wife, and he offers her to Jacques. They leave and I stay. After a bit, I have to piss, so I get up to go outside, and while I am wetting the ground I hear Jacques shouting for me to run. I turn to see that Jacques he is without clothing, naked and he is being chased. I raise my rifle and fire at the men behind him. I turn and run to the river when I feel a pain in my back and know that it is an arrow. I feel more pain in my back and chest, and then I hear Jacques scream again.

"After that, I remember you pulling me into the pirogue and here we are." He paused and then said, "Give me another drink."

"I wonder what the hell Jack could have done to poke that hornet's nest? Silas said, wondering. "You sure nothing looked off while you were in the chief's lodge?"

"There was nothing to cause such a response," Bernard said. "And now, I am like le porc-épic, the porcupine, no?" Again he tried to smile, and then asked, "Silas, is it very terrible?"

"We couldn't get one of the arrows out. It went in deep, close to your spine," he paused, "Not sure where the point is, might be near your heart."

Bernard closed his eyes for a moment and then finding the smile that he had attempted before, opened his eyes and spoke to his friends, "I too will go under, no?"

"Do not talk like that, mon ami," Antoine said, attempting to convince himself as well as Bernard that there was hope. "You will live to be an old man."

"This I do not think," Bernard said, and closing

his eyes he laid his head back and rested.

"What do we do now?" asked Ben.

"We need to know if the dammed Rees are done with us, or if they intend to finish what they started," Silas said. "Let's go up and see if Lapin has seen anything. We'll be right back Bernard." He stood and picked up his rifle, then jumped off the boat onto the river bank followed by Ben.

As they moved up from the cover of the river bed, they could see Estienne in the distance, headed back in their direction. Going down on one knee, they waited until he was close enough to talk.

"What did you see?" Silas asked.

"We are not very far from the village on this side of the Big River. We have not gone very far from them, and I think soon they will look for us."

"You ever go far up this here river when you wintered with them bastards?"

"Only a little further, maybe two, three days west and north. It makes the trail like a snake," Estienne said, motioning with his hand the side to side wondering of the river. "There is little cover and soon she will get too shallow to float even the pirogue."

Silas thought about their situation, and the predicament they now found themselves in. He knew that if the Arikara decide to look for them, he and his companions could not propel the pirogue fast enough to out distance them. There was almost six tons of cargo in the boat and they couldn't let that fall into the hands of the Indians, especially at the price of their lives.

"Estienne, do think we could make it cross country to the Yellowstone where Lisa is headed?" Silas asked.

"Ce n'est pas évident, *it is not so easy*," Estienne shook his head. "We are where the grass is short, and the land she is rough but open."

"But, can we make it? Do you think you could

find the way there?"

"Oui, but it is a big country out there."

Silas weighed their options, and though the leader of this small group, decided to ask for the thoughts of everyone.

"Let's get back to the boat and talk with Antoine and Bernard," he said.

They moved back across the open prairie to where the pirogue was beached. Antoine jumped up, rifle in hand at their approach, and was relieved that it was not Indians.

"We don't have a lot of choices," Silas began, "I won't make this decision on my own, I feel you each have a say in what we do. I'm pretty sure them Rees will come looking for us, they know we're down two men, and we got all this cargo they're itchin' to get their hands on.

"I was thinking we cache the goods somewhere along this river, and then find another place to beach the boat, hide it and then double back and make for the Yellowstone over land."

"What about Bernard?" asked Antoine.

"We make a litter and carry him," Silas said.

"I would like to lift some Ree hair," Estienne said.

"I'm afraid the Arikara would love to give you the chance to try," said Silas, "But right now we save our own hair. What say you all? Do we try to float all the way back down stream and hope they don't catch up with us or head west overland?"

"West," Antoine said.

"Oui," added Estienne.

"Looks like I go where you all are headed," said Ben.

"Then it's settled. We find a good place to cache the cargo."

Scouting up river, they found a place where the pirogue could be unloaded and the cargo cached, hidden from the Indians. All but one crate was buried, and this one Silas made sure was left on the boat. The location of the cargo was marked on trees close by. Next they searched for a place the now empty boat could be pulled out of the water and hidden as best as possible. With luck, both the pirogue and the cargo could be retrieved in the spring.

Once the pirogue was on dry land and hidden, the men intended to set out following the Grand River to its headwaters. From there, they would attempt to reach the Yellowstone River where Manuel Lisa was building his fort. The exact distance was unknown to them. But what they knew was from the rough maps created after consulting with the Lewis and Clark men now with Lisa. Silas calculated they had nearly three hundred miles to cover. He rationalized that the rough estimate of the distance they had intended to travel up the Missouri and then down the Yellowstone, was twice that. Moving on foot they could possibly travel as much as twenty or thirty miles in a single day, this would be without the burden of carrying their injured partner, Bernard. Silas was resigned not to leave him behind, and not to attempt the journey on foot.

"How far did you say the Ree villages are from here?" Silas asked Estienne.

"Maybe, two miles, straight across la prairie," he answered.

"I have an idea. Do you think you can sneak up and relieve them Rees of a few horses?"

"Oui, but do you not think they will follow us?" Estienne questioned.

"Maybe so, but maybe they won't miss them for a time. At least long enough for us to get some distance between us and them."

"We can try."

"Good. You and Antoine take off now. It'll be dark in a few hours. Give them Rees time to settle down and then you pick out some horse flesh and head straight back here. We'll put on some miles before sunup tomorrow."

The two voyageurs set off in the direction of the Arikara villages while Silas and Ben stayed with Bernard and made ready to travel.

"Silas," Bernard called out hoarsely, and waved the man over with his hand.

"Yes, Bernard?"

"I have a favor to ask mon amie."

"Sure, what do you want?"

"I do not think I will be going down the same trail as you, I am to go another way."

"What do you mean?" Silas asked and then understood what Bernard meant. "No, you're gonna' make it fine."

"No. I wish I had a priest to hear my last words."

"I'm sorry, Bernard." Silas shook his head.

"I know that you can say the words for me, no?"

"I can't do that." Silas protested.

"S'il vous plaît, mon frère!" Bernard pleaded, "J'avoue à Dieu que j'ai péché. I wish to make the confession."

Silas, though reluctant, shook his head in assent, and said, "Dimittuntur peccata tua, in nomine Patris et Filii et Spiritus Sancti," pleasing Bernard.

Ben was some distance away, and not understanding what was transpiring, he tried not to intrude on what seemed to be something personal. He could hear, but not quite make out the words Bernard was speaking in his mixture of French and English, while Silas sat listening, his head bowed in silence.

The sound of the river flowing past and the rustle of the few stubborn leaves that still clung to the cottonwood trees, were the only sounds that disturbed the chilly fall air. Ben thought that if the situation were a bit different, this would be a very pleasant place. He even thought that it would have been nice to share a place like this with the girl Jean. He smiled. Thinking about her warmed him and he wondered what she was doing at that moment. Did she think of him, he wondered, or had she forgotten him to move on to someone else, someone who would stay in St. Louis? Ben knew she was her own person and that she would make her own decisions, deciding what she wanted and with who.

Silas stood and walked a short distance away. He stood there his back to Ben and Bernard, looking out from the cover of the tree line onto the short grass prairie. After a few moments, he turned and spoke to Ben.

"We best find a place to dig a grave." This shocked Ben and he looked from Silas over to Bernard whose face no longer showed pain, but the relief death offers those suffering.

They tied Bernard's blanket around him forming a shroud, and then began to dig a hole for the body. Before laying the body in ground, Silas and Ben emptied the crate that had been left on the boat. Its contents, saddles, bridles and headstalls were laid aside. They then took the wooden crate apart, placing the boards in the bottom of the grave, to make a bed for their dead friend. The remaining boards formed the sides and top of the makeshift coffin. The sun was setting when they had finished filling in the grave, and wiping out all traces of its location. There would be no marker, only the memory of the man would remain.

Standing over the spot, Silas began to speak in a language that Ben had never heard and could not understand, "Requiem aeternam dona ei, Domine."

The moon rose a bit larger that night, shedding some light on the empty darkness along the river. Silas and Ben waited patiently, the minutes passing slowly, turning into hours. Silas sat peering out into the emptiness, his back against a tree, his Henry rifle resting across his lap.

"You think they got caught?" Ben broke the

stillness.

"No tellin', we'll give em more time. If they're not back by sunup, we'll head out on our own." Silas waited a few moments then said, "You try to get some sleep, I'll keep watch, and wake you when they get back or if anything happens."

Still apprehensive, but with faith in Silas' judgment, Ben found a place among the trees and made himself as comfortable as possible. He rolled up in his blanket, wishing that there was a fire to help ward off the cold night air, but he knew a fire would act as a beacon to announce their hiding place to the Arikara. So, with a mattress of fallen cottonwood leaves and the wool blanket covering, he soon found sleep. His dreams were first of working at the forge in his uncle's shop. He could feel the heat from the coals as he pumped the bellows, the forced air feeding the fire causing the coals to turn from orange to white hot. It felt good and almost comforting on his face, arms and chest, and there beside him was Jean Drury, smiling at him. He turned to take her in his arms, but still smiling she put her hands on his chest to hold him away from her.

"Always remember me, mon chouchou, though I will be no more than that memory. There is someone waiting for you," she whispered and then she was gone. A cold wind rushed in, blowing away the forge and its warmth, replaced by a cold fog, and shadowy figures crossed back and forth in his slumber.

There in the mist floated Bernard Laurent, Jack Cox, and Seth Griffin. Set in their pale-gray faces were hollow eyes that seemed to gaze through Ben. He spoke to them not so much with words, but with a silent prayer, begging them to leave him in peace, telling them he was sorry about their dying. As in an attempt to answer him, Griffin and Cox turned and walked away, merging with the mist that floated in the air. Alone, Bernard looked away and pointed to some far off destination. He then opened his lips as if to speak some advice or warning, but no sound came out. He mouthed words that formed no meaning, offering no comfort for Ben, and then he melted into the mist, his message not understood. Ben strained his eyes to look where his friend had disappeared and a shape took form and moved toward him out of the mist. At first it seemed to be someone crawling along the ground but as it grew closer Ben could see it was a huge cat, a catamount. Though Ben had never seen one, he knew what it was, and it looked just like the animal scrimshawed on his powder horn. A chill ran through him as the cougar's eyes locked onto his and the big cat let out a shrilled scream.

"Pissst..." The soft hiss from Silas brought Ben awake with a start. "They're back. We best pull foot, no time to waste."

Estienne and Antoine had returned with horses stolen from the Arikara. Silas informed them of Bernard's death, and though they were saddened, there was no time to mourn. It was imperative they put as much distance between themselves and the Indians.

Once they saddled the horses and were mounted, they moved the horses back and forth over the area of Bernard's grave to wipe out any trace of the resting place. They did not want their friend's body dug up and mutilated, or left for the wolves to devour. This done, they departed and followed the Grand River west, the sky behind them signaling the coming dawn.

The four men were unaccustomed to riding horseback. And it took some time adjusting to the Indian ponies, daring not to push the horses into too fast a pace but keeping them at a steady trot. By the time the sun was well up in the sky, they had covered almost a dozen miles with the broken terrain offering some cover. The river flowed back and forth, as Estienne had said, like the path of a snake, sometimes more north and south than west increasing the distance they traveled. Silas motioned to his companions to slow down so they could talk and they moved in close to each other.

"We might want to give these horses a rest," he said, surprised that the sturdy little horses had lasted so well thus far. They all stopped and dismounted, letting the horses pause and graze on the short dry grass.

"You think they know you took the horses?" he asked Lapin.

"I am sure of it," Lapin said, "We did not get away with the horses without being noticed. There was a guard watching the herd. A young boy, I do not think I kill him, but he will have a headache, no."

"Either way, they'll know and come looking for the horses. It doesn't matter to them who took 'em," said Silas. "We'll rest a bit down next to the river, let the horses graze and put some meat in our bellies."

They took cover among the cottonwoods, elms, and willows that grew along the river's course. The further west they went the river's course, meandering as it did, would make progress slow and decrease their chances of outdistancing any pursuit the Arikara might offer.

They talked, pooling their combined knowledge of what was known about the country and its inhabitants, again, this mostly learned from the five men of Lewis and Clark. They knew that on the journey back from the western ocean, the two explorers had separated and William Clark followed the Yellowstone River from its source in the mountains back to the Missouri River. Several rivers flowed into the Yellowstone; Clarks Fork of the Yellowstone, the Bighorn, the Tongue, and the Powder. Past where the Yellowstone added its water to the Missouri, the Little Missouri joined its big sister.

Ben, Silas, Estienne and Martin needed to make it

to the confluence of the Yellowstone and the Bighorn where Lisa was building his trading post. This meant they would have to cross three of these rivers that flowed from the south; the Tongue, the Powder and the Little Missouri. Following the course of the Grand was not practical, so they decided to head as straight west as the terrain allowed. This would put them in open ground for the most part, but they would cover more of it.

When the men had eaten some dried meat, washed down with river water, and the horses were rested, the journey directly west began. Once they left the confines of the river's path, the country lent itself to faster travel but was still rugged, consisting of rolling hills and plains cut by ravines and dotted with steep flat-topped buttes, some of these rising four to six hundred feet high.

Despite the terrain, the four men covered well over another forty miles before sundown. If the sky remained clear, the near-full moon would offer enough light for them to put even more distance between them and the Arikara, so they decided to rest for an hour or two allowing both men and horses to recover their strength.

With the sun dropping into the western horizon, Silas pulled a silver chronometer from his haversack. Its well-worn cover and crystal showed both age and special care. Ben had witnessed Silas look at the pocket watch several times a day during their trip up from St. Louis. He found it curious that for a man that otherwise seemed not to care about keeping track of details like the time of day, Silas took special care of the watch, winding it just the right amount and keeping the mechanism clean.

Silas made a mental note that the sun was setting at close to half-past four in the afternoon. He had checked the time before they left the Grand River at sunup and it had been seven o'clock. The moon was growing toward full and there would be plenty of light to travel for the next few nights if there was no cloud cover. But it was November and there was no telling when the weather would change, bringing the permanent snows of winter. Silas did not want to be caught out in the open prairie if a storm developed.

By pushing themselves and the Indian ponies, the men traveled through the night and on through the next day. Without knowing their exact location, they had reached the forks of the Grand River some one hundred miles from where they had started. Here they decided to take an extended rest to eat and sleep through the night. They felt that the Arikara might not have followed them this far, and it would be safe to let their guard down.

As if some sign of hospitality, a lone pronghorn antelope topped the rise on a hill above the river. Ben glanced over at Silas and the older man nodded his head as if giving permission. Ben raised the Lebanon County rifle to his shoulder, pulled back the steel jaws holding the flint, and centering the sites on the buck, he squeezed the trigger.

They built a fire, heated water from the river and made coffee while the antelope meat roasted on the fire. For the first time in three days, they put warm food into their stomachs. Ben was amazed at how something as simple as a hot cup of coffee made the world look completely different, and the taste of the lean red meat was better than any meal he had ever had.

After they finished their meal, they picketed the horses, put out the fire and turned in for the night. They would take turns, one at a time standing guard until morning. Before rolling into his blanket, Ben had a chance to talk to Silas.

"Silas, can I ask you something?"

"Sure."

"Back there, you said some words over Bernard's

grave. What was that language you were talkin'? It didn't sound like French, was it Spanish?"

"No," said Silas, "It was Latin. I guess you could say it's the granddaddy of French and Spanish, Italian too."

"Latin?" Ben was a confused as before.

"Yep, Bernard asked me to say some words over him. I knew enough to grant him at least that. Now, you better get some sleep. You have horse watch at midnight, then Lapin and I'll take the last turns."

Ben rolled over, and in the darkness he could hear the four-legged predators of the night fighting over the remnants of the pronghorn that had been drug away from the camp. He wasn't sure, but knew it was either the gray wolves or the small prairie wolves that were beneficiaries of his marksmanship. He closed his eyes, listening to their snarls, yelping and finally lonesome calls, a wild lullaby as he passed into the dreamless sleep of exhaustion.

Just before dawn, Silas roused his companions. They rose, saddled the horses and were on their way before the eastern sky turned yellowish-orange, the few clouds dissipating as the sun warmed the air. Reaching the first rise away from the river, they stopped to look out across the terrain in front of them. To the west were more rolling hills and gullies. Directly to their right sat a small flat-topped butte rising less than one hundred feet from its surroundings.

"Looks like the same from here on out," Silas said, taking out his pocket watch to look at the time, noting it was half-past seven. He had just placed the watch back into his haversack when his horse, wide-eyed, lunged forward and let out a scream of pain. Silas was almost thrown from the saddle and held tight, pulling on the reins to regain control of the animal. He then found the cause of the horse's destress, the feather shaft of an arrow protruded from the horse's croup just behind the loin. Before the cry of pain from the horse dissipated in the cool morning air, the arrow was followed by more and the sound of war whoops and a few gun shots took its place. The arrows flew around the men and the whiz of lead flew past them.

"Head for the high ground!" Silas yelled, and kicked his heels into the horse's flanks spurring it in to a run toward the butte. The four men followed with just a quick glance behind them to see a large party of Arikara breaking from the timber bottom and headed toward them.

Upon reaching the top of the butte, Silas scanned their surroundings and realized there was no natural cover. Though on high ground, they would still be exposed and vulnerable to attack. They had to act quickly if they were to survive against the superior number gaining on them.

"Make a breastwork of the horses," he called out, dismounting his horse and pulling its head close to him. He drew out his belt knife and slit the animal's throat. The horse struggled but was overcome by the fast loss of blood and fell to the ground, lashing out at the air with hooves for the briefest moment, and then lay still providing a place for Silas to take cover.

By this time the other horses were milling around in terror, the smell of blood in air, and hits from both gun fire and arrows. Each man in turn brought his own mount down and followed Silas' example, at this point it being more a blessing to the suffering animals releasing them of the pain inflicted by the Arikara. Each of the ridden mounts went down first, the pack horse was last.

"Pick your shots, and don't everyone fire at once," Silas said, firing from his prone position behind the horse carcass, his shot taking down one of the most advanced attackers.

Ben, kneeling took aim and also fired, hitting his

mark, knocking a warrior from the saddle. Estienne and Antoine followed suit, each calmly choosing a target and firing and then reloading.

With their numbers decreased by four the Arikara pulled back to where they thought they might be out of the range of the White men's rifles. They milled around, talking among themselves, a few coming out taunting the men on the butte to come out and fight.

"Nique ta mere!" Antoine yelled, hurling back an insult in French, making the obscene gesture of grabbing at his crouch.

Lapin, laughed, and commented, "You probably have already had his mother, no?"

Taking careful aim each of the men on the hill would wound or outright kill one of the Arikara when they came into range and it was not long before the attackers fell back to a safer distance, venturing out only when their courage was worked up and their judgment poor. Each of these solo warriors offered a target that was easily dealt with. It was not long before the Arikara, short on patience, sent out more targets than could be fired upon by the whites at any one time and the accuracy of shots fired in haste decreased the effectiveness of the defender's aim. It was also determined by the Indians that the white's supply of powder and lead must be low. The Arikara gathered one last time just out of range and decided to make the best of this assumption.

Still outnumbering their quarry by ten to one, the Arikara broke from their huddle and spread out, encircling the small butte. It was obvious that they intended attack from all sides, and the short distance from the bottom of the rise seemed to make it clear that they would over power the whites.

Silas pulled his belt pistol, and checking the priming, laid it within reach, copied by his companions. He also spilled the few lead balls he had left out into his palm from his shot pouch, and placed them in his mouth. When pressed for time, he would forgo measuring the gun powder he needed to load his rifle. Estimating the amount of powder he poured it directly down the barrel from the powder horn, and then he spit in a lead ball, seating it home with the ramrod. Ben, having no pistol, set his knife and tomahawk close at hand. He shook with a mixture of fear and anticipation for what would come next.

As expected, the Arikara attacked from all directions as the four men crouched behind their fortification struggling to hold them back. The Indians pressed forward taking advantage of the time it took the whites to reload their muzzleloaders. Arrows aimed upwards in an arch fell from the sky, landing among the men. It was obvious that time was on the side of the Arikara.

Each of the men behind the wall of horse flesh was determined to sell their life at a cost to the Indians. The assault slackened and Silas stood, his pistol in one hand, and knife in the other. Ben seeing his mentor rise up copied him and took up his knife and hand axe. Looking down the slope, they could see the Arikara pulling back a bit, and from the river bottom came what appeared to be reinforcements for them, the number of Indians increasing by three times.

"Merde!" exclaimed Lapin, "we go under for sure now. At least I will leave a pretty top-knot to hang in someone's lodge, no."

"No one would want that mop of hair you call a scalp," Silas remarked.

Ben could not understand how these men could joke so close to their own death, but then it didn't surprise him and he was proud to be with them at the end.

More war whoops and gunfire erupted from the two groups of Indians as they first moved toward each other, and then several of the first group turned and sought the shelter of the tree line along the river.

The White men stood in astonishment as it was now plain that the two groups of Indians were fighting amongst themselves. Lapin raised his hand to shade his eyes in an attempt to better see what was happening.

"Mon Dieu!" He exclaimed, "Those are Crow!" and he let out war whoops of his own, dancing around in joy!

SAM J. PISCIOTTA

CHAPTER 10
FORT RAYMOND

For Manuel Lisa, there couldn't have been a better place to build Fort Raymond. Here, at the confluence of the Yellowstone and the Bighorn Rivers, was everything he could possibly want. It was near the winter hunting grounds of the Crow Indians, the lowlands offered plenty of timber for construction and nearby was an ample supply of a low grade coal that could be used for heating the little fort. The design of the trading post would be simple, three sides made up of low buildings, all connected, their exterior walls forming the outside of the fort, and the opening, facing the junction of the two rivers, would be walled across to form the front with a gate in its center. At two opposing corners, one in front and one in back, there would be a second story, creating a place to post guards and lookouts. These also offered a place to defend the fort from inside, allowing those inside an unobstructed view down the outside of all four walls.

Work had commenced as soon as the main party had arrived less than a week ago, and Lisa was satisfied with the progress made so far, though he still pushed the men to complete the work as quickly as possible. He wanted to send out emissaries to the Indians notifying them of the trading post's presence, and that must be done before winter set in. He knew these men needed to be trustworthy, strong and intelligent. Not only would they be his representatives to the Indians, they would have to be adaptable to any situation they found themselves in. They must be able to survive on their own through to the spring, finding food and shelter, and hopefully winter with the

Indians. He had already chosen who he would send; Edward Rose, Peter Weiser, George Drouillard and John Colter. These men would head out in different directions, with the hope they would return with customers and information about the availability of beaver in the surrounding territory.

With some luck, the construction would also be at a point where Lisa could send out a few groups of men to trap the nearby streams before they froze over. The groups consisting of six men each would venture up the Yellowstone, the Bighorn and their tributaries, setting beaver traps and harvesting the furry "bank notes," as they represented the wealth that the mountains streams offered.

For decades, St. Louis-based traders had gone up the Missouri River, but they had never ventured much further than the area of the Arikara and their financial returns had been meager. The region on the Missouri River, where the Mandan and Arikara lived offered few beaver or other fur-bearing animals. As far as Lisa was concerned, these Indians were not particularly ambitious or successful hunters so they had few pelts or buffalo robes on which he could make a profit. Here, next to the mountains was the true beaver country. Lisa knew that the Indians of this country would be good customers trading the furs they brought in to the post, but sending out his own engagees would cut out these middlemen. With what he knew of the Crow, Manuel Lisa could see no problem with his people taking the bounty the mountain streams offered. The Blackfeet were a different story, but every venture carried its own risks.

Lisa's concerns about the Blackfeet were bolstered by the fact that the North West and the Hudson Bay Companies out of Canada were expanding westward. Until now the British were in undisturbed control of the fur trade of the upper Missouri, and they fostered opposition, if not outright hostility, toward the

Americans by supplying the Blackfeet with firearms.

The hold of the British on the upper Missouri would now change as Lisa had outdistanced the St. Louis traders in the south and was going up against the British in the north. He would break into where the true riches could be obtained. Manuel had come a long way from being a storekeeper in Vincennes.

*

Taking advantage of the mild weather so late in the year, the sixty Crow warrior's intent was to stock up on buffalo meat for the coming winter. Several women and a few younger males accompanied them to help with the hunt and the processing of the meat. Coming across a group of Arikara was purely by chance, and an opportunity not to be passed up. The taking of the Arikara horses and scalps was an added bonus.

Their leader, Painted Otter, was not chosen for his abilities to lead men into battle but as a wise and accomplished hunter. There was no time to discuss if there was one among them more qualified, so Painted Otter attacked the Arikara as he would a running herd of buffalo. He quickly ordered his group to strike at both sides of the Arikara as well as a head-on assault, easily routing them in mere minutes.

With the Arikara either fleeing or dead on the battlefield, the Crow turned their attention to the White men on the small rise. Painted Otter and a dozen of his fellow Crow first circled the little butte then pushed their horses up the slope to determine if the fight was to continue.

Ben stood with his companions watching the Crow as they rode up and surrounded them, the horses of the Crow pawed at the ground, their blood still up with the heat of battle. Though not painted for war, the Crow looked more terrifying than the Arikara, and Ben could see a big difference between the two tribes in just their appearance.

The Crow clothing was more elaborate than that

of the other tribes Ben had seen. The one who seemed to be their leader wore a long shirt made of soft, tanned elk or deer hide, the animal's leg skin left to dangle at the sides adding to the movement of the man wearing them. The shirt was decorated with dyed porcupine quill bands as was the triangular bib at the front opening. He wore leggings adorned with quilled band also and moccasins covered with porcupine quills dyed red.

Another distinction of this man, and his companions, was their hair style. The man's hair was without braids, left long at the sides and back, with the front cut short, standing up straight in a pompadour held in place with bear grease. At the sides of this chief's head, he wore vertical hair bows, also decorated with quill work and long dangles. Some of the other Crow had their upright crests coated with red or white clay, and their hair hung down below their waist. In all, these were a completely different breed of Indian, and Ben was awed by them.

The Chief dismounted his horse and walked forward to the breastwork of dead horses. He looked around taking in the scene before him and then at each of the men sizing them up. Two had pale skin, one with reddish hair, the other with hair like the color of the sun. The other two, were darker skinned with dark eyes and hair, and looked like the Frenchmen who came out of the north He was suspicious of these four as they could very well be British who gave guns to enemies of the Crow, the Blackfeet.

He spoke to them in Crow, *"I am Painted Otter, of the Children of the Large-beaked Bird, the Kicked in the Bellies band."* He paused to see if any of the Whites understood the language of the People. One of the dark-skinned one's smiling, spoke in broke Crow, augmented with sign language.

"We are happy to see you. We are friends to the Apsáalooke. *We come to trade with the* Apsáalooke.

We have a big lodge on the Elk River." He pronounced the Crow's name in their own language to the best of his abilities and used their name for the Yellowstone River.

"This is a good thing," said Painted Otter, *"Why are you fighting with the Corn Growers?"*

"We tried hard to avoid a fight with them, but we had taken some of their horses and this they did not like." Lapin laughed softly hoping the chief would have some sense of humor. If the Crow saw humor in this, he showed no sign of it.

"It is a good thing to take the horses of the Corn Growers." He looked down at the dead horses. *"But I do not believe these are of much use to you now. Come, we will talk and smoke together."* He vaulted onto his horse and rode down the hill, followed by the other Crow.

From the packs, Silas pulled the few meager trade goods they had kept from the entire store of items they had hidden. This was some red flannel, a few hanks of white glass beads, and he carried Bernard Laurent's Deringer Rifle. The next few hours would determine whether these meager gifts would be enough to win over the Crow, or if these Indians would simply rob them of all their possessions. The Lewis and Clark men with Lisa had told of their encounter with these people. On the return trip from the West, the Crow has made off with the entire ramuda of horses meant for Captain Clark and his men.

The rest of the day was spent in setting up a camp along the river, the small hunting lodges of the Crow erected by the women so fast they seemed to rise up out of the ground. A few Crow hunters ventured out and returned with fresh game. Soon haunches of venison roasted over the fire. Buffalo robes were spread on the ground, and the Whites invited to take part in a feast and the celebration of the victory over the Arikara. The Crow had taken thirty Arikara scalps and as many horses.

Panted Otter and a few other Crow men sat under the sparse shade offered by the bare-limbed trees with Lapin, Silas, Antoine and Ben. Before any talking commenced, they passed around a long-stemmed pipe with a red stone bowl containing a mixture of tobacco and bear root. After the pipe was passed Lapin introduced his companions, the names meaning little in the language of the Crow except for Lapin who introduced himself as Rabbit. The Crow themselves would give some type of name to the whites; Red Hair for Silas, Big Yellow Hair for Ben and for Antoine Martin, Crooked Nose, for his nose that had been broken many times leaving it to sit somewhat to one side. Lapin made it clear that Silas was their leader and this suited Painted Otter.

Silas offered the chief the red flannel and glass beads, and then held out Laurent's rifle. As Painted Otter took the rifle, Silas made the hand sign for "gift," using his right hand, moving it from his chest out toward Painted Otter palm up.

The Crow chief nodded his head in approval and made the hand sign for thank you. It was now time for the Crow chief to offer something in return and he gave Silas five of the Arikara horses to replace those they had lost.

"You have said that you have a big lodge on the Elk River. Do you have plenty of the Whiteman's possessions there?" he asked.

"Yes, we have many goods to trade with the Apsáalooke. *If they would bring in the skins of the beaver, buffalo and other fur bearing animals, we will trade many wonderful things."* Lapin said.

"This is good. I think we will go with you to this big lodge."

It would be almost two weeks before they reached the trading post. Traveling with the Crow meant that the Whites had less chance running into trouble, and gave them time to get better acquainted with their proposed customers. Of all of them, Silas and Ben learned the fastest; Lapin and Martin being content with what knowledge they already possessed. It was not long before Silas had a good working knowledge of the Crow language, and Ben had learned enough to get by.

Silas learned as much as he could about the Crow. Among the Indian nations, they had fewer allies than enemies, but their territory was worth defending as it was richest in the natural resources that the Crow counted on for survival. From their oral tradition, Silas gathered they had once lived east of the Missouri River, possibly on the other side of the Mississippi. Like other tribes, they had moved slowly westward in search of buffalo and it was then they adopted the horse, allowing them to move out on to the Plains and hunt buffalo more actively. The Crow became noted horse breeders and dealers, developing large horse herds. Being a small nation, they were subject to raids and horse thefts by other tribes such as; the Gros Ventre, Assiniboine, Pawnee, Ute, Arapaho, Cheyenne, Lakota and Blackfeet, of these, the last three being the greatest enemies to the Crow. Other tribes such as the Plains Cree, Assiniboine, Saulteaux, Ojibwe, and Métis also counted themselves enemies of the Crow. Only small nations such as the Flathead, Nex Perce, Kiowa and Shoshone were friendly to the Crow, and they warred against the enemies of the Crow.

*

The soft glow of a campfire through the trees tempted Dob with its promise of warmth as he sat shivering in the darkness. The temperature was dropping and he knew if he spent one more night without a fire he would die. He had wandered around in circles for the past four days, not knowing where he was or where he was going. His only motivation was to get far away from the place where the others in his party had been killed.

The Blackfoot war party had struck without warning catching most of the trappers with no chance to defend themselves. Only Obadiah Cash, and Dob had managed to react in their own defense. They were close to the picket line when Cash noticed a painted warrior attempting to sneak up to the horses. With little thought and lightning reflexes, Cash brought his Henry Rifle to his shoulder and fired, knocking the Indian backwards. Dob dove for cover behind a fallen tree.

"Blackfoots!" Cash yelled, but his warning was drowned out by the war cries echoing from the surrounding trees. Thirty painted warriors broke into the clearing where the trappers had made their camp firing their Trade Guns, bows, and swinging war-clubs or tomahawks. Only one or two of the six men around the campfire made it to their feet before being brought down. The rest died where they had sat.

Cash had no time to reload his rifle, only enough to pull a large hunting knife from the beaded sheath at his waist before he was faced by a large Indian brandishing a stone-headed club. They met, each grabbing for a hold on the other and staggered back toward the cut-bank of the river below the camp. As Dob watched, Cash and the warrior plunged over the river embankment.

Dob looked for better cover and spied a downed cottonwood trunk, its inside hollow from rot. He crawled over to it, and climbed inside. From this hiding place he watched, in horror and fear, as the men he had lived and worked with for the past seven months were killed and then mutilated. Cash had warned them that if they were not vigilant, they would pay dearly for trespassing into Blackfoot territory.

"Keep your nose to the wind!" he would tell Dob as he taught the boy the art of trapping beaver. "It ain't often a man gets two chances to make a mistake in the Rocky Mountains." Cash had been the only one who had taken any time with Dob. It might not have been that he liked Dob, more than likely he felt some form of empathy for the greenhorn with the devil's mark on his face. But, this did little for either Cash or Dob as the Blackfeet raged through the camp.

One of the last to fall was Fred Carpenter, the camp keeper. Knocked unconscious, he was dragged toward a tree and his hands secured to its trunk with rawhide thongs, and his feet to stakes driven into the ground. As the Indians ransacked the camp, one squatted in front of Fred and stayed there as if studying the boy. This warrior's face was painted black with a strip of yellow across his eyes.

When the trophies of severed fingers, scalps, horses, and firearms, along with anything else of value, had been secured, the Blackfeet started to leave the campsite, all but one. The lone warrior who had been looking at Fred did not move. Even when one of his companions spoke to him, his gaze never left the boy tethered to the tree. He replied something, that Dob couldn't understand, but it chilled his blood.

The second warrior moved off and the first reached out and slapped Fred across the face in an attempt to wake him, but it had no effect. Repeated attempts, with more force, brought about some results. Fred blinked his eyes, and the realization of his situation came to him. A look of fear crossed his face, and he began to looking around at the scene of carnage around him. His first thought was to scream for help, but there was no one to help him, save for Dob and he was not about to leave the security of the downed cottonwood.

The Indian spoke to Fred. Now and then he tilted his head to one side, much as a dog would, in an attempt to understand something.

"I do not understand you long knives," he said in

his own tongue, *"You come into the land of the People, and believe you can take what you want with no thought that you must give something in return. Is this not how you see it brother?"* He looked away from Fred as if speaking to someone else.

He looked back at Fred. *"You yell loudly, but have no reason. You show you have fear. You do not act like a man. Even a Crow woman is stronger than you. Let us see how much you can scream."* This said, he drew his knife from the sheath at his belt and cut away one of Fred's pant legs. Slowly, he then began to cut small slices of flesh from Fred's thigh. The boy screamed in pain as the Blackfoot methodically worked, cutting as if he was taking meat from a deer.

Fred lost consciousness again, but the Indian was not satisfied. He waited a short time then awakened the boy a second time. This time he cut flesh from the boy's chest and arms. Fred had reached a point where the pain seemed no longer to matter. Sobbing, softly he called for his mother, saying he was sorry he had left home and begging her to forgive him.

"Look Brother, he seems to pray now." the Indian spoke again to his nonexistent companion. *"He is stronger and now I can take his strength, and we can share it."* With one hand, he reached out and took hold of Fred's hair; with the other, he drew the knife around the boy's skull and then pulled free the scalp. Fred moaned, as blood slid down his forehead and into his eyes, mingling with his tears.

The warrior, again with his head tilted to one side, evidently decided he had achieved the results he sought, and plunged the knife into the under the boy's rib. Reaching inside the chest, he tore out the boy's heart, its last beats felt in his hand.

Fred's head fell to one side and his dead eyes appeared to be looking in Dob's direction. Dob feared that somehow he would now be found, but the Blackfoot moved over to where the camp fire had been and sat down. He leaned forward and brought flames back to life by blowing on the embers. He reach for a long stick and running it through the heart, began to roast the organ. As he turned the stick slowly he spoke again as if he had a companion next to him.

"Though he was not brave at first, I believe there is some strength in his heart. You and I brother will take this strength as our own."

When the meat was sufficiently cooked, he began to consume it, stopping between bites to hold it out, offering a portion to his invisible friend.

His hunger filled, he stood, mounted his horse and slowly rode away from the campsite. As he moved away, he spoke to the specter only he could see, his words uttered so low they barely made a sound.

By nightfall, fresh snow had begun to fall, building up until late the next morning. It was only then that Dob pulled himself out from the log and began to search for anything the Blackfoot had left behind.

He found nothing of use and was left with only the clothes on his back, his knife, his rifle, and no powder or lead. He then began to wonder which way to head, and without a notion of where he was he moved off in the opposite direction taken by the Indians.

It was thus that he had spent the past four days, cold and hungry, driven only by fear. By chance, he had noticed the fire in the evening's dimming light as he stumbled through a grove of aspen. He moved toward the flame's inviting warmth, an uncontrollable shaking running through his body. His desperation for warmth and food was overriding the fear that the campfire belonged to the very Indians who had killed his companions.

He approached with caution, carefully placing one foot at a time slowly in front of him just as Cash had shown him. He held his empty Wheeler rifle in his shaking hands. He was not ten yards away when he could see the figures huddled around the fire, and one of them called out.

"You best come in before you freeze to death out there."

Dob stopped, the fear welling up inside him, welding his feet to the ground.

"Come on in," the voice called out, "We been listening to you fumble around out there for the past hour." With this, one of the figures stood and beckoned Dob with a wave of his hand.

*

A blanket of snow covered the country along the Yellowstone River, transforming it, creating a completely different world. The mild weather of the past month had given in to the first onslaught of winter and these first snows were wet and heavy, the warm earth melting a good portion of it. The rest would harden and freeze to be the base for snow fall that would follow throughout the winter. Manuel Lisa was pleased the weather had not delayed completion of Fort Raymond. Now he worried about the long overdue Silas Scott. Scott should have arrived by now. More important than Scott were the papers he carried from the Governor.

From the bastion, Lisa looked down the Yellowstone River, expecting the pirogue containing the last trade goods to round the corner but there was no sight of it. He turned and scanned the white landscape to the southeast and what appeared to be a herd of buffalo crested the rise. As it came closer he realized that it was a large group of Indians and he called out, "Sound the bell! Indians approaching! Secure the gate!"

It had taken the better part of two weeks after the battle with the Arikara for Crow hunting party to escort the White men to the newly completed fort. Their arrival and the presence of Ben's group with them, took everyone at the fort by surprise, Manuel

Lisa most of all.

Before the Indians had settled in near the fort, Lisa called the four men into his quarters demanding the reason they had arrived by land, and with none of the goods they were in charge of.

Silas explained the entire turn of events from St. Louis all the way to the meeting with the Crow. He had saved the important documents, carrying them in his haversack and these he turned over to Lisa. Lisa resigned himself to accept the hand dealt to him, with a mixture of frustration and anger over the missing trade good, balanced out with Silas bringing in the Crow to trade.

He placed hope that the goods and the pirogue cached by Silas on the Grand River could be retrieved in the spring. Only time would tell. For the moment they would settle down for the winter, wait for the spring trapping season and hope that the envoys to the Crow in general would bring in more business. There was also the hope that the few groups of trappers that had been dispatched already would return carrying heavy packs of furs.

Ben searched among the men still at Fort Raymond looking for Dob, and found that he had been sent out with one of the trapping parties and would not be back until spring. He resigned himself to wait, if nothing else the past months with Silas Scott as a mentor, had taught him patience.

Ben was assigned to help the blacksmith at completing the few iron items that still needed to be made for Fort Raymond, and it felt good to put his hands back to work creating something. His only complaint was the inferior grade of coal they were forced to use.

Three days passed and all seemed quiet. Ben was at his job in the forge when an alarm call sounded from one of the log bastions. Everyone retrieved their rifles and manned their assigned post at the walls.

From the distance a lone figure approached the wooden stockade. He was next to naked, his clothes tattered and torn, his body weak as he stumbled through the snow toward the fort.

From the wall, Lisa watched this man and when he had reached within a few yards Lisa called out, "Open the gate." As the wooden gate swung on its hinges, the emaciated figure staggered in and fell to the ground.

One of the men at the gate bent down and turned the man over. "It's Diah Cash!" he shouted.

"Take him inside," ordered Lisa.

Others rushed to Obadiah, picked him up and carried the unconscious man into one of the buildings. Once his wounds were dressed and he was warmed with blankets by a fire, he awoke. He was given hot broth to drink and when he had recovered his wits, Lisa began to question him.

Obadiah told about the Blackfoot attack on the Musselshell River not fifty miles away, and that he thought there might be others still alive. He also said that it was a small Blackfoot raiding party of about two dozen.

"We was just caught off-guard," Obadiah said.

Lisa furious, his anger overcoming his better judgment, decided to act. He was determined to seek revenge as soon as possible. His only problem was a shortage of manpower. He called on Silas to discuss a plan of action.

"Mr. Scott, take ten men with you and move as fast as possible. Track down the vermin and deal with them."

"Yes Sir, I'll leave as soon as we're saddled." Silas had a brief thought, and then asked, "Might we ask the Crow if any of them want to come along? That way, I wouldn't need so many of our own men. I could take maybe four or five plus myself."

"Do that, Mr. Scott."

It took little for Silas to decide who to take with him. He would take Estienne, Antoine, Ben and another man Edward Brown. He would speak with Painted Otter and see it any of his warriors wanted to go before he chose any more of the Manuel Lisa's engagees.

The young men of Painted Otter's band were more than willing to get into a scrap with the Blackfeet, but cooler heads prevailed and the number that finally decided to go with Silas was an even dozen. Before midday, they were ready to leave.

As they rode away from the fort, a lone rider caught up with them. It was Obadiah Cash.

"Diah, what the hell you doin'?" asked Silas.

"Goin' back to get me some Blackfoot hair, anyways, you'll find the camp easier if I show you the way.

"I 'spect there is no talking you out if it. Let's ride.

CHAPTER 11
BLACKFEET AND BRITISH

"Your wound does not bleed anymore," Walks Long said, commenting on his observation, noting that the hole in his friend's chest appeared dry. It did not bother either of them that no one but Walks Long could see or hear Calf Standing, and what Walks Long saw was an apparition, a specter of what Calf had been in life. Walks also saw that his friend had slowly changed since his death. His flesh had dried and his features were sunken in, his skin lay tight against his bones. His lips had pulled back from his teeth giving him a permanent grin, and his eyes were dark holes, void of any light.

"This is true," Calf said, *"It only bothers me when I am hungry."*

"Soon Cold Maker will come from the north, and I will not be able to feed you."

"I am made to believe that you hunger for the taste of the Whiteman's heart as much as I do, perhaps more," said Walks.

"I do not like the taste of their flesh. It reminds me of bear meat, but not as sweet."

"Bear meat is not fit to eat," reprimanded Calf.

"You are not the one who is truly eating it. You say I must eat the flesh and heart of the Whiteman, to satisfy your hunger, to make you strong." He paused and looked around at the other warriors in the camp to see if they were staring at him. Most had become accustomed to Walks' peculiarities and some believed he was holy, while others believed he was possessed of an evil spirit.

"It does not matter," Calf said, *"You must eat again*

180

before we return to where our village will winter."

"It was only by chance that we came across the white men who were hunting Ksisk-staki, the flat tailed one. I do not believe we will see more white men until the grass turns green."

"You must FEED me!" Calf insisted, his anger evident. *"I cannot rest if I hunger!"*

"Why do you not leave me alone?" Walks asked.

"Because you hate the Whiteman as much I do. Because you cannot rest until they are driven from our land."

"And what of the white men at the trading house in the land of White Father George? *Are they not also our enemy?"*

"Yes, they are our enemy also, but they give us guns, powder and lead. We need these to fight our first enemies, especially the whites who come from the south. We are the Real People, and there will come a time when there will be no white men, no Raven People, Sheep Eaters, or Flathead in our lands."

"Walks Long, I would talk with you." The voice of another warrior broke into Walks conversation with the specter. He looked up to see Broken Horn walking towards him.

"We have wasted much time away from our winter village. We were meant to hunt for buffalo and all we have found is a few white men," Broken Horn said, receiving no reaction from Walks. *"The snow has fallen and it will fall again making travel hard. Now we have no meat to take home, only a few scalps, some horses and the traps used by the Whites."*

"You see no good in taking the scalps of our enemies?" Walks questioned.

"There is good is that, but we must bring back meat. Cold Maker will not hold back the snow for much longer. He has waited far too long as is."

"What would you have me do, make the buffalo spring from the soil?"

"No, I would have us return to the village. It is bad enough that we have chosen to winter so far south, we should not have come further into the land of the Raven People."

"Do you fear them?" Walks stood and moved to within an arm's length of Broken Horn. This would have intimidated most men, but Broken Horn was braver than most, and he in turn moved closer to Walks.

"I fear no man. I fear the blindness that comes with hate. It is one thing that can destroy a people. You do not respect our enemies, you only hate them."

"I need not respect them. They are but dogs to be butchered."

Broken Horn, knew that he was wasting his time talking to Walks Long. He spoke as he turned to walk away. *"Fear or not, we have found no buffalo and we will return to the village near the White Father's trading house."*

As Broken Horn walked away the specter spoke to Walks, *"He is a coward."*

"He is not a coward. He does not understand that our people must be protected from the Whiteman. We will return to the village near the English trader's house, and winter there. As I said, when the grass turns green we will come back and hunt the White men again."

The sound of horses running pulled Walks Long to his feet for a better look. Two riders rushed into the temporary camp pulling their horses to a skidding stop.

"There are more white men coming this way, and they are accompanied by Raven People!" one of them said. The Blackfeet sprang to their horses and prepared to ride out and engage their enemies, the Americans and the Crow.

*

With Obadiah Cash as a guide, the campsite of the trappers was easy to find. The scene, though covered

182

by new snow, was still horrific. The remains of those killed had been ravaged by predators and scavengers, and the body of Fred Carpenter, the camp keeper, was still secured to the tree where he died. No survivors were found and there was no hope any would be.

Ben's search was more intent than anyone's. He had found out from Obadiah that Dob was one of the those left behind during the Blackfoot attack. Ben was driven by a mixture of feelings. On one hand, he wouldn't have been disappointed if Dob was killed by the Indians, on the other, this would have cheated him from exacting his own revenge. There was no sign of Dob, and very little of half of the men who had made up the trapping party.

"It appears you were the only one that made it out alive, Obadiah," said Silas.

"It 'pears so," Obadiah said. "I 'spect I was lucky."

The Crow warriors had made their own search of the surrounding area and many were disappointed that the signs left by the departing Blackfoot were old and this seemed to cool their lust for blood. A few of them rode up to the white men.

"Where are the Pikuni so that we may fight them?" exclaimed one of the young Crow. *"We came here to take their scalps and horses."*

"They had word that the children of the Big Beaked Bird were coming and have run away," Silas said, his newly learned Crow serving him well.

"If there are no Pikuni to fight, we will return to the Whiteman's house," another said. *"We do not need to chase smoke in the cold days."*

Silas had no comment for this. He knew that he had been lucky to keep the interest of these young warriors as long as he had. It was plain to see that the Blackfeet had not spent much time at the camp site and they were probably a long way off. With no one for the Crow to fight, there was no need for them to go any farther.

"You may return to the warmth of your lodges," he told the young Crows, *"My friends and I will look a bit more for the Blackfoot."* This said, the majority of the Crow turned and rode away leaving six of their number to that of the trappers and to decide a course of action.

"We have plenty of daylight left. You boys want to see if we can figure where them bastards headed?" Silas asked.

"Hell yes," said Edward Brown, "The boys that died here were my friends and I haven't had a chance to get me a scalp."

"Do you wish to follow the trail of the Blackfoot one more day?" Silas asked the remaining Crow.

"We will go one more sun and then return to the warmth of our lodges," replied one of the Crow.

"We all agree that we go on then?" Silas said not expecting a reply. "We'll go another day and see what we find. First, we try to take care of what we can here and bury these boys."

The frozen crust in the ground offered a feeble resistance and a mass grave was soon dug for the remains of those who had been killed. A collection of rocks were used to pile on the grave forming a large cairn.

Leaving the grave on the Musselshell behind them, the trappers headed northwest following the trail of the Blackfoot party. The weather had cooperated and though cold and overcast, there was no new snow to cover the tracks they followed. Riding on into the following day they made a camp on a small creek which seemed to flow due east toward the Musselshell River. In front of them was a small mountain range about twenty miles long, arching to the northeast and consisting of numerous low peaks broken by stream drainages.

They talked amongst themselves and decided that it was fruitless to follow the Blackfoot further. Camp was made and in the following morning they would turn and head back to Fort Raymond.

"You think it's best we head back, eh?" Obadiah said to Silas.

"No real chance of us catching them. Even if we did, not knowing exactly how many of them there are, I'm not sure we're strong enough to put up a good fight."

Ben sat by the fire, his thoughts a mixture of what had taken place over the past month. For the first time, he had seen men die at the hands of the Indians and he had taken lives himself. Not close up, not close enough to see the faces of those he shot, but he was still troubled by this. He questioned himself about what he would really do when and if he caught up with Dob. He had no doubt that Dob was still alive. There was no body to prove that he died with the other trappers back on the Musselshell, but Dob had a way of surviving. Ben wondered if now he would never know for certain.

With the rising sun, the small party rose and in a sullen mood took their time in preparing to leave. The Whites brewed coffee and roasted some meat, while the Crow sat, talked and smoked their pipes. It was almost mid-morning before they saddled their horses and turned to retrace the trail back to Fort Raymond.

Crossing the creek bottom and approaching the edge of the tree line the party was brought to a halt as a shrill war cry broke the stillness. Turning to look in the direction of the cry, they saw a fast approaching group of Blackfoot warriors, more than three times their number.

"Take cover in the trees!" Silas shouted, and no sooner had they reached the shelter of the pines when both arrows and bullets landed among them. Edward Brow cried out in pain, and fell from his saddle, a bullet wound to his back. Antoine was the first to vault from his horse and go to Brown's aid, dragging him to the cover of the trees. In doing so, he was exposed and a bullet found its way to his shoulder. Wounded, Antoine still managed to reach safety pulling his companion with him. By this time, all the trappers had abandoned their horses, taking cover behind the trees and firing shots in the direction of the Blackfeet.

Two of the Crow had fallen, one dead before he spilled from his horse, the other mortally wounded. Two of the other Crow went to this man's rescue bringing him to safety, while one of the others, enraged let out a war whoop of his own and charged the line of oncoming Blackfeet. He had made it half way to his enemies when he too was cut down. When the Blackfeet reached his body several leaped from their mounts and descending on the Crow, scalping him and mutilating the body. Cries of anger erupted from the remaining Crow as they returned fire with bows and smooth-bore guns.

The Blackfeet were repelled only long enough for them to formulate a plan of attack. They divided up into three groups, one each to flank the sides of the defenders and the third to hit them head on. Overwhelmed by the superior number, the trappers and Crow were soon engaged in hand-to-hand fighting with the Blackfoot. Ben fired his last shot almost point-blank at one Blackfoot, before he dropped his rifle and resorted to his knife and tomahawk. Closing in with another Blackfoot, he struggled to fend off blows from the warrior's stone-headed war club. The circled each other like boxers attempting to get the advantage or exploit a mistake made by their opponent. Ben dodged a poorly aimed swing of the club, and stepped inside the Indian's reach, driving his knife deep under the warrior's ribcage. His opponent seemed startled, his face showing shock and the then he fell at Ben's feet.

Silas was likewise doing battle, and emptying his

pistol he resorted to knife and tomahawk as did the other two trappers. The remaining Crow dove headlong into the Blackfeet each making them pay dearly before all but one forfeited their lives. This single Crow was knocked senseless, and was taken prisoner.

Amid the sounds of the fighting a scream could be heard from Edward Brown who had been found by the Blackfeet and was scalped alive before being placed out of his pain by the blow of several war clubs.

The five whites fought until completely worn out and then were overpowered. All five were roughly ushered together, a rain of blows putting them to the ground. Obadiah lost consciousness, and if not shielded by the others he would more than likely have been beaten to death. The heat of the battle somewhat cooled, the Blackfeet stopped to plunder the dead, and chase after the trappers horses. Tied hand and foot the whites, bloody and beaten, waited to see what their fate would be.

"What do you think they are waiting for?" Estienne asked Silas.

"Probably deciding if they want to kill us all at once or one by one," Silas answered. He looked over at Ben and was not surprised to see an absence of fear in the young man's eyes. He'll do alright when he faces the end, Silas thought.

"Show 'em you got grit," he said to Ben. "When your time comes, try not to scream, don't give them that pleasure."

Ben looked at Silas and shook his head in assent, though he was trying hard to repress a scream at that moment. Outwardly he seemed stoic, but inside his stomach churned with fear. He hoped that Silas would go before him so that the man he had come to respect wouldn't see he didn't have the sand to stand up to torture. He had never felt the kind of fear that was welling up inside of him at that moment. He started to shake and just as he thought he couldn't stand the waiting any longer, one of the Blackfoot warriors strode over to the captives and stopped directly in front of him. He squatted on his heels and stared into Ben's face. His face was painted black with a stripe of yellow across his eyes, and tilting his head to one side he looked Ben over. Taking hold of a lock of Ben's hair he ran it between his fingers, as if test its texture, curious but not surprised by the blonde locks. He began to talk, at first Ben thought to him, but then the Blackfoot turned as if speaking to someone next to him, but there was no one else close by. The warrior carried on what seemed to be a conversation, almost an argument with this non-existent person.

Ben was sure that the man in front of him was crazy, or at least feeble-minded. It was while the Blackfoot was examining him that something happened to Ben. Ben's nerves calmed down, and his fear seemed to melt away. It was the realization that these Blackfeet were not superhuman savages, but men, no more. This should have increased Ben's fear, because he knew normal men were capable of unspeakable acts. But because these Blackfeet were men, there was a chance Ben and his friends could survive.

Once the Blackfeet had finished gathering what plunder there was, and had taken care of their own wounded, they built travois and loaded up their injured as well as their dead. They prepared to leave, and pulling the lone surviving Crow and the whites to their feet, tied them in a line neck-to-neck, with a rope and led them off as they rode away.

The Blackfoot set a pace just faster than a walk and the prisoners had some difficulty in keeping up. If one fell, he would drag down one and then another of the men he was tied to. They all would be drug along the ground for some distance before the Blackfoot who held them in his charge would stop his horse and allow them to regain their feet. This was usually accompanied with a sharp tug of the rope or blows from the rider's quart as a reprimand.

The party moved off in a westerly direction, skirting the low mountain range and pulling their captives behind them. When the Blackfeet stopped to make camp at dusk, Ben and his companions were totally exhausted. Antoine suffered the most. When the captives were allowed to rest they merely fell to the ground. It was the first time that Antoine could receive any care from his friends.

Silas pulled the Frenchman's coat and shirt up to inspect the wound. He first noticed that Antoine was running a fever, and though the bullet hole wasn't bleeding badly, the area around it was swollen and red. All this was a sign that the wound had become infected, and without some medical treatment, Antoine would soon be dead.

The Blackfeet settled down, cared for the horses and then prepared themselves a meal. When this was done, one of them came to check on the prisoners, almost as an afterthought. Silas attempted to communicate with this man motioning toward Antoine. The Indian looked at the Frenchman and seemed not to understand or care. Silas switched from English to French.

"Our friend needs help. He is badly injured. We must clean his wound." This, the Blackfoot seemed to understand, and he replied in poor French.

"It no matter. He die now. He die later." He walked back to his friends and paid no further attention to the whites.

"What will we do?" Estienne asked Silas.

"It would help if we could get that bullet out and clean the wound. But I don't want to go poking around in there with my fingers."

"We have to do something," Estienne said, "Or he will die."

"Probably be best to go that way. You seen what they did to Fred Carpenter," Obadiah said.

"I think they have something else in mind for us," Silas said.

"Oui, they lost many warriors by our hands. If they are like the other Indians I have known, they will give us to their women and let those harpies have their vengeance on us," Estienne said.

"No matter. For now, we have to do something about Antoine." Silas looked about, but with no knowledge of the local plants he was at a loss as what on hand could be used. He turned to the single Crow prisoner, and in Crow asked, *"Do you know of a plant here that could stop the blood from turning bad?"*

The Crow reached for a small leather pouch that hung around his neck, pulled it free and without a word handed it to Silas. Silas struggled with his bound hands to pull open the pouch, and in the twilight tried to look inside. The bag was filled with some kind of dried herb, the smell was familiar but Silas couldn't identify the plant. He looked at the Crow as if asking what to do with the contents.

"Mix with water and make a poultice," the Crow said. Silas understood water, but didn't understand the word poultice in Crow. The Crow could see Silas did not comprehend and attempted French words, *"Put water, make paste."*

"He is saying to make a *cataplasme*," Estienne said, "A poultice."

"Ahh," said Silas. "Give me your open palm Estienne." The Frenchman held out his open hand and Silas poured the powdered herb into it. Now, Silas thought, I need water. With little hesitation, he scooped up a handful of snow and placed it on the powder. Estienne cupped his hands together and with what little heat he had in them, warmed the snow and ground the mixture into a moist ball. When he was done, he handed it to Silas who placed it into Antoine's open wound. Strips of cloth were torn from his shirt and the injury was bound tightly.

"Now, we'll just have to wait and see," said Silas. He then turned to the Crow and with his bound hands attempted to say thank you in sign language.

The Crow nodded his head and said, *"Though you are a* baashchiili, *you are respected by the People, Red Hair."* He used the Crow term to describe the whites, "Yellow Person." Then he added, *"I have hope that your friend lives."*

"I also have hope," said Silas. *"What are you called among your people?"*

"I am Alaxchia-ahush, *Plenty Coups."*

"That is a strong name. Plenty Coups, do you know where the Blackfeet might be taking us?"

"I do not. We are on the Buluhpa'ashe, *the Plum River. The Yellow River is far behind us. We will reach the Big Muddy River soon."*

The Missouri, thought Silas, and he wondered how far they would travel before the Blackfeet would stop. He looked at Antoine and said a silent prayer for his friend, knowing that if he was made to travel too far he wouldn't live long.

*

Dawson Thomas was tired and cold. He had ridden south from Fort Maskwa to find the group of Blackfoot hunters in hopes that he could persuade them to return to their winter village located on the Missouri River near the fort. The factor of the fort, John Ranald, was adamant that the Blackfeet come back as he didn't want them running uncontrolled through the Missouri River Territory.

Having been completed the previous fall, the new post was just over a year old. Word had reached the North West Company in Montreal of the American Manual Lisa's intent to establish a trading post somewhere on the Yellowstone River and this would be very close to the area where Fort Maskwa was now located on the north side of the Missouri River at the mouth of the Judith.

The broad river bottom at the fort's location was almost five miles long and three wide, making it a perfect place for grazing stock in the summer; and the availability of wood from the river supplied materials for the construction of the fort. William Clark named the Judith for his bride-to-be Julia "Judith" Hancock, but the Cree and Blackfoot called it the Plum River, and this was the name used by the North West employees.

Thomas had been employed by the NWC for the better part of ten years, immigrating to Canada after leaving the British Army. Few opportunities existed for an ex-soldier in England, and the lure of obtaining financial stability drew him to the fur trade. He had fallen victim to the British attitude of class and title during his service for King and Country. He had not felt comfortable working for the Hudson Bay Company, due to their British sense of hierarchy coupled with nepotism and outright animosity toward the Americans. With the NWC, he felt he could advance on his merit. He found the NWC was more to his liking. As for the Americans, it was not that he was fond of them, they were the competition, not mortal enemies.

There was also the fact that the North West Company was outdoing Hudson Bay and could possibly be the future of Canada. Under William McGillivray, the Company continued to expand, and to profit. In in just one year, 1800, the Hudson Bay Company profited £38,000 in trade compared to the North West Company's £144,000. The North West Company also had a foot on both sides of the border. It maintained a branch in New York City allowing cargo ships owned by the NWC to sail under the American flag. This allowed the Canadians to get around the British East India Company's monopoly and ship furs to the Chinese market.

Thomas figured that within a few years he may be factor of his own post. Far away from Montreal, he would live like a gentleman, unfettered by the snobbery and prejudice of people like those that looked down on anyone who was not born with a title or money. Most of all, he would be able to get out from underneath John Ranald. Ranald lived like a feudal lord, with the Métis and the Indians as his subjects. It was impossible for Dawson to shine with his own accomplishments as Ranald took credit for any achievements, and passed on the blame for any failures. Dawson didn't hate him, but had no respect for the man, finding him a bully and a coward.

Thomas and his men traveled south, skirting the Judith River, suffering from the cold and the recent snow storm. While camped his second night out, an American had stumbled in, cold, wet and hungry. Dawson took an instant disliking to the young man. It was the look about him, and his face carried a large red mark down the left side. It was also that this dark-haired man with pale eyes seemed to have no sorrow over the loss of his companions, most likely killed by the very Blackfeet Dawson was looking for.

The young man said his name was Robert Bergmann, but he would answer to Bob, Rob or whatever was easy. He was also quick to renounce his fidelity to the "Dammed Spaniard," as he called Manual Lisa. He claimed that Lisa worked him beyond what he had signed on to do and felt that made his contract void. It took little for him to swear allegiance to the North West Company. Dawson knew that the first chance Bergmann had he would not only shirk his duties, but most likely desert.

Dawson also wondered how Bergmann had survived the attack by the Blackfeet. His account of the battle painted him as putting up a valiant fight, attempting to defend his fellow trappers and barely making it out alive. If it had been the same Blackfeet that Dawson was looking for, it seemed very unlikely the young man would have escaped unscathed. It was more likely he had turned tail and ran, saving himself.

For the most part, Dawson was disgusted with Bergmann. If he hadn't been a Whiteman, Dawson would have left him in the wilderness to die. As it was, he fed the young man and gave him a horse, gun powder and lead.

One of the NWC men who had been sent to scout ahead returned to the advancing column carrying news that he had spotted the Blackfeet approaching from the south. Dawson called a halt and they made a temporary camp to await their arrival, and he would enjoy a cup of hot tea while he waited. A fire was built for this express purpose.

As the Blackfeet approached, a few of them dashed forward making a display of bravado with a sham charge, halting their ponies with a skidding stop mere feet from the NWC party. They whirled around shouting their war cries and brandishing the scalps they had recently collected. As the NWC men had witnessed this before, they were only mildly impressed, but Dawson noted the Bergmann edged away from the commotion and made his way to where the horses were picketed.

Dawson stood and waited for the main party of Blackfeet to arrive. As they approached, he held up his hand in greeting, palm outward. He paused only long enough for the leaders of the hunting party to dismount and follow him to the fire.

The two leaders of the group were both known to Dawson, one was called Broken Horn, a fairly level-headed man with a keen sense of how things worked between the Whites and the Blackfeet. The other Blackfoot was Walks Long, and Dawson had kept contact with him to a minimum. Everyone agreed that this man was insane. He acted with little emotion, killing on a whim with sadistic brutality. This set him apart from his fellows in only one way, the lack of emotion. He also had a tendency of talking as if carrying on a conversation when no one was near him, sometimes even arguing with himself.

"It is good to see my Pikuni brothers," Dawson spoke in Blackfoot as well as using hand signs. *"Have you had good luck in hunting the buffalo?"*

"We have had poor luck," said Broken Horn. *"We have been as far as the Yellow River and found no buffalo, only the* Napikowann, *the Long Knives, from the south."* He pointed over his shoulder and Dawson's attention was drawn to the now visible white captives. He moved over to them and looked them over. He noted they all had been beaten, and that one was in fairly bad shape.

"Are you Americans?" Dawson asked.

"Yes, we are," answered Silas. "My name is Silas Scott, this is Benjamin Voss, Estienne Lapin, Obadiah Cash and that's Antoine Martin, he needs some attention, has a bullet in him."

"Do you work for Manual Lisa?" Dawson asked.

"That we do," replied Silas. "You gon'na help us out of this mess, or are you a son-of-a-bitch tit-sucker to these bastards?"

Dawson smiled. "You're pretty free with your talk aren't you?"

"No need acting like a lickspittle, might as well be up front with you and have you know where I stand. Just as soon get it over with if you're gon'na let these bastards kill us."

"I don't think it will come to that," Dawson paused. "My name is Dawson Thomas. I'm employed by the North West Company at a trading post north of here on the Missouri River. If I can, I'll get you free and we'll tend to your friend. You just sit tight." He went back to Broken Horn and invited him and the other Blackfeet to sit, smoke and eat. When they were finished with the formalities dictated by Indian etiquette, Dawson was free to discuss the prisoners.

"*What will you do with the Long Knives you have taken captive?*" he asked, again speaking in Blackfoot and hand signs.

"*It has not been decided,*" said Broken Horn, "*I would have killed them rather than drag them all the way back to the village as some in the party wish.*"

"*What will Broken Horn do with these men at his village?*"

"*They will be given to the women who grieve at the loss of their husbands and sons.*"

"*I do not think the White Grandfather would approve of this,*" said Dawson.

"*The Grandfather has given us guns to fight these whites from the south, has he not?*"

"*Yes. What harm can these men do to the Blackfeet?*" He didn't wait for an answer, "*Look at them. They are weak and will die before you reach the village.*" He paused and went on, "*I would offer you, and your warriors, gifts from the trade house for these white men, and their property.*"

"*I would keep their rifles, they are better than what my men have.*"

"*The rifles of these men take much powder, you are better off with the guns we have given you, but you may keep one for yourself as a gift from me.*" Dawson hoped that Broken Horn would accept the offer of goods and one of white men's rifles.

"*I do not think the grief of the women will be healed by a few blankets and beads,*" Broken Horn said. Now Dawson knew that he had convinced the Blackfoot to do a trade, the only thing now was to negotiate a price.

"*You may keep the Crow for your women. I am sure that will cool their blood.*"

It was decided that each of the whites would be released to Dawson for payment of goods from Fort

Maskwa. Broken Horn would get his choice of one of the white men's rifles and he choose the heavily brass ornamented Trade Gun that belonged to Antoine Martin.

Dawson went to the captives and informed them that he had paid their ransom. He also let them know that they would accompany him and his men back to Fort Maskwa, where he would help them recuperate. They would be indebted to the NWC for the expenses incurred and had a choice to either sign on as engagees with the NWC, or sign an agreement that the debt would be paid by Manuel Lisa. That decision could be left until they reached the fort.

"What of the Crow?" Silas asked, "Will you pay for him also?"

"I'm sorry. He wasn't part of the deal. There is no way these Blackfeet will let that Crow live."

Silas went to Many Coups and offered his hand, as a parting gesture. No one noticed that Silas had taken a small leather bag from around his own neck and slipped it into the Crows hand. It contained Silas' flint and fire steel, one side of the striker had a sharp edge. This small knife by itself was no weapon, but could be used to help a lone man escape and possibly survive.

It was the next morning before the entire group moved north toward Fort Maskwa. The only man left on foot was Many Coups, and as before he was led off with a rope around his neck.

Ben felt sorry for him and wished there was some way to save this man who had helped Antoine, but there was nothing in his power that he could do, he hadn't even been given back his rifle. Dawson explained it would be best to wait until they reached the fort, and there was no need for the rifles to be returned as they were in friendly country.

Ben let the motion of the horse under him lull him into a peaceful rest as the group moved along. He was oblivious to the pair of pale eyes that watched him from behind. Dob had not been this close to Ben for almost half a year, and now he felt trapped.

CHAPTER 12
FORT MASKWA

Led by North West Company engagees, Ben and his companions traveled further north, away from the Musselshell River, and deeper into Blackfoot country. Each day they moved, the weather became colder. Storms would seem to gather on both sides of them and then close in behind, as if shutting off any idea of retreat back to Fort Raymond and any friendly Crow villages in the south.

Ben swayed back and forth in the saddle, rocking to the motion of the horse beneath him. His fatigue, and the beatings he had received at the hands of the Blackfeet, made him drowsy and nod off as he rode. His head would slowly drop to his chest and then he would wake with a start, coming to half-consciousness and the reality of his situation. Little had been said between Ben and his companions since their "rescue" by Dawson Thomas, but all four men pondered their fate.

Estienne, ever easy to make friends, had engaged the NWC men in conversation, especially the few Frenchmen and the Métis engagees who seemed to return Lapin's kind and carefree manor. In this way, Estienne was able to gather information about their destination and an idea as to the character of Dawson Thomas and the factor of Fort Maskwa, John Ranald. It seemed that Dawson was a fair man, but could be a formidable foe if crossed. John Ranald was a Scotsman and by all descriptions a hard man, single-minded and brutish, wielding his power like a highland lord over his fiefdom. He was uncompromising, and certainly dangerous.

In their own quiet way, Silas and Obadiah were also busy collecting information. Silas was sizing up the type of men who worked for the NWC. They were a mixture of Métis, French and Canadians, not much different from those employed by Señor Manual Lisa, save for the Métis. Silas had met a few Métis, who were a mixture of European and Indian blood, and unlike any other mixed breeds they had become a true race of people with the distinction of this name and a language of their own.

The early European trappers and explorers were the fathers of these people, and the mothers of the Métis were usually from one of the several Indian tribes of Canada or of mixed descent from these peoples. There was an important distinction between French Métis born of Frankish voyageur fathers, and the Anglo-Métis descended from English or Scottish fathers. These marriages are commonly referred to as 'marriage à la façon du pays', or marriage according to the custom of the country.

The Métis were respected as valuable employees of the fur trade companies due to their skills as voyageurs, buffalo hunters, interpreters and their knowledge of the lands.

Obadiah also sized up these men as well as the mood of the Blackfeet who they traveled with. He didn't trust any of them and was weary of any pretenses or false sense of security. There was one man in particular among the NWC engagees who caught Obadiah's eye. He seemed to keep his distance from the Lisa men and pulled his coat collar up and the sides of his wolf-ears cap down to keep his face covered as much as possible. This in itself wasn't noteworthy due to the cold, but every time Obadiah looked in the man's direction he would turn away or try to hide more of his face.

Obadiah searched the appearance of this man to see if there was a clue to his peculiar behavior when he spotted the man's firearm. It was a Wheeler rifle, just like the one carried by Dob Bergmann. Then Obadiah saw the cold blue eyes of Dob peering out from under the brimless cap.

Obadiah gave his horse a slight kick to speed it up and pulled in next to Silas and Ben, his eyes shining with the news he had for his friends.

"Look over yonder at the chechaquo back there in the wool wolf-ears cap." He pointed over his shoulder with a thumb. "I'll be a jackass if that ain't Dob Bergmann!"

Both Ben and Silas turned in their saddles in time to see the man pull back his horse and move out of sight behind other riders. Like Obadiah, Ben wasn't sure it was Dod, until he saw the cold blue eyes looking back at him.

Ben started to yank on his horse's reins and turn toward Dob when Silas took hold of the mount's halter stopping him.

"Hold on son," he cautioned. "Don't get in a rush and rile up these North West boys. For the time being, hold back. He knows he's caught. Let him stew in his own fear. We can deal with him later."

*

Traveling as fast as possible, the party made it to the Missouri River within two days. The broad plain sheltered from the wind and deep snow by the surrounding hills was inviting. Though his fate was still unsure, Ben felt relieved at the site of the stockade walls belonging to Fort Maskwa, the North West Company flag flying in the breeze above one of the bastions.

The fort was twice the size of Fort Raymond, but built similar with two watch towers, bastions, at opposite corners. From the height of the trail approaching the fort, Ben could see there were buildings along three sides of the interior, some two stories high, and a corral took up the remaining space on the fourth side. The main gate opened to the south toward the Missouri River with the mouth of the Judith just upstream. Close by, on both sides of the Missouri and the Judith, were numerous teepees that Ben assumed belonged to the Blackfeet.

The Blackfeet broke off from the main party going to their camp and the sound of Indian women trilling with their tongues soon filled the air. It was a sound that could turn a Whiteman's blood to ice water, but was a joy to the ears of the returning warriors.

Silas looked back to get one last glimpse of Many Coups as he was dragged into the circle of lodges and disappeared amid the throng of milling Indians. There were more war whops as well as cries of anger and hatred for the lone Crow now surrounded by his enemies.

The remainder of the riders crossed the Missouri and rode directly to the fort. A shot was fired from a swivel gun mounted in the front bastion sounding their arrival and the gate swung open, allowing the party to enter. They stopped in an open area between the buildings, and then turned their mounts towards the coral.

Once everyone was dismounted and the horses were tended to, Dawson Thomas led Ben, Silas, Antoine and Estienne toward the largest of the buildings inside the compound, instructing them to wait for him outside. He then entered what he called the "Big House" leaving them standing in the cold.

As they waited, they observed the normal routine of any fur trade establishment; work being done at the smith's forge, furs being bundled and processed in to bales at the fur press set dead center in the large open space, and the wheels of a Red River cart being greased.

It was from one of the side buildings that a woman emerged into the outside light. She was obviously an Indian woman, but unlike any Ben had seen before. In fact, she was unlike any women he had ever met. He watched her as she walked past the men working at the fur press. Ben was transfixed, both mentally and physically by her very presence. As she walked, she was also noted by everyone else, most chancing only a quick glance as if fearing her gaze.

She was dressed much like the other women at the fort, wearing a long woolen-flannel dress that reached just above her ankles, exposing intricately decorated, high-topped moccasins. Around her shoulders was a white point blanket with green, red, yellow and indigo stripes at the ends. From the top of the blanket folds, her hair with the sheen of a raven's wing, shone blue-black, framing her face. Her features were thin, and strong, her nose softly aquiline, and her high cheek bones touched with a natural flush that shined through her olive completion.

She walked with a grace that could only be compared to the movements of a cat; smooth, effortless, and without hesitation. She looked neither right nor left, her gaze straight ahead, pointed in the direction of the "Big House." She approached the door, opened it and entered disappearing into its darkness. Ben stood staring at the spot where she had vanished, something compelling him to follow her, and he took one uneasy step.

"Be careful with those eyes of yours boy," Silas warned. "A woman like that, special as she looks, belongs to someone, someone with either power or money."

"Oui," echoed Estienne, "That one, she is not your typical squaw."

One of the North West Company engagees overhearing their conversation offered his own comment in French, *"Yes, it is better that you do not look at that one she is like the catamount, the cougar. Her name is Kat-reen, but she is called Kat by everyone except the bourgeois."* He pronounced the word "booshway."

"Catamount," thought Ben, then he shook off the feeling that had overpowered him, but the spell had been cast and he longed to get another glimpse of her.

The door of the Big House opened again and Ben hoped the woman was coming back out into the light, but his expectations were dashed by the appearance of a large man, well over six feet tall, followed by Dawson Thomas.

They both stopped on the front step of the building and in the light Ben had a better look at the man. He was without a frockcoat, wearing a red waistcoat over a white shirt, and a watch chain dangling from a button hole in the vest went to one of the front pockets. On his feet were knee-high boots which he wore over a pair of plaid wool pants. Not only was he tall, but built stout, somewhat reminding Ben of his own father in stature. His curly hair was steel-gray and long, falling down past his shoulders. A beard of the same color, with a hint of rust-red, covered his cheeks and chin making it hard to distinguish were the beard stopped and the hair on his head began. Above the beard were cheeks flushed red, and below his bushy eyebrows were eyes of gunmetal-blue, cold and hard-looking.

He stood, feet apart, with his ham-like hands on his hips as if he were sizing up the quality of a horse or a beef.

He turned, and in a thick Scottish brogue spoke to Thomas over his shoulder, "Mr. Thomas, I thought ye said there was five of 'em?"

Thomas looked past his employer and stepped down from the stoop, moving off toward the corral in search of the lost American. He returned quickly with Dob Bergmann in tow, pushing him toward the others. Ben's eyes locked on to Dob's and Dob instantly dropped his gaze to stare at the ground.

"Now then, I'm John Ranald, factor of this here

trading post. I understand that my man, Mr. Dawson Thomas, rescued ye from an eminent fate of death by the hands of my good friends the Blackfeet?" He paused, not expecting an answer. "It appears that ye will be my guests until we figure out what to do with ye. Come in and put something warm in yer bellies."

"Excuse me, Mr. Ranald," Silas said, "one of our men has a severe wound, and needs attention." He pointed to Antoine Martin who was standing with the support of Lapin.

Ranald looked at Antoine, again as if studying livestock. He then spoke to Thomas. "Have him taken to the employee's quarters and send for Mr. Owen to treat him." He turned back to Silas and explained, "Mr. Owen is our resident surgeon, though not a true doctor, he knows a bit about medicine, and does well enough at stitching up a wound."

Thomas passed the orders to two NWC men who took Antoine to where he would receive the medical attention promised. Ranald turned back to the door behind him followed by Ben, Silas, Estienne, Obadiah and Dob. Thomas was last through the door and closed it behind them.

They entered into a large room, with a long table, set with chairs. Above the table hung a crude chandelier, holding a dozen candles, a sign of opulence. These illuminated the table top that was already set with pewter plates, table knives and three pronged forks. To the side were two smaller tables bare of any table settings, each with rough-hewn wooden benches.

"Have a seat at first table," Ranald said, motioning with a hand toward the big table. Each of the men took a chair with Ranald seating himself at the end of the table. Ben again saw a similarity between Ranald and his father. He thought of how this man sat at the head of the table, like Benjamin Voss, displaying the same superior and condescending manner. Ben took an instant disliking to the man.

"Rochelle," Ranald barked the name, this single word conveying an entire message understood by someone unseen. A door to the side of the room opened, and backlit by the light form an adjoining kitchen, a woman emerged and moved toward the table. At first Ben thought it might be the woman he had seen outside, but as this figure came closer to the illumination of the chandelier, he saw it was not her. This woman was older and harder looking. She stopped at Ranald's left hand side awaiting his bidding.

"Bring tea, and the hot soup with bread," he ordered. He then spoke to his guests. "We eat simple here, meat isn't for every meal ye know. But I as ye are guests, I'll treat ye with fresh white bread!" Ranald waited for a brief moment then continued. "Ye know who I am, now it's yer turn. Who are ye, and what is yer business?"

Silas spoke first, well knowing that Thomas had probably told Ranald he and his companions were employees of Manual Lisa.

"My name is Silas Scott, this is Benjamin Voss, Estienne Lapin, and Obadiah Cash. We are engagees of Señor Manuel Lisa." Silas thought it best to offer as little information as needed.

"And, who might ye be?" Ranald asked Dob.

"I'm Robert Bergmann," he spoke barely loud enough for all to hear. The others at the table waited for him to add more but he fell silent.

"And Mr. Robert Bergmann, who do ye work for"

"I was workin' for Lisa, but my friends got killed." He looked up sheepishly at Obadiah.

"I see," said Ranald. "So, these here aren't your friends?" Ranald smiled.

"He's a coward and a thief," blurted out Ben, surprising everyone at the table. Silas placed a hand on Ben's forearm as a reminder to hold back his temper.

"A coward and a thief, are ye now?" Ranald asked. "What do ye say to that?"

"I...I...I ain't no coward!" Dob said, his anger overtaking his better judgment.

"He's a liar too!" Ben added, and he stood shaking off Silas' hand.

"We'll not have blood at my table," Ranald warned, his eyes turning a colder blue. "Now sit down, Mr. Voss." Ben regained his seat, but his gaze never left Dob.

"This matter between the two of ye can be settled later."

Rochelle came back to the table carrying a large kettle filled with hot tea and a large loaf of bread with a golden-brown crust. Behind her, two other Indian women appeared one with bowls and spoons and the last carried a ceramic bowl filled with hot soup. This was served starting with Ranald and then moving around the table to the others. The men ate, dipping their spoons into the hot broth, except for Ranald who took up his bowl and drank his soup directly from it, the slight overflow dripping out the sides into his beard. This he wiped away with the back of his hand.

"Now, let us get better acquainted," Ranald said. "You say yer name is Scott, but I don' hear much a trace of that clan in yer voice."

"I left Scotland at a young age," Silas said.

"Oh, do ye know much of clan history?"

"I do. It was something taught to me at early in life."

"Then ye know of Clan Ranald of Lochaber, a branch of Clan MacDonald of Keppoch." He thought this fact would make some form of impression on Silas. Seeing it mattered little, he continued. "Ye should remember that our two clans have a shared history. Was it not a Captain John Scott, who commanded the British 1st Foot at Highbridge in

Lochaber on the River Spean in the year seventeen and forty-five? As I recall, the Jacobites defeated his forces and took him prisoner. He was wounded and then aided by members of Clan MacDonald of Keppoch who arranged for his wounds to be dressed at Cameron of Lochiel's Achnacarry Castle. It that na right?"

"Yes, I believe so," answered Silas.

"Aye, and to pay back this kindness, another Captain Scott of Guise's 6th Regiment, Caroline Frederick Scott by name, took Mac Donald prisoners at Fort William, hanged them in salmon nets and drowned them in a mill flume at Lochoy."

"I believe that too is true," Silas admitted. "It is a good thing that was long ago, and we are far away from Scotland with no animosity between us."

"Aye, right," said Ranald, meaning he didn't quite believe this. He changed the subject, "Now the way I see it, I will give ye my hospitality, a warm place to sleep and hot food, but I can only be sociable to a point, The North West Company is not a charity.

"Mr. Thomas, as my representative, has ransomed you from the Blackfoot. This has been at a cost. I'm a business man and this post must run on a profit. I will offer ye all employment to pay back what I am owed. Once this debt is taken care of, you can stay on or go as ye wish."

"Your offer is generous, but we are already committed to Señor Lisa. We cannot, will not, break our contract with him."

"Do ye all feel that way?" He looked at Dob, who shook his head no. He called out to Rochelle once more and said, "Clear the table and have my journal brought to me." The table was cleared, and then the woman who Ben had seen in the court yard entered the room.

She carried a small portable writing desk, and set it on the table in front of Ranald, and stayed, standing beside him. She had shed the point blanket and now

Ben could see the beautiful figure that had been hidden beneath the bulky wool. She was leaner than he had thought, but built strong. Ben looked at her from head to toe and then back. She was long-legged, her hips voluptuous, and accented by a narrow waist cinched with a wide leather belt worn over a red wool sash. The swell of her firm, high breasts rose and fell with her breathing, and several strings of glass trade beads round her neck reflected the candle light as they moved.

Finally, his eyes went back to her face and she was looking directly at him, her eyes reflecting her distaste of his gaze. He was instantly embarrassed and ashamed of himself. His reaction was noted by Ranald. He followed Ben's gaze back to the woman and saw she was looking directly at Ben. What Ranald witnessed displeased him and his face grew redder. He spoke in evident anger.

"Katherine," pronouncing her name KAT-rreen, "Away with you." She turned and left not daring to look back.

Ranald brought his own attention back to Ben and the rest of the men at the table. Opening the portable writing desk, he withdrew his ledger, pen and ink. He set these in front of him and thumbing to the first blank page began to write, making notations in neat columns. As he wrote, he spoke without lifting his eyes from the account book.

"I think it would be best if ye were to leave first thing tomorrow." He paused, looked up at Ben and Silas, and then placed his attention back to the book. "I will have ye sign a voucher for horses, firearms, powder and the like to be charged against Señor Lisa. I'm sure his bank will make good on this?"

"We have our own blankets, rifles and such, you'll not need to charge us there," Silas interjected.

"Aye, that is true, but the Company rescued these at a cost from the Blackfeet, and I understand ye will need powder and lead."

"What of Antoine Martin," Silas continued, "He'll not be in shape to travel for some time."

"That's true. But, it might be best if he recoop at his own post and be the burden of Señor Lisa. As I said, you should leave first light. No telling how fast the weather can change in these parts this time of year."

"I'd like to stay," Dob blurted out. "I don't think my life is worth a damn if I go with them."

"We can allow that, but if ye turn out to be what these fellows say ye are, I'll turn ye out for the wolves." Ranald saw that there was a problem between Dob and Ben, and felt allowing Dob to stay would be a way of causing Ben hurt. It was a way of punishing Ben for looking at Kat. He also intended to remind her that she needed to keep her eyes to herself.

Ranald finished making the entries in the ledger and then turned his attention to a blank sheet of paper in front of him. He drew up an agreement noting the items they had just discussed and turned the paper over to Silas.

"Read this and sign it, all of ye that is, if you agree to the terms," he said.

Each of the men looked over the paper and signed their names, except for Estienne who made his mark, a small stylized rabbit.

"Mr. Thomas will show you where you can bed down. Ye can have coffee and bread in the morning before you leave."

Dawson Thomas led them to the living quarters of the engagees of Fort Maskwa. There they also found their firearms and personal possessions that had been taken from them by the Blackfeet. Antoine Martin lay on his bedding near the large fireplace. The fort's surgeon had tended to him and he was resting peacefully. His haversack, shooting bag and belt with its knife hung on a wall peg above his head. His gun was missing, having gone to the Blackfoot Broken Horn as part of the ransom paid by NWC.

Lapin went over to him to check on his condition and found that his friend was sleeping soundly and that his fever had disappeared. This was some consolation to their predicament for at least Antoine was safe.

Once Silas had found and donned his belt, knife and pistol, he felt a bit more secure. Ben found his own rifle, knife and tomahawk, satisfied that they were now back in his possession.

Silas spoke to Ben, "Come take a walk with me." He turned and went out the door, followed by Ben. They made their way across the compound and ascended a flight of stairs taking them to the roof of the building and offering them a view out across the river bottom toward the Blackfoot village. They stood behind the chest high pickets and Silas pointed to the lodges, glowing in the diming light of the dusk.

"You hear that?" he asked. "That there is the sound of them bastards celebrating the killing of our men and the Crow we led up the Musselshell. Those she-devils know how to torture a man and make him live a long time while they do it. They'll be tearing the flesh off Many Coups one small piece at a time."

"I wish we could help him," Ben said.

"Me too," Silas shook his head. "I gave him my striker with the sharp edge on it. It was not much, but it may help somehow."

"I hope so, he tried to help Antoine."

The sounds of voices and drumming from the Indian camp stopped suddenly, creating an eerie silence across the entire river bottom. Then a shout of alarm followed by more voices echoed from the village. A large group of people both mounted and on foot exited in the direction of the hills to the south. In the semi-darkness Ben and Silas could make out a lone figure far out in front of the growing mob that had left the village. They soon over took this single person, surrounding him and after a brief struggle, brought him to the ground. Another cry from the midst of the group was a mixture of rage and disappointment. Silas let a wry smile cross his face.

"My bet is that was Many Coups down there. I'd say he made a run for it and died fighting, cheating them bastards out of a chance to torture him."

"You think it made much difference to him?" Ben asked.

"I'd like to think so," Silas said.

"We gon'na get out of this, Silas?"

"Hell son, we got a long way to go, and there's no tellin' when we'll reach the final destination. When it's your time to go, not much can change it. Doesn't mean you have to go belly up. No matter what anyone says, we do have a choice in our own destiny."

"I don't know about leaving here, I..." Ben wasn't sure how to express what he felt.

"You talking about the little shit Bergmann?"

"Yep, seems like I finally caught up with him and I'm turning around and letting him go."

"I wouldn't say that page is written, Son. We'll see him again, and we ain't gone yet."
*

Before dawn, Silas was kicking Ben, Estienne and Obadiah awake. "Time to get out of them blankets. There's hot coffee waiting for us over at the dining room."

"What about Antoine?" asked Estienne.

"Let him sleep until we're ready to leave, he'll not get much rest once we leave."

Entering the dining room, they found no table settings at first–table like the night before. Rochelle was there and instructed them to seat themselves at one of the smaller tables. She brought them hot coffee, fresh flat bread and slices of cold venison. As they were eating, John Ranald descended a flight of stairs from his quarters on the floor above.

"Good day to ye," he said in an overly cheerful manner. "I pray ye slept well under my roof with a warm fire."

"That we did," Silas said.

"Good. Good. We wouldn't want ye ta be leaving thinking that the North West Company ill-treated good folk, even those of a competitor." He moved over to the head table and took his seat there. Rochelle was close behind setting a cup on the table and pouring hot tea from a kettle for him.

"I'll eat now," he told her, and she disappeared into the kitchen.

It was not long before the door to the kitchen reopened and Kat emerged carrying a plate of steaming food. She ignored Ben and his companions and walked directly to Ranald, placing the food on the table in front of him. Ben couldn't help but watch her as she moved across the floor. The graceful movement she had the day before was gone, replaced by unsteady steps. Each step she took was obviously painful. She started to return to the kitchen when Ranald stopped her.

"Stay," he ordered, and she obeyed returning to stand at his side, her hands clasped in front of her, her gaze downcast.

Ben kept his eyes on her, wondering what might have happened. He looked to Ranald and saw the man was returning his gaze, and smiling. Ranald then reached up and with an opened callused hand lifted Kat's head up a bit, letting the light shine on her face. Her left cheek was bruised, and her lower lip was cut and swollen.

Ben started to rise to his feet and Silas reached out placing a strong hand on his shoulder, forcing him back into his seat. "Sit still," he whispered, "You've caused that gal enough trouble with your wondering eye."

"But I didn't mean no harm," Ben protested, keeping his voice low so that only Silas could hear.

"This is his house. More is at stake here than you know. It may not be right, but we have to leave it be."

Ben couldn't eat another bite, his stomach churned and he felt he had to do something. He felt he had to apologize to the beautiful woman for the injury he had caused her, but he knew Silas was right and anything else he did would only cause more harm.

*

Ranald stood in the bastion and watched the Americans ride away. He wondered if he had not taught the tall blonde a lesson, but he had to be satisfied with the punishment he had dealt out to Kat. She had resisted at first, denying she had been making advances at Ben, but Ranald knew better. Ranald had called her what she was, a slut, and handled her as she deserved. The slight beating and then the forced sex, had put her back in line, back to the obedient and faithful concubine she was.

He turned to Katherine who was standing beside him and spoke, "That is the last we'll see of him. A good thing too, I was in a mood to kill him, and that would have been messy.

*

Ranald's eyes were not the only ones that watched the Americans cross the river and head south. Walks Long stood just outside the circle of lodges, running things through his head and discussing them with his ethereal friend.

"*Why does the Trader Chief tell us to kill the Long Knives from the south, and then let them go free?*" asked Walks Long.

"*I have no understanding of these men,*" said Calf Standing.

"*Is it that he wishes them to die away from his big*

lodge?" said Walks Long.

"I would think it would be good to hunt them, and then we can eat again."

"That is all you care about. Why do you not rest?"

"I cannot rest until all the whites are gone."

"It is decided then. You and I will follow them, and one by one we will kill them."

"Then we will eat?"

"Yes, then we will eat."

*

Starting in the Little Belt Mountains, the Judith River stretches for over a hundred miles flowing through isolated breaks, white cliffs, and deep coulees to reach the Missouri River. Up the Judith was the route Ben and his friends would take south through what was called the Judith Gap, on to the Musselshell River and then to the Yellowstone and Fort Raymond.

They rode for half a day in silence, and had stopped to water the horses. When they mounted back up and started to ride on, Silas saw that Ben was headed back in the direction of Fort Maskwa. He kicked his horse into a trot to catch up with Ben, pulling in beside the young man.

"Where you headed?" he asked Ben.

"Back," is all Ben said.

"For what, ta get that worthless pile of shit Bergmann?" Ben didn't respond, and Silas figured it out. "You're gonin' back because of that gal! Are you crazy? That man will kill you son, and there ain't two ways about it."

"It ain't Dob or her I'm goin' back for. I'm goin' back for myself. I need to finish things, and they're all back there."

"I guess if your goin' back, I have to go with you. Can't let you go alone," Silas insisted.

"No, I can't ask that of you, not you or the others. You need to get Antoine and the others back to Fort Raymond. Send word back to my uncle that I found

Dob and I aim to take care of him. I need to do this on my own." He kicked his heels to the horse's flanks and rode away.

CHAPTER 13
ATONEMENT

The sky had turned from a soft haze to an angry slate-gray as Ben rode along the river. His feelings were a mixture of determination, anger and a small amount of fear. He thought about Silas' question, was he going back for Dob or Katherine? Ben's purpose for the past nine months had been in search of Dob, and now Dob was within his reach. Ben knew that taking Dob back to Pittsburgh was unrealistic, and he would have to find justice in another form, but what, kill Dob? He wasn't sure if he could do that.

And there was Katherine. Did he owe this beautiful woman anything? She most likely didn't even know his name, and he had no reason to have feelings for her. If she feelings for him, they might be anger in blaming him for the abuse Ranald had inflicted on her. But Ben had no way of knowing if this was true. It was of no matter, Ben felt guilty, and obligated to set something right.

Allowing his horse to set the pace back to Fort Maskwa, these thoughts filled his head, and he paid little attention to his surroundings, one of the biggest mistakes a man could make while alone in the mountains. He failed to notice that someone was paralleling his path. From the time since he had turned back to the north, he was followed by Walks Long as a wolf would stalk its prey.

Silas had constantly warned Ben, "Keep your nose to the wind. You don't often get a chance to make the same mistake twice." And now, Ben had slipped into a self-made trap that only fate could save him from. Walks Long moved closer and closer trying to decide if he should use his Trade Gun, or quietly ride up and strike Ben with his stone war club. He chose to move in as close as possible and take Ben with the club.

It was either fate or just a whim of Mother Nature, that saved Ben. The clouds grew darker, snow started falling and the wind picked up. It was not long before visibility was reduced to mere yards, separating Ben and Walks Long with a veil of white. Ben reached round and pulled his white blanket loose from behind his saddle. He wrapped this around himself and covered his head to ward off the wind and snow, and unknowingly added camouflage. In the blinding whiteness he was soon completely out of Walks Long's sight

From his seat behind Walks Long, Calf Standing complained, *"You have lost the Whiteman. How can you feed me if you let him go?"*

"I will find him again," Walks said, thinking of knocking his unwelcomed companion off the horse.

"You never were a very good hunter," quipped Calf, "Your eyes are weak."

"They are good enough to see you," sneered Walks.

"You have no choice. I am a ghost spirit and will be with you forever."

"We will see," said Walks, *"We will see."*

Ben rode on through the storm, allowing the horse its head, and taking them both back toward Fort Maskwa. By the end of the day, He had reached the southern hills overlooking the broad floodplain of the Missouri River, the fort standing dimly in the distance. Ben urged the horse forward.
*

Kat stood in front of the small wall mirror in her cramped quarters. This was the first chance she had to be alone since the previous night when Ranald had beaten her and taken his pleasure with her. She looked at her bruised cheek and the split lip, not surprised by what she saw. Though worse than normal, it was not as severe as some from the past. She had left Ranald in his quarters, passed out in a drunken stupor. By the following day he would act as if nothing had happened, his anger and lust played out.

She poured hot water from a kettle into a tin wash basin sitting below the mirror on a little table. Letting her clothes drop to the floor, she took a wash cloth, soaking it in the hot water and rubbed soap into it. Slowly she started to clean herself, starting with her face. Gingerly, she removed the dried blood from her lips and then ran the cloth over her face and down her neck. She fought the urge to scrub for she had learned that washing might take the smell of Ranald from her flesh, but it would linger in her nose no matter how hard she ran the cloth over her body.

She worked her way down her frame, going over the new bruises on her arms, her side, and finally her legs. Her inner thighs were tender; the bruises there seemed the deepest. Then, she cleaned between her legs. Here her flesh was the most painful. Here Ranald had been the most brutal.

Kat had learned long ago that it did no good to resist him, she had tried the first time and the result left her beaten so badly she could barely move for days. After that, she submitted to avoid severe beatings, but she submitted only her body not her spirit.

Her last obligation to herself was to drink a hot cup of tea made from dogbane and snake root, an herbal mixture her mother had taught her. This would insure that no matter how strong Ranald's seed might be, there would be no child born from the brutality he inflicted on her.

Finished, she donned a fresh chemise and climbed into her bed, the wool blankets soon offering a warm cocoon. As she had done so many times, she thought back to the days before she came to Fort

Maskwa. A time she had spent with her Métis mother and her French father. Her father had died, falling victim to a fever and leaving her and her mother with a debt owed to the North West Company. It was at that time that Ranald had taken over the debt and in his own mind bought the two women. His first advances were at Kat's mother, and she submitted only as a means of protecting her daughter.

As Kat matured into a beautiful young woman, Ranald's eye moved to her. He not only lost interest in her mother, but began to abuse her to the point where a final beating put the woman in her grave. Kat hated the man, but after a while the hatred was numbed by the pain of his treatment of her. She thought now and then of killing him, but she had settled into the life she now led, and for the most part, the beatings were not that severe. This time, he had escalated to not only the beating but by foregoing any pretense at his particular brand of romance. He tore at her clothing, forced her down on to the bed and took her with a violence she had not felt before. She wondered, had the tall blonde American with the blue eyes, caused Ranald to lose his normal composure? Had the way that young man looked at her fired up Ranald's insecurities? If so, Ranald would be more dangerous, and for the first time in a long while, Katherine felt afraid. The tall American was gone though, and she would soon forget about him, and hopefully so would Ranald. She closed her eyes and settled into a restless sleep, her dreams invaded by the tall American.
*

Ben spent a cold night on a large island midstream in the Missouri River, and downstream from Fort Maskwa and the Blackfoot camp. He hoped the light of day would give him a better perspective. The storm had abated, leaving a new blanket of snow on the landscape. The dawn broke with its first rays peeking out from under the clouds and casting a red glow across the river bottom.

Smoke rose from the various chimneys at the fort as well as from the smoke flaps of the Blackfoot lodges. There was little activity outside of these structures and Ben decided that the early hour of the day was the best time to approach the fort. The water level of the river was low, but cold. The icy water and the tension built up inside of Ben sent a chill through his body as he crossed the Missouri. The muscles in his back and shoulders tensed and his hands shook as he moved closer to the stockade walls of the fort.

Ben approached the fort from the side, coming around to the front gates just as they were being swung open for the morning. To the surprise of the two engagees who were manning the front gate, Ben seemed to appear from nowhere and rode in without challenge. He dismounted and tied the reins of his horse to the top rail of the corral. Then, with his rifle in hand walked directly to the Big House, opened the door and entered. In the dim light, he saw Ranald sitting at first table with Dawson Thomas at his side. Not far away, Dob Bergmann sat at one of the other tables, with a few other engagees. Everyone, caught off guard by the unexpected visitor, sat still save for Thomas who stood and spoke, "What has happened to bring you back Mr. Voss?"

"I figured I had some unfinished business here," Ben replied.

"There is no business here, other than my business," Ranald said, his tone sharp and clear with obvious anger.

"Then you and I must come to an understanding." Ben stood, shaking a bit from the cold, but more from fear turned into determination.

"Oh, an understanding ye say?" Ranald let an unsettling smile cross his lips. "Come, sit down and we'll see if we can't come to this 'understanding' ye want."

Ben crossed the room and sat down at the table directly opposite from Ranald. He laid his rifle across the table in front of him to keep it within his reach, all the time keeping his eye on the big Scotsman.

"Will you have a cup of coffee to ward off the morning's chill?" Ranald bid, not expecting or wanting an answer. He called out, "Katherine, coffee and a cup."

Kat entered from the kitchen and within a few steps she was stopped in her tracks by the sight of Ben sitting at the table. She regained her composure and went directly to Ranald's side.

"Pour me another cup and then one for our guest," Ranald ordered. She obeyed, trying to keep her eyes from looking directly at Ben, but as she poured the hot black coffee into the cup her gaze locked with his and her hand shook ever so slightly, enough to spill coffee on the table.

This brought a rebuke from Ranald, "Are ye clumsy as well as a slut?" Katherine pulled back away from the table knowing that she was close to receiving another beating.

"I don't believe that is the way for a gentleman to speak." The words left Ben's mouth before he had time to think.

"A Gentleman, eh?" Ranald let out a harsh laugh. "When it comes to the Métis sluts, manners are not required." He paused, and continued, "Are ye a learned gentleman then, Mr. Voss?" Ben did not answer.

"Do ye know who the ancient Greeks were?" Again, he did not wait for an answer. "There was a certain Titan goddess, Metis by name, and she was known for being cunning and crafty. Zeus, the main god, he didn't trust her so he swallowed her up whole. You see the only way ta keep her from turning on him was at keep her in close, ta put her in her place. Like the Metis of Greek stories, this bitch of a mongrel race

222

called Métis must be kept in her place." Before the last word was out of his lips, Ranald stood and had taken hold of Katherine by the hair, and pulled her to the table. He held her there and grabbed the neckline of her dress ripping the material. She struggled to cover herself and pull free from the big man's grasp, but his brute strength overpowered her and he forced her face down on the wooden surface of the table.

In that same moment, Ben sprang from his seat to move toward Ranald. But, before he took a single step he was struck from behind, an explosion of light filled his head and he fell to the floor.

The world seemed to float in the bright light of the sharp pain he felt at the back of his head. Though it seemed only a fraction of a second had passed when Ben regained his senses, he found himself on the floor with his hands bound behind his back. Thomas and Dob stood over him, and Ranald still held Katherine, face-down on the table.

"Pull him up," ordered Ranald. Dawson and Dob pulled Ben up onto his feet, supporting him, and holding him back as he struggled to break free.

"Ye should never have come back for the bitch," Ranald said.

"I didn't come back for her," Ben insisted, "I came back to make things right. I wanted to settle up with Dob, and..." he stopped.

"An'?" questioned Ranald. "An' you came back because you were all cow-eyed for this slut!" He retained his hold on Kat's hair with one hand, his forearm pressing down along her spine. With his free hand, he pulled Kat's skirt up out of his way. He then tore open the flap of his pants and forced himself on her. Katherine struck at him, but her attempts to defend herself were useless, Ranald would only press her face down harder on the table top.

"You're insane!" Ben yelled as he struggled against Dob and Dawson. With an almost herculean effort he broke free and rushed at Ranald. With his head down, Ben drove his shoulder into the big man sending him sideways away from Kat, and onto his back, Ben on top of him.

Ranald pushed Ben off and gained his feet while Ben struggled to right himself, his bound hands hampering his efforts. Ranald took an uneasy step back and with a kick of his booted foot struck Ben in the ribs, knocking the wind out of him.

"Take him, ye worthless bastards!" he yelled at his men. Dawson and Dob took hold of Ben and dragged him to his knees in front of Ranald. Ben sat back on his folded legs. His head still rang with the blow he had received but more painful was the sharp stabbing bite in his side that signaled a broken rib.

"Ye are a right scunner, ye are!" Ranald hissed, admitting that Ben had gotten to him and was more than just an irritation. He turned around looking for Kat, and found she had taken refuge against the wall where she stood in shock of what had just happened. Ranald strode over to her and again took hold of her hair and pulled her over to where Ben knelt. There he forced her to the floor close to Ben.

"Now, it would seem that I must give this bitch another anointing."

"It takes a brave man to beat on a woman," Ben said, bringing a deeper shade of red to Ranald's face.

"Hell slap it intae ye! Ye have this commin'. Hold 'im!" he said, and Dawson and Dob held Ben while Ranald swung his heavy first striking down at Ben's face, again and again.

"Please, stop! You're killing him!" Kat uttered a plea for the first time in years. "He didn't do anything."

This never-before outburst from her stopped Ranald in surprise. He couldn't remember the last time she had showed any feelings for someone that he felt needed to be taught a lesson.

"Ye speak now?" he said. "Ye care for this boy that much?"

"No, I don't even know him. I just want you to stop." She buried her face in her hands and sobbed. A smile crossed Ranald's face accompanied by a short sarcastic laugh. He had finally bested her, she had finally broken. It had not been the beatings she had received at his hands, but the empathy she felt for this blonde-headed young man.

"So, ye would like me to spare 'im, ye would?" Ranald knew he had a bargaining chip of sorts. "Just because you asked, I'll not kill 'em, I'll give him a chance, a better chance than he deserves. I'll set him free out there, if ye be waiting for me to return with a smile on yer lip, and yer arms open wide to welcome me back."

She shook her head accepting his terms knowing that setting Ben outside the fort this time of year was as good as a death sentence, but at least out there he would have some chance of survival.

*

From the front bastion, Kat watched as the group of riders moved away from the fort, Ranald at their head. She could see Ben weaving back and forth in the saddle, held steady by the two men riding on either side of him. They rode downstream toward the Breaks of the Missouri, and Katherine knew they would go no further than necessary, but far enough that Ranald felt was sufficient to let nature take its course with Ben.

She waited until they were out of sight and descended the steps going to her quarters where she packed her few possessions. This done, she made her way to the kitchen and assembled a bag of provisions; hard bread, jerked meat, tea, and some pemmican. This and her personal items she took to the bastion and hid among the barrels and sacks of grain stored there. Her final search was for Ben's rifle and other possessions which she added to her store of goods.

She knew that she would have to wait until Ranald and his men returned. And as he ordered, she would have to be waiting for him in his quarters. If she was not there, he would look for her no matter what it took. So that was where she would take action. If Ranald could be dealt with in his quarters she had a chance of getting away. She thought it through. A knife would be risky, even if she drove it deep into him, he could still fight back and possibly kill her. A pistol would make too much noise alarming the entire fort, and like a knife, a bullet may not prove sufficient. She would have to find a way to incapacitate the brute without anyone knowing. No matter what she did, she vowed he would never lay another hand on her.

*

Riding under the darkening sky, Ranald and his NWC men lead Ben away from Fort Maskwa to the east. Barely conscious, Ben sat in the saddle shivering as the wind picked up and the chill of the setting sun seeped into him. Ranald had taken away his coat and hat, leaving him in his shirt and pants. There was a stabbing pain in his ribs with each icy breath he took. His face was swollen from the beating Ranald had inflicted on him, one eye completely closed, and he could feel several teeth loose.

When the group had traveled for almost an hour, Ranald called a halt. He dismounted, followed by his men, and Ben was pulled from his saddle onto the ground. Two men drug him to where the big Scotsman stood and left him at the man's feet. Ben rose to his knees and then attempted to stand, but Ranald knocked him off his feet with another blow to his face. This time the blow hit him square in the mouth and nose. Ben felt the crack of cartilage snapping. With the pain, he felt the thick blood filling the back of his throat and the salty iron taste of blood in his mouth.

"Ye don't deserve the chance I'm givin' ye," Ranald said, telling Ben it was his own fault that had brought him to this. "I would have killed ye and be done with it, but the bitch needs to learn a lesson too. Ye see, she'll have to lay there under me and think about ye out here freezin' ta death, nice and slow." He turned back to his horse, mounted and motioned to his men to head back to the fort.

Dob held back and Dawson stopped, asking, "What are you waiting for?"

"He don't ever give up," Dob said. "Every time I think I've given him the slip, he shows up again."

"He won't come back from this. He'll be dead within the hour."

"He'll come after me, I know it," Dob almost whined.

"Get your ass moving or we'll leave you here to die with him," Dawson ordered. He had no sooner turned away from Dob when he heard the gun shot. Everyone in the party stopped and returned to where Dob and Dawson sat on their horses. Ranald bringing his horse to a skidding halt next to them.

"What the hell is going on here?" he shouted at Dawson, who was dumbfounded and could only look over at Dob.

"He'd come lookin' for me if I didn't kill 'im while I had the chance," Dob said, smoke curling up in to the cold air, from the barrel of the big Wheeler rifle in his hands.

"Damn ye, I gave no order for him ta be killed," shouted Ranald, and with a swing of his hand swatted Dob across the face with his riding quart, and then he pulled one of the big bore Sea Pistols from his belt and aimed it at Dob's head. The hammer of the gun sprang forward, the flint held in its jaws struck the frizzen and sparks fell into a pan onto damp powder. The failure of the pistol to go off only angered Ranald more and he had to restrain himself from throwing the pistol at Dob. "Curse ye and the day the Devil raked his claws across your face leaving that mark! I'll deal with ye later." Ranald yanked on his horse's reins and kicking his heels to its flanks rode off.

Dob looked at Dawson, who shook his head, and wondered what had possessed him take Dob Bergmann in, rather than leave him to starve or freeze to death. Dawson kicked his horse into a gallop and followed the rest of the NWC men back to the fort. Dob fell in behind Dawson, and every so often he would turn in the saddle and look behind him to see if Ben was following.

It was well after dark when Ranald and his men returned to the fort. Ranald dismounted his horse, and leaving it to be tended by his employees, entered the Big House. He made straight for his quarters on the second floor bursting through the door. There, he was surprised to find Kat standing at the foot of his bed, waiting for him. He had almost expected her to not obey him. His feelings were a mixture of disappointment that he would have no reason to beat her, and pleasure at the sight of her standing there, waiting for him.

He smiled and tore off his gloves, coat, and hat, tossing them to the floor. He pulled his pistols from his belt and placed them on the small table that served as his desk. He then moved to take Kat into his arms.

With no warning, Katherine swung her arm up from behind her, a blacksmith's hammer held tightly in her grip, and struck the big man on the side of his head. There was the dull sound of the iron hitting flesh and the crack of bone shattering. Ranald had no chance to defend himself and fell limp to the floor, the side of his face bloody.

Kat stood over him, the hammer ready to deliver another blow but the Scotsman didn't move. She felt her heart would leap from her breast, it beat so savagely. As she looked down on Ranald, his arms and legs splayed out, the years of his mistreatment flooded her mind. For a moment she thought of what the Blackfoot women would do to a prisoner, separating them from their manhood, mutilating them, and even inserting the man's severed penis into his mouth. Kat contemplated this, going as far as pulling the butcher knife from the sheath on her belt. But, the thought of touching him with her bare hand revolted her and she decided on an alternative. With his legs spread wide she kicked him in the groin as hard as possible. As one last parting gesture she spit on him.

She turned and put on a heavy blanket coat, then stepping over Ranald's body she started to leave the room. She stopped and took up the two .54 caliber pistols, and saw that the priming was missing from the pan on one, and damp in the other. Calmly she cleaned both pans out, and primed the guns with fresh, dry powder. These she stuck into the sash of her coat and left the room.

The snow started to fall in big wet flakes, and no one had noticed the two horses led from the corral and out the back gate by Katherine. She walked them slowly across the open ground away from the fort and in the direction Ranald had taken Ben. She had no idea why she would look for the tall blonde man, for she was sure she held no feeling for him; she couldn't allow herself to have feelings. Yet, she was compelled to find him, or at least his body.

*

In the growing cold, Walks Long wrapped in a buffalo robe, huddled in the night as he watched the Whiteman's fort. He had seen the trader chief lead away a group that included the man with hair the color of the sun, and later return without him. He had then seen a lone figure leave the fort with a two horses. He wondered out of curiosity, if he should follow this lone figure and discussed this with Calf

Standing, as they sat in the night's chill.

"*That one might be worth following, if it is a Whiteman, we could eat,*" said Calf's ghost.

"*True, but I am more interested in what has happened to Sun Hair. I would think that maybe that one goes to look for him,*" said Walks.

"*Then what are you waiting for? Go get your horse and let us follow.*"

CHAPTER 14
WINTER

Fleeting visions of the past day floated in and out of Ben's mind, creating a confusion of what had happened to him. He recalled lying on the floor of the great room at Fort Maskwa, the kick to his ribs and Ranald hitting him in the face with his fists. His next recollection was the movement of a horse under him, the rocking back and forth sending pain into his ribs, each step feeling like a dagger thrust into his side. Finally, he found himself laying on the snow covered ground, struggling to his feet in the cold and seeing riders moving away, save one, Dob Bergmann, who raised his rifle and fired in Ben's direction. Ben felt the blow of the lead ball as it tore into his shoulder, sending him down into the snow at his feet.

When he opened his swollen eyes, he saw only the blue-black shadows of the nighttime landscape covered with snow, the pale moonlight reflecting off the crystalline surface. He felt no pain, but he couldn't move, and he wondered if this was what waited in the after-life. He also wondered what his uncle and aunt would think about his never returning. Would they wait with hope that someday he would walk into the wagon yard alive and well, or would they give him up for dead, mourning his disappearance into the vast wilderness?

He closed his eyes and thought about the woman, Kat, and in his delusional state he envisioned her face looking down at him, her hands reaching out to him. And then he gave up and drifted off into the darkness.
*

Kat had no idea if she would find the blond American.

She only knew that she would head in the direction Ranald had taken him. She followed the tracks left by the North West Company horses in her search for Ben. The moonlight was little help, its first quarter just peeking through the broken clouds in the night sky, but casting shadows where the horses' hooves had torn up the otherwise smooth surface of the snow. She cursed herself for not having a better plan, feeling that the situation had been thrust upon her and that she had no other choice but to leave the fort and its security. The weather could turn at any time, and snow storms this time of year could last for days lying down snow as deep as a foot or more depending on the whim of nature.

After traveling for almost two hours, Kat came upon an area where the tracks milled around and no longer headed downstream. She dismounted her horse and began to search in the semi-darkness hoping she would find Ben, or at least his body. What she found was the dark stain of frozen blood on the white ground. A small trail of foot prints lead off at an angle toward the river and leading the horses she followed the unsteady tracks. She had not gone far when the shape of a body caught her eye and she rushed to it. With trembling hands, she turned it over and found that it was Ben. At first the thought of finding him dead created a knot in her stomach, and real fear gripped her. She bent down close, her ear next to his nose and mouth, to listen for even the faintest sign of breath, and at the same time placed her hand on his chest in search of a heartbeat.

His skin felt cold to the touch, and she let her hand linger on his chest, her ear almost touching his face, and she was rewarded with the slightest breath from his lips. She leaned forward and put her arms around Ben, pulled him tightly to her. She let out a soft sigh, and for the briefest moment, she smiled and a tear fell from her eyes.

Relieved that Ben was still alive, she looked him over to determine what injuries he had. The most evident was the patch of blood on his left shoulder. Here she found a bullet hole that had frozen closed, and the material of Ben's shirt completely attached to his skin. The only other injuries she found were from the beating Ranald had given Ben, both eyes were swollen and bruised, his nose was bent to one side and his lips were split. A frosty coating of blood had matted the sparse hair on his lip and chin, giving him a ghoulish appearance. Kat gently brushed a bit of the frost and blood from his face, but hesitated to attempt cleaning him properly. This would have to wait.

Her task now was to keep Ben alive, but he was too heavy for her to lift and place on her horse. She needed to find somewhere they could take shelter and there she would tend to his wounds. Once this was done, she would plan for their next move. She knew that if the weather held, she must get as far away from the fort as possible because the killing of John Ranald meant the North West Company would place a reward for her apprehension or death.

There were several small islands along this stretch of the Missouri River and with the water level down it would be likely that one could be reached without crossing the water. There was also the chance she would find some drift wood there for both shelter and fire. Kat took the buffalo robe she had rolled up with her and Ben's blankets and laying it flat on the ground rolled Ben onto it and placed the blankets over him. She then tied a rope to the front legs of the robe and pulled Ben along behind the horses in this improvised sled.

Not far from where Kat found Ben, she found what she needed to create a shelter. Driftwood had piled up at the head of one of the small islands in the river channel, and as she had hoped, the decrease in the river's flow had exposed a sandy and dry path to one side of the island. A large tree formed the bulk of the driftwood pile and was situated in a way that blocked the wind. Here she pulled Ben's makeshift litter, and created a place where she could tend to him. The baggage that she had brought with her, she piled at the head and foot of the bedding she had created, and a sheet of canvas served as a cover.

The shelter completed, Kat gathered more wood and built a trench fire across the open front. Now she was ready to tend to Ben's injuries. She heated water and cleaned the bullet wound in his shoulder first. Her efforts caused blood to ooze from the hole and she applied pressure with a clean cloth, stopping the flow. She applied wakinakim, a paste made from the inner bark of junipers and she then bound the bullet wound. Next, she cleaned his face. Gone were the strong straight lines of his jaw, swollen closed were his bright blue eyes. She looked him over and wondered what she had committed herself to. Now that she had started to care for this stranger, she could not back away; she could not leave him to die.

When she was satisfied with her nursing, she took time for herself, brewing a cup of tea sweetened with rich dark sugar, and sipped this while she ate a bit of pemmican. Her hunger sated, she built up the fire and crawled inside the shelter. She lay next to Ben wrapping her arms around him to give him as much warmth as possible and under the wool blankets and the buffalo robe she rested.

She had not intended to drift off to sleep, but the stress of the day and her exertion overcame her. The crackling of the fire, and the slight wind lulled her into a deep slumber. Life in the fort had dulled her instincts for survival in the wilderness, and exposed as they were, she would not hear the approach of danger. It was this false security that was broken by the sound of wood in the fire being disturbed. Kat bolted up, one of the big Tower pistols in her hand.

Across the fire pit was a figure, its hairy appearance reflecting the yellow glow of the flames, and for the briefest moment Kat feared it was a bear, possibly one of the great bears with powerful jaws and six inch claws which could tear a man to shreds. Fort Maskwa was named after these great and terrible bears, sometimes called white bears or grizzly by the American trappers.

Her fear and apprehension was relieved to see that the figure was not a bear, but an Indian wrapped in a buffalo robe, his face painted black and a yellow stripe across his eyes. He reached down and taking a piece of wood threw it onto the fire, causing sparks to fly up into the cold night air. He then seated himself and sat motionless.

"Welcome to my fire," Kat said in Métis, receiving no reply. She then repeated the phrase in Blackfoot.

"The woman welcomes us brother," said the Indian, confusing Kat.

"I have little to offer but you are welcome to what I have." She shifted sitting up on her knees and reaching for one of the saddle bags, pulled out some pemmican, and offered it to the man.

He took the dried mixture of meat and berries, tearing off a bite and chewing it slowly. He turned his head to one side as if listening to something out in the darkness. He looked back in Kat's direction and spoke.

"You tend to the Whiteman with hair like the sun." It was more a statement than a question.

"Yes, he is injured," said Kat.

"Will he die?"

"I do not know. I have done my best to treat his wounds." She was puzzled by this warrior's questions. She asked, *"Is this Whiteman a friend of yours?"*

"No. I had thought to take his hair and eat his heart." This set a chill through Kat's blood. *"But there is no honor in taking either if he is not fit to fight."* He

threw another piece of wood on the fire, and continued. *"I am Walks Long of the Pikuni Blackfoot. I will wait until he has recovered from his wounds, then we can make war on each other. You may rest now, and make him better. I will watch over you."*

"Thank you," Kat said, not trusting Walks Long, and she tightened her grip on the pistol.

"No. I will not kill them to feed you," Walks Long spoke into the darkness to his right. *"You will not feed tonight."* This confirmed Kat's opinion of the Blackfoot. She now knew for certain the man was insane.

Sometime during the remainder of the night, Walks Long disappeared. Kat was sure she had not closed her eyes for more than a few seconds, but when she looked up he was gone, and the sky above the horizon was turning yellow and orange under the gray-blue overcast. She rose and first checked on the horses and found that fresh cottonwood bark had been placed for them to eat. Kat could only guess that Walks Long had not only watched over her and Ben through the night, but had feed the horses as well. She was worried by the strange actions of the Blackfoot, but among many of the tribes, people who would be considered crazy by some were considered special and almost holy by others.

Kat was lucky to find two tree limbs long enough to create a makeshift travois. It would not be as sturdy or as efficient as one made from lodge poles, but it would work. She moved Ben onto this improvised litter, and searching for a shallow place, crossed the river. She had now to decide in which direction to go. Soon, someone at the fort would find Ranald's body, and it would only be a matter of time before a search party would be sent out for his killer. She had kept her tracks mixed in with those of the NWC men who had taken Ben out into the wilderness, and this would confuse any pursuers for only a short time.

Kat knew that there was a winter camp of some Cree and Métis near the Big Snowy Mountains. There she had a chance of finding a hiding place and wait out the winter. By spring, Ben would either recover or die. She would then decide her next step.

To reach the winter camp, she would have to backtrack toward the fort where just east of the mouth of the Judith, the small tributary called Animosh Creek flowed into the Missouri. She would follow its course southeast and hopefully find the well-worn trail that led out into the buffalo country south of the Missouri Breaks and above the Musselshell River.

Working her way back up the river Kat soon found the creek and turned away from Missouri. The trail she searched for forked about one mile from the fort, the right fork paralleling the Judith, and the left headed south-east, the direct she wanted.

The poor materials she had used for the travois failed several times and it was necessary for her to stop often and make repairs. She wished she had strips of raw hide she could wet and tie the rickety structure's joints together. When dried, they would shrink and bind the wood tightly. But she did her best and made better progress along the trail than she had expected, reaching the windswept plateau above the Judith River before sunset.

*

Paralleling the path of Kat and Ben, Walks Long rode engaged in conversation with the specter of Calf Standing.

"Why do we follow them if we are not going to kill them?" asked the pale apparition.

"I do not know."

"You do not know? What form of answer is that? Ride down there, kill the Sun Hair, eat his heart and then if you want crawl between the legs of the Métis woman."

"I have no need of the women. You know that."

"Why is that? I often wondered why you never take comfort with a woman."

"It does not matter."

"Yes it does. Do you not want children?"

"If I were to have children, you would attach yourself to them. So I do not think of those things."

"You must. I remember your man-part became hard when you killed your first enemy. It was a Crow, was it not? You became excited and shook like the leaves on a tree. I though you would wet yourself." The phantom laughed.

"You talk too much. Why do you not sleep like the other dead?"

"I will never rest until my hunger is satisfied!" hissed Calf.

*

The sky seemed to have lost the sun completely, only a pale glimmer of cloud-defused light made its way to the ground illuminating the country in front of Kat. The clouds hung heavy and low, promising snow and her hope was that the impending storm would not bring wind with it. She could travel in the snow, pulling Ben's litter along like so much driftwood behind the pack horse, but wind could spell disaster. Not only would the wind drop the temperature, if it blew hard enough, visibility would be lost and there would be no dividing line between the ground and the sky, it would blend into one white mass destroying all sense of direction. As to validate her foreboding, a breeze kicked up from the north, picking up snow from the ground and swirling it into tiny whirlwinds of ice flakes. She pulled her blanket coat tighter around her shoulders and the hood of the coat down further to cover her face.

With the wind at her back, she had traveled for most of the day and then stopped to check on Ben finding that he was perspiring and hot to the touch, but was shivering. He was running a fever, most likely due to bad blood from the lead ball still in his shoulder. She would have to make camp, put up a shelter and again clean out the wound and add yarrow root to help fight off the putrefaction. She found a gentle drainage with well-established trees and made camp.

She cleaned Ben's wound again, but this time she feared that she must attempt to remove the bullet. Hanging next to the large butcher knife in a sheath on her belt, she had a beaded, cone-shaped, case containing a long thin triangular awl with a bone handle. This she heated in the fire, and when she thought it was hot enough, with shaking hands, she began to probe the bullet hole for the lead ball. Surprisingly, she didn't have to dig too deep. Either Ben had been shot from a great distance, or the charge of powder used had been light, possibly wet. As a result the wound was not very deep. She added more yarrow root and a clean bandage cut from the sleeve of her dress. She then wrapped Ben up in a blanket and covered that with the buffalo robe.

Her hands were still shaking when she finally sat down next to Ben, a cup of hot tea held tightly in her fingers. She had never felt so alone, so lost as she did at that moment. She looked over at the blond-headed man, and wondered what kind of man he really was, she wondered if he was kind, or if he was like most men and all he would want from her was her body.

When fatigue finally overcame her she crawled under the covers and lay next to him, seeking to share to warmth. As she came close to his body she felt he was still shaking but that he was cool to the touch and that his fever must have broken. Without thought she wrapped her arms around him, pulling him tight to her and she was soon asleep.

Kat awoke with the coming dawn that like its predecessor was dull and gray. She stoked up the coals in the fire and soon had a good blaze going to heat water for tea. Of all the goods that were available through trade with the English, tea and sugar were the two that Kat had grown to love. They were her one small pleasure, even the smell of the large packages labeled "ZODIAC EXTRA FINE IMPERIAL TWANKAY No 111 SHANGHAI" was a pleasure for her.

As the water heated in her cup, she checked on Ben and found his fever had truly broken. His breathing was strong and even, and the bullet wound showed no signs of mortification. The bruises on his face had become more intensely purple and black, but she knew in a few more days they would start to turn a greenish color and finally yellow, signaling they were healing. The swelling would also go away and Ben's sickly pallor would give way to a healthy glow.

Satisfied that Ben would recover, she turned her attention to the horses. She found them where they had been picketed, the area around their feet pawed up by their hooves in search of grass under the snow. She made a mental note that the first thing she must find after breaking camp was water for the horses. It was more important to make sure they had water during the cold day than it was the hot ones. Horses suffered from lack of water more than lack of food, and to lose a horse could put her life in jeopardy.

She sipped her tea and looked over at Ben. It seemed that his battered face had somehow softened, he no longer had the hardened look of the engagees. He had somehow become more human to her. For the briefest moment, she thought of crawling back under the covers to be close to him, only to chide herself for considering such a foolish thing.

Her tea finished, she began to pack hoping that this would be the day she found the Métis camp. As she knocked the remnants of the tealeaves from her cup, she heard a noise from where Ben lay. Turning, she saw him looking in her direction through the slits of his swollen eyelids.

"Water..." His voice was weak, coming from his parched lips. Kat quickly poured water from a wooden canteen into her cup and took it to him. She helped him raise his head and he took a small hesitant sip of the cold water, this first icy cold drink burning his throat and choking him slightly.

"Easy," she said to him. "Drink just a bit at a time." He took a few more sips and closing his eyes, he sighed. He licked his lips and then spoke again.

"How long..." he stopped, licking his parched lips again.

"It has been three days," Kat said.

"Where am I?" He looked around seeing nothing but the small camp among the sparse pines.

"We are headed south to where there is a camp of my people." She surprised herself when she mentioned the Métis as "my people." She had not thought of herself as belonging to anyone save Ranald for some time.

"The fort...Ranald..." He was exhausted and found talking difficult, his shoulder and his ribs hurt. Each breath he took brought back the stabbing pain.

"We will talk of that later. Do you think you can drink some tea, possibly eat something?" she asked and he shook his head slightly.

Kat made another cup of tea and as the water heated she gave Ben a piece of pemmican which he chewed slowly. Once the tea was ready, Kat helped him drink it. The warmth of the rich brew and the energy provided by the dried meat had an obvious effect on Ben. He became more alert, and his memories became clearer.

"How bad am I hurt?" he asked, placing his hand over the soreness between his chest and his shoulder.

"Some bruises and minor cuts on your face, once the swelling goes down you'll be fine. You were also shot. I took out the bullet, it wasn't very deep." This brought back the memory of Dob pointing his Wheeler rifle at him and Ben let out a small laugh.

"He never did take care of his powder," he said. He saw that Kat was puzzled by this statement.

"Dob Bergmann, he never could keep his powder dry. I told him a bunch of times but he never listened to me, good thing I guess."

"We need to leave, there is a storm building in the north and we must reach the safety of the Métis camp. I do not want to be caught out in the open." Ben nodded that he understood and made an attempt to rise from his bed, only to fall back in pain.

"No, you are not strong enough to ride yet. You must travel as before, I will pull you behind the horse."

"I'm sorry, Kat-Kat-rine." He tried to pronounce her name the way he had heard it, "KAT-rreen," but it didn't seem to sound right. She shook her head.

"I am called Kat by most people. They do not think I know this but I do not mind. You may use that if it is easier for you to say, and in fact I prefer it."

"Kat. I like that." He tried to smile but the movement of those muscles hurt. Through his swollen eyelids he got his first look at her in the daylight. She was every bit as beautiful as he had thought before, more so in fact. Her long black hair shone even in the subtle light of the gray morning. Framing her face, it fell down past her shoulders, like curtains at the sides of a window, a window to another world. All this beauty was enhanced by her hazel eyes, their pale-golden brown radiating out from around the pupil, fading into yellow and blue rays in the iris that combined to make her eyes look green. These were not common among her kind, and were most likely the gift from her father's French blood.

Ben felt he could easily get lost in her eyes, but there was something there that was cold. At this moment he would have given anything to see brightness in them, to see a smile cross her lips.

Once more the wind picked up out of the north,

and Kat and Ben followed the trail out onto the level plain south of the Missouri River. Kat kept the small plateau's drainage to her right skirting it until the open plain spread out in front of her. She knew in the south would be a range of mountains rising up almost 2000 feet from the surrounding terrain, some of the tribes called these peaks the Moccasins. When she was closer to this range she would be able to see Judith Peak in the south. Somewhere between the too, sheltered from the north winds, would be the winter camp of the Métis and Cree. Though further south than usual and encroaching on Crow territory, the area would hold buffalo and possibly deer and elk. Kat hoped she would be able to find this camp without having to head too far south. The Crow and the Cree were enemies, and the Crow would not treat her well if she was found trespassing.

As she rode, she kept an eye on the skyline in all directions, and a lone figure caught her attention off to her right. She halted, and rising in her stirrups to get a better look she could see it was Walks Long. He was still following her and Ben, but had kept his distance. He had not posed a threat so far, however he made her nervous.

By midday, Kat caught sight of the Moccasins and she felt better about her situation. Yet as fate would have it, the sky grew darker, the temperature began to drop and the wind increased. Along with the wind came fresh snow, and as the wind increased so did the snow. It was not long until visibility was diminished to just a few yards. Kat had no choice but to stop where they were, and attempt to wait out the storm.

In the storm the horses naturally turned their backs to the wind facing away from it. Kat hobbled and tied them together, setting the baggage down to building a windbreak and covering Ben and her with the buffalo robe. Ben tried to help but was still too weak to be of much aid. They ended huddled together under the Buffalo robe, their blankets wrapped around them. At first, neither of them thought beyond the present moment, but as the minutes passed they both became aware of the closeness they shared.

Ben found himself embarrassed, for though Kat had slept next to him for three nights, this was the first time he was conscious of her nearness, the scent of her was intoxicating and excited him. Kat also felt uncomfortable, but could not place the feelings she was experiencing. She didn't like it and was frustrated that she couldn't break free from the confinement of their cocoon.

Kat was at the point of total exasperation when she settled for just a peek out from under the covers, if only for breaths of cold air to cool off the heat building inside her. Looking out into the whiteness, she thought she saw the figure of Walks Long sitting just a few feet away. This sent a chill through her and she trembled slightly. Ben mistook this trembling as a result of the cold and placed his arms around her.

Kat almost pulled away but her resistance melted instantly and she took comfort from Ben's strong arms. This was the first time in her life that a man had held her with her wellbeing in mind, and it confused her. She allowed him to hold her, yet she would not allow herself to rest her head against him. This would be total surrender and she was not ready for that.

It was in this way they passed the rest of the day, slowly giving way to the exhaustion that stress can bring and with that, sleep. The storm raged into the night, blowing itself out onto the plains to the south, and leaving a clear sky filled with millions of tiny pinpoints of light that make up the Milky Way. With the clear sky the temperature dropped further, and even in their buffalo robe and blanket covering, Kat and Ben started to feel the deadening cold.

"We need to get a fire started," said Kat and she

pulled aside the covering, the snow that had built up on them falling to one side. Kat had the foresight to put firewood on the pack horse, and this would be enough to give them warmth through the night. As she emerged from the shelter of their covers, her first sight was that of both horses laying snow covered, dead from the exposure to the storm. Kat's heart sank, and with a false sense of hope she looked in all directions wishing to see the Blackfoot, Walks Long. With no sign of anyone, Kat decided Walks Long must have found shelter from the storm or perished like the horses. The landscape was pristine white, the crystals of snow reflecting the light of the near full moon. There was nothing to do except work through the moment and survive the bitter cold of the night.

The dawn brought little warmth, and Kat and Ben filled their bellies with hot tea and the high energy pemmican. As the sun rose higher in the sky, the faint shape of the distant mountains could be seen to the south.

"We must head in that direction," Kat told Ben. "Do you think you can travel?"

"Sure, I'll do fine," Ben lied and Kat knew it. Ben still had not gained enough strength to travel on foot, but there was no other choice.

"How far do you reckon those mountain are?" he asked.

"On horseback, maybe a day," she paused looking at the dead horses. "On foot, two or three, depending how deep the snow is and if we run into drifts." She was being optimistic. She calculated that the distance was over twenty miles and if they did manage to make it that far, there was no certainty that they would find anyone at all.

They set to work sorting through the packs and deciding what to carry. Ben was surprised to see that Kat had his rifle, shot pouch, powder horn, knife and tomahawk. Ben wrapped his wool blanket around himself securing it to his waist with his belt. On his back he would carry one of the panniers from the pack horse containing their food.

Kat wore her copote, the hooded blanket coat made from a heavy English blanket. She would carry the buffalo robe, and her blanket on her back and two haversacks with her meager supply of medicines, the few pieces of tin wear, a shoot pouch and powder horn with the two British tower pistols she had taken from Ranald. On top of this load, Kat had placed a small bundle of their last firewood.

As a last thought Kat cut pieces of meat from the horse's hind quarters and wrapped them in the horses' skin. They would at least have some fresh meat to sustain them as there would be little chance of finding game on foot.

With the clear sky came another dilemma. The reflection of the bright sun off the white ground posed a risk of Kat and Ben becoming snow blind. Kat solved this problem by cutting pieces of the horse hide into bands they could tie around their heads, with only a small slit across their eyes to allow them to see. So, weighed down with their packs and bundled up, they moved across the plain. With Moccasin Mountain as their landmark, they headed south through the snow, no more than a few inches deep in most places but there were drifts up to three and four feet in others. Most of all they had to avoid where the snow had filled in gullies or drainages. There the snow could be too deep to navigate and become a death trap.

They made slow progress, and by midday they had to stop and rest, both of them nearly collapsed onto the ground. Ben was more than willing to stop but only did so when Kat suggested it. He did not want to admit that he wasn't sure if he could go further, the pain from his shoulder and ribs being almost unbearable.

He closed his eyes to help ease the strain and the

sting from the harsh light, and it felt as if there was sand under his eyelids. He wondered what they would have felt like if Kat had not made him the eyeshades he now wore. When he opened them to look out across the plain, his vision was blurred but he thought he saw the movement of a dark figure off in the distance.

"Look there. Do you see something?" he asked Kat, pointing in the direction of the moving shape.

Kat stood and shading her eyes with her hand peered off for what seemed an eternity to Ben. Then she spoke, her voice dry but clear. "He's back."

"Who? Ranald?"

"No. A Blackfoot called Walks Long." She sighed. "He was following us and I thought he had given up. He said he wanted to kill you but wouldn't do it unless you could fight back."

'Son of a...' Ben's voice trailed off. "Well, I ain't gonna' let him get close enough to talk about it." With this Ben rose to one knee, checked the priming in the rifle's pan, and pulled back the hammer. He leveled the rifle, finding it hard to steady his aim with his weak left arm. The sites seemed to weave in a circle around the ever-growing target as it approached, and he cursed under his breath. Just as he thought he had a clear shot, Kat reached over and gently lifted the end of the rifles barrel.

"Don't shoot," she said. "I don't think it is the Blackfoot."

Ben pulled himself up to stand next to Kat, his rifle still ready in his hands as the figure on horseback approached to within fifty yards and stopped. Looking at Ben and Kat for a few moments the man kicked his horse into a walk and came up to them. Across the saddles pommel in front of the rider lay a Trade gun, his right hand resting on it, a finger near enough to the trigger if need be.

From under the hood of a sky-blue blanket coat a

bearded face appeared, a clay pipe clenched in its teeth. The man, smiled and a voice boomed, sounding like thunder in the stillness. The words were in a language Ben had never heard but some of the words sounded like French.

"I thought you were a buffalo laying out here!" The man spoke Michif, a dialect unique to French-Cree creole Métis, using French nouns, Cree verbs, and some local vocabulary borrowed from the Ojibway or Dene. This was also a language with long words and fairly free word order, unlike any other spoken. Though a mixture of a these languages, many Métis could neither speak nor understand French or the native tongues.

"You are lucky this 'buffalo' did not shoot you," said Kat.

"Maybe that is true, but then how could I offer the hospitality of my lodge to you?" The man chuckled. He stood in his stirrups and waved his gun in the air above his head, signaling to his companions who were not far behind him. Four riders with packhorses came at a headlong gallop skidding to a stop next to the man, in a cloud of kicked up snow.

"You are Cree?" the man asked?

"My mother was a Cree, my father a voyager," answered Kat.

"And this one, he is English, no?"

"No, he is an American."

"Ahh..." He paused, wanting to ask more questions, but willing to wait until later. *"We have a camp not far from here. Come and we will give you a warm meal. Then we can talk."*

The pack animals of the Métis hunters carried very little, their hunting just started, and Ben and Kat's few possessions were placed on one of these and they shared another to ride. Once ready, they turned and headed back in the direction they had come from toward Moccasin Mountain.

As they rode, the man in the blue capote chatted with Kat. *"I am called Henri Thibault, we are a mixed camp, some Cree, a few Ojibway but mostly Métis. You are welcome to stay with us as long as you need."*

"You are generous. My friend has been injured and needs to heal."

"Your friend? He looks as if he received more than just an injury, to me it looks as if he has been badly beaten." Henri quipped. *"We can tend to his injuries and you can rest with us."*

Within an hour, the camp came into sight. It was nestled against the southeastern slope of the mountain, shielded from the north winds. The Judith Mountains rose from the southern horizon a mere ten miles away.

Before they entered the camp, Henri pulled back to ride next to Kat. *"You have yet to tell me your name, and where you came from."*

"I am Katherine, I was born in Montreal."

"Ahh. And how did you come about having a wounded American?"

"I must be honest with you. We have had some problems with the North West Company at Fort Maskwa. Once you have helped us, we will leave as soon as possible. We do not want to cause trouble for you and yours." Kat feared that if she were not open with Henri, he would not offer any help at all.

"I appreciate your candor, speaking plainly is valued by me. Our camp is a mixture of North West Company and Hudson Bay people, but we are all friends and there will be no judgment of strangers in need." He then moved his horse to ride next to Ben, who though unsteady, stayed upright in the saddle.

"What are you called?" he asked in broken English with a thick accent similar to that of Ben's friend Estienne.

"My name is Benjamin Voss. I'm a contracted trapper, an engagee for Manuel Lisa at Fort Raymond on the Yellowstone River."

"Ahh." Henri said, "I have 'eard there is an American post there, on the Big 'Orn, no?"

"Yes."

"Can you tell me 'ow you were wounded, was it Indians?"

"No, I was shot by a man who is a thief and a coward."

"I see," Henri said and felt this was enough for the time being.

There were a dozen conical lodges set in a haphazard crescent; each lodge had a pile of brush around its bottom to help cut the wind and help keep the lodges warm. These were different from the Crow lodges or the Blackfoot lodges Ben has seen. Their sides were set at a steeper angle and the smoke flaps were smaller and unadorned.

Scattered in the camp were several travois, drying racks and four two-wheeled wagons. These caught Ben's eye as soon as he entered the camp. They were somewhat like the carts he had worked on in Pittsburgh, the wheels on these little wagons were over four feet tall and not proportional to the cart like those back home. Ben's curiosity was piqued and he was determined to get a better look at them the first chance he had.

Henri led Ben and Kat to one of the lodges. Dismounting, he dropped the reins to his horse and called out in Métis, *"Jacques, come out, your Papa, he is home!"* From the lodge emerged a young boy in his teens, lean with dark hair and an olive complexation.

"Papa!" the boy shouted, happy to see Henri. *"You promised to take me hunting with you, did you forget?"*

"No, we did not go far and I have brought some company. Go tell your mother I am back."

The boy ducked his head back into the lodge door and called to his mother. He turned and came closer to where Ben and Kat sat on their horses. Emerging from the lodge, an Indian woman appeared and stood looking at Henri and his guests. She was short and heavy set with large breasts. Her ample size was emphasized by a broad smile that seemed to light up her face, and when she spoke her words were intertwined with a soft giggle. She was obviously delighted to see her husband and that he had brought guests.

"Love of my life, I have brought company." He turned to Ben and Kat and introduced the woman, *"This is my wife,* Pules, *Pigeon."* Then he turned back to his wife, *"Do we have room to shelter them?"*

"Oh, yes! Oh, yes!" she exclaimed. *"Come. Come. I have a stew on the fire and we can eat and get to know each other."* She looked to her son and said, *"Jacques, unpack the belongings and take care of the horses."* Then she ushered them into the lodge.

Ben had never been inside one of the buffalo hide structures and at first he found it confining until he moved to where he was instructed to sit, and then he found it quite comfortable. A small fire set directly in the center of the teepee offered heat and also served as the cooking area.

"My husband is a good provider and we never go hungry. There is more than enough room here for you and your woman," she said to Ben. Kat of course understood the woman who spoke Michif, and she translated for Ben. Their eyes met for just a brief moment and then the embarrassment passed, both of them deciding to say nothing.

Pules dished out hot stew from a copper kettle that hung over the fire and handed her husband and each of her guests the steaming bowls. As they ate, Pules chattered on, telling Ben and Kat about her husband, son and almost every little detail about the other occupants of the small winter camp.

"Oh," Pules said, speaking directly to Kat as if the

two of them had been friends for years, *"You will like Numees, she does the most beautiful quill work! I never could make the patterns come out right, but I do better with a needle and trade beads."*

"Speaking of needles," Henri said, *"I believe that Ben needs some sewing up."*

"Yes," said Kat, *"I dressed his wound as best as I could, but had no needle to sew it closed."*

"Oh, we must take care of that," Pules said, *"Let us finish eating and then we can tend to him."*

When the meal was finished, Henri sat back with a pipe and watched as Pules supplied Kat with needle and thread, and then Kat cleaned the hole in Ben's shoulder, stitched it up and added more wakinakim. Pules offered some clean cotton cloth and a new dressing was applied.

Jacques poked his head into the lodge door and started to pull in what little belongings that Ben and Kat owned. These were passed around the inside to the space Pules had cleared for them and it was there that Kat would make their bed.

Ben leaned close to whisper in her ear, "Tell them they have made a mistake and that I should sleep somewhere else."

"That will not be necessary," Kat whispered back, "It would be better if we stayed together. It would also eliminate the questions that would be asked about how we came to be together."

Satisfied with a hot meal and a warm place to sleep, Ben and Kat fell in to a much needed and restful sleep.
*

The glow from the camp fires inside the lodges made them appear like lanterns in the dark night. Sitting in the shelter of the nearby trees, Walks Long spoke with Calf Standing.

"Now what will you do?" asked the apparition.

"Now I will wait until the melting of the snow and

the greening of the grass. Then I will come back," said Walks.

"*I am hungry! Feed ME!*" screamed Calf Standing, his words piercing the night, causing Walks to cover his ears with his hands.

"*I will come back when the snow melts. I will find the one with hair like the Sun and I will feed you then. I have nothing more to say.*"

SAM J. PISCIOTTA

CHAPTER 15
THE MÉTIS

Dawson Thomas climbed up the exterior set of stairs to the second story of Fort Maskwa where the living quarters were located. Ranald, as the bourgeois or factor, had the largest room; the next smallest was shared by the head clerk, Robert Kentland and Doctor Owen, and there was a cramped, but private room belonging to Dawson. There was another small room, located at the top of the interior stairs and next to the bourgeois'. This had belonged to Ranald's woman, Katherine. These four rooms took up a good portion of one wall in the fort's second floor while the other three walls were comprised of the catwalks and two bastions. Dawson hurried to get out of the cold night air and inside where a warm fire awaited him. In his hand he carried the fort's ledger book, a complete accounting of the goods and services associated with the day–to-day operation of the establishment. He dreaded going over the numbers, and making notes as to the horses and supplies lost with the desertion of the Métis woman. Someone would have to be accountable for the loss.

The heat from inside the apartment hit his face with a welcome blast as he pushed open the door and walked in, stamping his boots to rid them of any snow that may have clung to them. Removing his fur cap, he slapped it against his leg to do the same. He took a few steps over to where a small cast-iron stove sat next to the wall radiating warmth generated by coals inside.

Dawson placed the journal on the wooden table and then stepped over to the bed and peered down at the injured man whose face was bandaged and swollen. John Ranald, the side of his head caved in, had lay close to death for the better part of a week.

Laboring for hours, the fort's doctor, Titus Owen had done his best to treat the damage inflicted by the blacksmith's hammer. He had removed the shattered teeth that could not be saved, set the broken jaw forcing the fracture to close, and removed the shards of splintered cheek bone before stitching the flesh together and applying a dressing. What he could not save was the devastated eye socket, and the orb it had once contained. Owen was at a loss when it came to a replacement for the cold-gray eye, at first filling the void with a small carved ball of wood, but this caused more problems. From past experience in the British Army, Owen knew that the Venetians made artificial eyes from glass. As neither a glass prosthetic nor the technology to produce one existed at Fort Maskwa, Owen was left with finding a suitable substitute. He knew that prior to glass, false eyes were made from gold covered with colored enamel. Gold also was not an option, too expensive and the process to cover it inn enamel was nonexistent so far from civilization. He then turned to the source of natural material used by the natives, the buffalo. With a bit of work the fort's carpenter carved and polished a small sphere made from a buffalo's leg bone. The carpenter had suggested engraving the likeness of pupil, but Owen discouraged this, fearing that if the prosthetic were to sit at even the slightest angle Ranald would look cock-eyed.

The damage to Ranald's face was the first to be tended by Owen, but during the further inspection of the factor's body it was discovered that his scrotum was filled with blood and swollen. Due to the amount of the swelling, Owen surmised that Ranald was either bleeding internally and the blood was settling in his testicles, or that he had received a heavy blow between the legs. Owen prodded Ranald's abdomen but could not confirm the existence or the extent of internal bleeding.

"I can't tell what caused this," he told Dawson. "We can pack the area of swelling with snow and see if the swelling recedes. If it doesn't, he's bleeding inside and I have no way of knowing how to go about fixing that. Truthfully, it looks to me that he got a good kick in the ball sack." He let out a small snicker, then remembering he was in the presence of Ranald's right-hand man, abruptly stopped.

"What I want to know Doctor, is will he recover?" Dawson asked.

"He has a chance, if there is no internal damage. When the swelling goes down in his face, we'll see how his sight is the eye he has left. There is also the chance of purification form any of his injuries. I've done what I can."

Owen had packed up his few medical instruments and retired to his quarters where he drank himself into a stupor. He dreaded that he would be blamed if Ranald would die, and if Ranald didn't die he would be blamed for the deformity left. Either way, his future was uncertain, but of the two choices, he prayed the Scottish bastard would die.

Now seven days later, Dawson's gaze was returned by the remaining gray eye of Ranald, peering wide at him. Though his supervisor could not speak, it was clear that he wanted to know the status of the situation.

"The storm has let up some, but it is still not practicable to venture out in search of her." This brought visible anger to Ranald and he attempted to rise, but the pain his movement caused wouldn't let him leave the bed. The swelling in his testicles had gone down leaving him with a shriveled sack of flesh, and a pain that could not be eased except by whiskey or laudanum.

"I've taken account of what she might have

thieved. She took her few personal possessions, the American's rifle, and two horses. It also appears she took your brace of new pistols." Again, Ranald's anger flared and he shook with the rage, taking hold new of Dawson's arm and squeezing it.

"I understand," said Dawson. "The pistols are not trifles and I promise if the winter doesn't kill her, we'll find her and bring her back to you." Ranald closed his one good eye as if accepting Dawson's promise.

"Rest, and I'll have Rochelle bring up some broth for you"

Ranald slightly shook his head and uttered a guttural protest. With great effort he hissed through his clenched teeth, "Laudanum...Whiskey."

"You have to eat something if you intend to live, and if you want to make the bitch pay for what she has done to you."

Dawson was not sure if he really cared if Ranald recovered or not. There was still a chance that the Scotsman's blood would turn bad, and if that happened he would have him buried and send a letter to NWC headquarters in Montréal. They would then either send a replacement or write back informing Dawson that he had been promoted. That would be the simplest outcome and the more acceptable to Dawson.

On the other hand, if Ranald survived there would be hell to pay for everyone within striking distance of the ill-tempered brute. Ranald would not be content with tracking down Kat and dealing out punishment to her. He would need to gain back what little respect he had lost, having been mutilated and humiliated by a woman. Until now, he had ruled more by fear than by respect, and being put down by Kat had proved he was vulnerable. It proved he could be beaten. Ranald would now be twice as dangerous, thought Dawson, and he would go to any length to repair his wounded pride.

Dawson Thomas concluded that it would probably be in everyone's best interest if Ranald would die; and though he had no compunction in helping the wretched man achieve this final outcome, Dawson had to draw the line on the killing of his superior. He felt that he would leave Ranald's destiny in the hands of fate, hoping that he would have to write that letter to Montréal.

*

Winter held its grip on the northern plains long after the first of the year with a succession of storms driven by strong north winds coming down out of Canada. For days at a time, everyone in the small Métis camp was forced to stay huddled inside their lodges. Due to this, Kat and Ben were in each other's constant company, and though they tried hard to act as if they were a couple, it took only a short time for Pules to see through the ruse. She had pointed this out to her husband, but Henri seemed either not to notice or it didn't seem to be important to him. But, intent on finding out the truth between Kat and Ben, Pules took advantage of the first opportunity to get Kat alone or at least away from Ben.

The weather changed with the arrival of a warm dry wind descending from the slopes of the Rocky Mountains, causing a rapid rise in temperature and offering a few days with clear skies and milder temperatures. Though still somewhat cold, it was a welcome break and almost everyone found some task to perform outside the lodges. As they had done several times in the past weeks, Pules suggested that Kat and herself go to visit her friend Numees. Kat, not seeing any subterfuge in this offer, was more than happy to get out of the lodge and away from Ben.

Spending so much time around the tall American had at first only bothered her slightly, but when she found herself being accustomed to his presence she became irritated by his every action. This also was noticed by Pules.

The three women sat outside the hide lodge of Numees, enjoying what little warmth the sun offered. They talked as Numees showed her technique for applying the colored porcupine quills to a strip of tanned buckskin. At first there was normal chatter about the other women in the camp, and their children and this brought about references to stories that taught lessons on behavior. Pules was the first to offer a story.

"I remember the story about a young man named Not Enough Horses who could not find a woman in his village to couple with him unless he married them," said Pules, *"He then set off to find someone without proper morals. Soon he found a beautiful young girl, who will let him take her. He brought her back to show her off to the other girls, and that night the couple made wild love! In the morning he wakes up to find that she was not a woman, but a coyote.*

"His whole village makes fun of him. But, he has still not learned his lesson. Once again he leaves and takes a woman who has no virtue. He has her again and again during the night, but then next morning he finds he was tricked and had been with a coyote a second time! This proves that because a woman is willing to give herself to you does not mean she is a coyote bitch and bite you in the end."

They laughed and Numees felt compelled to tell a story of her own regarding an old man who thought he could satisfy any and all women, and was taught a lesson by his wife.

"There was an old man who could not keep his eyes off the young girls, and bragged that he could satisfy any woman. To teach him a lesson, his wife disguised herself as a young girl and tricked him into making love to her. Thinking he was with another woman, he kept comparing her to his wife, saying her breasts were firmer, her legs straighter, her belly flatter,

and so on. When the wife disclosed who she was, the surprised man tried to say he knew it was a trick all the long, and was trying to be in on the joke, but the wife knew better and chased him through the village beating him with a stick. All the young women laughed at him and knew him for the fool he was."

"What man does not think he can satisfy any woman?" said Pules, and with this they moved on to discuss, faults and attributes of their husbands, including their sexual prowess.

They shared a few lewd stories, some about other women and men they knew. As they talked, and laughed Numees noticed Ben and Henri standing next to one of the Red River carts.

"Kat, tell us about your big American. Is he like the Métis men or maybe the English?" Numees asked. Kat looked at the woman, surprised by the question and unsure what to say. Her glance then went to Pules who sat smiling at her.

"You can tell us the truth, Little Sister," said Pules, *"It is obvious that you and Ben are not as man and wife."* Her smile remained and she placed a hand on Kat's arm.

"I do not know what you mean. We have only refrained from sex until he has recovered from his injuries." Kat lied poorly, and the other women laughed.

"It is his shoulder that is injured not his man part!" Pules giggled.

"And, if it is as big as he is tall I would not let any injury keep me from riding him like a wild horse!" Numees laughed so hard that tears formed in her eyes.

Kat found herself trapped. She looked back and forth between the two women and had no way of explaining what her situation was.

"It is plain that the two of you have feelings for each other. He looks at you as if you were the moon and the stars, and you..." Pules was stopped by Kat.

261

"I have no feelings for him." She surprised herself. *"He means nothing to me."*

"You may say this, but I see into your heart. You tell yourself you do not have feeling for him but I have seen you smile when he is not looking at you."

"You have lived among us, will you not tell us the truth?" asked Numess.

"It is true, I have not been completely honest with you," Kat said, and then she began to tell the two women the truth. She finished by saying, *"I am sorry. At first I said nothing because I did not trust you, then when I had come to know you I was afraid it was too late to tell you everything. Now I realize that our presence here in this camp may put you all in danger. I have killed the factor of Fort Maskwa and they will send someone to punish me. They will also punish anyone who has helped me."*

"Let us decide whether you are to stay or go," said Pules.

"Yes, we will decide this at another time. We are a free people and we do not have to fear the British," said Numess.

The subject was dropped and the conversation turned back to other people in the small camp. As Numess and Pules chattered, Kat looked across the open area between the lodges and watched Ben as he talked to Henri. She thought how shabby he looked. Turning back to Pules, she asked, *"Do you believe someone in camp might have deer skins that I can trade for? He needs new clothing.,"* She motioned toward Ben.

"I am sure there are. And, yes, he is in need of clothing, a new shirt, some leggings and a good pair of moccasins."

Kat looked back at Ben and she felt a warm flush of blood rise to her cheeks, and this time rather than chastise herself, she only held back a smile.

Ben too was feeling the effects of confinement in

the buffalo hide lodge of Henri and Pules. He had also noticed that the boy Jacques had formed a crush on Kat. In a strange way, Ben found empathy in the boy's feelings and solace that he was not alone in having his advances rebuffed. Ben's feelings for her had remained the same. He was still in awe of her, but no longer self-conscious and had accepted that she would remain cold to him. He thought she might feel trapped by the circumstances of their flight from Fort Maskwa.

While they were still confined in the lodge, they had spoken to each other in English, hoping no one else would understand their conversation. Kat had told Ben that she had killed Ranald but had not gone into detail, and he had not asked her too. He did ask why she had come to aid him, and for this she had no answer.

Ben apologized for having been the catalyst for her final confrontation with Ranald, and he promised he would attempt to see her to some place of safety. Now in the Métis village, Ben thought she might have found that safe haven. Then he reminded himself that it was she that had saved him and brought him to safety, not the other way around.

Kat did her best to convince Ben that he had not been the cause of what had happened, but that he had only offered her the small push she needed to attain the freedom she had been seeking for some time. They both agreed that as soon as spring came, they would go their separate ways; Ben back to Fort Raymond and Kat to travel with the Métis. This seemed to be the logical thing for them, but neither of them had considered Kat's feelings for Ben would change.

As Ben recuperated, the time he spent with Henri improved his knowledge about the upper Missouri territory and the Métis people themselves. Though not a true tribe or nation of people in their inception, they had become a culture all to themselves. The majority of the families in the winter camp traced their lineage back to the mixture of French voyagers and either Plains Cree or Ojibway women. Henri was proud to consider himself not only Métis, but what was called a "Hivernant," a term derived from the French word for winter, and referring to those "rovers" who wintered away from the permanent settlements to hunt buffalo on the plains.

Ben was a quick study and found that he had a knack for learning languages. He had picked up some French of the river men and the engagees that he had met, but that learning was intermittent. Here, with little else to do, he found Mitchif, the language of the Metis Creole, came to him easily with the help of Henri and Pules. He also learned what bit of Blackfoot that Henri knew and a bit of Dakota.

Henri also schooled Ben on these other people of the upper Missouri country. For his part, Henri associated with the Cree and Ojibway, and though the North West and the Hudson Bay Companies courted the favor of the Blackfeet, Henri stayed away from them as much as possible. Henri also passed on his knowledge of trapping beaver, and offered Ben half-a-dozen traps with chains, each weighing five pounds. Most of what Henri had to tell Ben about trapping beaver enforced what he had already learned from Silas Scott, and Ben began to look at Henri in somewhat the same vein as Silas. Their mannerisms were similar in respects to how they dealt with people, and Ben even noted Henri had a habit, like Silas, of picking up a hot coal with bare fingers to light his pipe.

Two of the beaver traps were in need of repair and Ben, speaking in a mixture of English and Mitchif, remarked to Henri, *"If there was an anvil and some coal in the camp, I could fix these easily."*

"You know how to work the metal?" Henri asked.

"Yes, I was an apprentice to my uncle in a wagon shop in Pittsburgh," Ben said with modest pride.

"We have no anvil, nor coal, but we can find a smooth, flat rock and we can make charcoal. Would charcoal make the heat you need?"

"It depends on the wood we use, charcoal takes the same amount of air as coal, but it is dirty, a lot of fly ash, lots of sparks and popping. Not as much working heat as coal, but it would work. Do you have any hard wood?"

"There is a broken axle on one of the carts that is made of maple." Henri beamed.

"That will work just fine. Let's go look at that axel and start a fire." Ben was happy knowing that good charcoal could be produced.

They walked over to one of the carts, and though he had been in the camp for over two months, it was the first time Ben had a chance to examine one of the two wheeled carts up close. His eye quickly scanned the vehicle and as a builder of wagons he was impressed by its construction. The cart had a box measuring a little over six feet in length, half that in height and width. Its axle was over six feet long, its wheels two feet in diameter. The two shafts attached to the box were each twelve feet long, running from the box to the where the horse was attached. The entire cart was assembled with not a single piece of metal, being constructed with wooden pieces fashioned together by sinew, rope and rawhide thongs, called shaganappi by the Métis. Their hubs were usually made from elm, wheel rims from ash or oak, and the axle from maple. Even the nails on the carts were wooden.

Of special interest to Ben were the four foot tall wheels. These large, spoked wheels were dished inward to provide greater stability and handling similar to those of large freight wagons Ben had worked on in his uncle's shop. In lieu of an iron tire, the Métis had again used rawhide secured with shaganappi, wrapping it around the wheels to bind the separate pieces together and create a hard tire.

Henri told Ben that if a cart broke down, all that was needed for their repair was a stand of trees and the few hand tools the Métis carried: an axe, a saw, a screw auger, and a draw knife. He also said that, one cart pulled by a single horse could carry as much as four pack animals, and cover up to forty miles in a single day if need be.

This seemed like an exaggeration to Ben, but he would give his host the benefit of the doubt. The carts made a terrible squealing noise when they moved because their wooden axles and wheels could not be effectively lubricated. Ben also noticed that one loose wheel had been tightened around the axel by wrapping raw hide around the end of the axle. When dried, it became hard as the wood and would last until a new axel or wheel hub could be made.

Their first task was to build a fire and break the old axle into smaller pieces. They constructed a form of kiln around and over the fire with rocks and earth. Once this fire was going strong, they added the pieces of maple wood. After the hard wood caught fire, they closed up their makeshift kiln, leaving a small hole for smoke to escape. The smoke emitted was white and they monitored it for the next four hours until the smoke turned bluish. This meant the initial burn was complete and the coal was now burning. At this point, they sealed up the hole and cut off air to the burning wood. They now had to wait until the next day and collect the charcoal left from this process.

The work producing the charcoal felt good to Ben. His ribs were healed, and he had been lucky the gunshot wound to his shoulder had been at low impact, and missed the main artery that fed blood to his arm. His shoulder was stiff though, having not had the exercise needed to regain full movement. This he intended to remedy by extending the arm and bending the joints as much as possible, over and over.

He knew that it would be a slow and laborious process.

While the charcoal was curing, Ben and Henri scoured the camp to collect the tools and what little iron was available to do the repairs on the traps. As was natural, their search also brought out the needs of others in the camp to have repairs made for various items. The final task was to construct some type of bellows. This was accomplished by creating a sack from a complete deer hide, tanned and sewn up to in the form of a sack.

On the following day, Ben could hardly wait to inspect the charcoal and was happily surprised to see large chunks that he could use in his makeshift forge. With Jacques' and Henri's help at the bellows, Ben set to work. He found that charcoal took the same amount of air as coal to heat, and though the process created somewhat less amount of working heat, it was sufficient for the purpose intended. Ben repaired his traps, and then turned his attention to work for others who had gathered in the cool morning air to observe his skills as a blacksmith. At first, Ben's shoulder ached from the movement, but the joy he was receiving by working the metal made the pain worthwhile. His pleasure was evident by the smile on his face as he worked.

Jacques was constantly at Ben's side, watching every move he made and fascinated by the way Ben used the heat to turn the metal dark red and then orange and finally bright yellow. With each blow of the hammer and the flying of sparks, the boy's eyes lit up.

"Can you teach me to do this?" Jacques asked.

"With time, I could teach you what I know, but I am not a real master like my uncle. Maybe someday you can meet him and he will teach you!"

"I would like that very much!"

Kat sat outside the lodge busy cutting fabric, which once sewn together would be a new shirt for

Ben. Pules had given Kat three yards of good quality cotton cloth made in India that she had been saving for her husband, but Henri did not need a shirt as badly as Ben. Pules had also given Kat four pewter buttons, one for each cuff and two for the neck opening.

Taught by her mother to sew, Kat had made many shirts over the years, mostly for Ranald. But since those she had made for her father, this was the first that she sewed with pleasure. She took greater care as to the tightness of the stitches and kept them straight. Once she was finished, she would turn her attention to a new pair of britches for Ben. Though most Métis men wore leggings and a breechclout, she had the skill to replace Ben's worn out wool pants with the same style in buckskin. On the legs of these new trousers she would leave just a hint of fringe an inch or two long.

Pules watched Kat as her fingers nimbly passed the needle and thread through the material. She commented on Kat's skill, *"You are not only accomplished but quick at sewing."*

"It has always been one of the things I have been good at. If I would have been allowed, I might have made a living at it, but it was not to be."

"You were treated badly?" Pules was carful with her question and would have understood if Kat did not answer.

"You can say that." Kat stopped her work on the shirt and looked up at Pules. Slowly, she confided in the older woman, telling her the complete story of her past. She did not go into detail concerning John Ranald's mistreatment, but left no doubt that he had abused her many times. Is was after hearing this that Pules understood why Kat was so reluctant to be close to Ben, but as was her nature Pules asked another question.

"What of Ben? Do you think you can become close

to him?"

Kat turned her gaze back to where Ben worked at the forge. *"Yes, but I fear the touch of his hand. What if I feel repulsed, or worse yet, what if I feel nothing?"*

"Ahh. Perhaps that is the chance you have to take. I do not think any woman should have to go without the gentle touch of a man's hand, and looking at that young man, I do not think he would ever harm you."

"Maybe not."

Ben, unaware that he was the topic of the conversation between Kat and Pules, glanced over and noticed Kat looking in his direction. Without thought, he smiled at her, and this brought a blush to her face that even her dark olive complexion could not hide. Her eyes went down to the work in her lap and she suppressed a smile of her own.

"He is not bad to look at, but would be better looking if he were to shave the down off his chin," Kat said, referring to the sparse growth of blond hair on Ben's cheeks and jaw, and then she let a smile slip out.

The sun and the warm wind had raised the spirits of the entire camp and seemed to offer hope of the spring to come. That mood was changed though with the appearance of a single man on horseback, who seemed to appear out of nowhere. To everyone except Kat, he was a stranger. She recognized Walks Long as soon as he rode between the lodges.

The Blackfoot rode to the center of the small camp and sat motionless on his horse, his attention on the group of men around the make-shift forge. Henri walked over to him, holding up his open right hand, palm out in a greeting.

"Greetings," Henri said in Blackfoot. *"Welcome to our village. Come sit and smoke with us."* There was no reply to the offer. Walks Long only sat looking at Ben. The Indian then slid from the horse and passing Henri walked over to where Ben stood, a hammer held

269

tightly in his grip anticipating trouble. It was the same Blackfoot warrior that had peered into his eyes when he was a captive on the Judith. When the Indian was close enough for Ben to see his face clearly Ben recognized him.

"It would appear that Sun Hair has recovered from his injuries," Walks Long commented to the specter of Calf Standing who had now taken to clinging on Walks' back, his skeletal arms wrapped around the neck of his friend.

"Sun Hair?" questioned Henri believing the Indian spoke to him.

"Is he still an American or is he now a Métis?" asked Walks.

"What does it matter, kill him and let us feed," hissed Calf into Walks' ear.

"This man is a guest in my lodge," Henri said. *"As are you, if you wish."* For the first time it seemed that Walks Long noted Henri's presence. He spoke directly to him.

"I will not stay here," Walks went back to his horse, mounted and then rode out of the camp. Kat and Pules had come close to the men standing with Ben and Henri, and they too watched as the Blackfoot rode away.

"What was that all about?" asked Pules.

"I have no idea, but it seems that he knows Ben," said Henri. *"You know that man?"* he asked Ben.

"Yes, he was one of the Blackfeet that took me and my friends prisoner over on the Judith."

"He is the one that I told you about Ben, called Walks Long," Kat interjected. *"He came to us when we were on our way here. I think he is touched with an evil spirit."* She saw no reason to relate that Walks Long had said he intended to take Ben's scalp and eat his heart, thought she did add, *"He told me that there was no honor in killing Ben when he could not fight back"* This sent a slight chill up Ben's back, but also

made him determined to fully recover his strength. If this Indian wanted his hair, Ben figured it would only be right to make him work for it.

"Well, my hairs not hanging on his belt yet, and if I have anything to say about it, it will be the other way around." Ben let a half smile cross his lips and this eased his own tension and that of those around him. Kat, seeing this change in his demeanor, was impressed by the resolve Ben showed and her feelings for him grew a bit more.

By the late afternoon, Ben had finished his work at the forge, and with Henri and Jacques he went to clean his hands and face in a pan of hot water that Pules had prepared for them. Ben had removed his shirt to wash and the bullet wound to his shoulder looked as if it were almost healed and had begun to scar over. Ben ran his fingers across the wound thinking how easy it would have been for the lead ball to have hit him a few inches over and entered his heart. Again, he was grateful that Dob was such a poor shot, and that the load of powder used had also been poor. As Ben was drying his face, Kat placed a hand on his shoulder and he turned to her.

"I have something for you," she said, and held out the new shirt. Ben took it and held it out in front of him to examine it. He was impressed and touched.

"I feel as if I need a proper bath before I put on something as fine as this. He smiled at her, and for the first time she smiled back.

Not wanting to completely surrender her composure she remarked, "The least you could do would be to shave." She then walked away to help Pules prepare the evening meal.

With the setting of the sun, the temperature quickly dropped and the warm air surrendered to the clear night sky. Pules and Kat had the evening meal ready when Henri and Jacques entered the lodge. Both had smiles brimming wide, evident of some secret they were holding back. Puzzled, both Pules and Kat looked at them and then the flap of the lodge door opened and Ben entered. He wore the new shirt that Kat had made him and his face was clean shaven, though evidence of his lack of practice with a razor was obvious.

"*My, you do look handsome,*" Pules remarked.

"*Thank you,*" Ben said. He looked over at Kat, and after the first flush of embarrassment passed he move to sit next to her. They then shared the evening's meal and after eating they decided to pass the time playing a game called Musinaykahwhan, or "Playing the Leader." Henri brought out a small board with an etched cross containing thirty-three small holes. There were little green-painted pegs carved in the shape of men, one larger than the rest, that were inserted into holes in a square board. The game pitted the oke-mow, or "Leader" against the other player's thirteen little pegs. The players moved the pegs following the lines of the board. The little pegs progress steadily forward to surround the oke-mow, while the oke-mow endeavored to escape and capture any unprotected little pegs.

They took turns at the game with Henri and Jacques the first to play, and after a bit everyone was enthused about the strategies both father and son used to beat one another. Jacques finally defeated his father, capturing his oke-mow, and everyone cheered. For the first time, Ben saw Kat laugh and he felt as if a weight had been lifted, that the wall she had built between herself and everyone had finally broken down.

When it was time for bed, Kat and Ben took their normal place at the side of the lodge, sharing the wool blankets. They settled in for the night, Ben on his back with Kat between him and the lodge wall. Rather than lay with her back to him as usual, she faced him and as their eyes met in the dim light she wished him goodnight.

"Goodnight," Ben replied, and for a brief moment Ben considered leaning over to kiss her. But he held back, not wanting to chance losing what little ground he had gained this day.

Kat rose up on one elbow and surprised Ben again. She leaned in and kissed him on the cheek, then rolled over and snuggled her back up against him.

SAM J. PISCIOTTA

CHAPTER 16
SPRING

Bear Head was unhappy with the way the council of headmen had ended. The majority of the men who had assembled in the lodge of the band's most respected leader, Steals Crow Horses, agreed that it was time to send out small groups to scout for buffalo. The grip of winter had eased and the ice on the rivers had begun to break up and float downstream. Though the Moon of Empty Bellies had passed, the store of dried meat in the winter camp of twenty lodges was low. The majority of the men agreed it would be prudent to bring in fresh meat as soon as possible. Everyone was restless and anticipating the greening of the grass and the return of the big buffalo herds from the southern plains.

Of a different opinion, was a small group lead by Broken Horn who wanted to go in search of the invaders to the land of the Blackfeet, the Americans. He proposed taking at least a dozen of the young warriors in journey west away from the Missouri, or as they called it, the Big Muddy River to the Yellowstone deep into Crow territory. Many of the young men were excited about such a venture seeing a chance to achieve war honors and possibly add horses to their herds. Another incentive was the chance to ride with Broken Horn and of course Walks Long. Walks Long said little in council, or for that matter spoke to anyone at all except to what many thought was a ghost. The young men knew that he was touched by that sprit and if there were enemies to be found, Walks Long would be guided by it and find them.

Four groups left the Blackfoot camp near Fort Muskwa headed in different directions three out towards the buffalo range to the east, the last led by Broken Horn went south into Crow country. Though Walks Long rode along with this last group, he paid little attention to any of its members. In his mind were thoughts about the white man, Sun Hair. He spoke to Calf Standing of his plan to go back to where the Métis camp was and seek out this man, kill him and eat his heart.

"I do not understand why you did not kill Sun Hair when we last saw him!" Calf Standing scolded Walks, as he clung to the warriors back.

"You have bothered me all winter long. You are nothing but dried flesh and bones, why does your tongue still wag like the tail of a cur dog?" Walks' words were filled with hatred for the one he had once called friend and brother.

"It is your fault that I do not rest, it was you that ran from the Long Knives and let them plunge their knife into my heart!" hissed Calf.

"It was your own greed for the Long Knife's guns and horses that got you killed."

"AHHHHHEEEEEEE!" The high-pitched scream passed from the lipless mouth of Calf Standing, piercing the air and causing Walks to lean forward and cover his ears in pain.

"I WILL NOT let you rest until you have fed me the heart of every Long Knife in our country!" Calf tossed his head about, his dried skin and neck bones barely holding the emaciated skull to his shoulders. As his weight swung back and forth it pulled Walks with it, almost toppling him from his saddle. Walks flung an arm back in an attempt to rid himself of the unwanted specter, but Calf dug his boney fingers into Walks and held fast.

The entire scene of Walks Long, flaying about with his arms at the empty air around him, was witnessed by the other members of the party, and those closest to Walks either held back or sped up to place distance between the touched warrior and themselves. Two of the youngest stopped, turned their horses around and headed back to the village, one saying to the other, *"No good can come from a war party that has this man in it. If we go with him we will all be killed!"*

No one seemed to take much notice of the two young men deserting the war party. If they had, they would not have thought badly of them, it was a matter of choice not an act of being cowardly. Those who remained followed the two war chiefs with little trepidation, knowing both men were fierce in battle and that they always came back with war honors.

The patience and trust the warriors had in their leaders was rewarded within three days travel from their camp on the Big Muddy River. A scout who had ridden out ahead of the main party of two dozen Blackfeet came back with the news that he had spotted a camp of the American trappers along a tributary of the Judith. The war party sped up and when close to the camp, they dismounted and fanned out to approach the camp in a broad front. Broken Horn instructed them to wait until they heard the first gun shoot, and then they were to rush in and kill the whites.

As they came within a hundred yards of the camp, one of the warriors spied two of the white men making for the camp. The trappers did not see the Blackfeet and seemed only on intent of heading in the same direction as the war party. Both trappers carried several skins of *ksisk-staki,* the beaver, as well as their firearms and traps. With little thought, a young warrior brought up his bow, aimed at the back of one of the trappers and let loose an arrow.

*

Silas Scott pulled the wool blanket tighter around his

shoulders to ward off the mornings chill and hopefully catch a few hours of sleep. He had spent the predawn hours checking his traps and resetting those which had either been tripped or had held a beaver. Of the dozen traps he had in his "set", ten had offered up the bounty of the fur rich streams. He was satisfied with the fact that he was beginning to help reap the riches that were held by the streams and rivers of the Stoney Mountains. Now, laying snug in his blanket cocoon, he was as close to content as he had been in years.

Manuel Lisa had not held it against Silas for abandoning the pirogue and its valuable cargo on the Grand River. Lisa was headed back down the Missouri to St. Louis with the furs that had been brought in from the fall hunt, and those traded to him by the friendly Crow Indians. Along with Lisa was Antoine Martin, who had recovered from his gunshot wound over the winter, and knew where the pirogue and its cargo had been hidden. With luck, the little flatboat and the couched goods would be found safe and intact.

After returning to Fort Raymond, Silas had informed Lisa of the NWC post, and the presence of the Blackfoot village on the upper Missouri. When he explained to his superior about the debt Ranald intended to collect for ransoming Silas and the others, Lisa dismissed the idea stating that the Scotsman could "va t'faire enculer chez les Grecs!"

Silas' understanding of the French language left no doubt that Lisa had no intention of honoring the agreement made with the NWC's factor. Especially a contract he considered signed under duress.

The past two weeks had put any thoughts of Ranald and the NWC in the back of Silas' mind, and for now he only concentrated on keeping his men safe while trapping. The tried and safe method was to set the traps either in the predawn or late evening hours, as the beaver were more active during the night time and any hostile Indians were active during the day. The trappers were also sent out in pairs, one could work while the other kept watch for any sign of danger, and not just that of Indian attack.

Not three days past; Estienne Lapin and a man named William Grace had just finished pulling their traps in preparation to move to another stream when they were attacked by one of the Grizzly bears that inhabited the area. The bear, fresh out of hibernation, was hungry and the smell of the fresh beaver carcasses had attracted its attention. The bear, startled as much as the men, hesitated only long enough to consider the trappers a threat, but one that it could deal with, and it charged them. Both Lapin and Grace fired their rifles, and then their pistols before the animal fell not a dozen paces away. As quickly as possible both men reloaded their guns and waited for any sign of movement from the bear.

They had been lucky, and the bear lay dead from the few shots that had hit it. Other men had not been so lucky. George Drouillard had told Lisa's men many stories about encounters with the "white" bears. On one occasion, he and Captain Clark had fired ten rounds into a grizzly before killing it and five of those had hit the bear in the lungs. They were a large and terrifying animal to encounter and the two men had escaped harm by luck only.

Luck was the one thing that the trappers could not count on. Every few days the trappers would try to make it back to the main camp, and from there, they would decide if the area had been trapped out and discuss moving on to another site. Starting with the previous day, everyone had returned except for Lapin and Grace, but there was no sense in worrying for another day or so. They might have run onto a spot rich in beaver and would be in as soon as they had trapped it out.

It seemed that Silas had just drifted off into a

peaceful, dreamless sleep when there was a shout of alarm bring the camp awake.

"Injuns!" Came the cry, and before Silas could open his eyes there was the sound of gunfire and war cries coming from the surrounding trees.

Lapin and Grace ran into the camp and took cover with the other trappers who were already returning fire. Grace had an arrow protruding from his back, but like his fellows he stood his ground and calmly fired his rifle and then reloaded to fire again. Silas, up from his blankets, had taken cover behind a fallen tree and he too took aim and fired when a target offered itself. Lapin dove in beside him breathless.

"The damn Blackfoots! They shot Willie in the back," he said, while reloading his rifle. Then he popped up to shot in the direction of the Indians.

"You get a look at how many there are?" Silas asked.

"I was busy running away from *de salauds*. It is like the gates of Hell they have been opened, No?"

"Well, let's send them back," Silas said taking aim and firing once more.

Three of the Blackfeet fell dead and four more were wounded in the charge on the trapper's camp. Even with superior numbers, their loss of surprise had also lost them their advantage. It was not long before they decided to retreat, and retrieving the dead and wounded, they fell back. The trappers, benefiting from this, followed them and killed one more of the attackers. After some distance the trappers were assured the Blackfeet would not return.

As the Blackfeet headed off to lick their wounds, Walks Long held back. When he was sure that the white men had returned to their camp he made his way back to the scene of the battle, cautiously working his way to a point behind the trapper's camp. From a concealed spot, he watched as they took stock of their losses; two men had minor wounds, and Will

Grace had the arrow lodged in his back. Walks Long watched as the wounded were tended to and the others broke camp and packed in anticipation to move.

He followed the trappers as they made their way back toward the Judith River and on to another set of small streams. They kept a sharp lookout to their rear, with two of them lagging behind to watch and wait for a while. When they were sure the Blackfeet were not following, they rode hard to catch up to the main group. They traveled through the day until well after dark and then they made a cold camp, with no fire.

Walks Long waited in the darkness, noting that night guards were set to watch the horses and they changed every two hours. As he watched, his constant companion, Calf Standing, still clinging to his back badgered him.

"I believed you were a brave warrior," he chided. *"I was made to think that you would kill all the Long Knives in the camp and feed me!"* Walks Long did not reply, he only sat and watched the dark camp. *"Did you not hear me?"* Calf Standing screamed at Walks Long. With the agility and the speed of a timber rattler, Walks Long swung around, and in his mind dislodged the apparition then reached out to take it by the neck. He could feel the dry skin crack under the pressure of his grip. He could feel the snap of vertebrae he believed he held between his fingers, and for the first time in years he smiled. The emaciated face he held before him was grotesque, but showed a look of fear.

"AHHHHHEEEEEEE!" Calf Standing shrieked, the sound as always sending a driving pain into Walks' head. But this time he did not flinch, he shook the form in front of him scattering bones and rawhide-like skin in all directions. If there had been anyone to witness the event they would have seen the Blackfoot

shaking his clenched hands in the empty air in front of him. No sound would have broken the nights calm, and no scream would have alarmed the white trappers not fifty yards away. Walks Long was filled with rage, but he composed himself and turned his attention back to the trapper's camp.

To Walks' ears the night was now calm. Slowly though, there was a sound of movement in the grass and without looking Walks Long knew that the scattered pieces of Calf Standing were finding their way back to each other, and shortly Walks Long felt the cold boney hands pulling at his buckskin war shirt and on to his shoulders where the voice came again.

"You know you cannot be rid of me. I am to be with you until the day your hair hangs in the lodge of some Crow or on the belt of one of these Long Knives." And then he laughed, the long dry sound passing between his bared teeth.

Walks Long was usually patient but he was irritated that he had been distracted by the confrontation with Calf. Once he ignored the reanimated Calf Standing, he calmed down and concentrated on the camp, he was rewarded by his patience. A lone figure rose from his blankets and moved away from the group, in the opposite direction of the picketed horses and the night guard.

Walks moved in closer to the man and studied him as the man undid his pants and began to urinate. Walks Long calmly walked up behind the man, and when within reach he swung a stone war club, striking the man in the side of the head. He did not put his entire strength into the blow, as he wanted the man alive.

With the coming of the dawn, the camp began to stir to life. The last horse guard came in and the group gathered to discuss whether they should stay in this area or attempt to put further distance between them and the Blackfeet. It was not long before they noticed that one of their numbers was missing.

"Where is Tate?" Silas asked.

"He's probably taking a shit or something," replied one of the men. Silas walked over to Tate's bed and placing a hand between the blankets discovered that the bed was long cold.

"He's been gone awhile," said Silas. "Let's pack up camp while a few of us circle out and see if you can find him." Silas saddled his horse, mounted it and circling out from the camp site he made a slow search for the missing man. His first discovery was a small beaded tobacco pouch that he knew belonged to Tate. This he found on the ground close to camp, and near it a few drops of blood. The young grass, and the sparse snow which still remained on the ground, showed signs that something had been dragged in a direction away from the camp. Silas dismounted his horse and followed the drag marks on foot. Every so often there would be more blood, not a large amount, but enough to show brightly against the whiteness of snow. Here and there Silas also spotted footprints, moccasin-clad foot prints, but not the type worn by the trappers. Those men, who had traded with the Crow at Fort Raymond, wore the style of that tribe, an almost crescent shape with a curve on both the instep and the outside. These tracks had a straighter instep, like those worn by the Blackfeet, and it was obvious that the wearer was not trying to hide his tracks.

After following the footprints and the drag marks for almost one hundred yards, Silas came upon a small grove of young lodge pole pine. There he spotted what appeared to be Tate sitting with his back against one of the trees. Silas pulled his Henry rifle from its buckskin sheath, pulled back on the hammer and checked the priming in the pan under the frizzen. Snapping the frizzen closed, he moved forward carefully, his rifle ready in his hands.

As he neared Tate, he could see that the man's head rested on his chest, the crown of his head was stained with blood where his scalp had been removed and blood covered his chest and belly. Silas moved cautiously over to the body and found that Tate's chest had been cut open leaving a gaping hole. Silas took an involuntary step back not being able to suppress the shock of the site in front of him.

His next reaction was to look around as if expecting the perpetrator of this heinous act to step out from the trees and confront him. His senses were tuned to the slightest sound, smell or sight that may announce this presence, but the only sound was the slight breeze rustling through the pines. With caution, Silas withdrew the knife from his belt and cut Tate loose from the tree. He lifted the body, placing it on his horse across the saddle, and slowly walked back to camp taking the dead man back to his comrades.

When he entered the camp, everyone was still packing up to move on, but all preparations halted when they saw Tate's body.

"Mon dieu!" exclaimed Lapin, "They have cut out his heart!"

"Shit, that happen 'an we didn't even hear nothin'!" one of the trappers said.

"You think there are more of them out there?" another man asked.

"Not sure," replied Silas. "My guess is there is always something out there. Let's get Tate buried and then we'll move on."

They dug a grave for Tate and after laying the blanket wrapped body in the hole they covered it with soil and piled a thick layer of stones on it to prevent wolves from digging him up.

When they had finished Silas stood over the grave and spoke the words over Tate's grave that he had uttered over Bernard Laurent's on the Grand River,

"Requiem aeternam dona ei, Domine." He turned away from the cairn of rocks and mounted his horse. As the small brigade of men rode away, Silas wondered how many more times he would utter those words.

*

Attracted by the scent of another beaver, the large male swam toward the place where it had made several trips in and out of the water. As he approached this at the water's edge, he hesitated, his keen hearing compensating for his poor eyesight, he hunted for the interloper into his territory. In searching for the location of the challenger to his supremacy over the beaver pond, he edged forward placing his foot down in order to raise his head for a better sniff of the small stick that had been dipped in castor and stuck in the ground. Before his foot could settle on the muddy bank, it hit the square pan of the beaver trap releasing the "dog" that held the springs of the trap open. Like a flash of lightning, the two powerful springs mounted at the hinges snapped shut, the jaws of the trap ensnaring his leg. In panic, the beaver's instincts took over and he headed for deep water, dragging the trap and its attached chain. The opposite end of the chain was securely fastened to the stream bottom by means of a stout stake, driven into the stream's bed. When the beaver reached the end of the chain and could go no further he found himself weighted down by the five pound trap and the length of steel chain. Unable to reach the surface with the added weight the beaver soon drowned.

It was in this way that Ben found his third catch of the morning. He had waded up stream to where he had set his trap and found the trap missing from its place near the bank. He moved out into the deeper water where the stake was driven and pulling on the chain retrieved his trap and the prime beaver it held. He pulled the animal out of the water and held it up for Kat to see and was rewarded with a smile from her.

Downstream, not thirty yards away, Kat had kept watch as Ben checked his traps. In her arms was Ben's rifle, and within her reach a 20 gauge Northwest Trade Gun and one of the English Tower pistols. Her job in this new partnership was to stand guard and warn Ben of any trouble, be it man or beast. She had proved to be a good shot and Ben felt secure with her sharp eyes scanning their surroundings. Ben carried the remaining Tower pistol, that had belonged to Ranald, tucked into his belt. If trouble arose he would make for the shore as fast as possible, but he relied on Kat for his safety in the water.

He made his way to the bank again downstream and threw the beaver carcass onto the ground. He then made his way back and reset the foothold trap in the shallow water at the edge of the stream in a spot where the beaver path met the water. He reshaped the shelf where the trap was to set, about eight inches below the surface, and he took care to place the trap off center wanting the beaver to trigger the trap by stepping on it. If he had set in in the center, there was a chance the beaver would simply walk over the trap. Lastly, he dipped a small green branch into the bait bottle he carried around his neck. The wooden container held the pulverized castor gland of a beaver and this scent would lure another unfortunate beaver to the set.

Ben and Kat had done well over the past month, and had trapped, skinned and stretched almost seventy pounds of the furry back notes. Ben was ecstatic over his success this first time trapping, and Kat was proud of his abilities and proficiency at the task. Along with the mutual respect, their relationship had grown into a comfortable coexistence. Both had deep feelings for the other, even romantic inclinations, but neither had pursued those feelings.

Kat was still getting used to the freedom of not

having to submit to the physical demands of a man, and though Ben was not at all like Ranald, she could not yet bring herself to be intimate with him. For her, even the thought of a man's arms around her was still unsettling. Compounding these feelings, new thoughts crept in and these bothered her. When she watched Ben work she found that it pleased her. When Ben was not in sight thoughts of him came to her and she would get a warm rush through her body. At times, it amounted to a hunger for his presence and this unnerved her. For a short time after these feelings occurred, she would be cold to him. This puzzled Ben and he wondered what he had done to displease her. In a day or two she would be back to her normal self and he would pass it off as his own lack of knowledge considering women.

Ben had become practiced at hiding his emotions, maintaining a good-natured attitude he was able to hide the growing admiration he had for Kat. He too felt an ach in his chest when he thought about her, but more so he felt a longing for her, for the touch of her skin. Of everything, this was the most frustrating for him. His previous experience had not prepared him for a woman like Kat, so he managed to go day-to-day both happy and miserable in her company.

For Ben and Kat, the days passed with this unspoken portion of their relationship just below the surface. Like the beaver traps Ben placed in the streams, it was only a matter of time when one or both of them would place a foot on the trap's pan and the jaws would snap shut. This would come about without warning, and in a manner neither of them expected.

They had reached the point when they must decide where to take the furs they had collected. Ben proposed Fort Raymond, due to the fact that he felt honor bound as an engagee to Manual Lisa, he felt obligated to return with his catch and Kat agreed to go with him. They had stretched, fleshed and dried the beaver hides, bundling them into tight of packs. They were prepared to leave the area of the Musselshell River, and cross over to the Yellowstone.

It was late in the day and Kat suggested they wait until the following dawn to break camp. The day was warm and Kat decided that she would like to take the opportunity to bath, and she had no idea when the next opportunity would come about. Ben too decided that the idea was good, but with the knowledge there may be danger for either one of them alone, he suggested that they take turns while the other stood close by rifle in hand.

Choosing a beaver pond that was in a somewhat concealed area, Ben went first, removing his clothing and wading out in the water. He did his best to clean himself using a soap Kat made from yucca root. With his bath finished, Ben took the time to shave, knowing that it would please Kat, and when she inspected the end results she gave him a slight smile in reward.

Kat bent down and placed a hand in the water to test its temperature. She first dropped a blanket to the ground and sat to remove her moccasins and leggings. She then rose and removed her buckskin dress, dropped it on the blanket, lastly at the water's edge she placed the Tower pistol.

Ben listened to the sound of each move she made, visions of what was taking place passing through his head and his heart beat a bit faster. Kat slowly stepped into the frigid water and goosebumps ran up her legs and engulfed her entire body. An involuntary cry escaped her lips and Ben turned to look in alarm.

Her back was to him, and though he tried to look away he was mesmerized, drawn by her beauty to stand watching as she slowly moved deeper into the water. It was only when she completely submerged herself that he did look away, a bit ashamed of himself, but more so excited. He wondered how much longer he could go on acting as if he didn't long for her. He felt he had to tell her how he felt. If she did not feel the same way, Ben decided they would have to part ways after reaching Fort Raymond.

Lost in his thoughts, he was surprised by the touch of a hand on his shoulder and he spun around to find Kat standing behind him, his green blanket wrapped around her. She stepped closer and stretching up on her tiptoes, she surprised him by kissing him on the mouth. She then turned without saying a word, walked back and retrieved her belongings then went to their camp.

Ben stood for a brief moment and then followed her through the brush to the campsite. There he found her sitting on their bedding under the arbor that sheltered them during the hours they slept. Ben laid his rifle and shooting bag aside and knelt next to Kat. They looked deeply into each other's eyes, the question of what would happen next reflected in their gaze.

The feelings Ben had held back the past months welled up and he was compelled to take a chance and reached out a hand, caressing her face.

Closing her eyes, Kat turned her head in his hand and kissed his open palm, and a slight shiver ran through Ben. She leaned forward and again kissed him on the mouth, a bit longer this time but just as tender. Ben took her in his arms and kissed her back. The kiss was at first as tender as hers but became more passionate, releasing the hunger that they both felt. Kat dropped the blanket exposing her bare flesh, and she shivered from the cold air and the excitement held inside her.

They spent the rest of the afternoon on the green blanket under the arbor, nestled in the comfort of each other. For them both, it was as if there had been no one else in their past; they experienced something new and the excitement and passion over whelmed them.

To remain at the campsite for a few days was tempting for both Ben and Kat. They didn't want to lose the feeling of their newly shown love for each other, but it was not safe to tarry in one place for too long. The chance of being found by either the Blackfeet or even the NWC men was too great. Thus, Ben and Kat packed up and moved down the Musselshell River eventually finding the place where the Blackfeet had jumped and killed the trappers from Fort Raymond last fall. From this location, Ben knew his way back to the fort, not three days away.

They spoke for the first time about the past few months and the debt they owed Henri Thibault and his wife, Pules. When parting from the Métis camp, Ben had expressed his distress at not being able to pay Henri back for the hospitality that he had offered, let alone for the three horses and provisions that had been given to Kat and himself.

"Do not worry about being in debt to this old man, in my youth I drank and pissed off a great deal more then what I offer you and that beautiful one." Henri paused and then thinking of a way to be repaid he said, *"I will ask something of you. Name your first son after me and tell him about me so that you will never forget me."*

"I will do that my friend. Though I do not know if I will ever have children." Ben answered.

"Ahhh, young man," Henri said as he looked to where Kat and Pules stood saying their goodbyes, *"I believe you will have many children!"*

Ben's estimate of the time it would take them to reach Fort Raymond was close, but without saying it outright, Ben and Kat took their time and it was four days before the Yellowstone River came into sight. They crossed the Yellowstone upstream from where the Big Horn flowed into it and made their way up the small rise to the picket fort. It was still early summer, and Ben had no idea what or who he would find behind the walls. Compared to Fort Maskwa, Fort Raymond was not as luxurious, being half the size and built more on a temporary basis. But still, in made Ben's heart leap to see the Stars and Stripes fluttering in the breeze above the front gate.

*

From the north side of the Yellowstone River, Walks Long watched as Ben and Kat climbed the hill up to the fort. For the past two months he had been hunting, not game to bring back to the village, but American trappers. Hanging from the handle of his war club were a dozen scalps, strung in a line from the stone head of the club to the handle. All but two of these he had taken this spring, and with each scalp he had also fed Calf Standing a heart.

"*You have let him slip away again,*" hissed Calf Standing. Walks pretended to ignore him. "*I know you can hear me, how can you not? I am a part of you.*"

"*Yes, you are a part of me, and if I could cut you away as one cuts the flesh away for the Okan I would be free of you.*" He spoke of the custom of cutting flesh for the Sun Dance.

"*How can you talk of such a sacred thing, when you do nothing for the People? You think only of yourself.*"

"*You talk about yourself, not me. When did you gain honors as a warrior? When did you hang from the sacred pole and bleed for the People?*"

"*I had no chance to do these things, but I was with you when you did them, it was me who pushed you. You will never be great without me.*" Calf Standing laughed, his boney jaw clacking against his skull.

"Niso'kawaiksi! *All my relatives! Take this from me.*" Walks Long cried in desperation. He prayed that he could be released from the ghost of his dead friend and implored the help of those who had passed over peacefully.

"*There is no one to help you,*" said Calf Standing.

"*What can I do to be rid of you?*" asked Walks Long.

"*Take the hair and the heart from that one,*" Calf said, pointing a boney finger at Ben.

"*I have told you, I cannot take his scalp unless it is one on one. I must face him, not take him like the rest, who have cowered like frightened dogs before me.*"

"*Then do so. Go now to the log house of the Yellow Hair and call for him to come out.*"

And so Walks Long crossed over the river and rode close enough to the fort to be heard. He rode his horse back and forth and in a loud voice called out, "*I am Walks Long, warrior of the Pikuni Blackfoot, of the Skunk Band! I have taken many scalps from the Long Knives who come to my land. This is the land of the People! You have no right to be here! Send out the one with hair like the sun and I will fight him. Have him come out if he is a man.*"

Standing on the roof of the building next to the front wall Silas Scott and several other men from the fort watched as Walks Long rode back and forth yelling in Blackfoot. The men had just closed the gate behind Ben and Kat when the Indian appeared and started his tirade. Barely over the sight of Ben who they had thought dead, was the second surprise of the Blackfoot, and more excitement than the fort had seen in months.

"What you figure that caterwauling is all about?" asked Obadiah Cash.

"Not sure, but is he does seem to be all lathered up about something," said Silas.

"Somebody ought ta do something about him," one of the men said and with this brought his rifle up and fired at Walks Long, the shot going wild and landing nowhere near its mark. Several of the others on the roof laughed at his poor shot.

Joining the growing crowd on the rooftop, Ben and Kat made their way next to Silas, and when they saw Walks Long they both knew who is was that taunted the white men.

"Let me have a go at him," another of the spectators said and like his predecessor his hasty shot also went wild, bringing about more laughter. Neither Ben nor Kat laughed, and Silas only shook his head at the poor shooting.

"I wonder what bee got under his bonnet?" asked Silas to no one in particular.

"I know who that is," remarked Ben.

"And who is that?" Silas asked.

"That's Walks Long. He was one of the Blackfeet that took us over on the Judith."

"You mean that Blackfoot followed us all the way back here?" Silas asked.

"No, I think he followed me and Kat. Not sure why, but he saved us over the winter when we left Fort Maskwa."

"What the hell you talkin' about?"

"I'll tell you everything later, when we have a chance to sit down." Ben didn't want to share everything in front of all the others gathered on the rooftop.

"I've had about enough of this horse shit," said Obadiah and raising his own rifle, he took his time and fired at Walks Long. The shot was true, but in the time between the pull of the trigger and the lead ball hitting its target, Walks Long had spun his horse to one side and the .50 caliber round hit the war horse in the head. The horse reared up and toppled backwards landing on top of Walks Long.

A cheer went up from behind the stockade walls and several men slapped Obadiah on the shoulder in praise of his marksmanship.

"Damn fine shot, Hoss!" said one.

"Sent that Red Nigger straight to hell," remarked another.

Obadiah took no solace in the shot, for him it was just one small step in getting even with the Blackfeet for all they had done to his companions over the past months. Like most of the rest on the rooftop, he turned away and walked down the steps to the fort's courtyard.

Ben, Kat and Silas remained looking out across the field to where the dead horse lay, waiting to see if the rider had been killed also. After some time, they too left the roof and joined the others below.

*

Walks Long opened his eyes and saw only darkness. As his eyes adjusted, he determined that it was night and figured that he had been knocked unconscious. He also found himself pinned under the weight of the dead horse. He had no feeling in the leg under the horse, and placing his free foot on the saddle pushed against it and finally extracted his leg. He could bend the leg and decided it had only lost its feeling from lack of blood while pinned under the horse. He sat up and after a short while stood on shaky legs.

"What of me? Free me also!" Calf standing was almost completely covered by the horse carcass, one arm and his head were all that was visible to Walks. Walks let out what could only be described as a short snort of a laugh, and turned to walk away.

"I knew you would try to leave me," said Calf, *"Just like you left me when the Long Kinfe shoved his knife in my chest."* Calf now limped by Walks side and then with one swift movement vaulted onto Walks back.

CHAPTER 17
COMPANY MEN

With the rising of the sun, word about the shooting of the Blackfoot rapidly spread through the gathering of Crow lodges upstream from the fort. Before long, a throng of Crows; men women and children, gathered around the dead horse in hopes of finding the deceased Blackfoot. Disappointed that there was no body to collect souvenirs from, they satisfied themselves with taking pieces of the saddle blanket, tack and locks of the horse's mane and tail.

One of the Crow men, who had been to the carcass, went up to the fort and informed the occupants that there was no dead Blackfoot, only the horse. Obadiah showed some disappointment in that he had not dispatched one of Bug's Boys back to hell.

Ben and Kat had spent their first night back at the fort inside the stockade walls, and both had felt some angst in the company of some many people. They had spent the past few weeks alone, sharing each other's company, and were not comfortable in the confines of the fort. Another disquieting matter was the attention that Kat was receiving. It was somewhat akin to that she had received at Fort Maskwa, but here more open, more obvious. More than one lewd comment was overheard by the couple, and was disregarded, until one of the trappers, by the name of Cuddy Mackay, approached Ben with an offer.

"Hey Son, what you want for a screw of your squaw?" he asked. Ben attempted to ignore him and turned to walk away. Persistent, Cuddy spoke again, "You hear me boy? I said I want that squaw and I'm willing to trade fer her."

Ben turned back to face the man, stepping close to him, and replied, "The woman is not for sale." Ben held back the anger that was welling inside him.

"Hell boy, any Injun slut has a price, let me deal with her if you ain't got the stones." He started to push Ben aside and move toward Kat. With speed that surprised both Kat and Mackay, Ben grabbed Mackay by one shoulder and pulled him back throwing him to the ground. Mackay's surprise was replaced with rage, and he slowly rose to his feet, drawing the butcher knife form its sheath on his belt.

"Looks like I'm gonna' have to teach you some manors, and when I'm done I'll give your little slut a lesson on what a man is." and then with no hesitation he sprang at Ben, swinging the blade in an arch toward Ben's stomach. Ben stepped back just in time, and swinging his fist brought it heavily down on Mackay's chin, knocking the man back to the ground. Mackay lay on the ground, shaking his head to clear it from the blow, and then reached out for his knife that lay close by. As his hand reached the handle, Ben's moccasin clad foot pinned it to the ground, extracting a cry of pain from Mackay. Ben looked down at the man, and with a swing of his foot kicked Mackay on the jaw, this time knocking the man out cold.

Ben stood back and looked around to see if there were any other takers, and was met by only silent stares. By this time, other men had gathered around and Manuel Lisa pushed his way through the crowd.

"What is going on here?" he asked.

"Cuddy there got a bit fresh with Voss' woman, and then pulled a knife on Voss," said Silas who until this point had let Ben fight his own battle.

"I'll not have fighting over a woman," Lisa said. "Voss you had better control your woman."

"She's not the problem," Ben said.

"She is if it disrupts the running of this establishment."

"Might be better if we quarter ourselves out side then," Ben suggested.

"No matter to me as long as order is kept. We are losing men fast enough to the god-damned Blackfeet, and I don't need you all killing each other." He turned and walked away. The crowd broke up and Mackay was left to regain consciousness on his own.

"You know, that I do not need you to defend me," Kat's words stunned Ben. "I could have taken that man by myself."

"I figured I was doing that man a favor by saving him from you," Ben said, regaining his composure and attempting some humor. "If I'd let him past me, you'd have gutted him, and we'd both be in trouble." He smiled at Kat and she returned his smile.

"Can we take credit for the furs we brought in and then bargain with the Crows, possibly trade for a small lodge cover and poles?" Kat asked.

"Don't see why not. Let's go talk to Señor Lisa and see what we can get."

They headed in the direction Lisa had taken, to the first floor of the fort's blockhouse where the furs were stored and found him there supervising the inventory in anticipation of sending them downriver to Saint Louis.

"Señor Lisa," Ben addressed his superior, "May I have a word with you?"

"What is it Voss?"

"I was wondering if I could get credit on my wages for the furs I brought in yesterday?"

"Have they been inspected and weighed?" Lisa asked.

"Not yet, we came in late yesterday," Ben answered.

"Unpack them and make sure they are dry and free of debris. We will then weigh them and see about your credit."

Ben and Kat left Lisa and sought out Silas Scott,

as Silas was well known in the Crow camp and could help them mediate a trade for lodge poles and a suitable cover. But first, there was the necessity of having the furs Ben and Kat brought in, graded and weighed to see what credit Ben would have with the company.

Ben moved the packs of pelts over to the counting house and there Benito Vasquez, Lisa's second in command, determined that they were of good quality but considered them "castor sec", or parchment beaver, rather than prime hides called "castor gras" or coat beaver which were more valuable. Castor gras designated pelts were taken in the spring by the Indians when the hair was at its prime. These were trimmed, and several of them were sewn together and worn with the fur next to the body. After constant friction against the skin, the longer guard hairs fell off and sweat from the Indians added a glossy sheen. The skin became well-greased, pliable and yellow in color. These pelts were seen as more valuable because they lacked the guard hair and the felt had been enriched and thickened through contact with human skin.

When Ben's pelts were weighed, it was determined that he had brought in seventy-five pounds of beaver and was given the credit of $2.00 per "made beaver" or nearly $1.25 per pound. This equaled to $99.00 in his favor, payable in goods at fifty per cent on the invoice cost. In the few weeks Ben had trapped, he had earned more than what he would have made working at his uncle's forge in Pittsburg for an entire year. For Manuel Lisa and his partners, those pelts would bring between $5.00 and $7.50 per pound in New York.

With his new found wealth, Ben felt like celebrating, and suggested taking advantage of the credit and obtaining a jug of liquor. Though not totally against the idea, Kat's cooler head prevailed and they settled for some needed supplies, some goods to trade with the Crow and only as a compromise to Ben's desire to celebrate, a pint of the strong whiskey. Ben did get his way in one other purchase, a small item for Kat. He selected a small looking glass set into a hardwood frame.

"Now you can see what I see, the most beautiful woman in the whole world," he told her. Kat only blushed and took the gift.

With a large copper kettle, some glass beads, and a few butcher knives, Ben, Kat and Silas headed out of the fort to the nearest Crow lodges. An alarm to their approach was sounded by a throng of dogs who were fierce and half-wild. They created a racket that filled the air until they were sent running by the toss of a stick from the matron of the first lodge they reached. The stout woman stood eyeing the dogs as they retreated and then turned her attention to the trio as they stopped a polite distance away.

"Hello Sister." Silas raised his hand in greeting and spoke in Crow to the woman as if he knew her. In response, she tilted her head back and peered at him down her nose. "Not a good sign," thought Silas. He tried again, *"I am looking for the maker of the finest lodges among all the Absaroke. I am made to understand that I may find that person here?"* The woman obviously softened and her demeanor changed.

"I am Little Doe," she finally spoke.

"How did you know she was the best lodge maker?" Ben asked Silas.

"Didn't, just greasin' the wheels a bit," Silas said and he winked at Ben, and then he turned his attention back to the woman.

"You are Little Doe? By your reputation, I thought you would be an older woman. Are you sure are you not her daughter?" Silas smiled. The woman smiled back and a slight flush rose to her dusky, sun-bronzed cheeks.

"What do you want?" Little Doe asked.

"We come to trade for hides to make a lodge cover.

Do you have finished hides you would be willing to part with?"

"You do not have a woman to tan hides for you?" she asked.

"No, I make my bed among the traders at the Whiteman's lodge. It is for these two who are newly married and do not have relatives to help them with a new home." Ben and Kat were surprised at Silas' words. They had never given much thought to the idea of being married and were not sure if that was the way to describe their relationship.

Little Doe eyed the couple standing with Silas then asked, *"Why does the woman not ask to trade?"*

"She is not of the Absaroke, and not accustomed to the ways of the People."

"Of what people do you belong?" Little Doe asked Kat.

"My mother's family were of the Ininiwok, my father a Frenchman. I consider myself Métis."

"We sometimes make war on the Métis." Little Dow made the hand sign "half-wagon, half-man" for Métis. *"But your people make war on the Cuts Throats and the Striped Arrow People. They are true enemies of the Real People, so you are a friend to me."* She spoke of the Sioux and the Cheyenne who were bitter enemies of both the Crow and the Cree. *"We will talk, you and I. Men only make matters worse, with their words like honey."* She glanced at Silas with a knowing smile.

"I would like that," Kat said and dismissed Ben and Silas saying, "The two of you can go."

The men, put in their place, left Kat and Little Doe to get acquainted with each other and negotiate the trade for what Kat needed to build a lodge.

Once the trade for the lodge cover was completed, Kat found she had made a new friend in Little Doe. The copper kettle, glass beads, and butcher knives were not quit enough in payment for the hides, but

Little Doe was more than generous with offering the hides Kat at a bargain.

Kat sought out a quiet spot away from the Crow camp and put herself to work sewing the hides together into the half circle that when stretched around the long poles would form the cone-shaped lodge. While she was busy with this, Ben returned to his duties at the fort. No one lived for free and Ben was still an engagee.

Ben and Silas went to the counting house in the fort, and Silas assisted Vesquez in grading and weighing the furs that were brought in by the Indians and the other employees. Ben helped at the fur press, a crude machine constructed of logs driven into the ground. A frame was then built over this to create a lever and a platform to press down inside the square and compress the furs into a compact bale, called a "pièce". The skins were placed inside the frame fur-side to fur-side, hide to hide, in order to prevent damage to the hair. The less valuable skins were placed on the outside of the bale. To make each bale, the furs were placed in the press and using brute force, weight was applied on a long pole to give the bale a compact square shape. Ropes were then run from the bottom of the press over the top and then tied to secure each pièce. The average weight of each pièce was from 90 to 100 pounds, the number of beaver skins in a pack depending on the season in which the animals were trapped and the thickness of the fur.

The work was tiresome and backbreaking but the time went by quickly with the amount of work that needed to be done. It was apparent that the emissaries Manuel Lisa had sent out the previous fall had been successful and the small bands of Crow began coming in to trade as soon as the winter weather had cleared. There were piles of beaver and other animal skins that had been converted into trade goods. Each made beaver brought a variety of goods: a brass kettle, ¾ a pound of glass beads, two yards of flannel, eight knives, or a blanket to list only a few. Of all the goods, the Crow were more than pleased to receive guns, gun powder and lead. Obtaining firearms would give them an advantage in hunting and a better chance to defend themselves against their traditional enemies the Blackfoot.

Lisa was also happy at the success he was experiencing. The furs brought in by the Indians and those taken during the winter and spring by his hunters confirmed the Spaniard's expectations of riches from the region.

Late in the day, George Drouillard came into the fort, having completed his second trip since the previous fall to acquaint the Indians with the new post. He was the first of the four men sent out for that purpose and was a wealth of knowledge. His first trip had taken him up the Yellowstone River to the Stinging Water, where he turned east, down it to its junction with the Big Horn. He then ascended the Big Horn for a short distance and retraced his route back to the fort.

His second trip out took him again along the Bighorn River, the Little Big Horn, the Rosebud and the Tongue He then swung west into the big Horn Mountains and back up to the Yellowstone returning to the fort. The Indians he had met were receptive to coming to the fort and Lisa was pleased with the half-breeds success. Drouillard had good reason to succeed. He was the personal representative of Lisa's partners, Menard and Morrison, and their interests were his responsibility.

Drouillard described the country he had traveled through noting its topography and the richness of beaver laden streams. He also described the wonders of the thermal activities to the southwest. He spoke about seeing geysers of steaming water shooting into the air, hot pools of bubbling mud, and boiling, sulfurous ponds.   But few believed his stories, unconvinced by his straight manner of talking, and thought he was only spinning a yarn.

Their attitude changed the next day when John Colter arrived.   Colter had also followed the Big Horn upstream to the southwest, where he saw the same mineral hot springs which Drouillard had passed and described to Lisa.   Colter then turned up the south fork of the Shoshone River and crossed the continental divide.   From there, he went west before circling back, traveling through the Absaroka Mountains, Wind River Mountains, and the Teton Range coming back through the area were the geysers and hot springs were before following the Big Horn downstream to Fort Raymond. It was while he was at the upper end of the Wind River Valley he located the main camp of the Crows. Unknown to Colter, Lisa's fourth emissary, Edward Rose, had found the same camp after Colter left and the mulatto had spent the rest of the winter there.

As for Colter, his description of what he had seen was   far   more   elaborate   and   descriptive   than Drouillard's, and the men began to believe such wonders did exist.   Though Drouillard had offered a more detailed report of his travels, Colter was given credit for what they all began to call "Colter's Hell."

Like the others, Ben was spellbound and amused while listening to Colter spin his tale about his visit to Hell.   Colter spoke about going down a hole in the ground and meeting the Devil himself.   He also said he had seen politicians and preachers there who he had known,   which   brought   a   good   laugh   from   those gathered around to listen.   In the stories, it became hard to tell what was fact and what was fiction, but it seemed to matter little.

Within the next few days, the third man sent out by Lisa, Peter Weiser returned.   Weiser had gone over the same pass that William Clark had taken two years back leading Weiser to the area around the Three

Forks of the Missouri, and then he ascended the Madison River. He told Lisa that the pass led to beaver-rich country on the Snake waters to the south. His report was as promising as Colter and Drouillard's. He had brought with him a pack of furs from one of the Crow bands and promised more were to come. Lisa couldn't have been more pleased.

As the days passed, the amount of furs taken in trade increased and it was time to pack the keelboats for the trip back to St. Louis. Lisa sat with his most trusted men and discussed plans for the coming months. It was decided that Lisa and Drouillard would go down river with the furs and sufficient man-power to get back to St. Louis. Vasquez would remain in command of the fort with about forty men and they would be equipped to head into the mountains to trap. The little trapping that had been done near the fort over the winter and the following spring convinced Lisa that he had been correct in utilizing his hunters rather than rely upon the Indians to bring in furs. It was evident that there would be more profit to be made if the men brought in the beaver hides themselves rather than trade with the Indians.

Another thought was that more capitol would be needed for the following season. Refinements to how the business was run would also need to be made if it was to continue in the mountains. To succeed, more posts would be needed along the Missouri to keep the tribes pacified and the river open to traffic. More trappers would also be needed for entrance into the territory of the Blackfeet which would have to be done by force if necessary. But in an attempt to win over the Blackfeet, Lisa decided to send John Colter to them and make the same offer to trade as he had to the Crow. With this mission, John Colter left the fort and would head toward the Three Forks of the Missouri to seek out the Blackfeet and win them over.

The final packs were loaded into the boats, and

Ben was looking forward to some leisure time with Kat in the little lodge they now called their home. Along with Silas and several of the other trappers, he stood listening to Lisa speak about the plans for the coming fall and winter. While he spoke, a call from the lookout on duty in the blockhouse drew their attention. A small group of Indians was approaching. As they grew nearer, they were recognized as Crow and in their lead was Edmond Rose.

Rose was the son of a white trader and a half-breed Cherokee-Black woman. His upbringing had left him with a savage readiness and penchant for fighting. One such fight had left him with a scar across his face leading to the Crow calling him "Cut Nose." Though rough looking, he had the ability to extricate himself out of any precarious situation. Amply supplied with trade goods and gifts when he left Fort Raymond in the fall, Rose had soon realized the power he could wield through generosity of giving those goods away. He had spent the entire winter in the Wind River Valley and now returned to the fort in grand style. He was dressed in Crow fashion, having been adopted by them, and was now treated like a chief among them.

While Colter, Drouillard, and Weiser had suffered the hardships of the past winter traveling hundreds of miles, Rose had languished in the Crow camp enjoying a warm lodge, plenty of food, the admiring companionship of the Crow men and charms of the Crow women, young and old alike. Lisa was not amused.

Demanding Rose to account for the goods he had taken with him, Rose dismissed the wanton misuse of company property with a shrug of his shoulders and a smile. Enraged, Lisa threatened Rose, but the Spaniard's temper was no match for Rose's and Rose dove into him, taking hold of Lisa and throwing him to the floor of the counting house. With one hand, he held him to the floor while reaching for his knife with the other. The room was crowded with men, including Ben and Silas, and there was little room to maneuver. Several men, including Ben and Silas moved fast and pulled Rose off of Lisa before he could harm Lisa but in the melee John Potts was severely cut.

Held down by Ben, Silas and three others, Rose struggled to free himself, and it took all five men to restrain him. It seemed as if he would tire them out before he gave in but with one final grunt of resignation he relaxed his efforts. George Drouillard gave Lisa a hand up from the floor then turned to where Rose was held against the wall. Faced by the bigger man, Rose's demeanor changed. He knew Drouillard was no coward and if there was a man among those present who could best him it would be the half-breed Shawnee.

"You gonna' cause any more trouble?" Drouillard asked.

"Na," replies Rose.

"Let him go," Drouillard said.

Ben was the first to let go of Rose and one by one the others followed, each getting a look from Rose as if he were noting who had opposed him. He then turned his back and strode out the door to the Crow warriors waiting outside. He vaulted into the saddle and rode off with them in the direction of the Indian camp.

"Tend to Potts," Drouillard said and then turning to Lisa asked if he was harmed.

"That son-of-a-bitch isn't worth a single bolt of cloth he took with him last fall, and he has probably done more harm for trade than good."

"Should we run him off?" Silas asked, not afraid of Rose.

"No, I don't see him worth the trouble," said Drouillard.

"We have other matters at hand," said Lisa. "George, we must send the men out to spend the winter trapping and John Colter off to the Blackfeet.

Then our business here will be done and we can be off down river."

Ben was rewarded with only a small portion of the free time he was hoping for, within two days he would accompany Silas and a group of men who would travel in the same direction as John Colter toward the Three Forks of the Missouri. Somewhere along the way the men would break up into small groups and trap through the coming season as Colter went on to find the Blackfeet.

Colter had initially hoped Potts would accompany him but the little German would have to stay at the fort and recuperate from his injury in the fight with Edward Rose. Once he left the company of the other trappers along the way, he would again travel alone.

Kat had packed the lodge and lodge poles on two horses, and all the newly acquired belongings were in her charge. With some pride she looked over the meager possessions, for this was the first time in her life she had ever owned more than what was on her back. She was ready to go long before the group of trappers was halfway organized for their trip toward the Three Forks.

Like almost everyone else at the fort, she and Ben watched as the first of the keelboats loaded with $9,000 in beaver pelts, pushed off to begin its journey in the opposite direction down river to St Louis. There were shouts of good luck and Manual Lisa gave a small wave from the stern of one boat. There was the boom of the swivel gun from the Fort's wall and at first many thought it to be a salute until the grape shot landed in the water next to the keelboat causing those on board to duck.

All eyes went to where the shot originated and there stood Edward Rose, a smile on his face. It was plain that he had not meant the shot as a salute and was somewhat disappointed that he had not hit Lisa. He left the wall, and mounting his horse, rode off with the same Crow warriors he had arrived with.

"Good riddens," said Ben.

"Don't count him out too soon," said Silas, "You and I both know that a bad penny has a way of turning up."

*

Over one thousand Blackfeet had assembled in preparation for a late spring hunt and this was a fortunate opportunity for the North West Company to obtain hides in trade from their favorite customers. Dawson Thomas was pleased to be back out in the field and away from Fort Maskwa. The still recuperating Ranald had made life unbearable at the fort, and Thomas was more than happy to turn his mind toward the business of the company rather than Ranald's vendetta toward the woman. As far as Thomas was concerned, he could care less where the woman had gone, and wouldn't mind if she was never found. Leaving Fort Maskwa and his supervisor behind was almost exhilarating for Thomas and would have been an enjoyable journey, except for the company of Dob Bergmann.

Thomas considered Bergman a loathsome little cur and made no effort to conceal his contempt for the man. More than once, he had ordered Dob out of his sight rather than having to work alongside him or deal with him in any way. But for this trip, Thomas had no choice, and Dob joined the company at the insentience of Ranald.

With two dozen engagees, Thomas had brought in a large pack train of goods to trade with the Blackfeet, most important; were the English Trade Guns, gun powder and lead. These were the choice items that Thomas had hoped would tip the balance in favor of the NWC against the newly arrived Americans. Not only would it arm the Blackfeet against their traditional enemies the Crow, Flatheads and others, it would help put pressure on the Americans to leave the rich fur fields to the NWC. A good season could possibly help the NWC resist the incursion of another competitor, the Hudson Bay Company. If the current trend in business continued, the NWC could fall and be engulfed by HBC. Thomas couldn't see this happening but there was speculation and talk of a merger.

The boxes of trade goods were set out in neat stacks with a sample of each in plain sight. Sheffield knives, hatches, files and iron arrowheads gleamed in the sun. Wool blankets in colors of white, green, red and sky blue, sat in piles with bolts of flannel and cotton cloth next to them. Packages of glass beads, mirrors, vermillion and verdigris lay as an enticement to the Blackfeet women, who though they did the work of tanning the elk, deer and buffalo hides had little choice in what they were traded for. The smart Blackfoot man knew better than to ignore those items that caught the eye of their women.

Thus, a brisk trade arose and the amount of beaver and other types of skins increased to the satisfaction of both trader and customers. Thomas and his men could barely keep up and he chided himself for not bringing more goods. He also hoped there would be enough room in the two wheeled carts to carry the hides taken in trade, for having to cache the hide in some hole in the ground was risky. Buried hides or goods were always subject to the elements or thieves.

Thomas was overseeing the journal entries and correcting his clerk when he heard his name called.

"Hoo, Daw'soon!" It was Broken Horn, smiling at the white trader as he approached.

"Hello, Broken Horn, my friend," Thomas addressed him in Blackfoot, "To see you makes my heart happy."

"My heart good too. You bring powder an' lead?"

"Plenty of powder and lead, my friend." Thomas

assured him.

"*Good, my braves need powder and lead to hunt, and to make war on our enemies.*" Broken Horn switched to his own language. "*Come to my lodge and we will smoke.*" Thomas knew the offer was not just social, but that he would more than likely be required to bring a few gifts to the Blackfoot war chief. This he didn't mind, for with a little tobacco, some sugar and of course gun powder and lead, he would maintain good relations with a fierce ally.

"*I will come to your lodge,*" Thomas said, and telling his clerk to "mind the store" he picked up an empty box and threw in a pound of powder, some bars of lead, a Sheffield butcher knife, some sugar and as a special treat, a packet of candied ginger root. This last item he knew the Blackfoot chief had a particular fondness for.

The two men sat on a buffalo robe in the shade of the lodge, and after Thomas had given his host the gifts, Broken Horn reciprocated by giving Thomas an tanned elk skin coat with strips of intricate quillwork crossing over the shoulders. Thomas was impressed by the value of the gift, for the workmanship of flawless, and the patterns beautiful. He accepted the coat with true gratitude. They then sat smoking and talking more as friends than as business partners.

"*There is talk among our people of trading with the Napikowann from their house on the Yellow River.*" He used the Blackfoot term for white men.

"*Have I not treated our brother the Blackfeet well?*" asked Thomas.

"*Yes, I am made to think so. Some of our young men are made to think that they would receive more for their furs than you offer.*"

"*They will not receive more from the Yankees, and remind them that the Yankees will also trade with the Crow, the Flathead and the Shoshoni, just as they will with any people who will bring them hides.*" Thomas

310

had no intention of letting Broken Horn know that if business remained good, the NWC was looking to expand, and possibly build posts in both the Crow and Flathead country.

"I am made to worry that our enemies are receiving guns to make war on us. But I alone cannot persuade the young, one way or another," said Broken Horn.

They talked of other things; hunting, horses, and of course women. There seemed to be little that could break the calm of the early summer day and the peacefulness they both felt while they smoked their pipes, but a cry rang through the camp. Several young men who had been out hunting rode into the village excited to spread the word that less than a day's journey away they had found a large group of Flatheads moving along slowly with their women, children and old people.

Though there were several hundred of the Flathead, the number of Blackfeet warriors in the camp outnumbered them ten to one. With little organization, almost every able-bodied man in the village prepared themselves for battle, mounted their best war horses and rode off in the direction of a sure victory.

Thomas shook his head in disappointment. It seemed as if the trading was at an end, for the only people left in camp where women and those men too old or too young to fight. He returned to were his trade goods were and ordered his men to start packing up the hides and furs. For the first time, he noticed that Dob Bergman was missing, and he half hoped that he could leave the wretch behind. This wish was dashed when Dob emerged from the cover of some nearby bushes, adjusting his pants. Close behind him came a very young Blackfoot girl, much too young in Thomas' opinion to be caught alone with a man, let alone Dob. As Dob got closer, Thomas reached out a hand and took hold of him by the arm.

"You harm that girl?" Thomas asked.

"Na, just had a little fun with her is all. And, I gave her a string of beads," Dob acted as if there was nothing to be worried about and Thomas wanted to believe him.

"You cause me any grief and I swear I'll turn you over to them Blackfoot women. You know what they do to a man when they get riled?" Dob seemed unafraid, or at least not to care. He figured that the girl had to lose her virginity sooner or later, and why shouldn't it be to him. Anyway, he would be long gone by the time anyone found out about it, and surely the girl wasn't going to tell.

*

Silas Scott was pleased with the group he had ended up with for the coming trapping season. Along with Ben and Kat were his friends, Estienne Lapin and Obadiah Cash. Five men that they had worked with at the fort also accompanied them; Samuel Magee, a man named Lynch and two Frenchmen, Boucher, and Nadeau. The last man, was not so valued, Cuddy Mackay. Silas felt he had still come out ahead, with Mackay being the only one he was sure he didn't like and didn't trust. His only problem would be how to pair up the men when it came time to separate and trap in pairs.

They traveled up the Yellowstone and crossed over a low pass that Colter had used earlier in the year. He told them that on the other side was the Madison River, the eastern most of the three forks of the Missouri. Once on the west side of the pass, Colter left the group and headed off in search of the Blackfeet to spread word of Lisa's offer to come to Fort Raymond and trade.

Two days later Colter showed back up accompanied by almost five hundred Flathead Indians, an entire village. He had run into them, and after telling them about Fort Raymond, they had asked him to guide them back there and Colter could not refuse.

The Indians set up camp alongside the white trappers' and the atmosphere was almost festive, the Flatheads appeared honest, in general of high character and were very friendly towards the white men. It was not long before there was a sort of competition on who could host one of the trappers in their lodge, Ben and Kat along with John Colter and Silas were asked to one of the head men's lodge. For the all the trappers, save Colter, these were the first Flathead Indians they had ever seen. They were completely different from the other tribes, in almost every aspect; clothing, hairstyles and some customs.

"Why they call 'em Flatheads?" Ben asked Colter.

"Don't know. They call themselves Salish. When I was with the Captains, the other tribes called them Flatheads. Never did see why, I seen other Injuns put their babies in a cradleboard and tie a board on their head to make 'em flat like. But that was way out toward the ocean an' I never seen that among these here folks."

A few of the trappers intended to avail themselves of the Flatheads generosity and thought they might sample a few of the women. They were disappointed, for the Flathead women were not as easily persuaded to lay on their backs like the Arikara or Mandan women. One of those who was rejected was Cuddy Mackay, and in a foul mood he decided to return to his own bed to brood. As he walked, he spotted two women moving off into the trees and decided to follow them. They were gathering wood and slowly moved apart from one another, one completely out of sight.

As Mackay got a better look at the woman he saw it was Kat and a sadistic smile crossed his face. Her man wasn't here to save her now and by the time Ben found out it would be too late, and Mackay would already have what he wanted.

Her arms filled with wood, Kat was about to

return to the lodge where Ben and the others waited for her and the host's wife. She had taken only a few steps back toward the village when Mackay grabbed her from behind, lifting her off her feet and throwing her to the ground. Letting go of the wood, Kat had barely enough time to break her fall with her hands, but she quickly turned over and pulled her knife from its sheath on her belt. Her surprise turned to anger as she saw it was Mackay who had assaulted her. He stood over her and began to undo his pants fly.

"I'm gon'na give you what you been needin' an' that man of yours can't give ya."

Kat couldn't raise off the ground to defend herself so she kicked at him, her blows ineffective, and Mackay only laughed at her. Then, his laughter was cut short and a shocked look crossed his face. An arrow had struck him in the neck just below the jaw and protruded out the other side. His legs buckled and he fell forward pinning her to the ground.

Kat summoned the strength to roll him off and gained her feet. Across the stream she saw a mass of Blackfeet warriors headed toward the camp. She turned and sprinted back to the village calling out a warning that roused the Flathead, and they came out to defend their women and children from their hated enemy.

The white trappers joined in on the side of the Flatheads and were instantly impressed by their bravery against superior odds. Amid the flying arrows and lead, several fell on both sides; one of the wounded was John Colter, who took a musket ball to his thigh. Crawling into the bushes, Colter remained cool and continued firing on the Blackfeet.

Kat had reached Ben's side and they stood together, Ben firing at the attackers knowingly killing at least one Blackfoot outright. There was no way to know where the other trappers were as they had been spread out throughout the village when the assault began, and only Silas was in sight of Ben.

Like Ben, Silas was firing as fast as he could and the thought of being overrun by the Blackfeet crossed his mind. It began to look as if it was only a matter of time before the Blackfeet overpowered the Flathead camp.

Ben's mind brought him back to the small hill on the Grand River where they were close to being killed by the Arikara and then the Crow came to their rescue. Now as then, he was willing to face death with honor. His only regret is that his life with Kat would be over.

Almost as if Ben had willed it to happen through the thoughts of that day, the tide in the battle changed with the arrival of several hundred Crow Indians and the Blackfeet began to draw back and finally leave abandoning their dead. The victorious Flatheads, and their allies the Crow, pursed the Blackfeet killing any that were left behind.

Ben stood not believing what had happened, stunned that the Crow had actually appeared. He felt Kat as she leaned up against him, her arm around his, taking comfort that the two of them had survived the slaughter. Silas came over and asked if they were unharmed.

"You two sound?"

"Yep," said Ben. "I 'spect we're just fine."

"We best go see if there's anyone from our boys hurt," Silas said.

"Mackay is dead," Kat said flatly.

"Yu see him go under?" asked Ben.

"Yes, he was the first one down." Kat added nothing more.

When the last of the killing was done, it was determined that the combined force of Flathead and Crow were still fewer than that of the Blackfeet, but the surprise of the Crows arrival had turned the battle.

The atmosphere in the village changed to a full

blown celebration with a scalp dance and feasting through the night, the mourning for Flathead and Crows who were killed overshadowed. After the other trappers were accounted for, other than John Colter, only Samuel Magee, who had been with Lapin, was slightly wounded. Magee's anger at having lost blood to the Blackfeet was tempered by the admiration of a Crow woman who had taken a liking to him and dressed the cut on his arm made by an arrow.

The battle with the Blackfeet, and Colter's injury, made any further attempt by him as an emissary to those people fruitless. This he discussed with Silas.

"I'll take these here Injuns back to Fort Raymond. I figure before fall I'll be healed enough ta head back out, maybe set some traps and make the rest of the year worthwhile."

"I figure the rest of us will go on as planned, there's enough of us for safety and too few to draw much attention. We'll split up, cache by day and set our traps in the predawn and dusk."

"That'll do 'er," said Colter. You watch your hair, Silas Scott."

"You watch yours John Colter.

The following day, the white trappers split from the Indians and made their way toward the Madison River to set their traps and bring in as much beaver as they could by the following spring.

CHAPATER 18
THE GALLATIN

Following the Gallatin River upstream, the small party of trappers made its way into the beaver rich country untouched by white men. The weather hadn't grown cold enough yet to turn the beaver's fur thick in anticipation for winter, but the nights were getting longer and the temperatures were dropping. Soon, the ice would be forming on the edge of the streams like tiny fingers reaching out to claim the rushing water, and the beaver would have to store up food to be prepared when they could no longer venture out of their dens up onto the shore.

Like the beaver, Ben's party would plan for the coming cold months, not only for trapping, but for food and shelter. With this in mind, they scouted out a secluded valley that would provide both shelter from the winter storms and adequate food to see them through until spring. They chose two such sites miles apart with the intention of splitting up to trap and then join up again in the spring. Ben and Kat stayed with Silas, Estienne Lapin, Obadiah Cash and Fox Crying, the Crow woman who had taken a liking to Estienne. Samuel Magee split off with the other three men and a Flathead woman who had attached herself to one of the Frenchmen.

The camp was simple, the trees offering the needed materials to build a rugged but small cabin with a low roof for all but Ben and Kat. Kat erected the hide lodge and when she was satisfied with the interior, she cut willows and created a form of woven fence around the outside of the lodge. This would cut the wind, stop snow from drifting up against the lodge, and the area between it and the lodge cover could be used to store fire wood.

Fox Crying was more than happy to have Silas, Obadiah and Estienne to look after, though she considered herself Estienne's woman she saw the other two men as his brothers and deserving of her attention and care. The three men were more than happy to share her attention, Estienne and Obadiah on a more intimate basis than Silas. After she became use to keeping house in a square structure rather than round lodge she felt at home. She became close friends with Kat and called Kat "Sister" or iishbíia –bia, Panther Woman. She also helped Kat to better understand the Crow language and customs.

In turn, Kat thought of Fox Crying in the same way she had Pules Thibault, finding the young Crow woman sweet, innocent and open. As a way of making her feel closer to the entire group, Kat attempted to teach Fox both English and Métis, finding that she was a quick study and was able to carry on conversations in either of the languages in a matter of weeks.

The duty of cooking meals was shared by the two women but Kat also went out with Silas and Ben when they ran their trap lines. Obadiah and Estienne paired up to trap and at times this left Fox Crying alone in the camp, but this didn't bother her as she spent the time mending shirts, making moccasins and beading. She laughed when Kat apologized for leaving her alone, saying that those were the time she could talk to herself without anyone thinking she was crazy.

The routine of the men leaving for a few days at a time to trap and then coming back to the camp became common, and there were times that one of the trapping duos would not see the other for a week or two. This would change when the hard storms descended from the north and froze over the streams and rivers. Everyone would then settle down to wait out winter.

The lodge and the cabin were set next to each other and Ben and Kat spent much of their time in the cabin with the others. This gave them all time to learn more about each other.

Estienne Lapin was the most open, sharing almost every detail about himself, bragging about some about his fights with either Indians or other men, but mostly his prowess and conquests of the fair sex. He also alluded to having wives in Montreal, St. Louis and New Orleans. Most of this was said in all honesty, but with a wink, taken in jest.

Obadiah Cash spoke of his life in Kentucky and the family he had left there farming near Lexington. He admitted that he had never been cut out to be a farmer as he liked whiskey and horses too much to spend his time behind a plow. It was both of these vices that had driven him west to escape the debt he owed from a horse race.

Kat and Ben's stories were fairly well known by the others and what little they did not share was unimportant. Silas, like Ben and Kat, shared only a bit of his past telling them that he had been born in Scotland, had lived in France and was educated in "books". His schooling, he said, truly began when he came to America and in the wilds of Georgia was taken under the wings of an Irishman named Colm Craigavon and a Cherokee called Yellow Turtle. It was there that he learned his woods-craft, and it was there among the Cherokee that he had felt the most alive and at home.

"That language I heard you talk, Latin. Where did you learn that?" asked Ben.

"That was part of my learning as a boy both in Scotland and in France," admitted Silas.

"Amérique, Latin. That is the language of the priests, no?" said Lapin, "I remember it from when I was a child and the priest would hit me on the knuckles with a stick if I did not say my prayers in the proper way! What I would not give to have that bald-headed old man here, now, in front of me and a stick within reach!" And with a swing of his hand he made a motion as if to strike Obadiah with the imaginary stick, bringing a laugh from the whole group.

"Tell us about yourself, Fox Crying," Obadiah asked.

The Crow woman seemed puzzled by the request. No one had ever asked her about her past, it was something that had never occurred to her.

"I am Crying Fox, I am of the Kicked-in-their-bellies clan. I wish only to be bi i'tsi, a good woman."

"How did you receive your name?" asked Obadiah.

"My father had asked a respected warrior to give me a name, but my mother's sister gave me my name. This woman said that I cried like a fox kit when I was born. So, I am Crying Fox.

The six became a small family sequestered in the arms of the winter storms, forged together by necessity but bond together by friendship. The days passed and there was a certain relief when it final became time to think about venturing out to start the spring trapping. Small trips out to look over the surrounding territory were a welcome chance to leave the confines of the cabin and even for Ben, the lodge.

As the days became longer and the ice on the streams started to thin, it was time to set traps and harvest the best pelts of the year, those thick with winter fur. Soon the trappers were bringing in dozens of hides, and in the security of the little valley, they fleshed and stretched the beaver pelts creating the Rocky Mountain dollars. A hide when stretched on a hoop of willow was the same shape as a silver dollar, and also represented coinage in their value.

For the most part, Fox Crying and Kat ventured only short distances from the cabin and lodge, keeping watch not only on this base of operations, but also the growing piles of furs. One of their tasks was to take the dried pelts off the willow hoops and prepare them in packs ready to transport back to Fort Raymond. As they worked, they chatted, though the conversation was more one-sided with Fox doing most of the talking. She would ramble on for hours, and under other circumstances it might have annoyed Kat, but Kat had grown so fond of the little Crow woman that it didn't seem to matter, and half the time Kat barely listened.

It was one of these times while Fox was talking away in Crow that she asked Kat off-hand, *"When will you tell your husband?"*

Kat stopped working and asked back, *"Tell my husband what?"*

"That you will have a baby.

"How did you know?" Kat asked.

"I am not blind, and has he not noticed your growing belly over the past months?"

"I do not think so, and no, I have not told him."

"Oh, does it belong to one of the other men?" Fox giggled.

"No." Kat was offended. *"I sleep with only Ben. I believe that men are blind to many things until it is right in front of them."*

"I did not mean to say something to hurt you, I only asked...you know I have been with both Rabbit and Diah. Though I would love to have a baby with red hair like Silas." She smiled at the thought.

"I am sorry, Fox, I do not know what has come over me. I have not been myself.

"That is the baby changing you. It happens. I have seen it many times. Have you not been around other women who were pregnant?"

"Yes, at the Englishman's fort, but I kept more to myself and did not spend time close to them."

"I have been with many women who had children, my sister and friends. I will be with you when your

time comes. And, you will help me at my time."

"You too will have a child?"

"Yes, that is another reason I knew you were with child."

"If you have been with Rabbit and Diah how will you know who is the father."

"Ahh, if the child has dark hair it will be Rabbit's, if it is curly and light like Diah's than it is his." Fox went on with her work, and then spoke again, *"We should make a new saddle for each of us. We will both need one that is more comfortable, and a bit larger. Then again we may have to walk as the horses will be burdened with all these beaver hides."* She then drifted off on another completely unrelated subject and Kat's attention shifted to her own thoughts.

Kat decided that as soon as Ben returned she would tell him that he was going to be a father. She wondered if it would please him or not. She had known that some men would desert their women when they found out they were pregnant, others would lose interest and find another woman to bed with. Kat tried to convince herself that Ben was not that type of man, that he truly loved her and that he would be happy to know they were about to have a child.

Ben and Silas worked in the predawn to pull up their last few traps. The sets had offered up fewer and fewer beaver signaling that the streams they worked in had been trapped out and it was time to move on. The weather was changing also, there was little to no ice left at the edges of the streams and the trees were starting to green up, buds forming on the branches. The grass was starting to poke its way up through the remaining snow and it would not be long before they would be seeing new life of spring in the mountains. Deer would soon be dropping their young and those animals that slept during the winter months would soon start to emerge in search of food.

One sign of an early riser from hibernation was

the tracks of a large grizzly bear that Ben ran across and pointed out to Silas. By the size of the foot prints, it was a large boar, the hind feet at over a foot in length left little question as to the size and this was confirmed by the claw marks found on a nearby tree at over seven feet from the ground.

"What you figure he's huntin'?" asked Ben.

"Don't rightly care, so long as it ain't us," Silas joked. "Let's just hope he's moved on and we don't run into him."

"You think we ought to head back to the cabin? We have about as much as we can carry in furs." Ben said.

"Yep. I'm thinkin' we've pretty much trapped out this whole valley. I suspect that Rabbit and Diah have done pretty much the same where ever they are. I agree, we should head back and get ready to go over to the Yellowstone."

"Think we'll meet up with Sam Magee between here and the pass?"

"Could be, but if we don't, they'll make their way back. Now let's get our possibles together and get out of here, anyway I'm hankering for some of that stew that Crying Fox makes, I'm tired of eatin' cold food."

They gathered up their meager possessions, traps and furs and before the day was half over they had headed back toward the cabin.

When Ben and Silas arrived to the main camp, Obadiah and Estienne had already returned and they too had been successful in their last trip out. By rough calculation, Silas figured that they would be bringing in sixteen packs of beaver furs. They discussed their next step and decided to head down out of the high country and return to Fort Raymond with their packs of beaver hides.

The mood was joyous and Obadiah voiced what the other three men were thinking, "Sure do wish I had a drink of liquor to celebrate!"

"There'll be plenty of whiskey once we get back to the fort, no?" assured Estienne.

"I would 'spect so," added Silas.

Kat and Fox were as excited as the men, and though Kat had wanted to wait and talk to Ben alone, Fox could not hold back the secret she was holding.

"We should also celebrate the coming of the babies!" she exclaimed. This caught everyone's attention and all eyes were on Fox.

"What are you talking about?" Obadiah asked.

"We will have babies before the moon when the berries are good!" she answered.

"What do you mean, we?" asked Ben.

"Panther Woman, and myself of course. You cannot have babies." Fox beamed with a broad smile.

Ben looked at Kat, surprised by the news. Kat was hesitant to look him straight in the eye. Ben reached out to her and taking her hands in his asked, "Is it true, you gonna" have a baby?"

"Yes." she said. "I wanted to wait and tell you when we were alone, but..."

"When? When is the moon when the berries are good?" Ben asked.

"Mid-summer," she said, then asked, "Are you pleased?"

"Pleased? I'm happier then I have ever been my whole life." He looked back at the others and said, "I'm gonna' be a father!"

"Yep, you sure are," said Obadiah, then he looked at Fox and she understood the unasked question.

"It is either you or Rabbit," Fox said.

"It could not be yours Diah," said Estienne, "Your tool, she is too short, it must be mine!" and Estienne laughed.

Obadiah smiled and then added, "We'll see what the child looks like. If nothing else it can have two fathers to spoil it! Will it come the same time as Kat's?"

"I think it will be after Panther Woman's, maybe in the moon when the chokecherries are black."

"Either way, between the two of us, the child will be taken care of," Obadiah said. This seemed to satisfy Fox.

Within two days, they were ready to leave the safety of the little valley they had called home for the past months. As Fox had predicted, most of the horses were required to haul the baggage and bales of furs. Kat and Fox mounted on new saddles, rode on the two horses that pulled travois and the men walked leading the others loaded with packs.

It took the first two days to work out all the little kinks in the tack and to find the right adjustment for weight and balance in the packs, but the group made good time heading for the low pass that would lead them over to the Yellowstone River.

Blazing a new trail through the trees no one noticed Crying Fox drop back and dismount her horse. The rope that secured the baggage on the travois her horse pulled had become loose and she had to stop and tighten them up. It was not long before the rest of the group was out of sight and she was alone.

*

Of the eight members of the Blackfoot war party, only Walks Long seemed calm. The others were excited and their blood was hot, stirred up by the talk of the British traders of the North West Company and the recollection of the white men fighting alongside the Crow and Flatheads the previous fall. Each man among them looked not only for war honors and trophies that battle offered, but there was another incentive. The trader chief Ranald had promised enough powder and lead to shoot twenty times in exchange for each Yankee scalp the Blackfeet brought him.

Walks Long could care less about the Whiteman's promised gifts, and if he had put any value on them, they were not what he wanted when he took the life of one of the trappers he had come to hate. In reality, it was clear to all the Blackfeet that the North West Company wasn't that different from the Long Knives. Like the Americans they offered guns and powder to anyone who would trade with them, and Walks Long decided that it would be best if all the Whiteman were driven out of the country of the People.

"*Why do we move so slowly?*" the persistent ghost of Calf Standing asked. "*I am tired of riding with these women.*"

"*They are not women, they only look at the world in a different way than you.*" Walks said, "*They are warriors of the people, some have not yet gained honors in battle, but they are not women.*"

"*I care not for honors, I want to be fed.*" Calf shrieked.

"*You know nothing of honors won in battle, you have no right to criticize them.*" Walks said in disgust.

"*It is your fault that I was killed, you left me behind and the Whiteman plunged his knife into my chest! Look!*" He spun around from where he had clung to Walks back to sit in front of Walks on the horse's neck. "*See, here is where the knife went in!*" He pointed to a jagged tear in what was left of the leathery skin that covered his emaciated figure. With the sweep of his right arm, Walks Long knocked the phantom to the side and onto the ground. He could hear the hooves of the horses that followed him step on the dry bones as they passed over the prone figure. Walks let a seldom seen smile cross his face, but it faded as the skeletal figure of Calf Standing dropped out of the next tree Walks Long passed under and again clung to his back, his boney fingers digging into Walks' shoulders.

Walks Long was about reach back and take hold of the bony figure when word came down the line of warriors that a group of trappers had been spotted, and without orders the Blackfeet spread out and advanced toward their intended prey. The first of the Whiteman's group to be spotted was a woman, and before she knew what had happened, or could cry out, her body was pierced by several arrows. She fell to the ground and one of the Blackfoot was on her. He removed her scalp with one clean sweep of his knife before she breathed her last breath.

Walks Long along with the other Blackfeet swept out from the cover of the trees and overpowered the trappers killing them before any could return fire. A wounded trapper seeking cover in the bushes, attempted to crawl off but was found and drug back to the scene of the carnage where he was bludgeoned to death with a war club.

Walks Long had neither fired a shot from his trade gun nor swung his stone headed club a single time during the short engagement. He saw no reason, for there was no time for him to single out one man to engage and then extract his own special brand of retribution.

"AHHHHHEEEEEEE!" Shrieked Calf Standing into the ear of Walks Long. *"They have cheated me of my food!"*

Walks Long hung his head down holding his hands to his temples in an attempt to ease the pain. *"Why do you not leave me alone?"* he screamed. His outburst drew the attention of the entire war party and they stopped to stare in his direction. Walks Long looked around seeing the expression on their faces and anger crossed his face, his eyes became wide and he addressed them.

"My brother is right! You are all women. You are as dogs that eat scraps thrown from the feast." He went to his horse, mounted it and road away.

This was only the beginning raid for the Blackfeet and they rose up all along the area of the Three Forks in an attempt to kill or drive out any trappers they found. Any white men found alone or in small groups, was hunted down and killed. Each foray against the interlopers into their territory rewarded them with scalps, horses and the other possessions of the trappers to take back to their villages.

Walks Long rode far off on the flank of the Blackfoot village as it moved to a new location with fresh grass along the Middle Fork of the Great Muddy River, the river hidden below steep banks. His mind was working over his hatred, for not only the Whites, but for the phantom that clung to his back. He wondered, if he were to kill himself if would it rid him of the Spector?

"You know I hear what you are thinking," Calf Standing hissed into Walks' ear.

"I do not care what you hear," replied Walks.

"You loved me as a brother once. Why do you now wish to get rid of me?"

"You torment me! I am alone even among the People. Some who are touched by a spirit are revered, even considered sacred, but you are no blessing, you are a curse."

"You hurt me, Walks Long. I blame you for my death. If you had not insisted on me going with you to steal horses I would have lived to be an old man."

"I did not insist, you would not stay behind, and I felt responsible for you."

"Ahhh, see now you know that it was your fault I was killed by the Long Knife."

"Leave me cursed spirit, I..." Walks argument with the spirit was cut short by the sudden excitement of the moving village. People were rushing over to the bank of the river and gathering there. Walks Long turned his horses' head in the direction of the disturbance. When he arrived and looked down into the river bed, he saw that there were two trappers, one standing on the bank next to a canoe and the man in another canoe a few feet from the bank.

All those gathered were yelling at the men, some telling the one in the canoe to come to shore. One Blackfoot waded into the water and reached out to take the man's gun, but the trapper standing pulled the gun free and tossed it back to his companion. This man then pushed away from the bank into deeper water. Without warning, another of the Blackfeet warriors fired an arrow hitting the trapper in the canoe, striking him in the hip. The man screamed out in pain and raising his newly retrieved rifle fired, killing the closest Blackfoot.

A cry went up among the gathered Blackfeet, and in a frenzy, they opened fire on the man in the canoe riddling his body with bullets and arrows. They then descended on the canoe dragging the corpse to the shore where they continued to take out their hatred by mutilating the body further, and cutting him to pieces.

Other Blackfeet had taken ahold of the trapper on shore and were stripping him of his clothes, others struck him with hands, or picked up rocks and threw them at him. Someone picked up a portion of the deceased trapper body and flung the bloody bit at the now naked man.

They then hauled him up to where he would be visible by the whole village and planned to torture him for the enjoyment of all. A heated discussion arose to determine the manner of torture and death to be used until Bear Head, Steels Crow Horses and Broken Horn intervened with cooler heads.

"I have a more entertaining thought," Bear Head said, *"Let us set him out and hunt him as we would the wolf."* Then he went to the Whiteman and spoke to him. *"Are you a good runner?"*

The man seemed puzzled and possibly didn't understand the Blackfoot language, so Bear Head repeated the question in Crow.

"Among my people, I am not considered fast," the man replied.

Bear Head lead the man out from the crowd onto the prairie pointing to a dead tree that jutted up against the skyline in the distance and said to the man, *"Go there, and when you have reached that place you must run for your life as my warriors will then follow you."*

Slowly the trapper walked away from the yelling mass of Indians, toward the tree in the distance. With each step of his bare feet, he was careful not to step on the sharp rocks or the prickly pear cactus that covered the ground. When he reached the dead tree he paused to look back, then broke into a dead run.

*

John Colter knew the country he was in and reckoned that he was only about five miles away from the Madison River. If he could make it to the river, he might have a chance of survival. He tried to rid thoughts from his mind of his friend, John Potts, being torn apart by the Blackfeet. Now Colter's only thought was his goal of the Madison River. Naked and shoeless, he was determined not to let the rugged terrain beat him and more determined that he would not be taken alive by the Blackfeet.

He reached the dead tree and paused only long enough to take a fleeting glance back and see the mass of Indians waiting for him to start running. "Best get to it," he told himself, and kicked into a dead run. The first few rocks and cactus he stepped on drove searing pain into his feet but the fear of being caught drove him on. His lungs began to burn but he pushed himself on, repeating the mantra, "Make it to the river. Make it to the river."

The pain in his feet and chest spread throughout his body and he felt something wet and sticky pass over his lips. He ran a hand across his mouth and saw that he was bleeding from his nose, the blood seeping out to cover his beard and chest. "Make it to the river. Make it to the river," he thought to himself.

*

Silas walked ahead of the others, his eyes scanning left to right, his ears tuned to any sound that seemed out of place. Even the absence of sound could be a sign of danger. He liked this time of year for spring signaled the beginning of things, the start of something new, fresh and untouched. His thoughts were not only occupied by the search for danger, he also thought about the two women in the group. A few days back, Crying Fox had dropped back from the group and everyone was concerned for her safety until they backtracked and found her.

It pleased Silas that amidst all the killing of the past two years, there would be comfort in the expectance of new life. He was happy for the others, but in a small way he was envious. A family was one thing he didn't see in his future. He had given his heart to a woman once and had that love ripped to shreds. He was sure he could never love again.

He was not sure if it was the stillness in the air, or the smell of death that drifted through the trees in front of him, but he was brought to a stop by it. He held up his hand to signal those behind him to stop also and dropping the lead rope of the pack horse he moved slowly forward, his rifle ready in his hands. Ben was soon at his side.

Looking up, they saw several ravens swooping in to land. On the ground in front of them were fresh tracks of unshod horses, and following these they moved forward to where the birds were gathering. The first sight that came into view was the body of a woman, the birds feeding on her prone figure. As Silas and Ben edged closer, the birds took flight but landed in the trees not far off. Ben knelt down on one knee to look at the body.

"I think this is the Flathead woman that was with Sam Magee," he said.

"Think so?" Silas asked.

"Not sure someone took her scalp. But it does kinda' look like her."

"Let's look up ahead, keep your wits about you," Silas said as he stepped forward followed by Ben. As they rounded the brush, they came into a little clearing. There they found more bodies, one being fed upon by a large Grizzly. Ben raised his rifle in the bear's direction, but Silas took hold of the barrel and stopped him from firing.

"Wasn't the bear that killed them, look yonder," he pointed to the body of a man that had several arrows protruding from his groin. "That looks like Sam Magee, and those look like Blackfeet arrows. Damn Injuns done this."

"We just can't leave them for bear bait," Ben protested.

"There's nothing we can do for them, and whoever did this may not be too far off. We don't need to bring them bastards down on us, too." The bear, alarmed by the sound of the men talking, raised its bloody muzzle up from its meal. Its eyes scanning the area, it spotted the men and stood on its hind legs creating an imposing and frightful sight. Satisfied the men were no real threat, the boar dropped back down and resumed eating.

"I don't see any packs or other possibles around," said Silas looking for sign of any of the belongings that had belonged to the Magee party. "Blackfeet must have taken all the plunder with them." Silas motioned Ben to back away, and the two men moved slowly away from the bear and back to their party.

"What did you find mon frère," asked Estienne.

"Magee and his boys," Silas said.

"They're all dead, killed by Blackfeet" Ben added, "The Flathead woman too."

"Merde!" whispered Estienne.

"Should we bury them?" asked Obadiah.

"No, a white bear has gotten to them and there

ain't much left. It's still there and the Injuns might be close by, too. We best give the area a wide berth, pass it by and get as far away as we can," said Silas.

"Be a good idea to maybe take a swing out to one side and have a look see. Maybe cross some sign telling us which way them red devils are headed," Obadiah suggested.

"Good idea, if you want to do that, but don't go out too far. If you get in trouble its best we're close by to help out."

Skirting the area where their comrades had been killed, they made their way to the east. Obadiah joined them near dusk and said he had found the tracks of at least a dozen horses, and they lead off to the north, headed down the Gatlin.

After two cautious days of travel they crossed over the pass and reached the Yellowstone River, where they felt some amount of security, and their pace of travel slowed somewhat. For the next two weeks the little group eased their way along the Yellowstone River, making it to Fort Raymond.

SAM J. PISCIOTTA

CHAPTER 19
FORT MANDAN

Arriving at Fort Raymond, Ben's party found that they were not the only ones who had news of the Blackfeet resistance to the American trappers. Of the groups of men who set out for beaver country immediately after Lisa's departure the previous summer, most had divided into small groups headed for the Three Forks of the Missouri, while only a few had went south toward the Seeds-kee-dee-Agie, or Prairie Hen River. Those who had returned carried the news that Indians had attacked in force, killing and robbing where they could, and had virtually driven all the trappers from the area.

The sixteen packs of furs that Ben and Silas had brought in were a welcome surprise as the pressure from Blackfeet had made it almost impossible for the other men to trap. The only other exception and hint of success, was just a rumor. Word had gotten back to Benito Vasquez the previous fall that a party, led by Case Fortin, the last group now known to be in the Three Forks region, had reported they had taken twenty packs of beaver. Vasquez estimated if they had eluded the Indians and were still alive, they could bring in up to fifty packs including the spring trapping. Those fifty packs of beaver gathered in a single season might be worth as much as $25,000. With the sixteen packs brought in by Ben and Silas, and a few packs Chapman had brought in from trading with the Crow, the efforts of less than a dozen men had brought in at least $35,000 worth of furs. There was also the possibility that a few of the scattered trappers would still come in and add to the profits. This was incentive for continuing to trap, especially the area of the Three Forks, but few men wanted to go back there because of the number of men who had not yet returned and were not expected to.

"What do you intend to do?" Silas asked Vasquez.

"We have been discussing this subject for days now," Vasquez said, including those who were gathered in the counting room. "Señor Lisa has promised to return with more goods and men. I expect he is on his way back from St. Louis already. I propose that we cache all of the equipment here, close up the fort and go down river as far as the Mandan village. Peter Weiser assured me that the site where he wintered with Captains Lewis and Clark will support our needs and there we will wait for Señor Lisa. While we wait, we can trade with the Mandan"

All those gathered agreed, though the decision was solely Vasquez's, he would get no argument. Not wanting the men to feel there were no plans for the coming future, Vasquez unfolded the plans he would propose to Manuel Lisa.

"We won't completely abandon trapping, I propose sending men under the leadership of Charles Sanguinet and Jean Baptiste Beauvais, south to trap the Prairie Hen River." This river, also called the Spanish River or the Rio Verde, was known to be rich in fur as well as out of the normal territory of the Blackfeet. Vasquez hoped the furs brought in by trapping on the Green River would bring a real profit for the company and insure its presence in the West.

"We giving up on the Forks, then?" asked Silas.

"No. We will be back. Señor Lisa promised he would return and that he would bring more men."

"If we go back in ta' the Three Forks, we're gon'na need an army!" another of the men commented.

"For now, let's prepare to leave." With this, Vasquez finished the discussion, and everyone went to work.

The next week was spent in securing the fort, burying equipment that be left behind and in the minds of some, surrendering the area to the Blackfeet. If this was not a result of their aggression, further proof showed up in the form of an emaciated figure staggering toward the gate from upriver.

At first the man was completely unrecognizable; his naked body was wasted by the deprivation he had suffered in the wilderness. His limbs were lacerated, bruised and bloody. As he grew close enough to see his face clearly, his gaunt face was barely visible under the matted hair and the beard encrusted with days-old dried blood.

The naked form of John Colter staggered forward and collapsed face down in the dust. The soles of his feet were swollen, being punctured by an uncountable number of cactus thorns and cut by sharp rocks. Several men including Ben and Silas, ran to him and only when they turned him did they half-recognize him. How could this be Colter? He had changed so much from when he and John Potts had left to trap together. The men picked him up and carried him into the fort to tend to his wounds. When he had recovered somewhat, he was able to relate what had happened to Potts and himself.

"I tried to tell him to come in ta shore. I figured they'd just rob us, you know, take our plunder. I figured we had a chance, but that stubborn German had to go and shoot one of them." Colter paused trying to put the memory of his friends death out of his mind. "I made it to the Madison, an' I hid under a pile of driftwood in the river. Them devils looked all over fer me, even standing right on top of me. After it was dark, I crawled out and started back here."

"You rest now," said Vasquez, "gain back your strength. In a day or two we're going down river as far as the Mandan village. We'll wait there for Señor Lisa to return from St. Louis."

Ben waited until he and Silas were alone to talk. He wasn't afraid for himself, but fear for Kat and the baby were foremost in his mind.

"Damn, that sure is some, isn't it? He made it almost three hundred miles, naked, unarmed and all on his lonesome," Ben said.

"Yep, that man has the hair of the bear in him," Silas remarked, meaning as the trappers would say, that Colter had the grit and stamina of a grizzly bear.

"Silas, I think it'd be best if Kat and I went down river with Vazquez," Ben said. "I think the baby is due any time now, and even going down to the Green River to trap might not be safe."

"Hell boy, there ain't no place safe, but I see what you're saying." Silas understood and could see no cowardice in Ben. "I haven't decided if I'll go with Sanguinet and Beauvais myself. I could do with a bit of work that doesn't require me to constantly be looking over my shoulder expecting an arrow."

"I'll talk to Kat. They'll need a lot of hands setting up down river. I'll tell her that they will probably need me more as a blacksmith than a trapper, at least until fall."

Kat had no objections to going along with Ben's plan. She discussed her true concerns with Fox Crying though, and the little Crow woman decided to go with her new sister.

"*We can protect each other from the Cuts Throats, the Sioux and the Mandan,*" said Fox.

"*We can also help each other when our time comes,*" Kat added. "*What of your man, or should I say men?*"

"*Ahh, I have decided that the little one in my belly belongs to Rabbit. The baby kicks like one of the long eared ones. If Rabbit wants to come with me, he can do that.*" She knew that Estienne would follow where she went, and stay at least until the baby was born. After that, she would have to wait and see. At any rate, she would have a baby with Estinnne's blood.

"Will you tell him and Obadiah what you have decided about the child?"

"I believe they both know."

And, so it was decided. As they had been an informal family over the past winter, Ben, Kat, Silas, Fox Crying, Estienne and Obadiah would go with Vasquez and help set up the new post near the Mandan village.

The boats remaining at Fort Raymond were loaded and set off down river. The distance between the Mandan village and Big Horn had taken twenty-one days to ascend up river, and took less than half that time on the return voyage.

A temporary post was set up at the site of Lewis and Clarks old Fort Mandan, and there the company sat and waited for Manuel Lisa to return. What they could not have known was that Lisa was coming back in force and in a different capacity than when he had left last fall.

When Manuel Lisa did arrive, the news he had for the veteran trappers was heartening. The initial success of the past season's returns had caused a change in attitude French traders in St. Louis toward Lisa. They had underestimated Lisa considered him an unwanted nuisance. Now their view of him and his venture into the upper Missouri had changed. If they wanted a share in the riches of the northwest fur trade, their only option at this point was to join him. Over the winter, they merged their interests with his and formed the St. Louis Missouri Fur Company.

The organization in this new venture included Lisa and his previous partners, Menard and Morrison, and in addition; Benjamin Wilkinson, Pierre Chouteau, Auguste Pierre Chouteau Jr., Sylvestre Labbadie, Reuben Lewis, Andrew Henry and William Clark. The sum of $40,000 was injected into the Company, with the expenditures and profits being shared equally by each partner. All but William Clark, who had been elected president of the firm, would accompany the expedition upstream.

In all, there were over three hundred new men in the party that left St. Louis. With them was a substantial quantity of merchandise, procured primarily from Auguste's brother, Pierre Chouteau. This large amount of goods would be the stock for Fort Raymond and four proposed posts on the Missouri; one at the site of Fort Mandan, two for trade with the Sioux and one for the Arikara.

Manuel Lisa was surprised that when he reached the Mandan he found Benito Vasquez there. The expected returns from the previous trapping season had failed to materialize. The partners decided that the trading posts planned would still be constructed with Fort Mandan being the Company headquarters. It was also decided that Andrew Henry would take a party overland directly to Fort Raymond, winter there, and the following spring move in force into Blackfoot country. Pierre Menard would take the boats and supplies up river to Fort Raymond, and Chouteau and Lisa would return to St. Louis to prepare for the following year.

Ben, Kat, Silas, Fox Crying, Estienne and Obadiah had settled down near the location of the old Lewis and Clark stockade of Fort Mandan. The men joined in to help rebuild and enlarge the enclosure to serve as headquarters for the St. Louis Missouri Fur Company. Ben found working at the forge again almost reviving. It took little for him to settle back into the rhythm of hammering the hot metal, shaping it to his will and forming the needed hardware, tools and utensils needed at the post.

Silas, Estienne and Obadiah helped set timbers for the walls and enclosed rooms, but only Silas found the work somewhat rewarding. Estienne and Obadiah both quickly became bored, and the call of the mountains streams and the freedom of the unfettered life of trapping was too strong to resist. They made arrangements to leave with the overland party lead by Andrew Henry. Fox Crying was undecided if she would follow Estienne and Obadiah or remain at Fort Mandan.

"Stay here with us." Kat tried to persuade the little Crow woman, as the two sat outside Kat's lodge. *"Your time is close and you will be safe here."*

"This I know, but I will miss my men, especially Rabbit, I believe I have come to love him more than Diah," Fox said. *"My heart also aches for the land of my people. I do not like it here among the Mandan and Hidatsa. Though their speech is familiar to that of my people, I feel they are too different and I do not want to live among them."*

"My heart will be sad to see you go, but I understand," Kat said.

"And I will be sad to leave my sister," Fox said placing her hand on Kat's. *"And now, I must give you something."* Fox opened the top of a parfleche and reached inside the rawhide bag. She pulled out a tiny pair of boot moccasins decorated with beautiful quill-work patterns in blue, white and green. *"These are for my nephew,"* she said, referring to the unborn child that Kat carried.

"How do you know that I am to have a boy?" Kat asked.

"I do not understand how I know these things. I only do. I will have a girl child and she will be as beautiful as your son will be strong."

"But, Crying Fox, I have no gift to give you," Kat said in apology.

"Your gift to me has been your friendship. Now let us put aside this talk and start work on a cradleboard, you will need one sooner than the moccasins and we only have a few days before I must leave."

*

Thick black smoke billowed up, casting a thick pall across the sky, the sun a pale yellowish disk barely showing through the haze. The Red River carts and the lodges in the small Métis camp burned amid the confusion of the violence that had just taken place. A few renegade Blackfoot warriors moved from body to body taking scalps and other body parts as bloody trophies. With them, was Dob Bergmann who, with his long black hair and paint on his face, appeared to be just another Blackfoot. He came to emphasize the claw-like mark on his face by applying red paint to it. The other side of his face, he had painted black, and from this red and black vestige his pale blue eyes shown almost white, giving him an inhuman appearance.

Painted and wide-eyed, he not only took part in the killings and looting of the village, he enjoyed it; he reveled in the power he felt in the killing and raping he practiced.

Just outside this spectacle of savagery sat John Ranald and Dawson Thomas on their horses. Dawson was appalled by what was taking place. Less than an hour ago, the small village had been a peaceful gathering of lodges along a quiet stream, and now it was a scene from hell in his eyes.

"You had no right to do this," Dawson told Ranald.

"I have every right to do what I wish. I make my own law here," Ranald replied, his one cold blue eye peering across the destruction in front of him.

"These people have no idea where the woman is," Dawson said.

"It is possible they don't, but is also possible that they are lying. Did you not hear the old man? He said she had been here."

"He said it was the winter before last, right after she left."

"Did you not also hear that the young cock was with her? He survived the winter also, most likely due to her witchcraft!"

"This is the end of it. I can't condone what is happening here." Dawson shook his head. "I have backed you up for the past year and a half, looking for the damned bitch. We are no closer to finding her now than we were the day she walked off into the snow storm.

"There is the company business to think about. Montreal has already sent us warnings that they may send out a new factor to replace you or we will be shut down all together. Come to your senses John. Let the bitch go." It was the first time that Dawson had taken the liberty to call Ranald by his Christian name. But this didn't anger Ranald, it was the suggestion that the big man had lost control of his mind that turned Ranald in his saddle to strike Dawson with the barrel of his rifle and knocking him to the ground.

"Don't you dare question my mental capacity!" Spittle flew from Ranald's lips and his single eye blazed with rage. "I'll burn down the whole of the Missouri country if I have to in order to flush out the witch. She took my eye! She took my..." he stopped just short of saying his "manhood," and then continued, "I want her lying in front of me naked and bleeding. I want her spread eagle, and the whole damned Blackfoot nation to have a turn at her. Then, and only then, I'll cut her throat if I feel generous.

"And, as for that bastard American that ran away with her, I'll make him watch the whole thing after I cut his balls off and shove them in his mouth."

Dawson picked himself up off the ground and mounted his horse. He turned his mount and urged the horse in the direction of Fort Maskwa not looking back. As he rode away he passed the Blackfoot warrior Walks Long, who it seemed, had also abstained from taking part in the massacre along the little creek.

For the past year, Walks Long had ridden off and on with the mixed group of Blackfoot renegades and the white men who rode under John Ranald. Once or twice he had taken part in the attacks on the American trappers, and on two occasions on small Crow villages, but the looting and raping had not appealed to him. The chances to face a lone man in some way and extract the bloody nurishment demanded by the specter Calf Standing had become fewer and fewer. He had found far more opportunities while hunting on his own.

During the past few moons, the figure of Calf Standing had continued to degrade in appearance. There was little of the leathery flint-like skin left clinging to the bones that rattled in Walks Long's ears with each step he took, or with the movement of a horse under him. The voice too, of Calf Standing had changed. It still retained its shrilling tone, but it no longer spoke in the moderate tone of conversation. It was either a consistent whisper in Walks' ears or the familiar shriek Walks had heard from the first time Calf had demanded to be fed. Walks contemplated this change and wondered if the frequent visits to the sweat lodge had changed the tone of Calf Standing's voice.

Though he was accompanied by a medicine man each time, these holy men were never at ease entering into the darkness of the lodge with Walks Long, and few ever did it twice. The sweat lodge was a sacred place where a man could cleanse himself spiritually, and it seemed that the presence of Walks Long drew only more unrest and uncertainty rather than bring peace of mind. A shaman that had helped Walks do a sweat the previous year had to stop almost as soon as they had placed the first dipper of water on the hot rocks in the center of the lodge. He had felt so much dread that he had to cry out "niso'kawaiksi", "All my relatives!" and toss aside the door flap. He rushed from the sweat lodge and he was so disturbed that he left the village for three days seeking solitude and clarity of his own spirit.

Walks Long, on the other hand, had always felt better and a little less of Calf Standing's presence with each sweat. But that would change within a few hours, and the boney fingers of his dead friend would dig deeper into Walks' shoulders and the voice would come back.

"I like that one," Calf Standing whispered to Walks Long, pointing a skeletal finger in the direction of Dob Bergmann. *"You should keep him close to you."*

"I have no need of a companion. You are more than enough for me," Walks Long said.

"You do not appreciate me, I look after you and what do you do? You forget to feed me!"

"How can I forget your hunger?"

"Look, Look! See how the cold-eyed Long Knife enjoys cutting the flesh from that woman!" Calf Standing's excitement angered Walks. Even as savage as he could be with his prisoners, he was revolted by what Dob was in the habit of doing. When Walks tortured a man, it was to gain his strength, his spirit. Dob, it seemed, gained only pleasure from the performance of such cruelty.

"He howls like an evil spirit," thought Walks, and for the briefest moment he saw how much Dob looked like Calf Standing did when he was alive. Except for the cold-blue eyes, the Long knife could easily pass for Calf Standing. But, Calf Standing had been eyeless for many years now.

*

Upstream from the carnage, Henri and Pules crouched, hidden in dense foliage Thibault along with their son Jacques and his young wife Maryse. The girl had a Blackfoot arrow embedded in her leg and Jacques had carried her to safety while his father, Henri, covered their retreat. The four watched as friends and relatives were cut down by the Indians and the NWC men.

"Why have they done this?" asked Pules.

"I do not know, Pigeon," answered Henri, peering over the sites of his rifle. "I heard them asking old man Renn about Kat and Ben Voss. Renn told them that they had been with us two winters ago but he had no idea where they were now. He said that he thought they had gone south to the American trading post on the Yellow River.

"It was then that the big man with one eye shot Renn in the face with his rifle. I do not understand what is happening."

"Did you see his face?" asked Maryse. "The side with no eye is grotesque. Is he the Devil the Black Robes talk about?".

"No, not the Devil but he is a demon." Henri shook his head.

"What will we do Papa?" asked Jacques.

"We will stay hidden here. Wait until it is over, then we will see if there are any survivors. Then, I think we will go south to the trading post of the Americans. There we may find Ben and Kat and tell them of what has happened. We will tell them that the one-eyed demon is looking for them."

*

Kat helped Fox Crying lift the packs onto the travois that she would use to carry her possessions and those of her "men." Both women, though hampered by their pregnancy, still worked as hard as ever and neither complained or asked to be treated any different.

Crying Fox did have to compensate for the change in her physical state by leading her horse to the nearby boulder which she used as a step ladder to mount the horse. She let out a small grunt and with more than the usual effort adjusted her dress and the blanket she would sit on and use to cover her legs with. Kat let out a small laugh of understanding. She too had found that mounting a horse had become harder and even the thought of vaulting into the saddle was impossible.

"*I hope your child can wait until you reach Fort Raymond,*" Kat told her friend.

"*I do not know if I can wait that long. It is as if I have carried this little one for many winters rather than moons!*" She smiled down at her friend. "*I may decide to just have the child now.*"

"*We both know that it is too early,*" Kat said.

"*Yes it is, and for you also,*" Fox replied. "*I do wish we could be together when our time comes.*"

Their conversation was interrupted by shouts, whistles, the whinnying of the stock and the entire cavalcade of trappers. Horses loaded with baggage began to move out, forming a long line behind "Captain" Andrew Henry.

"*I must go now,*" said Fox.

"*I will miss you, Fox Crying,*" Kat told her, and Fox kicked her heels against the horse's flanks to move into the line. As she moved off, she called back over her shoulder, "*I will miss you also Panther Woman. Remember we are sisters.*"

Kat watched as her friend moved off, swallowed by the mass of men and animals. Fox did not look back, and Kat thought that if she had it would have broken Kat's heart. Fox Crying was the closest thing to a sister she had ever had, and the emotion of her leaving was hard to bear.

Kat turned to walk back toward her lodge outside the fort when she was struck with a pain in her stomach. She stopped and placed her hand on her side, hoping that it was no more than the result of the exertion of helping Fox pack, and that it would pass. Within moments though, it increased and would not go away. It grew to a low, deep, sharp dark stabbing and she knew she was going into labor. She was tempted to sit down on the ground, and even curl up into a ball, it was so intense. This scared her and she feared something was wrong, that the baby was in distress.

She attempted to walk a few hesitant steps and then felt the wetness between her legs and down her thigh. Lifting her skirt, she touched the inside of her leg and looking at the moisture on her fingers, saw blood. She looked at the fort in the distance and was determined to make it back to Ben. She steadied herself and took two more steps before a weakness overcame her and she fell to the ground. Looking up, she could see the clear sky, it blueness almost too bright and then she lost consciousness.

When Kat opened her eyes she could only make out the dimness inside of a lodge. Totally exhausted from the labor, she had fallen asleep right after the baby was born. Her memories were vague, just outside the pain and fear she had experienced. She recalled being lifted up and carried by Ben. There were faces and voices, the sound of several languages mixed together; English, Crow French and either Mandan or Hidatsa.

"The child had not turned, it wants to back into the world," a bodiless voice said in a mixture of broken French and Hidatsa. *"I must help the baby. Hold on sister,"* Kat remembered hearing.

Kat was on the verge of panic. She had thought that she would deliver her child much like any other woman, with little to no help, and that like the strong individual she was, everything would take its natural course. Knowing that the child was breach, she feared it would be lost. She didn't care about herself, and through the pain she said, *"Save my child. If you must cut it free, I do not care about myself. Save my child even if it means I will die."*

"No, no, Child, I will turn him. I have done this many times," the voice assured, and then Kat felt strong hands on the outside of her abdomen, pressing

and forcing the child inside her to turn.

"Do not push yet," the voice warned. Kat felt an slight easing in the pain and then it returned traveling from her back to her stomach.

"Push now," the voice said, and Kat concentrated on the action, not the pain. Repeatedly she pushed and then she heard the voice again, *"There he is. Push one last time for me."*

Kat laid back and listened for the sound of her child crying after taking its first breath of air. She heard nothing, only silence filled the lodge, and her heart sank. Kat knew that she had lost a large amount of blood, and that many women died in child birth with that type of complication. She thought about the silence and wondered if she would hold her child on the other side of death. She looked up at the smoke hole at the top of the lodge. It was dark outside, and she wished she could see the stars. She closed her eyes and let the peacefulness of the soft darkness overtake her.

Kat turned her head and could make out the form of someone hunched over near the doorway. Her throat was parched, and she tried to swallow but there was nothing in her dry mouth.

"My child?" Kat said through parched lips, in Métis. This drew the attention of the figure, who when it turned revealed itself to be a very old woman. The woman made her way across the lodge and from her toothless mouth spoke a mixture of words in Mandan and French that were almost undecipherable to Kat.

"Where is my child?" Kat asked in French.

"Vous avez une forte fils." The woman's words were still poor but Kat understood that the child was alive.

Kat raised herself up into a semi-sitting position. *"Bring me my child,"* Kat requested this time speaking in French.

With the difficult movement of old age the woman

traversed the lodge and picked up a bundle from near the doorway. She brought it back to Kat and handed the child to her. The old women then eased herself down to sit by Kat's side. Kat moved aside the folds of the blanket and found the small oval face of her child.

"Voir, un garçon en bonne santé." The woman smiled, her face crinkling up exaggerating the many wrinkles in her skin, reminding Kat of a dried plum. A boy, thought Kat and she smiled.

"*He is healthy?*" she asked the woman.

"Oui, saine et solide," the woman said, her toothless mouth working the French words around in her mouth.

"*What is the language of your people?*" Kat asked, tired of deciphering the poor French of the old woman.

"*I am Hidatsa,*" the woman said. "*I am called Many Child Woman, because I have helped with many hard births for many, many winters.*" The child moved in Kat's arms and began to whimper.

"*He is hungry. You should try to feed him. He has had milk from one of our women, who nurses one of her own, but the milk of a child's mother is the best.*" She flicked her tongue to moisten her aged lips. "*They called me when it was determined that you were having a difficult time.*"

"*Thank you, Many Child Woman.*" Kat offered her breast to the child who took hold with a hungry mouth instantly, and began to feed.

"*Do you know where my husband is?*" Kat asked.

"*Yes, he is outside. He has waited since we found you yesterday. I will send him in.*" With difficulty, she gained her feet and left the lodge, leaving the door flap open.

Ben entered and moved directly to the side of his wife and child. He was hesitant to get too close, not knowing what to do. When he saw their child nursing and the content look of both mother and child, he smiled and leaned in to kiss Kat.

"Say hello to your son," Kat said.

Ben looked down at the child and could not believe that this tiny person was really his. How small the baby looked, and he asked, "Is he all right?"

"Yes, the Hidatsa woman said he is healthy and strong."

"And you?"

"I am fine." Ben knew she was not convinced herself, as the old woman had warned him that Kat had lost a lot of blood and that there was a chance she might be attacked by that evil spirit that poisons the blood after such a difficult birth.

"Good," said Ben. "I was thinking that we would stay here at the fort, at least until next spring. There is plenty of work to do at the forge and it will give you time to regain your strength, and the boy to grow some."

"That sounds good to me," Kat said, "But we can't call him 'the boy' can we?"

"No, I expect not."

"Have you given any thought for a name? We have no uncle or aunt to give him a name."

"I have been thinking about that," Ben paused. "I kind of promised Henri Thibault I'd name my first boy after him, but I'm partial to my brother's name, Zebulun. He was the only brother that treated me well."

"Why can we not name him for both?" Kat asked.

"That alright with you?"

"Yes, we will call him Zebulun Henri Voss."

"That's good. Zeb for short."

The child had quenched his hunger and had fallen to sleep, his lips still at Kat's breast. Kat handed him up to Ben and said, "I think I will sleep for just a bit. Take care of your son, Benjamin Voss." She closed her tired eyes and drifted off into a peaceful sleep.

Ben looked down on his wife and was sure that at

that moment he loved her more than ever. He left the lodge and took his son out into the light of day.

"Let's you and me go find your uncle Silas, and see what he thinks of you."

CHAPTER 20
RESOLUTION

Work at the forge was somewhat tedious and boring for Ben. Though he found the labor fulfilling in its capacity to create and repair items of iron, it was confining and wearisome. He had kept busy making the needed hardware and accoutrement for Fort Mandan and the necessary boat repairs, but now he was at the point where that work was finished. His only enjoyable diversion was the company of Kat and his newfound fatherhood. He delighted in holding little Zebulun, and the child would smile and coo while in the arms of his father. The past weeks had been hard as Kat had lingered close to death and her recovery had been slow. But, If she had been a weaker woman, she would not have recovered. Now she was almost back to her old self, but Ben had doubts about her health.

Accepting a sedentary lifestyle had begun to wear on Ben and it was evident to Kat that he was anxious to be on the move, not so much as to leave the security of Fort Mandan, but to get back into the mountains. Kat knew it would not be long until Ben would hint that he wished he had left with Estienne Lapin and Obadiah Cash.

Likewise, Silas Scott found himself bored and wishing that he had followed Captain Henry, Estienne and Obadiah in returning to Fort Raymond and then back into the Three Forks area. His only conciliation was the return of Antoine Martin from his trip to St. Louis and the appearance of Caleb Thompson who had recovered fully from his broken arm and returned with Antoine. Both men had come back upriver and were now planning to leave with the boats headed back to Fort Raymond under the leadership of Pierre Menard. With this in mind, Silas approached Ben and started a conversation in a round-a-bout manner.

"It sure is quiet around here," Silas said, as he lit his pipe. He inhaled and let the sweet smoke fill his mouth and then exhaled, a little cloud rising above his head and drifting off. He made no further comment, waiting for Ben to say something.

"I was thinking that same thing myself, not much to do here and I seem to feel hemmed in some," Ben remarked.

"Is a bit safer here though."

"It tis that, but with all the new men it might not be so bad back up in the high country." Ben was trying to convince himself more than he was Silas.

"You thinking about leaving with Menard?" Silas finally asked the question.

"Not really. I sort'a promised Kat we'd stay where it was safer."

"Seems like everyone who is anyone is headed out, not sure I want to stay here under Sylvestre Labbadie's hand. I never was meant to be a store keeper. I don't mind clerking, doing book work and such, but I kind'a miss the fresh air of being out there."

"You talked to Menard already, didn't you?" Ben looked at Silas and the older man smiled.

"Yep. Antoine, Caleb and I kind of worked our way into following the boats upriver, shadowing them and supplying them with fresh meat."

"Damn you, Silas, what am I gonna' do?" Ben lost his humor. "I got a new child and Kat really isn't back to being herself."

"I know son, but you see I don't expect you to leave with us. Yep, mighty selfish of me, but I just can't sit still with nothing to do. I want to get back up to Fort Raymond and then help establish another post up on the Three Forks."

Ben was heartsick and felt that Silas was abandoning him, but he couldn't blame his friend. It was what he himself wanted to do. The only setback was talking to Kat.

Ben found Kat busy inside the lodge, with Little Zeb asleep, snug in a cradleboard hung safely off the ground from one of the lodge poles. Ben didn't know how to approach the subject of leaving and started off commenting on Zebulun.

"He sure does seem happy," he said.

"He is content," said Kat.

"How you feelin'?"

"I am well, and have been thinking that I am ready to leave this place." This surprised Ben.

"What do you mean?" he asked.

"I miss Crying Fox, and do not feel comfortable here among the Hidatsa and Mandan. I wish to leave. I wish to return to Fort Raymond."

"Do you feel strong enough to travel all that way?"

"I am strong enough to go where ever you go and carry my child with me." Kat said, lifting any doubt Ben might have had and relieving him from the guilt he felt for wanting to leave.

"I was talking to Silas and he said he would be leaving with the boats, back to Fort Raymond. Him, Antoine, and Caleb are going to hunt fresh meat for the boats, kind of follow them up river. Maybe I could see about getting you an' little Zeb a place on one of the boats."

"I would prefer to ride a horse. I do not trust the boats."

"Alright then, it's settled. We'll leave with Silas." Ben's grin spread across his face and Kat knew she had made her husband happy. Her only fear was that she might not be as strong as she let on. She was determined to leave though, and she began to decide what she would pack and what she would leave behind.

Early the next morning, the task of moving the boats and equipment on the long haul by water to Fort Raymond at the mouth of the Bighorn began. Few men were able to perform efficiently the extraordinary labor of moving a fleet of boats upstream and getting them to their destination in good time and in one piece. The journey back to the post would be a tribute to the capabilities of Menard and his men.

The hunting party would aid in this by insuring the availability of fresh meat without delay to the boat crews. Two of the men would range out in search of game while the other two traveled with Kat, little Zeb and the pack horses and travois. Ben was hesitant the first time he was made to leave Kat and the child behind to hunt. But, Kat reassured him that they would be fine and that he must not only do his duty to the company, he must also provide fresh meat for her.

After crossing to the south side of the Missouri River, the hunting party cut across the open rolling prairie. This provided speedy travel for the hunters, and the streams that fed the Missouri River offered plentiful game. The party would hunt and take the game to the river, using dead reckoning to determine where the boats would be at any given time, usually not missing a rendezvous with them or having to wait more than the following day for the boats to arrive.

The bounty of the country was endless, offering deer, elk and buffalo. The hunters had even jumped a flock of turkey, bagging eight fat birds and the change in diet was welcomed by everyone. The heat of late summer was a drawback to the Eden the hunters were experiencing, and at times their only difficulty was finding drinking water other than what was in buffalo wallows. This was sufficient for the horses, but offered no relief to the hunters.

The vastness of the open prairie also held the threat of discovery by any Indians that may also be out hunting. Not knowing who may be friend or foe, a chance meeting with any group of the natives could result in outright robbery, if not death. The first close encounter with such a group happened several days out, just after mid-day. Antoine and Caleb were taking their turn ranging out in front of the party in search of game, while Silas, Ben and Kat rode along talking. Silas spied what had appeared to be a herd of buffalo on the horizon, but turned out to be a moving band of Indians. With little time to think or plan a course of action, the three quickly dismounted their horses and pulling on the reins, forced the animals to lie on the ground. Kat first retrieved Zeb in his cradleboard and then cut the travois free from the pack horse. This animal, free of its load, was then pulled down by Ben. The small group huddled on the dusty ground and waited for the unknown band to pass them by. At one point, the sound of the moving village reached the hiding spot and Silas, Ben and Kat prepared to fight.

The sun had moved past its highest point in the sky before it seemed safe to rise up and determine if the danger had passed. All that was visible of the slowly moving band was a cloud of dust left in its wake.

The terrain changed within a few days journey away from Fort Mandan, as they entered the country along the Little Missouri River, containing deep sinking sand, steep slopes, dry loose soil, and slippery clay that was more broken and difficult to traverse. Though harsh, the landscape was staggeringly beautiful in its own way.

Little Zeb seemed to thrive no matter what the terrain offered, and the child became endeared not to only his parents but to the other three men as well. Antoine Martin began to call the child "Mon petit loup," stating that the child ate like a hungry wolf cub when at his mother's breast. As each day passed, the child grew more and more aware of his surroundings and was soon smiling at seeing familiar faces, or hearing the sound of his mother's voice. When Ben spoke to the child, his large eyes seemed to sparkle and Ben was ecstatic that they were blue like his. Kat explained that that could change as the child grew.

"No matter, there's no question as to who his pap is!" Ben proclaimed with pride.

"If'in he's lucky, he'll take after his mother in looks," Silas said.

"Taint nothin' wrong with lookin' like me," Ben protested, "But, he does have the prettiest momma in the whole dammed Rockies!" At this, Kat smiled in her own modest and self-conscious way.

Zig-zagging back and forth across the country, and meeting the boats every few days, gave the hunters a chance to become familiar with the country, their path somewhat paralleling the journey they had taken two years earlier from the Grand River to the Yellowstone. They looked forward to arriving back at Fort Raymond and spending the remainder of the year trapping in that area. By the following spring, with the large number of trappers in the Company, and the goods and supplies that Manuel Lisa would be bringing up river, a full expedition into the Three Forks region could be launched and the Blackfeet would pose little threat.

*

Henri Thibault and his little family had traveled south to the Yellowstone River, and across the water near the mouth of the Big Horn lay the stockade they presumed was Fort Raymond. On foot, they had made slow progress, the young girl Maryse having to be carried either by Henri or his son Jacques. The arrow in her thigh had been removed and Pules had doctored the injury resulting in her improved health, but she was still unable to walk on her own.

From concealment on the north bank of the River, Henri watched the post for some time before crossing over to ascertain if it was safe. He had observed that there appeared to be no movement in or around the structure, and that the gate stood open. Cautiously, he made his way across the river bottom and up the slight rise to where he was within a hundred yards of the picket walls. Again, he waited and watched, and still there was no sign of life.

He stood and made his way to the gate, his trade gun in hand and at the ready. Walking through the gate, he found that his assumption that the fort was abandoned was correct. There wasn't a soul in the entire establishment. Once he confirmed this, he climbed to the roof and taking the blue scarf from his head tied it to the end of his gun and waved it back and forth above his head, signaling Pules, Jacques and Maryse that it was clear to come in.

When they arrived, Pules choose one of the rooms to make their quarters and started a fire in the fireplace. Her first concern was to make her daughter-in-law as comfortable as possible, and inspect the condition of the girl's leg.

"Henri, see if there are any provisions we can use," she told her husband.

"I have already looked through all the rooms and there is nothing useable," he replied. *"I will send Jacques out to scout the area, look for game and then we can rest.*

"We need fresh meat for Maryse to recover properly. Both of you should go look for game." Henri knew that there was little use in arguing with his wife and in short time he and his son left in search of food. They split up, Henri going west along the Yellowstone and Jacques south along the Big Horn. Within a few miles of the fort, Henri jumped a small group of deer feeding on the late foliage, and with a single shot brought down a fat doe. He quickly dressed out the animal, slung it across his shoulders and headed back to the fort.

He suspended the deer from a roof beam that protruded from one of the buildings and began the task of skinning it. Pules stood by patiently awaiting the opportunity to cut some choice pieces of the venison to roast. Occupied as they were, neither Henri nor Pules noticed the men who entered the gate and were alerted only when they heard the sound of horses behind them. Before they could react, Henri and Pules found themselves defenseless, hemmed in by two dozen armed men.

Henri turned to face them, the knife in his hand, his only weapon. He glanced over to where his gun lay against the wall and swore to himself at his own stupidity. Looking back at the group of men, he saw that they held Jacques as prisoner, his hands tied in front of him.

"Who are you and what are you doing here?' one of the mounted men asked.

"*Bonjour*," Henri said, forcing a smile. "*I am sorry, but I do not speak the English,*" Henri said. "*I speak Michif, a little of the French, the Ojibway, Cree and a bit of Lakota.*" Though Henri did speak some English learned from Ben, he thought it better to keep this to himself for now.

"*Then we will speak in French,*" the man said. "*I am Andrew Henry of the Missouri Fur Company and this post is Company property.*"

"*Ahh...That is good,*" Henri spoke slowly. "*I am searching for one of your men. Benjamin Voss.*"

"*You know Ben?*" asked another of the mounted men. "*I am Estienne Lapin, a good friend to him.*"

"*Yes, Ben is my friend. I am Henri Thibault. Ben and his woman spent the winter with me and my family, near the Moccasin Mountains.*" said Henri.

"This man he tells the truth, mon Capitaine," Lapin said to Andrew Henry. "I have 'eard Ben talk of him."

"*If Rabbit vouches for you, you may stay, but you*

must work for your keep," Andrew Henry said.

"Merci," Henri said. *"Will you now release my son?"*

"Untie the boy," the Captain ordered. Jacques was then set free, and his gun returned to him. Rubbing his chafed wrists, he went to his father's side a scowl on his face.

"They jumped me, I had no idea they were there until it was too late," he said to Henri.

"You are lucky they were not Crow. They would have killed you."

"I know, I was careless."

"We do not often get a chance to make the same mistake a second time. Learn for this." Henri patted his son on the back.

Andrew Henry's men went about reclaiming the fort after the absence of the past few months. Stores and equipment that had been buried were dug up, and the meager supplies they had were stored in one of the fort's rooms. Repairs were then started to secure the premises in anticipation of the arrival of Pierre Menard with the boats containing the remainder of the trade goods and supplies that were to last them until Manuel Lisa returned from St. Louis bringing relief in the form of, man power, trade goods, food, powder and lead.

Estienne made it his duty to make the Thibaults feel more at ease. His first chore was to assure them that they were safe, even in the presence of a few Crow that were with the mixed brigade of trappers. He also told them that they could stay in the room where they were, but would more than likely have to share it with others.

Henri said that he was grateful for the kindness and offered Estienne an invitation to eat with them when the deer meat was cooked, and the little Frenchman was more than willing to accept.

As they ate, Estienne informed Henri that Ben

and Kat had stayed at Fort Mandan and that they had a child. Henri was pleased to find out that Ben had kept his promise and named the boy after him. Henri in turn told Estienne about the renegade party under the leadership of John Ranald, and of the massacre of the Métis and Cree at the hand of the Scottish madman.

"We came here to find Ben and Kat to let them know that the Devil is still alive and that he hunts them. With him is the Blackfoot, Walks Long, and the one called Dob," Henri told Estienne.

"I think maybe Ben and Kat are safe at Fort Mandan, no?" said Estienne. *"Will you stay here to hunt and trap with us, or go to Mandan?"*

"My daughter must heal, and now that I know that Ben and Kat are safe, we will stay, if your Captain will allow it."

Within a few days, the fort was back to operational and as it was already too late in the year to consider any attempt at crossing over to the Three Forks area, Andrew Henry directed forays by the men in the vicinity of the post in search of beaver. This would be the extent of trapping, for it was necessary that the supplies Menard was bringing up river reach Fort Raymond in order for the post to be maintained through the coming winter. Henry had no choice but to wait until spring for the establishment of a new post deep in Blackfoot territory.

When news came that the boats had been sighted moving slowly up the Yellowstone, the mood at the fort lightened a bit in anticipation of the supplies they carried. Only three or four days away, the boats would insure the men made it through the winter and on into spring. Andrew Henry was pleased, and though he wished he were already at the Three Forks, he could wait until spring, and then the following summer when Manuel Lisa arrived with fresh supplies from St Louis.

Adding to the news of the boats pending arrival, a

small group of riders appeared and it was discovered they were the hunters for the boats on the river. Everyone, and especially Estienne, was pleased to see Silas, Ben, Antoine and Caleb. A surprise to Ben and Kat was the presence of Henri and Pules. The little Métis woman ran to Kat as soon as she appeared at the gate.

"Kat! I am so pleased to see you my sweet girl," Pules said as she took Kat's hands in hers and leaned in to kiss her on the cheek.

"My heart is glad to see you, too," Kat replied.

"And, who is this little one?" Pules asked as she looked over Kat's shoulder at the child in the cradleboard hanging form Kat's shoulders.

"This is Zebulun Henry," Kat said, swinging the cradleboard from her back.

"Ahh...little Henri," said Henri, *"he has a good name!"*

"I must go find Crying Fox to tell her you have arrived," Estienne said, and he went in search of her. Returning with her and Obadiah Cash. There were handshakes and back slaps among the men and the sheer joy of seeing friends was contagious.

"My heart is glad to see my sister, Panther Woman," Crying Fox cried at the sight of Kat and threw her arms around her friend. She held tight to Kat.

"I missed you also, Little Sister," Kat said and she pulled back to look into Crying Fox's eyes. She could now see that Fox lost some of her youthful look, she appeared somewhat haggard.

"Are you sick, Little Sister?" Kat asked.

"No, I am well, but my daughter is small, and I do not know what to do for her. There is no medicine man among the Whites who can pray for her," Fox confided.

"There is a friend here who may help. She is called Pigeon in the tongue of the Métis. Would you like for her to look at your child?"

And though a bit of apprehension existed at allowing a woman of a hostile tribe to touch her infant, Fox submitted to the advice of her friend.

Looking at the child, Pules found the baby's belly looked swollen, felt hard, and made a rumbling sound. She dug into her meager possessions and pulled out a small bag containing the inner bark of the aspen tree. Some of this she mixed with bear grease and rubbed onto the child's belly. Then, she placed more of the bark in a cup over the fire and let it seep in warm water, gently giving sips of the resulting tea to the child, by placing her finger in the cup and allowing her to suck on the finger.

"This may help," she said, *"Many children go through this, and the spirit that causes it leaves them soon. I do not believe the child is in danger."*

"Thank you," said Fox.

*

The boats were pulled up on the river bank side-by-side and the trail of men and pack animals carrying the cargo up the hill to Fort Raymond reminded John Ranald of ants hauling food to their mound in anticipation of the coming winter. At a rough count, he estimated the force of men at close to fifty or more. His little group of renegades would be no match in an all-out confrontation, but he knew that the Americans couldn't help but give in to the lure of trapping the surrounding area and that would mean they would send out small parties, vulnerable to attack.

He thought about the men that had followed him, mostly worthless as honest labor, but when it came to taking the fruit of another's toil, they were experts. In particular was his new second in command, Dob Bergmann. He still had no liking for the repulsive little bastard, but found him a useful tool replacing Dawson Thomas. Ranald discovered that Dob had transformed into one of those men that reveled in the unfettered morals of the darker side of the human nature. He had no qualms when it came to killing, torture and outright sadism. Dob's transformation in his appearance reflected this in his imitation of the Blackfeet way of dress, hair and face paint. There was no way to tell Dob from one of the Indians, save for the color of his pale blue eyes. The one saving grace Dob possessed was that he feared Ranald.

Ranald decided to spend a short time in the area of the Yellowstone River, using his men to harass the Americans, who would venture out from the fort to trap in smaller parties. He felt he had control of his renegades, and if they did their work efficiently, there would be no telling them from the Blackfeet who would most likely be doing the same.

Unlike Dob and the other men with Ranald, Walks Long seemed to come and go as he pleased. This was more in line with the true character of the Indians, but Walks Long was still an exception even to them. He would appear at the most unexpected time, do what he wanted and then disappear. At those times when Walks Long was in camp, Ranald noticed that there was some sort of connection between him and Dob Bergmann. He hadn't quiet figured it out, but it seemed as if the more Dob transformed into an Indian, the more Walks Long noticed him. This in itself was unusual because Walks Long paid little attention to anyone.
*

Once settled in at Fort Raymond, Pierre Menard and Andrew Henry sent out parties, ten man strong, to trap the tributaries of the Yellowstone and the Bighorn. One of these parties with Silas in charge included; Ben, Estienne, Henri, Calib, Antoine, and Obadiah with three other men, Wyatt, Corley and McGill. They were not to venture too far afield, but were to stay in the field either until the area was trapped out or weather made it impractical to trap.

The women of these men stayed at the fort, much

to the disappointment of all, but both Kat and Crying Fox had their children to take care of and Pules had Maryse to tend too. Jacques was left to be at the disposal of the women, and staying with his wife seemed to please him.

Silas' group did well trapping during the remaining mild weather of fall. While snow was accumulating in the high country, their weather was a mixture of a few sunny days, then cold rain ones followed by snow driven down from Canada. They had also been lucky in that there had been no sign of Blackfeet, and the thought among everyone was that the Indians had retired for the winter.

Somewhat homesick for the fort and its promise of a warm place to stay for the winter, the men had convinced Silas that remaining in the field held little appeal. He gave in to this without debate and it was decided that once the last of the group had returned to camp, the entire group would pack up and go back to Fort Raymond.

After another two days, Calib Thompson, Wyatt, Corley and McGill, had yet to return and Silas started to fret about them. Either they had found a stream rich in beaver or had experienced an encounter with the Blackfeet. Silas hoped it was not the latter. The following day, the entire group moved out in the direction that Calib had gone and by the end of the day their questions about their colleagues were answered.

Calib Thompson was the first to be found. It was obvious that he had been dead for several days. His body was pierced by several arrows, his arms and legs slashed, his scalp removed. The next to be discovered was, Wyatt and McGill whose bodies were likewise mutilated. Searching the area thoroughly, turned up no sign of the last man, Corley. Missing also were the traps, firearms, horses and furs that these men would have had. Nothing of any value was left behind by the

Blackfeet.

After burying Calib, Wyatt and McGill, Silas turned his little party back in the direction of the fort, and in his mind was the realization that every beaver pelt taken from the Stoneys would have a high price. He wondered if that price was worth paying.

*

Dob had sat for several hours watching Walks Long. He had sat at a respectable distance to observe what few had seen, the special ritual that this Indian performed with his captives. Dob was mesmerized and his heart pounded in his chest as he watched.

"Are you satisfied with your meal?" Walks long asked Calf Standing.

"Ahhh, yes. His heart was strong and it will sustain me," Calf hissed, then added, *"For a time at least."*

"Will you eat more?' Walks said, his voice impatient and louder. He was then surprised by Calf's voice, as it seemed to echo.

"Yes, I would like to eat." The echo came not from the vaporous, emaciated figure who sat beside Walks but from behind him. He turned and there was Calf Standing, his bones covered in flesh, no sign of death about him. He looked back to where he had just seen Calf as they ate, but the specter was gone, and Walks Long looked again at the person standing behind him. He now understood. Calf had returned to what he was before the Whiteman plunged a knife into his chest. The only difference was the cold blue eyes that Calf Standing now had. Walks Long rose to his feet and with a piece of Corley's roasted heart in his hand he walked over to the figure and held it out.

"You have changed brother," he said to the figure.

"Yes, I have," Dob answered in his broken Blackfoot words, pleased that Walks Long was calling him brother. He reached out and took the offered flesh from his new mentor and tore off a large chunk with

his teeth, chewing it with delight.

Walks Long was puzzled by the poor use of words by Calf Standing, but pleased that his brother could now eat on his own. Did this mean that he would no longer have to feed Calf Standing? Would he now be free of the specter that had clung to him for so many years?

With a bit of apprehension, he asked, *"Will you want me to feed you again?"* And the answer dashed his hopes of freedom.

"Yes, of course. I would eat as much as you provide!" Dob replied.

*

Manuel Lisa arrived in St. Louis in the latter part of November 1809, and his first chore was to procure goods for the return trip upriver in the coming spring. The past years' experience had given him the knowledge of Indian needs and desires, and he fully understood the sometimes impulsive or illogical character they possessed. With this understanding, he would be able to anticipate the yearly needs of the company with regard to each tribe.

Lisa was thwarted in his efforts in buying goods by tensions between the United States and Great Britain. President Jefferson had recently instituted an embargo of goods from that country, and St. Louis had nothing to offer in the way of supplies. As a result, Lisa went to Vincennes; where he picked up his friend, Touissant Dubois, and they traveled on to Detroit. Crossing the river into Canada, they found goods readily available on the British side. But, again due to the embargo, they could not be imported. With Detroit a failure, Lisa traveled further north to Montreal where he hoped he could find a roundabout way of getting the goods across the border. His efforts there were also unrewarded and he was forced to return to St. Louis empty handed.

Manuel Lisa had to face the fact that there would

be no Missouri Company expedition in the following spring and his partners Menard and Henry, with their hunters would have to be left to their own devices in the mountains. All the work that had gone into opening the upper Missouri region now depended on those men surviving through the winter and on into 1810 without aid from St. Louis.

SAM J. PISCIOTTA

CHAPTER 21
THE THREE FORKS

Fall gave way to winter and the majority of the trapping parties came back into the fort to wait until spring before venturing out again. Though the area had been harvested the previous seasons, the rewards of the fall hunt had been better than expected. The drawback was the rewards were eclipsed by the loss of several men to the constant pressure of the Blackfeet. Along with the men was the loss of horses, traps and any pelts those men had taken, a double blow to the Company. The expectation of breaking free from Fort Raymond and crossing over to the Three Forks area was on everyone's mind. With a post established deep in Blackfoot territory, and with the man power that Andrew Henry had at his disposal, it was believed that the Blackfeet could be beaten back. So they huddled inside the fort, venturing out only to hunt, and waited for spring.

By March of 1810, everyone wintering at the fort on the Yellowstone was more than ready to move west. Plans had already been made and as the days grew longer, the little close knit group of Ben and his friends had to make the decision as to what course they would take when the time came to leave Fort Raymond. It was obvious by their conversations that almost everyone would move west to the Three Forks, except for Henri and his family. With Maryse recovered from her wound, Henri had decided that venturing deep into Blackfoot territory was not appealing and he decided to take his family back to the territory of the Métis where it was safer. When it came time to leave Fort Raymond, the parting of

Henri's family and their friends was sad but not tearful.

"I will miss you Little Sister," Pules said to Kat. *"Remember you will always have a place in my lodge."*

"I know that. And, I know that someday we will see each other again," Kat assured her.

"Take care of yourself, my friend," Ben told Henri.

"And you take care of Little Henri," Henri said. *"Do not forget to tell him what a great man he is named after."*

"I will, I promise. Are you sure you do not want to come with us?"

"Yes, I am confident that the fork of the river that I must take leads me back toward Montreal and my people."

"We will meet again," Ben said.

"Au revoir," Henri said to the others in general, and shook the hands of Silas, Estienne, Obadiah and Antoine. He mounted his horse, kicked his heels into its flanks and moved off followed by Pules, Jacques and Maryse.

"What did he say about a fork in the river?" Silas asked Ben.

"He said that we each had a different path to take, like a fork in a river," Ben answered.

"That's true, Son. We best be getting ready ourselves to take our fork in the river."

Pierre Menard, with Andrew Henry, led the majority of the men away from Fort Raymond in the direction of the pass leading to the Three Forks of the Missouri River. Ben and Silas were looking forward to returning to the area they knew was rich with beaver, and their high spirits were shared by their companions.

Kat had settled into the comfort of having an extended family for the first time in her life. Though she would miss Pules, she still had Crying Fox and they were like sisters with little Zeb and Crying Fox's daughter Raven, treated as if they were brother and sister, cared for by both women.

Over the previous winter, Crying Fox and Obadiah Cash had become closer and at first they feared Estienne might be jealous. But the little Frenchman's eye had wondered toward some of the other Crow women near the fort, and he bowed out gracefully, accepting the role of uncle to the child. Obadiah in turn became a doting and proud father to the curly-haired little girl, calling her "Bright Eyes." Crying Fox was now sure that the spirits had corrected the path she must travel and that the child was not Estienne's but Obadiah's, and the three became inseparable from each other.

When the time came to move out from Fort Raymond, the large force of men seemed impervious to attack and the entire group had a sense of security that though warranted, was naive, not taking seriously the past experiences with the Blackfeet.

A day in advance of the group, hunters were sent out to obtain fresh meat for the main party. The first of these to range out consisted of two white men, Webber and Carter, along with a Shoshone Indian, his two wives and his son. On the second day out, Silas and Ben rode just in front of the main party as a precaution and advance warning if any trouble appeared and to keep an eye out for the hunters.

Alert to any sign of danger Silas and Ben heard the sound of someone approaching and both men stopped, their rifles ready. Soon Webber, Carter, the Shoshone and one of the women came into view. They were moving fast and halted when they met with Ben and Silas.

"We got jumped this mornin' by Blackfeet," Carter said. "We barely had a chance to get out."

"They just came in, killed one of the women and the boy, then they moved on, didn't even chase after us," Webber said.

"Go back and tell Captain Henry and Monsieur Menard what happened, we'll go on ahead and have a look see," Silas said.

Entering what had been the hunter's small camp, Silas and Ben came upon the nude bodies of the Indian woman and the boy, lying on the ground, their heads split open.

"They just killed 'em for no reason?" Ben asked.

"Looks like it," Silas said. "Or just to prove they can do what they want. I'm beginning to think these people are truly spawn of the Devil."

With the killing of the Shoshone woman and her son, the mood changed among the entire brigade of trappers. Each man in his own way had reason to hate the Blackfeet, all having lost friends and companions, but these killings fueled that hatred. There was no longer a lack of vigilance, and hunting parties were no longer just two or three men. By the time the pass over to the Three Forks was reached, everyone was determined to move into Blackfoot territory. If there was any resistance from the Blackfeet, they would beat them back, and make them pay for every life they took.

Alone, Pierre Menard held hope that the Blackfeet could be pacified, reasoned with, but Andrew Henry was certain there was no way they would accept the presence of the Americans in their territory. Menard and Henry discussed this and sought the council of the two men who had the most experience with the Blackfeet, George Drouillard, and John Colter.

Both of the veteran trappers were emphatic as to the futility of approaching the Blackfeet with the intent of making peace and opening up trade with them.

"The first time I ran into them, I was with Captain Lewis and they tried to steal our horses and guns. We ended up killing two of them in the attempt to retrieve our property," said Drouillard.

"Seems to me, that every time I come across a

Blackfoot, he's been trying to lift my hair," Colter added. "I'm not too sure anybody but the damned Brits can trade with them."

"I believe we need to be open to the idea. Unless they can be pacified, I fear nothing could be done in the way of trapping," Menard suggested.

"We can see what the response is to building a post deep in their territory. It may be a matter of having a post that isn't located in that of their enemies," Henry said. "But, it is of no matter, we see a better profit if our people trap the beaver than if we trade with the Indians. We are committed to that endeavor, and we cannot let the Blackfeet stand in our path."

It took almost a month to reach the confluence of the Gallatin, Jefferson and the Madison forks of the Missouri River. A site, about two miles south of confluence of the Jefferson and Madison, was chosen and work on the post, now called Fort Henry, proceeded rapidly with the picket walls almost complete by April. Menard was then able to release several of the men for trapping.

As at both Fort Raymond and Fort Mandan Ben was first employed at Fort Henry in setting up a forge. As at the two prior posts, Ben found settling in at the new fort unwelcomed, and the freedom of the open wilderness was calling both him and Kat. Little Zeb was already taking his first steps and he too seemed to have his parents thirst for exploration, disappearing from sight as fast as his little legs could carry him. A constant vigil was needed to save him from the hazards of fort life.

When the time came to send out the trapping parties, Ben and Kat, were more than eager to join one of them. With a party of almost two dozen they left the confines of Fort Henry and moved about forty miles up the Jefferson to trap. Along with them went; Silas, Antoine, Estienne, Obadiah and Crying Fox.

At first, fortune smiled upon them, providing an abundance of beaver to trap and the season looked encouraging. It was evident that they were in virgin territory unsurpassed in its wealth of beaver, and their daily catch was almost breathtaking. With success in their minds, they pushed back any thoughts of Blackfeet danger.

Kat and Crying Fox had grudgingly agreed to remain in the secluded main camp, reasoning that they and their children would be safer than if they were out with the trapping parties. Ben had also thought that as there would be half a dozen men in the camp, there would be more than enough firepower to protect his little family while he was gone. Over the past two years he had grown to know the men he worked with, and he trusted those left behind; Valle, Hull, Cheek, Ayres, Rucker and Fleehart by name.

The little camp was kept busy most of the time in stretching and fleshing out the hides brought in by the other trappers. When there was a lull in these chores, the two women took advantage of the freedom offered and would seek out some secluded place to bath the children and themselves, the frigid water cleansing the spirit as well as the body. It was a sunny spring afternoon when the women had just finished tending to the children and sat quietly chatting that the tranquility of their secluded place was disturbed by the sound of gun fire. Quickly they took up the children and found a hiding place, where they waited, guns ready if necessary.

In Kat's hand she held a North West trade gun and one of the big horse pistols she took from John Ranald was within reach. She was determined that if she was to be overpowered she would take at least two enemies with her.

*

With lightning speed, the Blackfeet with John Ranald and his three remaining renegades descended on the camp. The trappers were easily overpowered, two of them killed instantly and three taken prisoner. Only one had managed to escape, having been the furthest away from the attackers. He covered his retreat by killing one of the Blackfeet warriors with a well-aimed shot before disappearing into the brush.

The small camp was looted, and taken along with the three men was all the horses, guns, ammunition, traps and furs. Casualties on the Indian side were two killed, and the white men remaining alive would pay for that loss. One poor soul, was lead off by Walks Long. This Whiteman had fought valiantly with his knife, having emptied his firearm and discarding it after he had used the empty weapon as a club. After killing an Indian with his knife, he had been overpowered by Walks Long with a blow to the head from his war club.

Followed by Dob, Walks Long led his prisoner off in search of a spot to perform his practiced ritual. Every now and then, he would glace back over his shoulder, not seeing Dob, but the newly formed Calf Standing. To Walks, his spectral friend had lost all the appearance of death and decay including the blurry haze or fog that had engulfed Calf Standing when he had started to regain flesh. This did not puzzle Walks any longer. What did raise questions in the mind of the Blackfoot was that Calf now took physical part in the war on the Long Knives. Also, other Blackfeet warriors seemed to now see and even converse with Calf, and Walks wondered if these things were signs that Calf would soon no longer need him. Was it too much to hope for, to be free from the malevolence that had plagued him for years?

"Will you feed me?" the voice seemed to come from not only behind Walks, but also inside his head. He tried to ignore it.

"Walks Long, will we eat?" the voice again echoed between Walks ears.

"Yes!" Walks answered, his temper growing short. He spun around and faced Calf, giving a look that not only stopped Calf but made him flinch back in what was obvious fear.

"I only wish to share with you, Brother," Calf said in his broken Blackfoot words. *"We will grow stronger together, and I will always be at your side."*

"I do not think I can stand for you to be at my side much longer," Walks thought but did not dare speak the words out loud.

"When will we stop and eat?" Calf asked, again.

"I grow tired of your voice, Calf Standing!" Walks long uttered the name of his dead friend for the first time since the day Calf Standing had been killed by Reuben Field. Walks surprised himself when he voiced the name as it was practice to never speak the name of the dead least they be brought back as an evil spirit. It was this thought that struck Walks with the absurdity of his own actions over the past few years. Had he not sustained the spirit of Calf Standing, or at least, been responsible for the malevolent phantom's presence? Walks Long decided that he knew how to rid himself of Calf Standing, but it would take Calf's cooperation.

As for Dob, he was surprised, but pleased that Walks Long called him Calf Standing. In his own mind, he thought that the Blackfoot warrior had taken to him and had given him a name in the Blackfoot tongue.

A suitable tree was found by Walks Long and there he tied the white captive and began his ritualistic torture of the helpless man. Dob, in his new vestige as Calf Standing, sat patiently observing Walks Long, every movement he made, every action he performed. He had decided that in time he too could do what Walks Long did in exactly the same manner.

*

Before deserting the camp of the trappers, John

Ranald searched for any sign that Kat might have been there. He found signs that there had been a female presence there in some of the personal items scattered about in the raiders hurry to loot the camp. But one item overlooked by the Indians, caught his eye, a white point blanket, with green, red, yellow and indigo stripes at the ends. It was possibly a coincidence that a blanket like the one owned by Kat was among the items in the camp, but Ranald raised the blanket to his face and inhaled. The unmistaken and unforgettable fragrance of Kat filled his nostrils.

In almost a panic driven by the excitement of her nearness, Ranald ran what had taken place during the attack on the camp through his mind. The two Americans had fallen, three had been taken prisoner and one had escaped. Ranald was not sure if the man who escaped was Ben, but he decided that whoever that man was, it was worth heading in the direction the man had fled. So, with his minions and remaining Blackfeet warriors, Ranald followed the trail of the fleeing trapper in hopes that it would lead to Kat.
*

Breaking through the brush, Valle happened upon Kat, Crying Fox and the two children. His fright was overpowering and as he stumbled onto the two women he tripped and fell. He stayed on the ground, face down, thinking he had been caught by the Blackfeet.

"What has happened?" Kat asked.

"Blackfeet, killed everyone in camp!" Valle blurted out, now realizing he was with friends. "They can't be far behind me! We need to pull foot and head down river to the fort."

"*Blackfeet! We must run,*" Kat warned Crying Fox. Both women picked up their children, gather what they could carry of their few possessions and followed Valle as he moved off, fearing Blackfeet at their heels.

They had traveled only a short distance when they ran into John Colter and three others of the party. A quick report of what had just taken place at the camp, and the superior number of Blackfeet that were more than likely in pursuit, convinced Colter and the three men with him to join Valle, Kat and Crying Fox in a retreat down river. They had not gone far when a second group of the trappers appeared; Ben, Silas, Estienne, Antoine and Obadiah. Their numbers now increased; there was a better feeling of security and making it back to the Fort, now only some thirty miles away.

John Colter brought up the rear and as fortune had it, a sound from behind had caused him to turn in the saddle; the position of his head changing the same instance a bullet pierced the brim of his hat, just missing him.

"Shit! Blackfeet!" he yelled, and almost as one the entire group spun around to face the new threat and returned fire. The fuselage brought down several of the attackers and they drew back, offering only a brief glimpse of their numbers and appearance.

"Ride, we'll cover you and catch up," Ben called to the women, and Crying Fox and Kat kicked their horses into a run to out distance the fight. Kat chanced one glimpse back and though it did not register then, she later thought she had seen the faces of white men among the Blackfeet. One in particular sent a chill through her. It was a bearded man with long blondish-gray hair, and the built of John Ranald. She ran this through her mind and tried to convince herself that it wasn't Ranald, but a small bit of the old fear she had felt in his presence crept in.

The Indians, either driven back by the withering fire of the trappers or by the loss of their fellows, gave up and pulled back allowing the whites to escape. The trappers left with no knowledge of if they were still pursued or not and no idea of the number of those who were behind them.

When Fort Henry was reached early the next

morning, Valle's alarm at what had taken place worried Menard and he sent runners out to bring everyone into the fort, fearing that an attack there was eminent.

John Colter examined the brim of his hat were the bullet had torn through it barely an inch from his head. Though not a coward and not one to panic, Colter considered his luck with the Blackfeet had just about ran out. He flung the hat to the ground declared, "If God will only forgive me this time, I will leave the cursed country tomorrow and be damned if I'll ever come into it again."

The following day, when no attack materialized, good to his word, John Colter shoulder his rifle and other possessions then headed down the Missouri River to St. Louis.

From the fort, Pierre Menard organized and led a party to the scene of the first attack. Upon arriving there, they found and buried the bodies of Cheek and Ayres. Though they searched, they could not find the bodies of Hull, nor those of Rucker and Fleehart. They did find the bodies of two Blackfeet who had been abandoned by their comrades. These, they scalped and left for the wolves.

With the desire for revenge, Menard lead his men in pursuit of the Blackfeet, following their trail away from the Jefferson River. The following day they came upon three horses that had broken free of the Indians and one of these carried panniers containing four dozen beaver traps. This was some consolation for their losses, but not enough.

Another day's pursuit brought them no closer to their prey, and the consensus was to return to the fort and rethink how best to proceed getting back into the field and taking beaver. Most of the men seemed to feel that the parties sent out should be bigger, but Silas Scott pointed out that though large numbers were safer, it was impractical while trapping to have too many trappers in the same spot.

Ben suggested that they go out in large groups but break up into smaller bunches during the day to run their traps and then return to camp in the evenings. That way they could have the safety of numbers, clean out an area faster and then move the whole camp on to another location. This met with some approval but no real agreement on a plan could be found.

April turned into May and the debate went on. When no sign of Indians had been seen in a few weeks, the trappers ventured out in larger groups as Ben had suggested. Like before, Ben and Kat were with their close friends, in a group two dozen men strong, led by George Drouillard. Again they went up the Jefferson to trap.

Some progress was made by a few of the small groups that went out. Silas' group with Ben, and George Drouillard's with two Delaware Indians, both did well, but the fear of leaving the larger group made the majority of the men hesitant about going out at all. This cowardly attitude on their part finally roused Drouillard to disgust.

"You hang back, afraid to leave the fireside and the company of your friends because you're cowards. Blackfeet or no Blackfeet, I intend to go out and set my traps," he said.

"Hell, it just ain't safe out there with them Injuns about!" one of the men protested, forgetting that Drouillard himself was a half-breed.

"I'm not afraid of the Blackfeet, I'm too much of an Indian to be caught by an Indian." With this said, he left to set his traps and then returned to camp that evening. The following morning he ran his trap line and returned with six beaver.

"This is how you make money in the mountains boys," he said. "You can't cringe around camp and call that living."

Silas' groups with Ben were also successful but never ventured more than a few miles away from camp, and three out of the five kept watch while the other two set their traps. Though not as profitable as Drouillard's hunt, they were doing better than most of the men in the party.

Three more days passed with still no sign of Indians, and Drouillard ventured further from camp each day. He chose only the two Delaware to accompany him and was becoming bolder with each successful hunt. Silas and Ben were also becoming use to the apparent absence of the Blackfeet. Just before dawn Drouillard and his two Delaware companions had just left camp when Silas asked Ben if he wanted to go run their line.

"We can let Estienne and Antoine sleep, just Obadiah and the two of us can bring in anything we've caught," Silas said, and Ben agreed. It was almost a half an hour later that the three men walked their horses out of camp and went in the same direction Drouillard had taken up river.

The wind had picked up and though Ben, Silas and Obadiah were vigilant the strong breeze made it impossible to hear even each other. It was this strong wind that carried away the sound of gunfire, and they were not aware that the Blackfeet had struck again.
*

Ranald watched as the fight went on. The first two trappers had gone down, though they put up a brave struggle, both taking twice their number with them before they were killed. It was the third trapper, a big man that had cost the party of Blackfeet and Ranald's men the most. He had made it more than a hundred yards from the other two trappers before he was stopped. He then fought in a circle from horseback, killing two of the Blackfeet and one of Ranald's men. When his horse was shot out from under him, he carried on the fight with rifle, pistol, knife and tomahawk using the horse as a breastwork. From this position, he was able to kill four more of his attackers, before being overrun by sheer numbers.

When the big man finally was brought down, the Blackfeet took out their anger and frustration by hacking the body to pieces. Among them, Dob had held back until the man was down and then he rushed in wanting to be a part of the mutilation. Upon reaching the front of the group surrounding the trapper, Dob noticed the dead man's tomahawk laying on the ground. He picked up the bloody weapon and with it chopped the man's head free. Pleased with himself, he thought he would take the trophy to Walks Long as proof of how brave he was, and with it in hand he sought out the Blackfoot.

Dob found Walks Long where the first two trappers had been killed, examining their bodies. Walks could tell they were not white men, but Indians of some other nation. Their clothing was different than that of the Blackfeet, but not quite like that of the Long Knives. He wondered if they were the red-white men, called Shawnee. He recalled the big Shawnee who had been with the whites so many years ago when Calf Standing had been killed.

Dob rode up and slid down from his horse's back to stand next to Walks. Dob could barely hold in his excitement, smiling with the anticipation of Walks' approval. At first, Walks did not pay attention to the object Dob held in his hand. Then Dob spoke.

"I have brought you something special that I took in battle," he boasted.

"And what does Calf Standing have for me?" Walks asked.

Dob raised the head up for Walks Long to see, the lifeless face eye to eye. Walks stared at the face for a brief moment and then he recognized it. It was that of the tall, Shawnee that Walks was only just then thinking about. Walks held his hand up to his mouth disbelieving his own eyes. How could this be?

"How did you come by this?" he finally asked.

"I took it from his shoulders after he had killed many of our people," Dob said. *"He was a great warrior and now so am I."*

"Do you not recognize this man?" Walks Long showed an un-characteristic concern over what he saw in Dob's hand. *"He is the one who talked with his hands, the one who was with the Long Knives, when you were..."* Walks could not finish his words and backed away from the awful sight.

Was this another sign that Calf Standing was truly alive again? Was he taking vengeance on the Long Knives for his death? When he was done with the Long Knives, would he then turn to punish those among his own people who had let him die? Walks Long thought, "Would Calf look to punish me and eat my heart?"

*

It was Silas that first sensed something was wrong. He stopped and without looking, pulled the hammer back to full cock on his Henry rifle. He then waved his hand to signal Ben and Obadiah to come forward and stop next to him.

"I got a bad feeling," he said to his friends. "Hold back a bit and I'll take a look-see." He then edged his horse forward cautiously.

Moving through the trees, Silas found the dead bodies of two Delaware who had gone out with Drouillard. Both men had been pierced with lances, arrows and bullets, and were lying near each other. Silas pulled back and waved the others forward. When they joined him they moved further on, about one hundred yards, and found Drouillard and his horse dead. Their admired companion and veteran mountain man's body had been mangled, his entrails torn out, his body hacked to pieces, and his head cut off.

"Diah, you head back to the camp and tell them what has happened," Silas said. "Ben and I'll bury our dead and be back soon as possible. And Diah, you watch yer' hair!"

"I'll do that Silas," Obadiah turned his horse and headed back to the main camp.

*

John Ranald counted less than two dozen men in the camp, and from his hidden vantage point, he patiently watched the movement of everyone. It was not long before he spied the figure of a woman walking across the small clearing, a toddler ambling behind to keep up with her. His heart beat a bit faster, and he strained his one good eye to see if it was Kat, but he wasn't sure. The woman seemed smaller and didn't move like Kat, her walk was different. His hopes were dashed until another woman appeared meeting the first one and they talked to each other. It was her, and her name slipped from his lips, "Katherine. Now I have you!" He waited a bit longer attempting to find Ben among the men, but could not pick him out.

He pulled back from his hiding place and went to where the remainder of his men waited, with the new addition of thirty Blackfeet warriors. With a hushed voice he addressed them speaking in Blackfoot.

"They do not expect us. No one seems to know we have killed the three up river and there is no guard out." He paused, his one eye glaring at the men gathered around him. *"We will come in from two sides, kill all those you want but no one is to harm the women. They are to be brought to me."*

The excitement in anticipation of attacking the Americans was felt throughout the group of renegades and Indians. Dob's hands shook with excitement and fear. He glanced over at Walks Long and his gaze was returned with a cold stare. Dob couldn't understand why the Blackfoot had not been impressed by the head of Drouillard. Maybe he could gain Walks respect if he took a prisoner in the trapper's camp. Dob wasn't sure if he could best any of the men one on one, but if he was patient, he was sure if could find one weakened, or wounded. The he would feed Walks the man's heart.

*

The majority of the men were still in camp, and with George Drouillard gone to check his traps, those who would not pose their opinions in front of the Shawnee, were embolden to speak against him and what they saw as carelessness on his part.

"Sure, he's willin' ta go out there and trap," one man said. "He says he ain't afeared of them Blackfoots cause he's too much of an Injun himself. Maybe that so, but that don't help save our scalps, does it?"

"I say we pack up and head back to Fort Henry," another said.

"You are like the dogs that bark when the threat has past," Estienne said.

"Oui, if you have no stomach for this type of work, then you should be back in Saint Louis!" Antoine added. "These women have bigger ecrous then the bunch of you." He pointed over his shoulder toward Kat and Crying Fox.

The malcontents looked at one another and somewhat cowed, broke up and went about their business. Antoine spat in the dirt behind them as they retreated, then turned to his closest friend and spoke in French, *"I have a small jug of liquor in by bag, should we have a drink Rabbit my friend?"*

"Yes, a drink would help get the bad taste out of my mouth left by speaking with that lot." The two moved over to one of the half-round shelters they shared with Ben, Silas, Obadiah and the two women.

"Excusez-moi," Antoine said as he reached past Kat and Crying Fox for his belongings to retrieve the small crock. Kat smiled at him and shook her head.

"You two need to keep your heads clear in case

there is trouble," she warned.

"It would take more than what is in this little bouteille to affect great men such as Rabbit and myself, no!" He laughed, and uncorking the jug took a deep swig before handing it to Estienne.

The wind was still blowing hard when the first muffled shot was heard, and one of the trappers screamed in pain. The entire camp was slow to react, but in their heightened sense of apprehension they were ready to respond to the attack almost as soon as other shots were fired and arrows landed among them. The war cries of the Blackfeet could then be heard above the wind.

Estienne dropped the whiskey jug and reached for his rifle. Antoine, already shouldering his, fired at the first Blackfoot he saw. Kat and Crying fox both took up their children, then armed themselves and took cover behind the packs and saddles stacked on the ground near the shelters, Estienne and Antoine joining them behind the makeshift breastwork. The four then joined in with the rest of the camp in returning the fire of the Indians.

Most of the men in the camp sheltered behind baggage, not offering a target to the enemies' arrows or guns. Each man, even those who moments earlier were fearful of the Blackfeet, stood their ground.

It was not long before the withering fire from the American's rifles drove back the assault. Many of the men actually left the safety of their breastworks to push the attackers back, Estienne and Antoine among them. Kat and Crying Fox stood, guns in hand, watching the men drive off the Indians. Grateful that it appeared just a few men had been wounded, and no one had been killed except the Blackfeet.

Kat, happy at the easy victory, turned to look at Crying Fox and what met her eyes replaced her smile with shock. Behind her friend stood John Ranald. Though one side of his face was distorted and one eye was covered by a black patch, she recognized him. Before she could voice a warning or raise the gun she held in her hands, Ranald struck Fox across the back of the head with the butt of his rifle, knocking her to the ground.

Obadiah had just tied his horse to the picket line when the first shots were fired. His only thought after realizing what was happening was to get to Crying Fox and Raven. He ran toward the camp, and the first attacker he saw between him and his wife went down, a bullet in his chest from Obadiah's rifle. A second one fell, a shot from Obadiah's pistol striking him. Before Obadiah could reload, another assailant fired his rifle missing Obadiah, and then drawing his knife closed in and they wrestled, each armed with only their blades.

The man was not a Blackfoot like the other two Obadiah had killed, but one of Ranald's renegade engagees. Obadiah couldn't understand why a Whiteman was fighting him but he was determined to get to his wife and didn't care what color of skin the bastard had, he wasn't going to be stopped from reaching Fox and Raven. The man brought his knife around and cut into Obadiah's side, but the stubborn Kentuckian didn't let the pain faze him and drove his knife up into the man's ribcage.

They both fell to the ground and it was then that Obadiah felt the pain in his side. As he lay there he reached over and felt the wound. He contemplated the severity for only the briefest moment and holding his side he stood and looked around for Fox. He found her lying on the ground, semiconscious, with Raven sitting at her side.

"Are you hurt?" Obadiah asked her in Crow, as he dropped to the ground and cradled her in his arms.

Fox lifted her hand to feel the back of her head and brought away only a small amount of blood. Then she spoke, *"He has taken Panther Woman and the child."*

"Who has taken her?" Obadiah asked.

"The evil one, with one eye."

There was little time to question who Fox was talking about as the battle with Blackfeet was still on-going and the trappers, though still outnumbered, pressed their counter-attack keeping the Indians at bay. The sound of gunfire could still be heard at some distance from the camp when Ben and Silas rode in at full speed, vaulting from their saddles, their rifles in hand and ready.

They both took in the scene around the camp, noticing the dead Blackfeet and a few of their own wounded comrades. Silas pointed out the body of a Frenchman, and asked Ben, "You know that man?'

"No, never seen him before." answered Ben. "Who the hell you think he is?"

"Don't much matter, he's dead." Silas moved over to one of the wounded men who sat with his rifle across his lap, blood seeping out from a bullet wound in his thigh.

"What happened here?' Silas asked.

"They came in out of nowhere, mix of Bloods and some white men too," said the man.

"You need help?"

"Nope, just a tickle in my leg is all. Anyways, I got my rifle and plenty of powder and lead. The fight is over that-a-ways, if you want to get some hair." He pointed in the direction the gunfire was coming from.

Silas looked back to find Ben and saw him talking to Obadiah who was being tended to by Fox. He went to them to see how bad his friend was injured. Fox was just telling Ben that Kat and Zeb had been taken.

"Which way did they go?" Ben was asking Fox.

"He took Panther Woman and Henri that way," Fox said pointing toward the river. *"I am sorry I was hit and could not help her. She fought hard, killing that*

390

man over there." She pointed at the body belonging to one of Ranald's men.

"That's a Whiteman," Ben said.

"Yep," said Obadiah, "There's white men with them Blackfeet. Looks to me like Britishers and Frenchies. I killed one when he tried to gut me."

"Why would white men be with the Blackfeet?" Ben asked.

"Fox says one of the men that took Kat had one eye, big man with the whole side of his face all scared up."

"Ranald! I need to go after my family," Ben said.

"Then let's you and me be at it," Silas said and the two went in the direction Fox had pointed out.

Ben and Silas ran down the trail, searching for any sign of Kat and Zeb finding plenty of tracks. As they came to a fork in the trail, they stopped, not knowing which way they should go as the tracks split taking both directions.

"Looks like we'll have to split up, Silas," Ben said.

"Yep, we just need to keep our ears open and come running if we hear gunfire." Silas headed to the left and Ben to the right towards the river.

Ben's heart was pounding at the thought that John Ranald had carried off his wife and child. If it was him, Ben knew they wouldn't last long in his hands.

"Let my child go you son-of-a-bitch!" The sound of Kat's voice drew Ben's attention and he left the path, cutting through the brush in the direction the sound of her words had come from. As he broke out into the open along the river, he quickly took in the scene. John Ranald held Zeb, upside down by one leg, the child flaying with his arms and kicking at him with the other leg, angry at being handled so roughly. Not a few feet away, Kat, her hands bound behind her back, was held by a Blackfoot warrior who struggled to hold her still.

Ben's entrance into the little open space drew everyone's attention, and when Ranald saw Ben, he smiled. His jaw was crocked, the side of his face distorted and the ugly gap left by his missing teeth, made his smile look that much more hideous.

"Well now, it looks as if we have ourselves a family reunion," Ranald said. "Saves me the trouble of huntin' ye down, don't it?"

"Saves me no trouble at all," Ben said.

"Take the wean," Ranald said handing Zeb to the Indian, who pushed Kat to the ground, and reached for the child. Rather than take hold of Zebs leg, he settled for a handful of hair, and held Zeb at a safe distance. It was when the Indian looked up from the child to Ben that Ben recognized him. Dob's cold blue eyes shone out from the painted face, fear reflected in them.

"Looks to me like I have two things to settle here, don't it," Ben said looking at Bergmann. "When I'm done with this one-eyed bastard, I'm gonna kill you and be done with the whole thing."

Before Ben could raise his rifle, Ranald had crossed the short distance between them and was on Ben. Ben's rifle went off, the shot going wild, and he lost his grip on the firearm. The big man outweighed him and was still stronger than Ben. They went to the ground and Ben was trapped under Ranald. Ranald grabbed Ben by the throat with one hand, and with the other brought his knife up to strike at Ben.

Ben blocked the knife wielding hand with a sweep of his own and then was able to hold on to Ranald's wrist, keeping the knife only inches from his face. With the other hand, Ben attempted to loosen Ranald's vice-like hold on his throat.

Ben could feel the pressure of Ranald's grip around his windpipe, and the thought of ending his life this way and what awaited his wife and child after his death, angered Ben. He released his hold on the hand around his neck and reaching up, went for Ranald's face, and gouged his thumb into the Scotsman's sole good eye.

The big man screamed, releasing his grip and fell back, covering his face with his free hand. He gained his feet and with his knife in hand he blindly slashed out at the air in front of him in search of Ben, who had also rose to his feet and stood just out of reach.

"Aaaahhhh! I'll gut ye! Stand close and fight me!" Ranald raved.

"I've a mind to leave you blind to wonder around, helpless, and die the way you had planned for me, at the hands of nature," Ben said, moving as he spoke so as not to give Ranald a direction to strike. "But you see, I'm not heartless, and I see no good in prolonging a man's suffering." With this, Ben reached to his belt, pulled out the horse pistol that had once belonged to the Scotsman, and shot Ranald in the head. The once powerful man stood for the briefest moment, and then dropped like a stone at Ben's feet.

Ben tossed the empty pistol aside and turned to look at Dob. From the sheath on his belt Ben pulled his knife, and from the back of his belt, he extracted his tomahawk. He balanced the two weapons in his hands.

Stepping over to Kat, Ben reached down and cut the ropes that bound her. She then rose, rubbing her sore wrists never taking her eyes off of Dob.

The two of them stood looking at Dob who still held their child in his grip. Dob looked at the prone figure of John Ranald and could see no way out. He pulled Zeb closer, holding a knife near the little boy's throat.

"Y'all let me go and I won't hurt the child," he said to Ben and Kat.

"You hurt my child, and by God I'll skin you live, you little bastard," Ben warned.

"Bastard, huh? You always thought you was

better than me, didn't you Ben?" Dob's ice blue eyes blazed with a mixture of fear and hatred. "Always braggin' about that gun of yours, and how great your life was with your uncle. Tell me, did he burn to death in the fire I set?"

"I wasn't sure you set the fire, only thought you might have, but I know you tried to kill a good man that never done nothin' to you, never did you no harm. Well, Dob, you failed at that just like you've failed at everything." He looked Dob up and down, dressed and painted like a Blackfoot. "Hell, Dob, you don't even make a good Indian."

Their attention was drawn to the arrival of Walks Long who stood taking in what he saw in front of him. His eyes going from the body of John Ranald, to Kat and Ben, then to Dob and the child.

"What has happened here Calf Standing?" he asked.

"Brother, help me. Kill these two and then you and I can feed!" Dob said.

"Give the child to me," Walks said, and Dob, bolstered by the presence of the strong Blackfoot warrior, smiled with the anticipation of escape and Ben's death. He handed the little boy over to Walks Long. *"You would feed on a child?"* Walks asked, and then *"Have you not eaten enough? Do you not think it is time that you fed others?"*

With no emotion, Walks Long swung his stone war club striking Dob on the side of the head. Dob wavered, shaking, the shock of the blow engulfing him, and then his knees gave way and he fell to the ground senseless.

Walks Long moved over to Kat handed the boy over to her, and as he had long ago he looked deep into Ben's eyes. He reached up and touched Ben blond hair, and then he stepped back and looked at Dob who lay on the ground.

"I have had an evil spirit with me that caused me

to do many things. I have listened to him on everything except the killing of you," Walks said to Ben.

"You want to kill me know," Ben said in broken Blackfoot, *"You can try, but it will not be easy."*

"No, I do not want your hair. I am made to think though, it is better you leave the country of my people. Take your woman and your child. Go to where the sun rises and never come back." He turned his back to Ben and Kat, and grabbing Dob by the hair, pulled him over to a tree where he tied him. Dob, regaining some consciousness, looked around in confusion.

"What are you doing Walks Long?" he cried in terror.

"I am tired of feeding you, Calf Standing. Now that you have gained flesh, you will feed me," Walks Long said.

"No! I ain't Calf Standin'! Don't do this!" Dob screamed in English. "Ben, help me! Don' leave me with this savage! I don't want ta die!" he sobbed, "Not like this!"

As Ben, Kat and Zeb left the little clearing Walks Long built a small fire between the legs of Dob Bergmann and started his long practiced ritual of torture.

*

The Blackfeet had been driven off, but it would be only a matter of time before they would return and make the cost of harvesting the richest of the Stoney Mountains too costly for the white men. What remained of the brigade of trappers returned to Fort Henry, and there they decided on the best options to take.

There had been no word from Manuel Lisa, and no supplies or reinforcements had appeared from St. Louis. Pierre Menard had been commissioned to bring in a report to St. Louis, and he with the majority of the company intended to head downstream. Andrew Henry would move across the divide with the rest of the men, to hunt and spend the winter on the Columbia's waters well outside of Blackfoot territory. Like everyone else, Ben and his friends gathered to discuss what course they would now take.

"I believe I have had enough of this country," Antoine said.

Estienne agreed, shaking his head and only adding, "Oui."

"Maybe we go to Saint Louis, no?" he slapped a hand on Estienne's shoulder.

"I'm of a mind to head back to St. Louis myself," said Silas. "And then, back to Georgia. I got friends there I been hankering to see." He paused, and then added, "Shore hate to be bested by them Blackfeet though. Maybe I'll come back and try my hand up here some other time, just me and a few good men." He looked at the two Frenchmen, Obadiah and Ben.

"Don't think I want to head down stream," Obadiah said. "Sticks in my craw them damned Injuns runin' us off. I think Fox and I'll go with Captain Henry, an' hunt the Columbia. I hear the beaver is so thick over there you can walk across the streams and nary' get your moccasins wet." He chuckled.

"Well I always thought you possessed more bravery than common sense," Silas ribbed him. At last he turned to Ben. "What you thinkin' about doin'?"

"Kat and I been talkin' about it. I think we may go up to where Henri and Pules are. Kat has also told me about Montreal, and I think I'd like to have a look see at the city. After that, we may mosey on down to Pittsburg; introduce my uncle and aunt to Kat and Zeb. I do need to let them know that I'm still alive and have a family of my own." He paused and added, "Ought to tell them Dob got what he had commin' to him too." Ben smile, and gave Kat a squeeze.

"Looks like we come to one of them forks in the river you was talkin' about Ben," Silas said.

"Yep it does Silas."

"Well, no sense in lookin' at the back trail, we got many a mountain to climb before it's all over."

"Yep, that we do," said Ben, "That we do."

Other books by Sam J. Pisciotta

The Cold Rider
Children of the Wolf
Stray Dogs on the Mountain
Dogs of the Winter Star

Please visit your favorite retailer or,
Join other readers at Books by Sam J. Pisciotta
on Face Book:
https://www.facebook.com/StrayDogsOnTheMountain

www.ingramcontent.com/pod-product-compliance
Lightning Source LLC
Chambersburg PA
CBHW060144260626
47160CB00001B/119